DAVID L. BLOND

THE PHOENIX YEAR

D1492843

Wattle Publishing

Wattle Publishing Ltd
Third Floor, 207 Regent Street
London W1B 3HH
www.wattlepublishing.com

Published in Great Britain by Wattle Publishing Ltd in 2014

A catalogue record of this book is available from the British Library

ISBN 978-1-908959-28-7

Printed and Bound by CPI Group (UK) Ltd, Croydon, CRO 4YY

*"The healthy social life is found
when in the mirror of each human soul
the whole community finds its reflection,
and when in the community
the virtue of each individual can live."*

R. Steiner from The Fundamental Social Law by Peter Selg

About the Author

Dr. David L. Blond works as a private economic consultant specializing in quantitative analysis of economic data. Blond began his career working for the United Nations in Geneva, Switzerland. During the period of 1978 – 1985, he was a Senior Economist in the Office of the Secretary of Defense, and after leaving that position worked for various major global economic forecasting and consulting firms in senior positions developing some of the largest and most complex global economic models ever developed for use by private sector clients. He lives in Santa Fe, New Mexico.

DEDICATION

I'd like to thank my long suffering wife and children for putting up with my working on fiction, when I could have been prospecting for economic consulting assignments. Lastly, I'd like to thank my father Bernard, who never sold a single story, but never stopped trying until his untimely death at age 48 – more than fifty years ago. He encouraged me, at a very young age, to find enjoyment in writing fiction.

CONTENTS

INTERLUDE I

Little of her face was visible, shaded by the dim light and her broad-brimmed hat.

"You've read the contract carefully, Mr. Lee?" she asked, her English slightly accented.

"Yes, yes," Lee answered, impatient to finish this business. His potential profits could be huge, still he worried that there was something wrong with the deal.

"You must understand, Mr. Lee, the property is not owned, only leased. The merchandise ..." she hesitated, and then continued, "must be returned in good condition, and unblemished. Read the penalty clauses in case of damage carefully."

"There's always some damage," he said.

"Minor damage is acceptable. Anything more will be taken from the escrow balance we retain of your initial deposit," she said coldly.

Lee looked again at the multiple conditions laid out in the contract. He would be taking on responsibilities—training, transport, the normal payoffs to Customs inspectors and Government officials—yet there was profit to be made. Avoiding the normal costs associated with acquisition, and the special nature of the product, would more than make up for the extra expense.

"There's one more thing ... "

He couldn't tell if she had heard him. The woman seemed lost in thought, but then she smiled, or at least she seemed to smile through the gauze-like veiling.

"Yes, Mr. Lee? Another question?"

"Why? Your procurement and delivery costs must be more than what you will make."

She didn't answer. She pushed the contract across the table towards him. Lee signed both copies, handing one back.

She picked up the copy.

"The first shipment will arrive in a week's time," she said, pushing back the chair and standing up. He could see her beauty from the shape of her body under her sheer silk dress.

"And the quality?"

"You will not be disappointed."

1. A String of Round-eyed Pearls

The girl sat up suddenly, staring blank eyed, and screamed. It was the first time she'd stirred since they'd taken her hours before. Kim helped her back to the bed, where she fell back into a drug-induced sleep. It would be hours before she was fully alert, but Kim was impatient to find out what the girl knew.

She studied the pictures of missing women that she'd received from her boss, Turner, in Washington, earlier in the week. His group had identified forty-two likely victims, taken in the past three years from homes and offices. Each was linked to an important business executive or high Government official. Ransom notes were never reported by the families, but Kim was sure that demands of some sort were placed on such powerful people; the information and influence these people possessed had a value beyond simple monetary terms.

The face matched the girl from Dallas, daughter of the Chief Financial Officer, of a major electronics company. Earlier in the week, they had tried to snatch two others, but someone—most likely the Thai police—had tipped off the brothel owner, and the girls had been moved before they could act. This girl was the only one of the three planned rescue attempts that had succeeded.

"Can you hear me?" she asked, as the girl's eyes opened briefly, then closed again. Kim continued speaking. "I'm with the American Embassy. You're safe now."

"I'm dizzy," the girl said trying to lift herself off the bed, only to fall back, and close her eyes again.

"Look at me!" Kim turned her head roughly so she could look into her eyes. "Can you remember your name?"

"Sue." She struggled with her memory, fighting off nightmares. Images blurred as bits and pieces of the past filtered in. She started to cry, the tears streaming down her face.

"Try to remember your name. Sue? Susan? Suzanne?"

"Mills," she answered, surprised by how that name came back to her. All those months, the pain, the torture, and the endless stream of men had blurred into a painful collage of hate and fear.

She was there on the list: Susan Mills, taken near Texas Stadium, on her way to a Cowboys game. It still didn't make sense. Sex slavery was a business, like any other. Even the premium paid for white flesh by Asian buyers didn't justify the outlay. There was easier, and far less expensive, prey: Caucasian girls from Eastern Europe were plentiful, and cheap.

Kim heard the sound first, then the door exploded, falling into the room. She dived for the floor, reaching for her weapon, but it was too late. The room filled with a hail of bullets.

Curley Marston heard the bell ring, followed by frantic knocking.

He looked through the peep hole. Recognizing Kim, he opened the door.

"What the fuck happened to you?"

"Good question, Curley. Who knew where I was? Only you and Johnson, and I don't suppose you told anyone ... which leaves Johnson." She sat down on the couch, the soot from her clothes staining the white fabric black. Marston grimaced, but he didn't say a word.

"Do you need a drink?"

"Water would be great." Kim took the glass thankfully and downed it. He poured her another.

"She's dead, Curley, gunned down in the apartment, and they fire-bombed the building to make sure. Everything happened so fast," Kim explained, still shaken by the suddenness of the attack. She had barely escaped the room. Two men, armed with semi-automatic handguns, had entered and fired directly at the bed. She'd watched as the girl's head exploded from the bullets. Kim had crawled towards the open window just as they threw an incendiary grenade into the room. She'd escaped through the open window, down the fire escape and had left the building in the confusion of the moment.

"What about Johnson?" he asked, thinking of the young man, recently recruited from the DEA as an operative, who was enthusiastic, but so unprepared for the ways of the dark world in which they worked.

"I sent him back to the office hours ago," she said.

"Well, he hadn't come back by the time I left for the day." He smoothed back the few strands of hair he still had. At one time, he had had a whole head of hair that curled in Bangkok's near 100% humidity.

"Shit!" Marston said, suddenly thinking the worst. "You think it was Johnson that spilled the beans?"

Kim didn't answer.

"You think they followed him?"

"Possibly. His spy craft is ... let me put it nicely ... untested."

"Who was she?" Curley asked.

"The girl's name was Susan Mills. Eight months ago she was on her way to a football game in Dallas. Father's the CFO of a semiconductor company there. Our theory at the moment is that someone's using these girls as leverage to gain inside information."

"What's next? Any ideas?"

"It took almost a month to find the girl, and set up the raid." Kim stood up suddenly, convinced that it wasn't wise to stay there longer.

"You remember what this city was like twenty years ago?"

"What do you mean?"

"With the goofy girls parading around half-naked?" Curley said, smiling. "These new, boom times depress me. Asia's dying. It's becoming like fucking New York or LA."

"Ever wonder where those girls went?" Kim asked.

"To hell. The life wasn't attractive, but I miss them. The place is starting to look ordinary" he said with a sigh.

"It wasn't a life anyone chose," she said, holding back the bile from her stomach. As a fourteen-year-old, she'd slept on the streets, grateful for handouts from well-meaning missionaries. She'd sold her body for pennies. That was before the House of Easy Pleasure; before she had made the acquaintance of Hwang Sheng, Mai Lin, or Old Wu-ling.

"Where are you going to look first?"

She didn't answer.

He noted her silence. Kim didn't trust anyone. Marston knew that well enough.

"I have to leave." She stood up, placing the glass carefully on the side table. She walked to the half-open door of the bedroom. Inside, she could see the stretched-out form of Miriam Evans, Marston's secretary from the Embassy. Overweight and over-age, Kim thought; a natural partner for an over-the-hill agent like Marston. "Nice ass," she said, peeking in at the woman, then she turned and walked quickly towards the door before Marston could reply.

Charlie Chan ate dinner every night at the same table, in the same Bangkok nightclub. He had missed only a few nights in the last fifteen years. Each evening, between 8 and 10, he held court. The cost of this arrangement, including the meal, was far less than an office in a new, downtown, high-rise office tower.

"You're looking worried, my dear." He studied Kim across the table. A waiter in white livery delivered a steaming plate of *oc hap thuoc bac;* snails, in a rich chili sauce; a specialty of Vietnam. It was made especially for Chan each night. He picked up a snail with chopsticks and offered it to her. She refused.

"There are many evil people in the world, Chan." Kim noted his two bodyguards, who flanked him at side tables. "Of course, some of us are better prepared than others."

"Too bad about young Johnson."

She realized that Chan knew far more about this affair than he was telling.

"I want revenge, Chan."

He'd known her for more than twenty years, from when Kim was a just child. "Why would a beautiful woman like you," he smiled, and wiped his mouth, which seemed to be set in a bowl of fleshy jelly that was his round face, "wish to get into things from which there is only one way out?" He stopped, leaving the obvious unsaid.

"Go on," she was surprised he was talking freely without money being passed.

"I have heard …" he paused, staring at her, "that you are now getting too close to matters best left alone." Chan continued to carefully pick out the choice parts of his food with his chopsticks without looking up. "There are very important people—Government officials, private individuals with influence—who are becoming very rich from these girls." He smiled.

"Who's behind this, Chan? Why the white pearls? Why now?" She slipped ten $100 notes across the table. He didn't reach for them, but continued to stare at her.

"I want to live a long, rich, happy life." Chan said in a monotone. "I have worked too hard to end it now. Each day is precious to me, as it should be to you, Little Jade," using the name Kim had long tried to forget. He slid the bills back towards her.

"These people in high places, what are they after?"

"I don't know, and I don't wish to know either. You should leave the round-eyed pearls to their fate."

"What do you know, Chan?"

"Their attraction, quite frankly, is their uniqueness, for they are all children of the elite: American, French, British, German, even Japanese. And they are leased at attractive terms."

He stopped. He had already said far too much. There was only one more point left to make, for he truly liked Kim. "Perhaps your old employer—or was it lover?—could tell you more?" He smiled cat-like. "Sheng might like to know that you're back. He talks about you often enough."

Kim shuddered as she recalled the day she'd left Sheng's. He was likely to still have the scar from where she'd cut him when she'd escaped.

She had one final question: "Who killed Johnson?"

"He's dead. Don't bother about him. Go for the living, not the dead."

Slowly, she rose and went outside into the hot, humid air. The noise of the infernal traffic jam, with its honking cars, assaulted her senses as she mentally summoned the strength to revisit her past.

The Bangkok Central Police Station stood in the flood plain of the Chao Phraya River that ran through the city. Twenty years of uncontrolled development in this area meant that the rains, when they came, spilled across the concrete and asphalt, causing regular flooding. Kim slogged through six inches of water; the residue of a foot of water a few days before.

"Lieutenant Phanout Thal," she said to the Sergeant at the desk.

"Second floor, second door."

She climbed the stairs looking back at the lobby below. Wave after wave of human trash ebbed and flowed through the space. The usual suspects filled the downstairs of the old building: half-naked girls and boys brought in from the sweeps of the streets; a few young gangsters, wearing black shirts and white ties like old-time Mafiosi; and a couple of Western tourists, victims of street robberies, seeking help. The walls were stained green with mold, and the building had a musky odor. Thal had come out of his office and stood next to her, looking down.

"Hardly changed at all, has it?"

"No," she said, looking at the older man's face. She had known him for twenty years.

"What do you need, Kim?" asked Thal.

"In your office." She looked down the hall.

"If you insist," he said, leading the way.

Phanout Thal's office was small and dimly lit. The old wooden desk took up nearly the entire space. On the wall were notices of meetings and old calendars. It smelled of stale cigarettes mixed with human sweat. It was depressing.

"Not changed much, Thal," Kim said, looking around. She crossed her legs, feeling the slit of her skirt push up near her thighs. Human flesh, a girl's thighs, hips, even pussy didn't impress Phanout Thal anymore. He had seen it all in his time.

"Dirtier, I think."

"Life's dirtier," she said, feeling the intensity of his gaze.

"All Bangkok's floating on a sea of filth. Next rains, and we will be washed away."

She didn't respond. He reached down into his desk and pulled out a bottle of gin. Thal produced two filthy glasses, which he wiped with his equally dirty handkerchief. He poured two drinks. Kim reached across the desk for the glass and took a deep draft. It burned going down.

"So what brings you to me again?"

"I need information."

"A commodity that comes with a price attached."

"You're supposed to be a public servant, Thal."

"You're supposed to be a Commercial Officer," he parried.

"Touché!"

"And what information can I give the Americans?" He smiled, recalling how he had met the scrappy little Amerasian. They'd raided one of Sheng's places. What a tiger she had been then.

"Sheng runs a public house near the main kalong," Kim said. "Does he have some other establishment; something quite private, for more upscale clients?"

"Are you after the white pearls, Kim, or Hwang Sheng?" Thal leaned back in his chair enjoying this. He sucked on the mostly smoked cigarette, inhaling the stale smoke deep into his lungs. Someday, it would kill him, if the streets of the city didn't kill him first. He smiled, waiting for her reaction.

"Hwang Sheng has another house." She repeated the question, ignoring Thal's aside.

"He has the very lovely and very touristy House of Easy Pleasure," Thal said, deciding to help the girl that he had once befriended. The policeman paused, looked up at the worn plaster ceiling with its dark spots of mildew, accumulations of heat, humidity, and tobacco smoke, then back at the girl, whose features were nearly hidden in the haze from the smoke.

"Sheng has another establishment: Eden, twenty miles upriver."

"And what happens at that house?"

"As you know, Little Jade, knowledge has a price." He smiled.

She smiled, and pushed a couple of 1,000-baht notes across the table.

"In that establishment no expense has been spared. There Sheng stocks the rarest of the rare, precious jewels of Western society, serving the exotic pleasures of very special guests. No vice is forbidden."

"Why don't the police close this place down?"

"Because, alas, we remain a poor country, and these people have influence. Besides," Thal paused, "you, of all people, Little Jade, should not be shocked."

She ignored his comment about her past. "How can I find this paradise, Thal?"

Thal didn't answer. He smiled like a cat, showing the gaps in his mouth where his teeth had fallen out.

"I see you haven't found a good dentist." Kim tried to break the tension between them.

"Perhaps with enough of these I could." He patted the money.

Kim slid two more 1,000-baht notes across the table. "How can I get inside this place?" "Mai Lin works for Sheng now, but you must be very, very careful, Little Jade."

"I'm always careful."

"You may be older and wiser, but you still ask too many questions for which there are no safe answers."

Yes, Kim thought, I'm older and *I* have changed. Twenty years or more had passed since she had last been seated in Thal's office: twenty years of living a lie in America, pretending that her childhood had been ordinary. She had changed, that was true, but some things stayed the same.

"Be careful," he warned her again, standing up. He didn't move towards the door. She walked to the opening, stopped, looked back at this man from her past, and smiled.

He lifted the cigarette in salute.

2. KIM

There had been a time when Kim had not been so sure of herself. Dredging up memories of her past was painful. She was the offspring of an American CIA officer and the daughter of a French planter and a Vietnamese mother, making her three-quarters European. Her mother had met her father at the Embassy, where she worked as a translator, and was seven months pregnant at the fall of Saigon. She was supposed to get to the Embassy, but a crowd had blocked the way. She watched as the last helicopter lifted off from the roof. Kim's father had been dragged on-board at gunpoint when he refused to leave without her.

Kim's mother packed and took a bus heading out of Saigon, soon to be renamed "Ho Chi Minh City," for the delta and relative safety. When Kim was just two years old they had finally made the last part of the journey by boat to Thailand, ending up in a refugee camp. But there was no warm welcome there, no future husband to protect her mother and take them back to America, only the desperation of thousands of other homeless, frightened people. When Kim was seven her mother, weakened, and without hope, died, leaving her an orphan and alone, clinging to papers that proved who her father was: an American driver's license; love letters; a picture taken during a happier time, in front of the Embassy, with the American eagle prominent in the background.

There was little food for children in the camp. Orphaned children were worse off than those with parents to defend them. In the end, she had found a way out of the camp, making her way to Bangkok. She was taken in by the woman Mai Lin, who had taken her to Sheng's House of Easy Pleasure. She was eleven before her first flowering as a woman, when she had her first man. Despite their hardships, her mother had started her education early, even before they were in Thailand. As a result, Kim spoke English, French and Vietnamese. She had been taught to read and write as well. When she was with Sheng, despite her circumstances, she had continued studying, seeing it as the only way out of the situation in which she found herself. During the day she studied, reading anything she could get her hands on. Furthermore, Sheng had taken a personal liking to her, and as his "special girl" she would be given occasional gifts of books and magazines, allowing her to dream of a different life than the one she had been forced into. However, as Sheng's special girl, and the one he valued the most, she was also the one he did not want let go.

Had it been luck or fate when she had met the American soldier who had led her to her father? She had met him, as she met all men, in the foyer of the House of Easy Pleasure. He was new to Bangkok, a marine newly assigned to the American Embassy, and she had talked to him in English. Later that night, she had told him her story and had mentioned the name of her American father. Unlike so many others to whom she had told her story, he recognized the name. The Station Chief of the CIA mission in Thailand was a man of the right age with a similar name, who was legendary in the Agency for having survived the Fall of Saigon in 1975, leaving on the last copter out.

She had gone to Sheng, happy with the news that her American father was alive, and in Bangkok. But Sheng would not let her leave, and tried to stop her. Finding the knife on his desk, she had cut him across his face and fled into the night, making her way to the American Embassy compound. At fifteen, she had come to America, highly intelligent and educated in the ways of the street, men and the world. With tutors and private schools, she had caught up with her more formal education. By the time she was twenty she was ready to enter university, and by twenty-three, she had graduated. Within a month of leaving Dartmouth, she was being trained for the covert service, following in her father's and grandfather's footsteps.

But now, she had to revisit the life she had left so long ago, on the streets of Bangkok. The first step was to find Mai Lin.

3. FROM RUSSIA WITH LOVE

Philippe Bertrand watched the American economist, Michael Ross, approach. He looked exhausted. To Philippe, who had never taken the world that seriously, the American seemed to carry the weight of the world on his shoulders. The meeting was being held in an eighteenth-century chateau that overlooked the lake. He had known Michael for ten years, and though hardly close friends, they had spent a number of days and evenings together at government meetings, and university seminars. But, after nearly four years in the White House, Michael seemed far older and grayer, burned-out from the stress of trying to cope with an economy that was stuck stubbornly in low gear.

"You need a drink," the Frenchman said, once the American economist entered the house. "You look worried." He handed the briefcase to the security detail that would lock it in the vault until tomorrow's meeting.

"We won't be able to contain it much longer, Philippe," Michael blurted out. "Too many people are beginning to question the data." Earlier, he had been given a paper prepared at the direction of his old friend and mentor Heinrich Von Kleise, the richest man in Switzerland, which detailed the inconsistencies in the economic data, and their negative impact on the world financial markets. Along with the paper had come yet another invitation from Von Kleise to visit him in Kandersteg.

This apparent manipulation of the global economy had complicated the problems that the slow global recovery already had going for it. Weak demand, fiscal austerity pledges, rising unemployment, and fluctuating prices for primary products were all difficult things to deal with: problems made much worse by a rising tide of trade protection, political dysfunction in governments around the world, and conflicting philosophies on economics. But the latest alarming news was the corruption of the economic statistics that guided markets, and the manipulation of trading by passing on insider information, leading to rapid changes of markets throughout the world. Altogether, it had the makings of a global, economic Armageddon.

Entire markets could be manipulated by sending orders to far-flung private associates to buy or sell. The price of commodities had fallen once the extent of the slowdown was understood. A few months later, without any new data to support a change of heart, the price of primary products, from food to fuels, shot to new highs, driven by speculators and hedge-fund managers, based on imaginary, erroneous data that the global economic engine had kicked back into gear. When the truth was known, stocks had fallen back, and commodity prices collapsed. The price of gold that had almost reached $1,900 in 2011, was now selling at around $600. That fact alone, Michael thought, suggested something bizarre. Gold should be the investment of choice in a world where nothing could be taken for granted.

It was now 2016, and an election year in America, and Michael couldn't wait to leave government for good. He was exhausted after years of constant pressure. He wished only to return to the simple life of a college Professor and occasional economic consultant. The years in the White House, trying to solve the intractable problems of a slow-growing economy, a deadlocked government, and reluctant capitalists, unwilling to take a chance on growth, had taken their toll on him. He'd even volunteer to teach Econ 101 again to Harvard Freshmen if it meant a return to Cambridge.

"We can't keep up the fiction that everything is okay with the data much longer. Too many good economists are beginning to notice the inconsistencies."

Philippe nodded.

Stopping at the bar, Philippe handed Michael a glass of wine. "Take this drink. There's someone who would like to meet you."

"Michael," Philippe acknowledged the attractive woman who had just joined the two men, "I'd like you to meet Natalya Avramovitz, Special Assistant to the Minister of Trade and Industry. She's straight from Moscow, but has spent time in your country. We were classmates at Harvard Business School."

Michael stared at her with surprise because he'd seen her on the boat he'd taken round the lake earlier in the day. After arriving in Annecy in the early morning, he'd taken the trip on the small, paddleboat that plied the lake from one small village to the next. He had first taken the trip during his honeymoon, more than twenty years before.

"You were on the boat today" Michael stammered.

"Yes," Natalya said, surprised by the intensity of his look.

"You've met then?" Philippe asked, confused.

"Only at a distance," Michael answered, still holding her hand, unwilling to let it go.

Philippe had never seen Ross react to a woman in any way but professionally before. It was refreshing to see that the staid Michael Ross was in fact, human.

For Natalya, however, finally meeting Ross after so long, was different from how she had imagined it would be. She had seen him at a distance on the boat that morning by chance. What struck her now was that he was much taller and quite handsome up close, despite the tinge of gray creeping into his full head of hair. The fact that there was still an academic scruffiness about him, despite his years working for the President in Washington, just added to his appeal.

In some ways, he reminded Natalya of her father, Pyotr Avramovitz, known throughout the halls of the Kremlin as "The Professor". Her father, however, was far more assured, even predatory, with the many women in his life.

"Why did you run away when I approached?" Michael asked, recalling the feeling on the boat when he had stared directly into her eyes and had felt a connection. When he had tried to get close, she had left quickly.

"If I recall," she said with a smile, "you turned first, once I looked into your dark brown eyes." Then, taking his arm and leading him towards the shadows at the edge of the garden, with its magnificent view of the lake two hundred feet below, she added playfully. "I didn't realize that you were a romantic at heart. Do you make it a habit of accosting females on lake trips, or am I special?"

She looked up and smiled at Ross, showing perfectly aligned teeth. Her skin was light olive, her hair dark brown, almost black, worn so it nearly touched her shoulders. Her eyes drew him in without revealing anything about who she was or what she was, and yet they captured his imagination. It was not that he was inexperienced with women. He had been married once, though it had not worked out, and after a few years they had parted ways, but there was something intriguing about this Russian woman, whose accent was decidedly American.

Michael, who had never found small talk easy, found it flowed easily with this young woman. They talked at great length about France, her time in America and Russia. Later, they discussed the economy. Natalya had good insights and an economic philosophy in line with his own, believing in an interventionist approach to solving the world's many problems.

Natalya viewed this meeting with Michael Ross, the American President's Special Assistant for International Economics, as an important part of her mission. Her position was, she knew precarious, both within this group, in which Russia was barely trusted, and within the Russian bureaucracy that saw her as something less than fully Russian. She had spent more than half her life in the United States, first as a teenager, then at college, graduate school, and finally, four years at Goldman Sachs in New York, before moving to London, and eventually back to Moscow. She had been back in Russia less than four years, and had only returned at the insistence of her father. She was Special Assistant to the Minister of Trade and Industry, but was not entirely trusted by many in the Russian Government. Gaining the trust of someone with Michael Ross's influence would be a feather in her cap, so she needed Michael to like her, even love her, but there were risks with this too. In the business they were in—advisors to their respective governments—friends in high places were like gold in the bank, but in the paranoid Russian Government, friends like the American also carried risks. However, it was a risk she thought worth taking.

It was close to eleven o'clock when the dinner ended. Back in his room, Michael undressed, opened the door to the bathroom, and turned on the shower. The hot water relaxed him after a long evening of listening to the others talk. He sensed their fear that there were no easy fixes to the world's many problems. Ever since the Fall of 2008, when the Treasury and the Federal Reserve had allowed Lehman Brothers to collapse, the world economy had languished. Stimulus had come through Government actions: lower interest rates; quantitative easing and increased spending; and reduced taxes. But this had not been enough to get the private sector to take risks. The result was a growing burden of Government debt. While the Government ran up debts, the private sector hoarded cash, without investing in new production or hiring more workers.

"Here." Natalya handed him the towel as he opened the glass door of the shower.

"How did you get in?" Ross demanded, grabbing the towel quickly and wrapping it around his waist.

"You didn't lock the connecting door." she said, walking back into her room, leaving the connecting door open. He stood in the doorway as she undressed. There was something strangely natural about watching her remove her clothes; as if it was nothing out of the ordinary.

"I'd better go," Michael stammered, "before we do something that we both may regret."

"You're probably right," she said, closing the door slowly. Then leaning up against it, she wondered about her feelings for the American.

Ever since she had left the Koslov Academy as a teenager, she had been a very controlled person. It was a simple compartmentalization of the discipline and training that they had hammered into her at the secret Russian school for sleeper agents and spies. But over the years, even as she had become more Americanized, that discipline had continued to affect her, such as how she dealt with friends; seemingly keeping them close, but really at a distance. She never truly revealed who she was deep inside. There had always been the worry that, at any time, she might be given a mission. However, as the years passed, and the instilled hatred for America and its capitalist excess dissipated into a better understanding of America's great strengths, as well as its weaknesses, and as Russia changed to some post-Soviet style of democratic socialism, she had relaxed more. But on returning to Russia as a fully formed adult, and accepting retraining at Koslov as a condition of her employment and a show of loyalty to the State, her old fears had returned. She had had a few lovers, but no great loves.

She wondered if, with Michael, it could be different.

INTERLUDE II

Three small, private aircraft landed, within minutes of each other. A limousine met each one. No luggage was unloaded, and the engines of the aircraft were left idling.

The meeting room sat in a round glass and stone structure, located adjacent to the runway. The room was dominated by a large, marble-topped table. In silence, each man sat down.

Across the table they could just make out the outline of a woman wearing a broad-brimmed hat, her face invisible in the dim light at her end of the table.

"You have read the terms of the agreements," she said slowly, watching each man's face. One was Asian, one American, and the third European. "Are there any questions?"

"How can we be certain you will deliver on your promises?" the American asked.

"The first month is free. If you are satisfied—and I think you will be with the quality of the intelligence and the advantage it will give your members—then you will, I am certain, be happy to pay the nominal charges, as indicated in the contract."

"What are the risks?" the European asked, concerned thinking about the penalties for trading inside information.

"There are always risks in life," the woman answered evenly. "Sign or don't sign. It makes no difference to us. There are others who will be happy to take this opportunity."

The silence in the room was only broken by the hum of the air-conditioner. Finally, the woman spoke again.

"We expect reports from time to time about the size of the membership in the clubs. In return for providing you with this service at reasonable prices, we require the clubs to be exclusive and expensive to join. You may resell the information to anyone without fee once club members' needs are served."

"What do you gain? It makes no sense," the Asian asked.

"We have our reasons," she answered, pushing three packets across the table. On the smooth marble of the tabletop, they slid easily.

She watched as they checked the terms and conditions. Each of the three men managed a large hedge fund, with significant assets and lines of credit. Each was looking for an advantage in the market, and had been chosen for their greed. She waited patiently. Finally, each man signed the agreement and pushed the thick, legal document back across the table.

Then the woman stood up and walked out of the room.

DAVID L. BLOND

4. OF BANKERS AND BUREAUCRATS

Jenny Bennette had met Walter Holtz at the United Nations Conference on Trade and Development (UNCTAD) meeting on commercial debt-rescheduling, earlier in the day. She knew him by reputation. His International Facilitation Fund lent to Third World borrowers, and its lower rates and reputation as a "friend of the poor" allowed it to capture the lower risk loans, leaving the higher risk debt to the commercial banks. IFF operated, at least on the surface, as a non-profit NGO, seeking to promote the growth and economic development of the underdeveloped nations of the world.

But she suspected there was more to it than that. IFF played commodities markets: buying at discounts from countries they lent to; stockpiling commodities to limit supplies and drive up prices; and selling once prices had been forced well above their normal levels. In a space of ten years, they had become a powerful player, and a force that no commercial bank with loans to Third World countries could afford to ignore.

Jenny had accepted Walter's invitation for dinner out of curiosity. A loner by nature, Jenny knew few of the men who frequented the meetings and negotiations of which she was a part. Walter and his wife Katherine were legends in the industry. He had started as a minor UNCTAD bureaucrat, had met Heinrich Von Kleise's daughter Katherine, and with her family money, had left the UN and founded the IFF. As a couple they moved among the European intellectual and government elite. It was now, hours after starting the meal, that Jenny was anxious to know the real purpose of the evening.

"Let's cut to the chase," she said. "What do you want from me?"

"Help," he admitted. "We believe that with your help a debt-rescheduling plan can be developed that will be acceptable to the banks, and to the countries struggling under the weight of past mistakes."

"What do you get out of it, Walter? Are you after ten cents on each dollar owed, or something else?"

He smiled. She was a tougher sell than he'd first thought.

"Endless write-offs are not the answer, nor are defaults. We are searching for the middle ground; something that debtor countries can live with, politically, socially, and economically. It's time to jettison the Washington consensus that calls for austerity, as if this will somehow create growth and additional revenues to pay off debts."

She was interested now. She had long realized that without real restructuring many of the current "debtor" economies would never be able to repay the debts owed to the banks. The austerity demanded of them tended to lead to social collapse and economic disinvestment, making repayment even less achievable.

Jenny nodded.

"I would like you to join our team. You will bring the needed realism to our thinking on this matter. Will you consider it?"

"I really don't know what to say."

"Say 'yes', of course," said Holtz with a smile. "You have a chance to make a difference, Ms. Bennette," he added, looking her directly in the eye to make his point.

"I'll have to think about it. It's a big decision to leave the bank," she said, knowing that working for IFF would be like turning traitor. She would never get another job in banking after that.

"This isn't a defection; it's an opportunity to make a positive contribution. Have a think about it. It's late and you've had a long day already. We will take you back to your hotel now."

"Are you staying through the weekend?" Katherine Holtz asked her, as they were walking out of the restaurant.

"The meetings continue next week so I have no choice."

"Join us in Kandersteg this weekend then. I'm certain you will find my father fascinating."

She didn't have to be asked twice.

"I'd love to come," she answered, understanding immediately that this visit was a gift, but not one without expectations attached. The Holtzs didn't do anything that wasn't carefully orchestrated to achieve their goal.

"Then it's settled," Walter said with a broad smile. "We'll pick you up at your hotel, Saturday morning. Say at nine?"

Carlos Montoya looked at the young woman in the bed next to him. They had met in the bar at the De Berge Hotel earlier in the evening. Carlos had taken her to Divonne, in France, where they had gambled until the early hours, and then he'd brought her to his apartment off Avenue de Genève. His father might think his life a waste, using up his trust funds at a rapid pace. His half-brother, Diego, by his father's new wife, had been groomed to take over the vast Montoya holdings in Central and South America. Perhaps, if his father had been a little less severe when he was younger, things might have turned out differently. Still, his life was not entirely without purpose. The Holtzs valued his skills with people, especially women: the more prickly and difficult the target, the greater the challenge of the conquest. The girl now slowly opening her eyes had not been difficult.

The phone rang forcing Carlos out of bed to answer it. He slapped the girl hard on her naked bottom as he got up.

"Time to leave," he said with a smile, then left the room.

INTERLUDE III

Michelle studied the report from her contact point in Washington. The investigation of insider trading was becoming more serious, possibly compromising the plan, now that it was nearing its climax, which was scheduled for late October. She had to know what they knew.

Lifting the phone off the hook, she waited while the secure network was set up by routing the call first to a switch in Paraguay, then to Asia, and finally to Paris. Speaking in French, she explained the problem, and offered some suggestions.

"The American must not be harmed," she said, "or you'll not be paid. I want the briefcase, nothing more. Is that understood?"

She listened as the man protested, but at last, agreed.

Relieved at having taken care of that, she returned to the living space, and staring out at the distant peaks, she felt a sense of calm, despite the fact that there was so much to do, and so little time left.

5. Private Meetings, Public Purpose

Natalya barely listened to the others at the morning meeting. As she had lain in bed last night, after closing the door, she had started to assess, in her usual, analytical way, how she could win Michael's trust, and perhaps even more to her advantage, his love. The sideway glances he gave her at the meeting made it clear that he was taken with her, but she had also found herself drawn to him in a way that she hadn't experienced before, not just physically but also on an emotional level.

As she sat there thinking, she wondered if something could develop between them, and if her own paranoia about the Russia she had come home to was real. Russia was becoming increasingly less open to change and the free exchange of ideas. She was considered a suspect, her every move questioned. Even coming here had been a stretch, and her boss had approved it reluctantly. Contacts with the West were becoming more difficult, more dangerous. Natalya knew she needed more time with Michael before she could be sure of how she felt, and what was the right course of action to take.

"Is this a worldwide conspiracy, in your opinion, Dr Ross?" Stordel asked.

"I think the evidence points that way." Michael answered, wondering where the German was going with this line of reasoning.

"Couldn't it just be that, by outsourcing the collection and input of economic data to places to save money, we have left them poorly managed?"

Michael smiled. "A good point, but that is simply a weak link, not the source of the problem. Someone, we don't know who, is acting on intelligence that allows them to game the system, to make profits well beyond the ordinary. Of course, we have not been able to prove this except through statistical tests; hardly enough to convict anyone in court. We are investigating further, but it is clear that insider information is being procured and acted on."

"And this activity is not limited to America?" the Italian asked.

"No, of course not. Companies and markets are global, interlinked."

Michael sat down. Philippe called on the others in turn. Similar stories were told of markets out of line with economic fundamentals.

Natalya reported on the inflow of contraband, and linked it to the unexplained loss of Russian gold reserves. Audits of the stocks of gold held in Central Bank vaults had shown that these were nearly totally depleted. She had been warned not to report this, but found herself ignoring the advice.

"I will be shot if this gets out," she smiled, "so I trust in your discretion about what you report, but the gold is nearly gone, with little of it having been sold on public markets."

"And you are certain that the gold is gone?" the member from the British Ministry of Finance asked. A sudden intake of Russian gold on the market would have caused a collapse in the price, But gold prices had remained remarkably stable, if somewhat depressed. It was obvious that the gold had been transferred through private sale, and had never reached the London or Zurich gold exchanges.

"Yes," Natalya said. "I suspect that when oil and mineral prices started to fall, the Government had two choices: print roubles or sell the gold in exchange for hard currency, to buy the needed food, capital equipment, consumer goods."

Michael again sensed the fear as he listened to what each country reported. It was clear now that there was someone, or some group, that had control of the equity and bond markets. It was dangerous. The global economy was fragile enough without interference and collusion making a mockery of seemingly "free" markets. Banks were still reeling from bad debts, accumulated during the boom years. It would take little for the volatility that so far had sent stock markets soaring to start them crashing down. With governments and communities weakened, and unable to cushion the burden on individuals and families caught in the economic downdraft, people would be destitute once their money ran out.

There was one point, made almost as an aside, by the Japanese representative, Taka Akiyhma. It had not registered with the others, as it didn't deal with questions of markets or finance, but to Michael's ear, it was important. Taka began his presentation describing the recent bubble in the Tokyo and Osaka property markets. The near-zero rates had led to an overextension of credit to property developers and investors. This was worrisome, but then he added something else that struck Michael as even more dangerous to the world economy.

"I'm not sure this is important, but we have heard rumors of an alliance between dock workers unions across all the major ports around the Pacific. This organizing activity is going on under the noses of governments and private sector firms. There is a hint, too, of an October work action. I don't have to tell you how such a coordinated strike would close down world trade within three or four weeks, as much as the tsunami in 2011." Michael thought Taka could be right. He would get the Agency to check it out once he was back in DC.

Someone or some organization was manipulating the global economy, but to what end? Certainly, knowing in advance of when all the shit was going to hit the fan would be useful, but if all of these events came to pass at the same moment, then fortunes would be lost, and the global super-economy that had been built through globalization would collapse, sinking all nations, rich and poor alike.

Natalya watched the others depart, leaving just Michael, Philippe and herself in the room. Her bags were packed and to one side. She had not called the Consulate in Geneva to send a car, but had left it to chance as to how she would get back. Aside from a "hello" in the morning, she and Michael had not spoken directly during the day, but now, standing awkwardly with him, she was nervous. What if she had underestimated her own charm, or his feelings towards her?

For Michael, last night's interlude had been like a dream. Why had he not taken advantage of her offer? And now, after hours of sitting across from her, avoiding her direct gaze, he was standing next to her, tongue-tied, trying to find the words he needed to say.

"I suppose Natalya is going with you, Michael?" Philippe saved the situation as he noted the absence of transport for her. "I don't know what she sees in you, that she doesn't see in me."

"He's handsome, American, and unmarried; you're French, and married," she answered.

"Do you need a ride?" Michael asked, finally realizing that she was waiting for the invitation.

"Yes, thanks," she said. She leaned up and kissed Philippe on the cheek. "Until next time." Then she walked out to the car, leaving Michael to say his farewells to Philippe.

"What are you thinking about, Michael?" Natalya asked once they had left Annecy and were on the main road back to Geneva. He had barely uttered two words to her since they'd left.

"About you." He looked over at her, thinking how much his life would change if he was going to be with her. There wouldn't be anything at first, at least nothing overt. He knew that it would trigger the interest of the security agencies who would start to take an even greater interest in his personal life; not that his personal life had ever been his own since joining the Administration. Political opponents would also use it as a weapon against him, or worse still, the President, when they were at their most vulnerable. However, Michael also feared passing up a second opportunity of being with such a physically arousing, yet intellectually stimulating woman, and losing her for good.

"What about me?"

"Life, at least for me, seems to have suddenly become more complicated since I met you, Natalya."

"Why? Because I'm Russian, or because I'm a woman and women tend to complicate life?"

"Because you live in Moscow, Natalya, and I live in Washington." He pushed his foot down on the accelerator, passing a car that honked as Michael swerved around him.

"It's more difficult for me," she answered, wondering which part of her was speaking: the cold, analytical secret agent that had been taught over the years to treat men like pieces on a chess board, to be used as necessary; or that of the woman searching for more than intrigue and subterfuge.

"Turn at the next crossroads," she said, pointing ahead. "We need more time," she answered looking at him. "Flirting with each other isn't enough to make choices that will affect us for a lifetime. There is an inn I know where we can make sense of our feelings."

"Where are we going?" he asked, turning without stopping to think that this might well be some kind of trap. His feelings towards her were less complicated. "They'll be expecting me in Geneva. If I lose these papers the Government will have my head."

"Call from the hotel. Ask the Consulate to send a courier to pick up the papers and send them back to Washington."

Michael stole a sideways glance at her.

"Why did you return to Russia, Natalya?"

"I thought I could make a difference. My father asked me to come back. Besides, my classmates at Harvard and colleagues at Goldman Sachs always envied my access to key people in the Government, as well as my language abilities. Russia was 'hot', the place to invest, to make money, to get rich in oil, gas, and minerals. You had to have all kinds of contacts to do business. It was a new and exciting experience for me."

"In your country …" Michael stopped himself. He slowed the car to a halt pulling off the road.

"In my country," she said angrily, "they have cold prisons, secret police, impossible bureaucracies, thought control, dangerous mafias, and, Michael," she said angrily, "my orders are to entrap you. Isn't that what you are thinking?" Natalya stopped before she said more.

"I didn't say that!"

"But you thought it, admit it."

"I thought it, but … I'm sorry, Natalya," he said after a moment. Starting the car again, he pulled back onto the road. "There's something going on between us. I just don't know whether to trust my feelings, or to worry that I am being entrapped for some other reason."

He was right, she thought, but she was also being pulled in so many different directions that it was unclear to her who was actually being trapped.

"Speed up, Michael." she ordered, looking back at the red car that had been following them for more than twenty minutes. When they had pulled off earlier, the car had slowed just ahead and waited. Now, it was behind them again. Was it coincidence or was there something more? Her training kicked in and she reached in the back for her overnight bag. She had taken the gun for protection from the security officials at the consulate in Geneva before coming to the meeting. At least one Russian official investigating the loss of the gold had been found dead.

Michael pushed his foot down on the accelerator. The car's motor whined. The distance at first increased, but slowly, the red car closed in on them.

"I don't like it." Natalya said, looking back at the car now just twenty feet behind. She could see two men sitting in the front seat. Was it just nerves or was it just a typical, impatient French driver wanting to pass.

"It's just a car, Natalya," he answered, oblivious to the danger.

"Slow down. Let's see if it passes."

Michael looked uneasily at the gun that was now resting in her lap.

He slowed the car and the red car sped up, going wide around them before disappearing into the distance.

"You see," said Michael, "it was nothing."

Natalya wasn't certain of that for she had noted how the men had stared at Michael as the car passed.

"I don't know."

"Do you know how to use that?" he asked, pointing at the gun.

"Yes." She didn't explain. It was a long and complicated story.

The road narrowed, running in a one-way loop through the cobbled streets of the village. The hotel was up a slight hill from the main square. It was an old auberge, almost from another century, with a slanting roof to ward off the winter snows that blanketed the hills outside Geneva. The imposing hulk of the Salève —the flat-topped mountain plateau beloved for its hiking trails and vistas of the Alps beyond—cast dark shadows on the hotel's parking lot. An old sign displaying two stars hung out front. There were a few cars parked outside, but the red car wasn't one of them. Natalya relaxed and put the weapon back in her bag.

The room, like the hotel, was old. Michael lay down on the bed only to feel it sink towards the middle.

"Call the Consulate and ask them to send a guard to take the papers back."

Hanging up the phone after an angry exchange with the US Mission Security Officer, Michael lay back on the bed next to her wondering what would come next.

She was the first to hear the steps outside their door. Instinctively, Natalya tensed. She hadn't been convinced that the men in the car following them earlier had left them for good.

"Hand me the bag," she whispered, reaching for it across the bed, and over Michael as he lay staring at the tin-plate ceiling of the room.

He handed her the bag, but she didn't have time to open it.

The door flew open with a loud bang as the wood splintered as the lock was torn off its anchors. Natalya threw herself at the larger of the two men, as Michael wrestled with the first for the briefcase on the chair next to the bed. The man outweighed her by fifty pounds and he slammed her back against the wall, his huge hands gripped her throat choking off her air. Instinct now replaced thought and she reacted violently. Koslov had taught her that in a fight, especially a fight for life, the one with the stronger will to live will survive. Natalya shoved her right hand, palm up, into the man's chin, twisting him around as they exchanged positions, and snapped his neck back against the wall. The shock of that blow was followed by a second that hammered his head into the metal prongs of the ancient coat rack on the right of the bed. Leaving him hanging there, blood oozing from the crack in his skull, she looked to where Michael lay on the bed, moaning, his right arm was covered in blood from a knife wound, and the briefcase was gone.

She assessed his injury. Just the arm, a deep cut, probably requiring stitches, but not life-threatening. Taking his other hand, she pressed it against the gash. "Squeeze down hard." From the washstand she grabbed a towel, wet it slightly, and handed it to him. "You have to press as hard as you can. I'll be back."

Grabbing her gun, she ran out of the room, almost knocking over the hotel manager, following a trail of blood from the attacker. Michael had evidently wounded him during their struggle.

The moon was bright enough so the trail was easily visible. It led towards the village just down the hill from the hotel. The weapon felt cold in her hand.

There was a line of trees, neatly spaced along the narrow path leading up to the hotel. Without consciously planning, she started to run, in and out of the trees. He fired, hitting the trunks of the trees as she passed.

"Don't fire until you are certain of success," her instructors had said many times at Koslov.

Now she was close, close enough to hear him scramble down through the underbrush. He stopped, turned suddenly, and raised his weapon one-handed, but he was tired and out of breath, and she was a dim shape outlined by the bright lights of the auberge up on the hill. Natalya fired on instinct, two shots; both struck, twisting him around and sending him to the ground, dead, the briefcase beside him.

The call to Philippe had brought counterterrorism police to the scene rather than the regular Gendarmes.

"I don't know this man," the security officer in charge said, studying the face of Natalya's assailant in the light of the inn's front porch. The body had been carried down from the room, leaving a trail of blood on the carpet. "The other we know," he said, studying the man Natalya had shot.

"Who is he?" she asked, slowly regaining her composure. The emotion of the last few hours had taken its toll. She'd never killed a man before.

"He's in one of our many left-wing clubs. A bit more radical than our standard French Communist, but then he was likely working under contract. I don't think this was ideological; it was purely business. Someone paid for what was in the briefcase."

Inside the hotel Michael told and retold the story as the Consulate physician cleaned his wound and stitched it up. He had refused to go to the hospital. The Marine guard and the State Department Security Officer were taking everything down. The briefcase would be moved that night back to Geneva.

"I've told you everything I know about what happened," Michael said, getting up from the bed. Natalya walked back into the room. She expected the third degree. Telling her story again, she watched the State Department man for signs that he believed her.

"Why did you have the weapon?"

"I carried sensitive papers to the meeting. I'm licensed to use it."

"Why were you here, and not back in Geneva as you had planned? Did you latch onto Dr Ross for some other purpose, Natalya? We know who you are, and what you were trained to do."

Michael watched as the State Department Security Officer grilled Natalya, growing increasingly angry at the aggressive questioning.

"I think we should thank Natalya for saving our papers. I'll check in with the Mission in the morning. So, unless you have anything more to say, get the fuck out of here!"

"Dr Ross, we are just doing our job."

"Yes, and you have done it. Take the damn case and get it safely back to the Mission. I'll be there tomorrow. Now leave … or do I have to call the President?"

"We'll get another room," she said, standing up once the State Department official had left.

"I'm getting up. Perhaps, we can get some food downstairs."

"I'll check. Stay here, Michael."

He fell back reluctantly on to the bed. He watched her walk out of the door, and thought through what had happened: she had reacted, not as an amateur, but as a professional.

Natalya spoke to the owner of the hotel. There was another room, a smaller one at the rear of the building. As for dinner, he would cook them a meal they would long remember. After arranging this, she returned to the room to find Michael standing staring down at the red car, still parked in the courtyard below.

"There's another room in the back that we can have for the night."

Michael reached up and brushed back the strands of her hair, from her face.

"I look a mess," she said.

"Not to me. You saved my life. And you hunted down that other man, didn't you? You stalked him in the dark. You killed him too. Where did you learn to do that? Why?"

"It was in the past."

"When you lived in America?" he asked worried and upset. "Did you spy for them?" It was a question that worried him greatly.

"No!" she said. "I never spied, I never stole secrets, and I never killed anyone before tonight. When I was twelve years old, they sent me to a school where I spent two years learning these trades, perfecting my English, developing an accent that was authentically American. I suppose they thought I could be of some use later, within one of the many sleeper cells planted in America. The Cold War had just ended, but the mentality of the successors was much the same. America was an enemy, perhaps less so than before, but a future rival for world power and influence."

"Can I trust you?" He looked at her. If he couldn't, if he had to forget her, given all that had just happened, he would be lost, and he knew it. Yet, he had to ask. He had to feel that she was on his side, that she wasn't the enemy.

"If I answer 'yes,' will you believe me?" Her stomach was wrenched in tight knots. Why was he questioning her now? She had protected him. She had retrieved the papers at great risk, knowing that to lose them was to lose him.

"Yes," he said, lifting her chin carefully so that he might kiss her.

"Then, you can trust me, Michael. You can trust me with your life."

It was after midnight when the owner of the inn laid the last course of the dinner before the two guests. He watched as they sampled the soufflé laced with orange liquor.

"It is very fine, Monsieur," Michael said first. The girl followed in rapid-fire French, complimenting their host. The owner smiled, turned and went back into the kitchen to finish cleaning up the pans, leaving his guests alone.

"Must you return to America tomorrow?"

"Yes. I have so much to do."

"I'm taking a week off," Natalya said on impulse. "Spend it with me."

"I really have to get back to work."

"It's July, Michael, the world's on vacation. Even the President of the United States goes to the Cape this month."

"I have reports to get out, the semi-annual budget review ..." He started to list the tasks left to do before September.

"Everyone needs time off, time to think, recharge the batteries. And with the battering you took tonight, you need a chance to recover, Michael." Natalya reached for his hand. "We need time, Michael." A part of him said "no," but the better part wanted to say "yes."

"What will they think if we travel together?" Michael asked out loud.

"What will they think now that we have slept together?" she asked. "The damage is done. Spending a week can't make it worse. Besides, they need you."

"I'll decide in the morning."

As they left dinner and returned to their new room, the hotel owner watched the woman closely as she passed by the doorway to the kitchen. She was both beautiful and dangerous. Two men, likely killers both, lay dead by her hand.

"*Quelle femme!*" he mumbled under his breath. "*Quelle belle femme!*"

6. NATALYA

The next morning, Michael explained to Washington that he was taking a week off, but chose not to say who he was spending it with. Given the events of the previous evening, it would not have taken long for that bit of information to have been pieced together.

The love-making the night before had been hurried, more a hunger on both their parts than something sweet and innocent. Michael surprised her with a passion that was long repressed, and she found herself needing a man almost as much.

However, the next morning as they sat in the garden, they were silent, as if the reality of their different paths made anything more happening between them seem complex and possibly dangerous.

"Who are you, Natalya?" he finally asked. He was as frightened to hear the truth as she was to tell it.

"I was born in Moscow, in 1983", she began slowly, knowing that it was a long story. She didn't want to scare him away, but she had to tell the truth. US intelligence services undoubtedly had a thick file on her and would, no doubt, present the worst parts of it to Michael once he returned to Washington.

"My father is Pyotr Avramowitz; an influential man in light of the new economics of Russia, and the grandson of one of the original Bolsheviks."

Her great-grandfather, Lev Avramowitz, had known Lenin, Stalin and Trotsky. He had fought in the Revolution, joined the St Petersburg Soviet after deserting the army, taking with him thousands of men, and somehow, had managed to avoid the purges that had destroyed that generation of old Bolsheviks. With such a pedigree, her own grandfather worked as a diplomat, and when appointed Ambassador to Switzerland brought his family with him, enrolling Pyotr at Enigen, an exclusive Swiss boarding school in Kandersteg.

Natalya remembered little of her grandfather, as he was an old man, and had died when she was four. When she thought of him she remembered the smell of sauerkraut and tobacco, and how his beard felt rubbing against her face. Her first real clear image of that time was at his funeral. They had driven out in a big Ziv limousine with two older men, friends of her grandfather, and one of Pyotr's younger women, ostensibly, to keep Natalya in line. She remembered the line of black cars and the old men and women who stood by the grave.

She knew little about her father's years before her birth, except things that appeared in the blurbs on his books. He had studied Political Economy at Moscow University. His family's political connections had allowed him to go overseas to finish his degrees. He had a Ph.D. from the London School of Economics, and had taught Western Economics on his return to Russia for a year, before taking up a position in New York, at the United Nations. What her father had done for the UN was unclear. He was, like other Russian employees in international agencies, part of a larger apparatus to gain intelligence.

Her father was a rarity in those pre-*perestroika* days, a man with impeccable political loyalties, who appeared to be sympathetic to Western ideas of secular humanism and individual freedom, and yet also still passionate about Russia's unique form of socialism. Sometime after leaving New York in 1983, she was born.

"And your mother?" he asked.

Natalya had been born sometime after leaving New York in 1983, but had never seen her birth certificate, nor did she know who her mother was.

"According to my father, I was his alone. There must have been a girl, somewhere, that he got pregnant, and she didn't want the child. At least, that's my operating theory. For much of what passed as my childhood, I wanted a mother. The girls that Pyotr bedded and then discarded were not substitutes, and my father was coldly indifferent to a little girl's need for love and attention. He is called "the Professor," and was both feared and respected, but as a father, he was cold and heartless; a man that I really don't know.

"When the Soviet Union started to fall apart in 1989, Pyotr was there to help turn the economy around. He was friends with them all, the new elites that would replace the old, tired, Soviet apparatchiks. I remembered Gorbachev, Yeltsin and Yegor Gaidar coming to the apartment to meet my father. Often there would be violent arguments between the men followed by long nights of drinking. Although I was just six years old, I remembered having to clean up my playroom the next morning and collecting empty vodka bottles."

For Michael the question that he was afraid to ask concerned what she had done last night. She had been trained to kill, which wasn't usual for bankers or those working in the Ministry of Trade and Industry. Was her work in the Ministry just a cover and was she part of the intelligence community? If that was the case, could he trust her to tell the truth even if he asked?

"How did you learn to do what you did last night?" he asked.

"There was a time Michael," she said leaning back in the chair, "when Russia demanded things of the children of the elites, to prove their parents' loyalty. My father wanted my uncle and his family to go to America. My Uncle Victor was far too outspoken, more like my Revolutionary Grandfather, Lev Avramowitz. Perestroika was a mirage. It allowed the State to identify people who saw this as an opening and demanded more. My uncle was in trouble or was likely to be in more trouble, and my father saw a solution, and the solution was his daughter, so I was sacrificed to that need."

Michael was confused. Natalya had said all this almost in a daze, as if telling him was as painful to her as listening to it for him.

"Sacrificed?" He asked.

"Just before my twelfth birthday, my father offered my services to the state. They sent me to the Koslov Academy, a special school run by the FSB to teach children to be instruments of the State. It was hidden from the public, but known to the top echelons of the government. I already spoke good English, but by the time I left Koslov I could speak like any teenage American girl. They taught me to resist America's lure, to see freedom as a mirage and smoke screen for a kind of secret repression of the poor and disenfranchised, that everyone was chained to the value-chain of the corporate structure without a real social safety net. America was evil even if it seemed like the perfect society: free, open, rich; everything Russia was not. And they taught me rudiments of spy craft with the view that at some time in the future they might 'activate' me. It was program with flaws. We were children, not spies, and while the others might be naïve enough to believe that someday they would serve mother Russia, I was not so naïve Michael. I knew the truth. My father had told me the truth about Russia long before I went to the Koslov Academy. So, when he sent me there he told me why: it was the price the family had to pay for my uncle and his family to be allowed to leave for America; it was the price he had to pay to get me safely away from the turmoil that was coming in the transition from one form of oppression—the oppression of the State—to another, the oppression of the market."

There were things she left out: the pain, the isolation, the hazing, and the constant indoctrination, but she was smart and adapted quickly, playing the game as they wished her to play it. She scored well on the language tests, learned the idiom, and learned to think as an American child. They gave her American textbooks, and she went to class as if she was in an American school.

There was one final test; the ultimate test of an agent. Could she kill someone she didn't know, or didn't hate? She remembered the feel of the gun in her hand, the excitement of the chase, the rush of adrenalin when she had cornered the poor, scared man, hiding in the bush, exhausted and confused. But when she had him at close range, she couldn't kill him. She had turned from him only to see the instructor she called "the *Fox*" come up behind her. He shook his head, and taking his weapon, shot the poor man, but didn't kill him. He made her sit by his side, powerless to help, and watch as he died slowly, painfully. Last night had been different: the anger was there, knowing that he had tried to hurt Michael, and she had not felt anything but relief when he had dropped to the ground dead.

"I left Russia in the summer of 1995, with my Uncle Victor, Aunt Katia, and their two children, both younger: Katrina, nine, and Sasha, seven. Pyotr had arranged for a position for my uncle, teaching Engineering at an American university, and we settled in a nice, house in Wheaton. I went to Wheaton High School just outside of DC, but I was bright and my Russian education, especially what I had received at Koslov, was better than that in the States, so I quickly advanced. I was just seventeen when I graduated, and was accepted at Harvard on a full scholarship. You might say that I took to America like a duck to water. Was it Koslov's training or just the taste of a freedom? And ..." she thought of her overweight, motherly aunt with fondness, "of course, Aunt Katia spoiled me, calling me her lonely orphan. She gave me the love that I had been missing for so long."

Natalya continued to talk. She talked about Harvard, about business school, about her work in New York for Goldman Sachs, and later, in their Moscow office, before leaving to work for the Ministry.

"When I returned to Russia, after leaving Goldman Sachs in Moscow, I was sent back to Koslov for a three-month refresher, to prove my loyalty to the new Russia. Not much had changed, Michael. They were still training children to be agents, still placing them in America, Europe, and China, as insurance."

"My father," she said with a bitterness that surprised her, "was still pulling the strings for everything I did.

"Come, we must go. It's getting late and if we are to make the most of this week together, then we have to start soon." She smiled. "Don't be worried, Michael. Whatever I was, I am not now; whatever I will become, is unknown. Let's just enjoy our time together and see what the gods' decree. So come," she said with some finality, "it's time to go and see if there's a future for us."

7. KANDERSCHLOSS

When you worked for the President of the United States, a vacation was always a luxury. Whether in Washington or abroad on business, Michael was always on call, and there was never enough time in the day or night to finish the work.

The events of last night, however, had convinced him that life was too short. He didn't want to let Natalya go without giving them a chance.

"Where shall we go?" he asked.

"Grindelwald, in the Jungfrau," she said. "It's a good place to hike at this time of year."

"That's near Kandersteg?" Michael asked, remembering Von Kleise's long standing invitation.

"Yes, the turnoff is just before we reach Interlaken."

"Would you mind stopping off on the way, so I can say hello to an old friend?" he asked.

"Who are we visiting?

"Heinrich Von Kleise," Michael replied.

"My father and Von Kleise were classmates at Enigen boarding school, just outside of Kandersteg," Natalya volunteered. "It wasn't the type of school that you would think a dedicated Stalinist, who had survived the purges of the thirties, and fought as a Major General in the Great Patriotic War, should have sent his sons to, but my grandfather was an extraordinary man. He wanted his sons to be friends with the sons of the most influential men of their time. Thus he sent Pyotr, my father, and his younger brother, Victor, to Enigen. How do you know him?"

"We met, years back, when I was in Switzerland working, alongside his daughter and son-in-law, Katherine and Walter Holtz, at the UN Conference for Trade and Development. I can't say how many times he has tried to recruit me to work for him, but I've always refused. He told me I was crazy to return to academia when, together, we could change the world."

"Why did you turn him down? I'm sure he'd pay you well."

"Oh, I've thought about it. Who wouldn't? But I've always valued him as a friend. You can't work for someone and remain just a friend."

They stopped for lunch in Montreaux, at the end of the lake, and walked along the lakefront after lunch, mixing with the tourists. It was mid-July, the high season for tourism in Switzerland. Natalya tried again to explain to Michael just how confusing her life had been. Words alone could not explain her feelings for him, but she found telling her story again, without embellishment, was easy … as if it were meant to be. The events of last night had forced the part of her life that had always been hidden away to resurface. When she was finished, a great weight had been lifted from her shoulders.

"Why did you go back?" he asked.

"Pyotr begged me. He claimed he missed me, but I think he just wanted someone in Moscow that might be able to raise capital for Russia. Goldman Sachs was supportive of me returning. I had already helped out on a number of deals from London, but having me based in Moscow was viewed as a positive business move. All the stars converged, and so I went. I was certainly qualified. I had a Harvard MBA, and there were opportunities in Russia at that time for an entrepreneurial, American-trained, MBA. It was the new economy and growing fast. I was, after all, an experienced investment banker and advisor, and of course, I spoke the language."

"For a while I worked out of Goldman's Moscow office, but Michael, as you know well, doing business in Russia isn't as simple as it seems. There wasn't a course at Harvard on how to fend off death threats, or how to determine the appropriate gratuity to offer to avoid a slit throat." She laughed, remembering the visit from the representative of the Russian mafia that had come just weeks after arriving. "In the end, my father found me a sufficiently high enough position in the Ministry of Trade and Industry. In hindsight, I suspected that was his original goal in the first place."

"Would you leave Russia for me, Natalya?" he asked suddenly, stopping to face her. He feared the question as much as he feared the answer. In either case, they would face huge complications. Theirs would never be seen as a simple or harmless romance.

"Don't let that problem get in our way. It's too soon to ask." She looked at the sun, moving towards the western horizon. "Come, it's getting late, and Kandersteg is still a couple of hours away."

It was already dark when they reached the town square. What he remembered was that the house was high above the town, overlooking a lake. In one of the hotels they asked for directions. The instructions were specific, but the clerk suggested it would be unlikely they'd make it past the guarded entrance to the estate's private driveway.

The road climbed well over 1,000 feet, gripping the side of the mountain. It leveled off at a well-lit gatehouse, where the car was stopped by steel barriers. On either side of the road a high stone wall blocked the house from view.

"This is a private road," said the guard in German, repeating the warning in English, when Michael didn't appear to understand.

"I'm here to see Von Kleise. My name is Dr Michael Ross," Michael pulled out his passport.

"You're not on the list," the man answered, without looking at any list. "Please turn your car around."

"Call Herr Von Kleise. I'm certain he will be pleased to see us. He said I should come at any time. Really."

"You are not on our list," the guard repeated. "Please return in the morning." The man moved back towards the gatehouse. Natalya leaned over so the guard could see her face. She spoke to him curtly in German. He nodded, and returning to the guard house, placed the call.

"What did you tell him?" Michael said, laughing at how she had been instantly obeyed.

"I told him that he would be fired if Herr Doctor Michael Ross, the very famous American economist and high government official, and old friend of Herr Von Kleise, was turned away unannounced. I demanded he call immediately. Any delay, even for a second, would likely lead to his immediate dismissal."

"And he believed you?"

"Such people only listen to authority."

Von Kleise was waiting outside. Michael's coming was unexpected, yet most welcome. His eagerness, however, had less to do with the American than with the woman he was bringing with him. He had waited many years to meet Pyotr's daughter.

"I don't believe we have met, Natalya," said the old man, extending his hand. "Still, I feel that I have known you since the day you were born. Your father and I are old friends."

"I'm very pleased to meet you, too," she said, taking his hand, surprised by the warmth of his greeting.

Von Kleise turned to Michael with a smile. "It's been too long, Michael. You've made an old man happy. Please come in," he said, ushering them into the entrance to the house.

"I hope we're not intruding?" Natalya asked.

"Hardly," the older man replied, dismissing the suggestion with a wave.

Von Kleise's Kanderschloss descended in tiers down the hillside towards the lake, 500 feet below the house. Like a waterfall, growing larger as it went lower, it opened up onto a huge interior space, a living room with floor-to-ceiling windows thirty feet high. It was late, but there was still a small amount of light filtering over the mountains to the west, suggesting a view of the lake and mountains that must be magnificent in full daylight.

"The old part of the house was comfortable" Von Kleise explained, "yet, Natalya, I'm afraid, as I've become a man with responsibilities, charm was sacrificed to the need for more space for guests."

At the far end of the room, in front of a roaring fire, a small group of people sat talking. They stopped as Von Kleise, Michael and Natalya entered the room.

"Some old friends of yours, Michael," Von Kleise said with a grin, interested in what would happen when Michael and the Holtzs met again.

Michael shivered. It had been fifteen years since he had last seen either Walter or Katherine Holtz and then the meeting had been cold, professional, and almost hostile. Once they had been colleagues, even close friends, but they had joined opposite sides of the economic divide as to the best prescription for the global economy. Michael still believed that governments and banks could sort things out, while Walter and Katherine felt that more radical changes were necessary and justified.

"Michael," Walter Holtz moved swiftly across the room towards the staircase where they had stopped.

"It's been too long." Michael extended his hand, but Walter ignored it, and instead gripped him in a bear hug. He let go just as Katherine approached.

"Do I get a kiss after so long?" she asked, turning her cheek to him.

"Of course," Michael answered stiffly. Katherine Holtz was still a beautiful woman despite being fifty-two years old.

Then she looked Natalya, studying her critically. Her dark hair contrasted with Katherine's own light brown hair, but the green of her eyes mirrored Katherine's hue. Michael, Walter and Von Kleise noted Katherine's sudden surprise.

"Katherine Holtz. And you are …?"

"Natalya Avramowitz." She extended her hand, which was ignored. "I see," was all Katherine could stammer, and then quickly turned away, leaving Natalya momentarily alone. Walter rushed to the rescue, surprised by Katherine's rudeness.

"I am sorry about my wife. She's usually quite charming, isn't she, Michael?" Walter said, struggling to smooth the awkwardness of the situation.

Katherine turned back towards Natalya, who was still shocked by the rudeness of the older woman. "You're Pyotr's daughter, aren't you?" she asked, glancing at her father. *Of course, he knew.* How could she have believed all these years that Natalya's birth had been hidden from him? Yet, he had never mentioned it.

"Yes," Natalya answered tersely. "You've met my father?"

"Years ago, a lifetime it seems, in New York, before you were born." Katherine continued to stare, then turned and walked back to where the other two guests were seated.

Von Kleise understood that the American banker, Jenny Bennette, was being wooed to work for Walter and Katherine, and he knew Carlos Montoya's reputation as a fixer for their company, as well as being the son of a former classmate of Von Kleise's at Enigen.

"I am afraid that my daughter lacks social skills. Perhaps you would like to see the house?" Von Kleise asked, taking Natalya's arm and guiding her back towards the staircase.

Half an hour later, Von Kleise and Natalya returned to the room and walked over to where Michael and Walter were locked in heated discussion.

"They're arguing again," he said, looking sadly at the two men. "Once, they were good friends, but the world has changed for both of them. There was once as much fire in Michael as in Walter, but working in academia, and now government, has robbed him of his belief in his ability to change the world for the better."

"You have a beautiful house." Natalya said, trying to change the subject. She didn't want to talk about Michael.

Ignoring Natalya's comment, Von Kleise glanced towards where Katherine was sitting.

"Katherine and Walter, of course, are hoping I will die sooner rather than later. They have great plans for my money …" His voice trailed off.

After a moment, he turned towards Natalya, and with a curious looking smile, led her back towards the other guests. Later, seated in front of the huge fireplace, sipping her drink, and staring out at the wall of nearly opaque, mirror-like glass, Natalya tried to picture her life with Michael. If she had stayed in America, would she have turned into some version of Jenny Bennette? Certainly, she thought, returning to Russia had changed the direction of her life, yet it had not turned out so well, and her influence was waning as the economy suffered one setback after another. In some circles of the FSB, she was assumed to be a spy, or at least a sleeper agent awaiting activation. Her days were numbered, she knew that, and this unauthorized week with Michael would likely cement the views of those who opposed her father, and therefore her, back home.

At dinner the conversation became heated. Michael defended the American position on debt relief, noting Jenny's silence on this subject. The disagreement with the Holtzs had started at a *Club of Paris* meeting twenty years before. The Club, made up of debtor governments, creditor governments and private banks, had been in existence since the 1970s. At that meeting Michael, acting as a consultant to the American Government, had challenged IFF's motives and aims. That had ended their friendship.

When Von Kleise could stand no more, he put up his hands and stopped the discussion.

"This is my house, it is a beautiful evening, and we have no reason to shout."

Von Kleise turned his attention to the American banker. "Miss Bennette, how can we solve this problem? The banks need the money and so many countries, including some in Western Europe, are essentially bankrupt, and need the debt relief just to meet basic needs for food and fuel."

"A compromise between what the debtors can pay, and what the banks can afford to write off must be reached. Plus, there needs to be some subsidy for losses from either the ECB or the Federal Reserve. That is the only realistic solution."

Michael listened. The debt had been run up by a host of countries pressured into borrowing by banks with cheap money, seeking better returns. Sovereign debt was thought to be safer than putting the funds into junk bonds. When the economy collapsed in Europe, Southern European debtors within the Eurozone were unable to devalue their currency, preventing the flexibility to solve their economic problems themselves. Elsewhere in the world, although the scale of the slowdown that had begun in 2008, had eased, economic uncertainty continued, without a strong recovery in employment and stagnant wages, causing people to increasingly question the benefits of free trade and globalization. The United States and other countries had tried to save their own economies by applying tariffs and quotas on imports from China, but this had led the Chinese economy to collapse in 2014, as investment disappeared and companies failed, leading to mass unemployment. A trade war ensued and the global trading system teetered on the verge of total collapse. Old debts could no longer be paid back.

"That is not what your bank's president wants to hear," Von Kleise noted, "but I agree wholeheartedly with your sentiments. There must be a compromise, but there must be something more. There must be a way for these countries to compete without being taken advantage of."

"We all share the same goals, Heinrich," Michael answered, "only our approaches differ."

"And how would you solve that problem, Michael?" Walter asked sharply. "After all, it was the series of trade restrictions that you imposed after the 2012 election, that are at the root of the problem of slow global trade growth. What is your magic bullet that benefits all without harming any?"

It was a typically loaded question that he had no answer to. It was true, Michael thought, he had recommended the increased enforcement of trade rules, which had caused the slowdown in global trade growth. But the United States could no longer afford to be the dumping ground for any country's excess production, and continue to run an increasing trade deficit.

"I wish I knew," he said finally. "I'm not a miracle worker, Walter. Miracles, I leave to you and Katherine."

"Then we will gladly take up the challenge," Walter said. "Jenny, I hope that you will give IFF your counsel, and help us work towards the goal of a reasonable compromise between lender and debtor countries that we all know must be accomplished, if we are to reset the global economy back on a path to sustainable growth." Holtz stood up suddenly. "It's getting late and we have a long day tomorrow." Reaching out his hand for Katherine's, he helped her up. Carlos and Jenny followed in turn. Michael watched, with some relief, as the four of them left the room.

"Can I offer you both a cognac?" Von Kleise asked, once the others were out of the room.

"Not for me, but perhaps for Natalya?"

"I'm very tired, Heinrich. It's been a long day. Perhaps tomorrow night?"

"Then I'll show you both to your room. You must forgive Walter and Katherine for their fervor; they sometimes wear their hair shirts too openly."

Later, after his guests were in bed, Heinrich walked, as he did each evening, to the far side of his sprawling house, where a lone cable car waited to take him up to the retreat he had had built, near the summit of Bluemlisalpenhorn.

8. ENIGEN

Enigen, the exclusive Swiss boarding school that Natalya's father and Heinrich Von Kleise had attended in the 1960s, was near Kandersteg. The school sat on 100 hectares of land, just off the road that ran through the valley from Kandersteg village to the main highway running from Bern to Interlaken. Von Kleise had called Jean Grunlian, the current headmaster of the school, to arrange their visit. The headmaster met them at the entrance.

Michael looked around at the walls of the school that looked like a classic English boarding school built in the Victorian style; more like a fortress than an inviting place of learning. However, upon entering the building, he was surprised to see that the walls of the corridors were well-lit, radiating with bright, vibrant colors that seemed to change hue as they walked through them. The bulletin boards were filled with drawings and carefully written pages of text, all illustrated beautifully with drawings and pictures. Grunlian noticed Michael's interest and explained that these were the students' lesson books. Waldorf, or "Steiner schools" as they were generally called in Europe, did not use formal textbooks, but rather depended upon the students to summarize what they learned in notebooks that were collected and graded.

"Herr Von Kleise explained that you are the daughter of one of our graduates," Grunlian said, looking at Natalya.

"Yes, my father attended between 1959 and 1965, alongside Herr Von Kleise," she said quickly, and then asked, "Did the old Enigen look like this?" She, too, had noted the difference between the outside and the inside. It didn't seem like a place where someone like her father might have fit in.

"No!" he laughed. ""Imagine a school more in the tradition of an English boarding school with no color on the walls, no beautiful drawings, no dance, no music, no soul, just willpower and iron-clad discipline to make things happen. Even when everything was conspiring to stop you achieving your goals. Machte, the headmaster at the time, kept much of the curriculum that he had learned from teaching in the first Waldorf School at Stuttgart, but stripped out much of the art and music, replacing it with hard physical exercise and endurance tests, in the belief that it strengthened the will forces. If you want to learn about the old Enigen, then I will take you to meet Peter Strauss. He taught here for more than fifty years. He was here at the old Enigen and knew Machte. He still lives in a small house on the property."

"Peter." Grunlian shouted as they approached the small cottage, "there are people here who wish to know about the old Enigen."

They both watched as an old man, probably close to ninety by the look of him and the way he walked, emerge from the house. When they were closer, he stared at Natalya, seeing something vaguely familiar in her facial structure.

"She is Pyotr Avramovitz's daughter," Grunlian explained, seeing the old man's stare. Strauss had an uncanny ability to read faces; a skill he was demonstrating now as he studied Natalya. Her eyes were set like her father's, but the nose and mouth were those of someone else, someone far more familiar.

"Yes, I may be old, but I still remember the Russian ambassador's son; very quick study of mathematics, but so political. Ugh!"

Grunlian looked at his watch and then begged their forgiveness for leaving them alone with Strauss.

"Enigen," his eyes looked towards the dark buildings across the fields, "not the tame Enigen of today. No, that wouldn't do for Herr Dr Machte. Back then, Enigen was rather a cold, dark, hard place, where young men's wills would be shaped, and their future course in life set."

Strauss paused, as if to remember, choosing his words carefully. "It was very exclusive, for Machte would only accept students with influential parents, and boys that had a strong potential to achieve future power and wealth. He ruled them with an iron fist, demanding much, and then more. It was regimented, essentially military in its physical training. And for the most part, the students that made it through their first year, stayed. They were in awe of Machte, who trained with them and was as hard on himself as on them. Hard work, sacrifice, even pain, was tolerated to mold the spirit. Machte, unlike Steiner, focused on the will forces, not the heart forces." Strauss paused, deciding what to say and what to leave unsaid.

"On just a few occasions Machte would choose a number of particularly promising students for a special challenge. He charged them with a task, a great task that could not be accomplished in a year, not in ten years, only in a lifetime. He only chose the students with the greatest intellect and strongest wills. It was a simple charge he laid on them: to change the world in a meaningful way. On the fiftieth anniversary, their *Phoenixjahr*, they were to meet and justify their lives to the others.

"Over the years that I have been here, there have only been a few such meetings. What they discuss and why they bother to seek each other out after such a long period of time, I have never been privy too. However, I have heard that this year, in October, Herr Von Kleise has requested permission to arrange a meeting here. He has told Grunlian that he wants to host a small reunion. But Grunlian knows nothing of the old ways of Enigen. I might be old, but I am not oblivious to this place that has been my life. It will have been fifty years since he graduated, so I believe Von Kleise is planning a *Phoenixjahr* reunion. If he is, it will be the last, for Machte died just after Von Kleise and your father graduated."

Michael shivered. There was a cool breeze blowing off from the far-off ice-fields of the Bluemlisalpenhorn, but it might equally well have been caused by what Strauss had just said. A Hitler or a Roosevelt could have been produced there. Enigen, for the thirty years that Machte had been Headmaster, had sent graduates into the world indoctrinated with the conviction and self-belief that they were special and unique ... above all other men.

"Perhaps it is well that the old Enigen is no more. It has no place in this world." Michael said, thinking out loud. "Will forces can be used for good or for evil. Isn't that right, Herr Strauss?"

"Or," Strauss countered, "it is precisely for this world that the old Enigen existed."

9. CHANGING STRIPES

It had been an amazing weekend for Jenny—the trip to Kandersteg, meeting Von Kleise—and she had finally come to realize that her fifteen years spent renegotiating bad debt had made no difference to the world's financial system. What Walter and Katherine were now offering her was that chance to make a difference.

And then there had been the sex, she couldn't ignore that, she thought as she lay on the bed remembering the feel of his hands on her body, the way he had felt inside her. It had made her feel noticed, intimately affected by someone for the first time in years. And it wouldn't have happened without the Holtzs.

The International Facilitation Fund headquarters in Ferney-Voltaire, just across the border in France from Geneva, were housed in a modern glass and steel building. Walter and Katherine's offices were on the impressive top floor, with other offices on the lower floors. Walter gave Jenny a tour of the office, then they returned to Katherine's office for Jenny to review her formal job offer. She read the contract carefully, asked a few questions, and then signed it with a flourish, with Carlos and Katherine as witnesses.

Carlos showed Jenny to her new office, which although on the floor below the Holtzs' top-floor offices, was still larger and better furnished than any she had had at Continental Bank, with a view over the Jura Mountains. Bookshelves lined one wall, empty but for a few copies of *Euromoney*.

"Is this adequate?"

"Very nice." She fingered the polished wood surface of the desk, while staring at the mountains outside.

"Not anything like New York, is it?"

"No, no, much nicer than New York," she answered.

Jenny looked at her watch while calculating the time in New York. It was early morning there. "I'm going to call my old boss now. I'm looking forward to this."

She put her feet up, not caring how unladylike she looked, and spent a few minutes controlling her breathing. After this, she dialed Thornton's number and as it rang, she took another deep breath, thinking about how to best explain her decision without entirely burning her bridges with the bank.

"Thornton," a very rough, very male, voice answered.

"Dick, it's Jenny," she said quickly, exhaling the air in her lungs.

"How did it go?"

"Fine," she hedged.

"Were you more agreeable?" Thornton asked, remembering his late-night call to Jenny on Friday night, when he'd ordered her to get the US State Department representative to the debt negotiations. Thornton had been hearing from his Washington grapevine that the bank's hardball tactics at the Geneva negotiations were potentially putting their domestic business with the Administration at risk.

"Mike from State is convinced we can work together on this," she said, recalling how sweetly she had played up to the overly sensitive State Department bureaucrat. He had been there to ensure that the US bankers kept to the agreed goal of ensuring the debtor countries didn't feel exploited. It was America's new "good neighbor" approach, designed to overcome the resentment that much of the world felt after years of war and American arrogance, as well as to try to counter Chinese influence, especially in Africa.

"Did we get some agreement on a repayment schedule for the $11.5 billion in East African debt? Did we get some guarantees this time?" Thornton asked. The bank's portion of the outstanding debt was close to 2.5%, almost $300 million. Even a small amount repaid would convince the regulators that this part of the non-performing loan portfolio was now "performing." It would be a welcome boost to the bank's bottom line, and would guarantee a bonus for Thornton.

"We didn't. But Dick, I was doing as you suggested; I was letting the State Department negotiator feel in control. I didn't insist that East Africa be placed in the first rescheduling tranche. And I supported his argument that we give up the Central African debt on humanitarian grounds. After all, those people are already starving as a result of war and drought. He said we'd be unlikely to ever see any of our money anyway."

"The fucker!"

"I did as you asked," said Jenny sweetly.

"My ass, Jenny! How could you sell us out like that?"

"Fuck you! Bastard! You called me up in the middle of the night, ordered me to cooperate, and now you're shitting green gook, when I only did what you told me to do." She started to hang up, and then thought better of it. Jenny was amused. Thornton quickly backtracked, his voice becoming less frantic, and his breathing more even.

"Easy. Easy, Jenny girl. Easy does it. I didn't mean to harp on it, but damn it, Mike promised me that if you cooperated on the other stuff, and gave him support, then he would push for a reschedule of the East Africa debt early in the New Year."

"He did say that, at the next session of the committee, African debt repayments would be looked at again. It would be high on the agenda, but Dick, don't count on much progress. It isn't one of State's highest priorities right now, not with the Chinese being so willing to help Africa through direct investment."

"Damn!"

That was all that Thornton could say. She had made her point.

"Dick, I have something else to tell you," she said after a few minutes' reflection on what Mike had done.

"What other good news could you offer, Jenny?" he said, trying to be light.

"I'm leaving the bank. I've had enough of this stupidity," she said simply, without explanation.

"Did Mike appear to be telling the truth? That they'd revisit it in January?" Thornton ignored her statement.

"Did you hear what I said, Dick?" she repeated.

He didn't answer.

"I'm leaving the bank. I've been offered a dream job with IFF. Given the circumstances, I would like an immediate departure."

There was no explosion from Thornton. Instead, there was a deadly silence. Finally, Thornton spoke. His voice was controlled, even calm.

"I don't understand."

"They have offered me an opportunity to change the world. It's an offer that I can't refuse."

"What kind of opportunity?"

"They're going to propose a new idea that may revolutionize the question of how to best to handle debt rescheduling. We both know that it's long overdue. We need a new approach. The old one of making loans, taking fat fees upfront, and then blaming everyone else when they don't perform and make our balance sheet look crap, just doesn't work. I've spent the last fifteen years on the road with nothing to show. It's time for a cooperative approach that solves the problem for good."

"Nice beauty pageant speech. Who fed you that bullshit? I bet that slime bucket Walter Holtz."

"Goddamn it, Thornton! I'm making an effort to tell you ..."

"What the hell makes you think that you have solutions where the best minds don't?"

"Because ..." She stopped mid-sentence.

"Because what? If they want you to work for the IFF, then they have a reason to want you, Jenny. And it's not because you can solve the problem, but because you'll make whatever they propose seem kosher, acceptable to the money boys. It's a trap, believe me. It's a fucking trap and you, my love, are the bait, the sweetener. But it'll turn to crap, you can bet on that."

"Don't swear at me," she yelled.

"I'm not!" he shouted back. "I'm telling you the damn, honest truth. They're going to use you."

"I don't care!" she yelled, and then angrily slammed the receiver down.

A few minutes later the phone rang. She picked it up, expecting Thornton, but it wasn't.

It was the IFF mailroom. "There's a fax for you, Miss Bennett."

"Send it up to me!" she said curtly.

"Yes, of course."

A few minutes afterwards, she was reading Thornton's handwritten message written on bank stationary, transmitted 6,000 miles, using technology that had been around for over 40 years. It stated simply: "You're fired! Don't come back! Don't expect us to buy out your stock options!"

10. WELTANSCHAUUNG

It was Wednesday already; the week was going too quickly. On Saturday, Michael would have to return to Washington. The US stock market had fallen another five percent. The dollar had lost another 2% against the euro, yen and Chinese yuan. He'd been getting crisis calls daily. The last employment numbers had confirmed that the economy— both here and elsewhere in the world— was slowing to a crawl.

Natalya took Michael's hand, dragging him from the near catatonic state he was in after talking to the Secretary of the Treasury and the new chairman of the Council of Economic Advisors. "Don't they sleep in Washington?" she added with a laugh. "It must be three in the morning there."

"Come along," Von Kleise said, rising to his feet after Michael hung up on the call from the States. "A morning hike will do you both good, and I wish to show the two of you a place that I love."

Von Kleise set a brisk pace up the trail that wound its way from the back of the house up the mountain. The air was still cool, but the sun was hot and the sky cloudless. Soon enough it would be a warm day.

He reached the top first, and waited while Natalya helped Michael, who was less used to the mountains, climb the final 150 feet to the top. Alone for the moment, Von Kleise looked out towards the mountains that had been a part of his life for so long, towards the Oeschinenhorn. His eyes then moved instinctively to pick out the Bleumlisalp Rothorn that lay just below the summit of the tallest of the three Bluemlisalpenhorn peaks. It stood at a height of 10,500 feet, a sheer rocky outcropping above the Oeschinenhorn glacier. It was there he had built his mountain retreat, the Oberschloss, reachable only by cable car from the house.

"Over there," Von Kleise said, pointing towards the distant peaks of the Jungfrau far off in the distance, once the out-of-breath Michael had finally caught up, "you can just make out the Einhorn." As he pointed out each of the peaks, Von Kleise had a short story, including several that involved Natalya's father.

"Machte said we must be self-reliant to conquer the world. A man who had spent his life climbing these Alps, he taught each class to climb. Near graduation we hiked to the top of the Jungfrau from Grindelwald. A long, tiring climb it was, but Dr Machte, even at close to seventy, set the pace."

From where they sat on the ledge the glaciered slopes of the Bluemlisalpenhorn stood out in the bright blue sky.

"This little hill, 3,000 feet higher than the Kanderschloss, is called the Ob Barglvi. When I was a boy I hiked this trail nearly every day during the summer." He stood up and walked over the grassy knoll, searching for a particular spot. "It was here, Natalya, on this spot, that Katherine was conceived."

He ran his hand through the tall grass and wild flowers, which he considered to be the colors of summer, as he lay back on the spot, then told the story to Natalya and Michael.

"She was a young American girl visiting her great-aunt. The aunt came to Kandersteg for the summer each year. I was just young man. I had graduated from Enigen and was at the University of Zurich."

"Did you marry her?"

"She was pregnant before the end of the summer, so I did the honorable thing and offered to marry her, but she refused. She went back to America, and I later heard that there had been a daughter. She married her childhood sweetheart, who raised Katherine as his own child."

"All those years without word?" Natalya asked.

"I didn't ask. I had offered the honorable thing; she had refused."

"When did Katherine find out?"

"When she was seventeen years old Katherine asked questions, added up dates, and discovered that she either had been born very premature, or that her father wasn't the man that she had called *Daddy* for so long."

"She found you?" Michael asked.

"I was pleased to have a daughter. I had never married; I'd been too busy building a great fortune. I'd had women; to be sure, a rich man can always find attractive women to bed. Katherine was nearly eighteen years old, an intelligent child. She saw advantages to the Von Kleise name. She spent a long summer with me, just long enough to establish who she was and cement her relationship with me. Then she left for New York. She wanted to experience the world, but not from this little village."

He looked at Natalya closely for a minute, and then continued. "Katherine was still very wedded to America. I had friends in New York and I gave her an allowance. She went to work for an NGO in New York that worked with refugees from the many wars that were then raging in Africa. I was pleased, too, that she wanted to help the poor. In New York, she met a man, older, closer to my age really, but with great skill with women. They fell into a physical relationship and she became pregnant. Unlike her mother, she gave the child up."

Michael felt Natalya reach out her hand for his. He felt her grip tighten.

"What happened to the child?"

Von Kleise didn't answer for a moment. "I don't know. The man returned to his country with the child, and that was the last I heard of it."

For a long time after all three of them sat quietly. Finally, Von Kleise looked at his watch, after taking it carefully from his watch pocket.

"And you, Von Kleise," Michael asked, "are you committed to solving the world's problems?"

"Is that, as you Americans say, a loaded question?"

"No, I didn't mean it that way."

"Men of good will are always committed to making things better. It is simply bad business to have a global economy that is skewed towards the rich, while allowing the masses to live in dire poverty. The American obsession with efficiency and maximizing profits has meant that shrinking numbers of people are employed with enough income to support an acceptable way of life. Marx had it right; capitalism plants the seeds of its own end. Unless companies realize that paying a living wage is the only remedy for economic stagnation, then old Karl will have the last laugh. Only one billion people live securely, and even that number is falling. The remaining billions scrape out a bare existence on less than two dollars a day." Von Kleise looked at his watch again. "I think that we should go back. Professor Stueben will have arrived. If nothing else, he's punctual."

The airport at Cointrin, just outside of Geneva, was not busy. The main Swissair hub was out of Zurich. There were no crowds when they said goodbye. Michael hugged her tightly, feeling like a fool to let her go back. She waved to him as she was just about to past security and then she was gone. Inside, he was a mass of nerves and fear. The week had seemed like a lifetime, and parting seemed like death.

"I'll miss you, Natalya" Michael had said as they sat eating breakfast in silence, before going to the airport.

She had held back her tears.

"You'll come to Scotland?" he had asked hopefully, thinking about the next meeting there, in two months' time.

"If I can," Natalya answered, recognizing the futility of promising.

There had been yet another shake-up in the Russian Government while she had been away. Hard currency was getting scarce after the collapse in the oil price to $30 per barrel—well below Russian production costs—as demand from emerging markets had plummeted in step with the fortunes of China. Reading the reports in the *Financial Times*, she had grown scared. Three decades of free-for-all capitalism were coming to an abrupt end, and Russia would turn inwards again. The current Russian President, like Father Stalin, would keep his people safe and his cronies in power, by demanding increased security, always appealing to the need for strength during times of social and political unrest. The curtain was once again closing. A voice deep inside her had said "get out, get out," and yet she had decided to go back.

As she sat on the Aeroflot jet, waiting for it to take off, she tried to sort out her conflicting emotions of leaving Michael. Was it love or simply fear that was driving the relationship? Every moment, from first seeing him on the lake boat, to her turning to look back as she passed through security at Cointrin was retrieved and analyzed. Love and fear, both intertwined. Even her father might not be able to help her if Russia was indeed returning to its Soviet past. The nagging voice in her head kept telling her she should have stayed away, stayed with Michael, while she still could.

11. MICHAEL

As he sat in the business class lounge, nursing a vodka Collins and waiting for his flight to be called, Michael tried to piece together his own feelings for Natalya. Was it love or simply fascination with this strangely beautiful young woman? She was unlike anyone he had ever known. There was an intrinsic strength to her that was far greater than his own, yet he had sensed vulnerability too. The last hours together, waiting for her flight, had been tense. He had wanted to save her from her fate, but he had hesitated. The words had remained unspoken for both of them. At no time during the past week together had the word "love" been spoken, but love, and the fear of irretrievable loss, haunted him.

He had felt his stomach drop as had watched her pass through security and out of reach. He feared he might never get the chance to see her again and tell her his true feelings. She had been frightened of going back, he was certain of that, and yet he had not given her the "out" that might well save her life.

She had an unnerving effect on him. When he was with her, he was different. Small talk was normally difficult for him, but with Natalya, talking, even taking her hand had seemed natural. He loved her smile, the way she studied him, and then laughed when he was being too "professorial," as she called it. Once, in bed she had tickled him, forcing him to reciprocate, and they had run around the room like teenagers. Yes, she made him feel young and alive, and now he felt empty.

There would be people, like the man from the Consulate who had collected the briefcase that night when the two men were killed, who would suspect that this was a Russian plot to control an important American official. He would have to justify this week to so many, who would suspect that he had been compromised. Leaving the White House now would be a blessing, he thought, given that the Administration would be over in three months anyway. A new President would come in and select a new team. He could return to Harvard.

He thought about how different his upbringing had been from that of Natalya. His father had taught at a small, liberal arts college in upstate

New York. He had been raised in a college town, surrounded by well-loved, but underpaid professors. His friends were mainly sons and daughters of these men and women. They were overachievers, on a fast track to good positions in law, science, and medicine. He had excelled at mathematics and science in high school, and for a while, had believed his future lay in getting an advanced degree in physics, but after his first few weeks in freshman physics at Stony Brook University, New York, he had switched to economics. As one of his father's friends had told him long ago, you needed to choose the profession you believed that you could be world-class in, even if that self-belief was mistaken. He would have been a mediocre physicist, but he could be a world-class economist.

Stony Brook was not the place to get an economics degree and he transferred the following year to New York University. From there he had gone on to get his Ph.D. at Yale, studying under Tobin. His specialty was econometrics and modeling. He had found analyzing large amounts of data to be more interesting than raw theory and esoteric mathematics.

As Michael walked towards the departure gate, he thought back to another trip, leaving from New York for Geneva with his wife, Marilyn, to start his two-year contract at the United Nations Conference on Trade and Development, UNCTAD. They had been married for less than a year, with Michael working as a staff writer and house economist at a small, consulting company, and Marilyn had an unpaid internship at the Guggenheim Museum. It was a good first full-time job for Michael, and his clients were among the largest multinationals in the world. As a young researcher, he was able to contact and interview his pick of the US and European business elite. But he was restless. He was spending his days as a journalist, and all that training as an economist was going to waste. The job in the Research Division at UNCTAD in Geneva had been offered to him by one of his professors from Yale, who was now working there in a senior position, but it had still taken almost two years before being finally being offered the contract.

Switzerland had been a revelation to them both. They were young, in love, and in the heart of Europe. Paid in Swiss francs, they led a good life by the lake. In their first week in Geneva they had met Walter and Katherine Holtz. Michael and Walter were a matched pair, always thinking of new ideas to improve the way economies worked; Marilyn and Katherine also became close friends. For the next two years, they were together almost every weekend.

They were both ambitious, competing against each other to try to make a difference in the world. In UNCTAD's spectacular public lounge with its thirty-foot plate-glass windows overlooking Lake Leman and the far-off snow-covered mountains, they argued for hours over coffee about how to solve the impossible; to solve problems that held so many countries from developing to their full potential. Michael's natural instinct to fight for his beliefs led him to repeated conflict with his Division Director, and the plans he proposed to solve the problems of poverty, neglect and exploitation in what was then called the "Third World." In his Director's mind all ills were caused by the West, and the United States in particular.

Walter, on the other hand, was the golden boy. He had contacts outside the UN, served on international commissions that proposed new solutions to global issues, and in general, was seen as sympathetic to the problems of the poor countries. He proposed radical ideas for changing global trade and industrial activity, focusing on proposals to change the commodity terms of trade that, back then, were in favor of the rich countries that were exporters of manufactured goods.

When OPEC forced the price of oil to unheard of heights in the late 1970s, the impact was felt mainly in the poorest countries. Forced to pay more for food and fuel, they ran up huge debts that were, in the end, impossible to repay. Out of this misery Walter came up with the idea of buying up excess stocks of primary commodities, to keep prices above their natural level, ensuring poor countries could survive. The idea had floundered in the bureaucratic maze of UNCTAD.

"All they do is hold meetings," Walter had lamented, "nothing happens. Reports are written and then shelved, never to see the light of day again."

"Reports will never solve the problems of global poverty and wealth inequality," Katherine had chimed in. "We need to restructure global industry."

"Your father might not agree," Marilyn, ever practical, suggested. They had spent the weekend at Kandersteg with Katherine's father the week before.

"My father is a plutocrat," Katherine suggested. "Of course he would not agree, yet we are sure it is the right course. We must change the dynamics which place a few key countries at the top of the heap, and everyone else at the bottom."

Frustrated, Walter had left UNCTAD and with his father-in-law's money, he and Katherine founded the International Facilitation Fund, the IFF, and the rest, Michael thought, was history.

Michael thought back to those old, hopeless arguments as he looked out the window of the Dreamliner, now speeding up on the runway. There was no way to restructure world industry; no way to make multinationals do anything that they didn't already want to do; no way to blackmail the rich to give up sovereignty to some group of bureaucrats in Geneva or New York. So, entering into these debates was a waste of breath. Was that what he had thought back then, or only now? So much had happened since that time.

He and Marilyn had returned to the States after four years at UNCTAD. He had wanted to take a job in government, but her heart was set on going back to school, to study for a Fine Arts Masters at Harvard. Away from their carefree existence in Geneva, they grew apart, and unable to reconcile their lives and compromise as to where to live, they separated and divorced. Michael never regretted letting Marilyn go. All he recalled of his time with her was her shopping. For Marilyn Ross, shopping was something you did to fill time, and the unneeded items had piled up in the apartment in Geneva.

His first taste of Washington's politics came soon after he took up his position as Senior Economist on the Council of Economic Advisors. It was the late 1990s and the economy seemed bulletproof. GDP was growing strongly, the stock market had reached new records, and it felt like the boom would never end. The Government had been running its first surplus in nearly a century. All this positive momentum had made Michael nervous. Growth had been built on an illusion. Small start-up companies selling mainly "ideas and services" over the Internet were expected to power a multi-trillion-dollar economy, while relying on other countries, primarily in Asia, to make everything that was sold in the shops. The trade deficit had reached a new height—over $800 billion dollars in red ink as more dollars went out than came in. Economists seemed philosophically unwilling to recognize that this imbalance might require some kind of intervention, to protect domestic industries and slow the drain on the economy, resulting from the loss of jobs and technical skills.

However, the President at the time was at heart an internationalist, and believed fervently in free trade and open markets. But this American openness came at the price of American competitiveness and ability to make things. At the start of the 1990s more than 20 million people were employed in manufacturing, but by the end of 2012, just 14 million of those jobs remained. By the time Michael had left the CEA, to take up his first teaching job at Harvard in 2001, the economy had gone sour, and the stock market had collapsed as the Internet bubble deflated.

It was during his time at Harvard that he had written his first book. He recalled the warm note he had received from Von Kleise on its publication. He had commented on the title, *The Economist's Error: Why Globalization hasn't worked for Rich or Poor.* It had gone to the top of the non-fiction bestseller list for a few weeks, and had helped with his promotion to Associate Professor, and three years later, with his appointment to the tenured Charles Martin Chair of International Economics, with its six-figure salary.

Just after President Toure's re-election in 2012, Michael was invited to Washington to a meet with him. Michael laid out his thoughts on why US trade policy had led to the loss of manufacturing jobs, and suggestions for playing hardball with the rest of the world, to bring the nearly steady half-a-trillion dollar yearly trade deficit into balance. President Toure had responded by offering him the job as Special Assistant for International Trade and Economics. It was a call to put up or shut up; to take the job, or be branded as bag of wind, full of ideas, but unwilling to do the dirty work of trying to make change happen. Michael moved to Washington, rented a small house in Cabin John, just over the District line, and settled down into the routine of twelve- to fourteen-hour workdays.

As the plane started the descent to Dulles, his thoughts turned to what needed to be done in the next few weeks. The meeting in France had posed more questions than answers. The next meeting was at the end of September, in Scotland. He hoped that Natalya would be there, but given the way things had been left, he suspected she would not. The last few hours before she had boarded the plane had been difficult. They sat, mostly in silence, holding hands. He sensed her fear, but had dismissed this as he had listened to her small talk about what she had to do when she returned…how much work she'd left unfinished.

But now he knew he had misinterpreted that talk and made a mistake. She didn't want to go back, but he had hesitated to say the one thing that might have stopped her getting on that *Aeroflot* flight. It was easier for him if she left than if she stayed. He'd taken the coward's way out. Perhaps if he had told her the truth, that he loved her, that he wanted to spend more time with her, she might have stayed and they could have found a solution … but he had hesitated. As he had watched her disappear into the press of people entering the gate, a part of him had gone with her. Now, nearly nine hours later, he wondered if he would ever see her again.

12. EDEN

In the two weeks since the raid, and Susan Mills' death, Kim had focused on finding a way into Eden, Sheng's upmarket brothel on the outskirts of the city. She knew enough about the economics of a brothel, even a high-class one, to know that it didn't pay to kidnap and transport high-value victims from North America or Europe to Asia. There were enough stupid girls who would travel on their own money, lured by false promises, before being snared. They must be getting some benefit from these victims, or their families; most likely, inside information and control over corporations and governments, which would make the expense worthwhile.

"Sheng may remember me, Mai Lin," Kim said, sipping the hot tea, as Mai Lin sat peeling prawns for their dinner. Kim had moved to Mai Lin's apartment just after the raid.

"How could Sheng forget your face?" She reached for Kim's chin, squeezing it tightly. "Pretty face." She smiled. "Sheng remembers your cut too, Little Jade. Always mentions it. Says 'that Little Jade, you give me, bad girl, bad girl,' then touch scar. Hate looks, not pretty anymore, ugly Sheng." She laughed, finding the joke funny.

"My hairs shorter, my face older," she argued, looking in the mirror and wondering where her youth had gone. She was nearly forty-six years old, but Sheng could remember, that was true. "And who remembers one little whore girl when he's had so many over the years? It's been nearly thirty years since he last saw me!"

"Perhaps," Mai Lin said, thinking back to that day when she'd taken the eleven-year-old girl she'd found wandering in the street to Sheng.

Mai Lin still worked for Sheng, supplying cleaning and food staff to Sheng's various properties, both in the city and outside. Tomorrow, she'd place Kim in Eden.

"I have to go out," Kim said, remembering that she had promised Curley Marston a progress report.

"Where you going, Little Jade?" asked Mai Lin, trying to pry the truth from her.

"I dare not tell you, Mai Lin," she answered, hugging the big woman.

"It's the Americans isn't it?" Mai Lin said with a sneer.

She didn't answer, but instead, reached for her string bag and walked into the heat and intense light of the equator at noon.

"Go!" Mai Lin ordered her gruffly standing in the door. "Go!"

Everyone in Washington was against her taking the risk of penetrating Eden without backup or support. Still they needed answers, and Eden was likely to be where they could be found.

Curley Marston looked up when Kim walked into the room. She had shed a few pounds once she'd started to live with Mai Lin again; her face was thinner, almost gaunt.

"Had enough of rice and fish?"

She ignored the taunt.

"Washington's been sending a load of stuff for you. It's in the safe. Ask Marion to get it."

Once in the alcove, she started going through her dispatches. Most of it was routine. There was a second copy of the list, and some additional details on Susan Mills. They'd also sent 127 blown-up photos of missing women, along with annotations on family background and importance. At the bottom of the pile lay a sealed package marked, "For Kim Donovan's Eyes Only."

"What's in that?" Marston entered the alcove without knocking.

"I don't know, Curley, I don't know."

"Are you going to tell me when you do?"

"I don't know." Kim smiled meekly at Marston. "It all depends, I guess."

"I need to know what you're doing."

"Why?"

"Curiosity." He paused, then added, "maybe even that I care." He held back his anger, but it got the best of him finally. "Because, goddamn it, I need to know!" he shouted, exasperated by her unwillingness to give in, then he added "I'm supposed to be running Thailand. If you need support then I need to know where the fuck you are."

"This package is for my eyes only. See?" She showed him the label.

"It's going to get you killed!"

"Fuck you!" Kim said, loud enough for him to hear her clearly. He turned, flipping her the finger.

She opened the sealed package; a briefing from her boss, Turner. Appended to the front of the report was a photo of a middle-aged couple. She recognized the man immediately: Ben Masters, the King of New York's high-priced real estate. He was standing next to an attractive blond-haired woman. Kim read carefully what Turner had written. Over the years, Masters had acquired one of the largest real-estate empires in the world, covering not just New York, but all over the world. Six months ago Masters had been sent to jail for the disappearance of his wife Lilly, and daughter Beth, despite protesting his innocence, and the fact that their bodies were never found.

While in jail, his lawyer and trustee, Brett Latimer, had been issuing bonds and leveraging the properties to the hilt. Moreover, credit default swaps or CDSs, which provided insurance against default had been sold all over the world, guaranteeing the Masters' bonds. If the real-estate market fell, the bonds would default, and the CDSs would likely be forced to pay out overwhelming amounts. This seemed to be what certain parties that had bet upon Masters defaulting wanted. However, such an event could precipitate a second financial crisis, affecting all real-estate investments.

It now appeared that Ben had been framed, and Lilly and Beth were still alive. There was new intelligence that Lilly had been shipped out by air from JFK on a Thai Airlines flight six months before. If that was correct then she would almost certainly be at Eden by now, Sheng's paradise in the country. For Turner's strategy to work, then Lilly Masters had to be found and released. Lilly's return, and Masters' release, would give the Masters' empire, or at least the Treasury and the Fed, time to react.

"See these are shredded. And, Marion ..." Kim said with some venom, "I'll know if you read them and share them with Curley."

She then went back to see Curley Marston.

"What was in the package?"

"None of your business."

"What the hell is happening?" Marston stood up. He paced the office. "I'm supposed to be running this goddamn station. Instead, I play nursemaid to some ..." He left the final word unsaid, but she'd heard him call her a "gook" behind her back before.

"What did you say?" Kim demanded.

"Let's work together, okay?" Marston said, taking a deep breath and trying hard to remain calm.

For once Curley was right. As much as she hated to admit it, she needed backup. Turner wouldn't be pleased by her go-it-alone effort.

"I'll be out of touch for three, possibly four weeks, but I will be feeding information that Turner needs. Make sure that your network in the Central Market is accessible. I'll get something to Wu in a week's time. Have your people ready to retrieve it. And, Curley, get the information to Washington ASAP. Okay?"

"How will I know it's from you?"

"Old Wu will say it's from Little Jade."

"And if I need to get a message back?"

"Reverse it. And don't forget … everyone throws a coin in Old Wu's pot for good luck."

"And where will you be, Kim?"

"I'm going upriver," she answered without further explanation.

Sheng studied Lilly Masters as she entered the room. She had been in his camp for new girls near the Laos border for nearly six months. Her skin was now darker, which contrasted with her hair, which was bright gold, like the sunlight. Her lease price was a mere $300 a week, compensation for the woman's age. She was just over fifty. New York Magazine had named her the uncrowned queen of New York, back when she had helped her husband rise to the top of the ruthless New York real-estate market, but that was now a distant memory.

Despite her years, she was still a handsome woman. At one time, no doubt, she had been an ass-kicker and ball-breaker, but now she was simply a docile, broken human, frightened and very confused.

"You'll like it here, Lilly," said Sheng, using his best English. "Good place, high-class people come. You party real well. Just like before, but different." He smiled showing his missing teeth.

She didn't look at him directly. She kept her eyes averted down towards the ground, and without her contacts, she could only make out blurred faces.

"Do what asked, full stomach," he smiled warmly, touching his stomach in the universal symbol of satisfaction. "Not do right thing, then go hungry. Very, very simple, right?" She nodded. Lilly knew what would happen if she disobeyed. She remembered. It was not so much the pain she feared, but more the humiliation. She had groveled; had wallowed in her own shit. And she'd been horrified when one young woman, rebellious and defiant, had been broken by a goat, its pecker rammed up her ass as she screamed. Lilly had feared that the most.

"Come." Sheng took her hand. It was time she met Mother Cha.

Despite the money spent on appearances, Eden still was a brothel. Sheng had spent a fortune enclosing the entire three-acre site under a thin, transparent canopy, and then air-conditioning it all to keep its temperature cold by Thai standards. The grounds were landscaped into a series of lagoons, small waterfalls, and walkways, and then intertwined with grassy areas, with living trees and plants. The cost of running it was enormous; it was losing him money, even when the guest suites were all booked.

Sheng's brochures described Eden as a sexual spa. Clients paid thousands of dollars a night to live like Roman emperors, surrounded by a harem of beautiful, pliant, young men and women. What made it unique were the identities of the slaves: they were mostly trophy wives, lovers, and spoiled children of the global elite. Catalogues in the rooms, called "pillow books," described these inmates' prior lives, and like a tabloid, every racy detail was exposed, making the experience greater than the mere pleasure of the sex itself. Every fantasy, no matter how odd or even dangerous, was allowed.

Lilly, wearing a brightly colored Thai sarong tied at her waist below her bare breasts, walked outside into the bright sunlight. In the center of the large plaza area was pool. First, she studied the young men and women, tanned and athletic from near constant exercise, and then the guests, older, mainly males, but there were a few women, as well. She searched for the correct term for these women, finally coming up with "cougar." If she had stayed in New York, married to Ben, she might have been described as a "cougar" as well. As she was standing trying to decide what to do, a tall man, wearing a white sports jacket with an Ascot scarf sticking out of his silk shirt, called to her from a canopied table.

"Join us, please," he said, pulling out a chair.

"Come sit," the woman ordered. She put her hand on the empty chair next to her. They were seated under an umbrella, with a table set for breakfast. Ahead they could see the pool with the young men and woman, naked as the day they were born, cavorting in the warm waters with some older Asian men.

Lilly sat down almost in relief. The entire experience of coming to Eden, of meeting Sheng, of being away from the pain and humiliation of the camp was almost surreal. Her past life seemed far, far away, almost like a dream. So she leaned back in the cushioned chair, feeling the smooth silk-like fabric against her bare back, and relaxed. She even smiled.

It was all very civilized, and it made her feel suddenly hopeful. On the table were rolls, eggs, bacon, buttered toast, and there was the unforgettable smell of hot coffee. Her stomach growled noticeably. For six months she'd had little more than rice with bits of meat or fish mixed in to eat.

"Hungry?" the man asked, studying her intently. "Not been fed? We can solve that problem." He waved to a passing waiter and ordered coffee, eggs, bacon and biscuits. "Your name?"

She hesitated. Why did they want her name? Why was it important to know?

"You have a name?" the woman asked, her voice shrill and grating.

"Lilly." She could barely say it louder than a whisper.

"Masters' wife, right?" the woman asked. It was like they were all old friends meeting at the Trump Plaza for afternoon tea.

Lilly didn't answer. To disappear was one thing, to be found like this was another.

"You're in the pillow book," the woman said. her voice high and grating. The wrinkles from too much sun and age gave her face a kind of narrow, horse-like look, and her voice was pitched two octaves too high. "There are a few pictures from your salad days. Still, you look quite good. Lost some weight too."

"You know who I am?" Lilly was shocked and further humiliated.

"Yes, of course. No secrets here, not from guests. Not at these prices."

"I don't understand."

"Of course." The man poured a cup. He handed it to her. "Now, please tell us every sordid detail."

Lilly stammered. The hot coffee felt like manna from heaven. They passed her rolls. She felt wonderful, comfortable even, forgetful of why she was there.

"It must have started in New York, sometime last year. Correct?"

"I was in a cab," she said thinking back, "and then it was dark, and I couldn't breathe."

"Did you know that Ben is doing time for your death?"

"My husband?" Lilly had never considered that possibility. Rather she had imagined Ben fucking women while she rotted here. And what had happened to Beth? Where was she? It was interesting, she thought now that she was sitting, almost peaceful, her stomach full, in a setting that was at least appeared normal, that she had never really thought of either Ben or Beth. They were both lost causes in her eyes. What love she had for Ben had died years in the past, and Beth, her daughter, had been a problem for as long as she could remember: when she was thirteen she was already asking for birth control pills.

"Yes, tried and convicted of second-degree murder. Obviously, they didn't find your body, or that of your daughter Beth either. The tabloids called it a 'crime of passion.' They think he disposed of the bodies in one of his many construction sites."

"What happened to Beth?"

"We saw your daughter at Lee's place in Singapore. Much like this, good group of clients, not the riff-raff, more like a fancy hotel than the beach resort this place feels like. Your girl isn't afraid of trying anything new. She's a credit to you and Ben," the old woman added with a smile.

It was a nightmare. They were like friends of the family, describing a chance visit with an older child of the family who had made it good as a whore. She almost laughed.

"Brett Latimer's running the company now. Running it into the ground I hear," said an older man, approaching their table in a clipped, British upper-class, accent.

It had been Brett, not Ben who had set her up! Brett, her old lover, the one she had trusted. How ironic!

"Have you had enough to eat, my dear?" asked the woman.

"Yes, thank you."

"Good, I think that I will go find a young boy to while away the morning with." The woman stood up, motioning the others to remain seated. She looked across the pool area to where two boys were standing, totally naked, like bronzed gods.

"Is Lilly mine or yours, Charles?" the Englishman asked.

"Take her," Charles answered, standing up noticing a younger, prettier, young woman standing idly by the pool.

INTERLUDE IV

"My understanding" said the woman dressed in black, her face hidden by a large hat and a gauze-like veil, her English accented with a slight lilt suggesting to Latimer that her native tongue was one of the Romance languages, "is that you need money. Lots of money."

"No, what you ask is impossible."

"Not impossible, difficult yes, but then you'll find a way to accomplish this."

"But Ben will see through it."

"He has other things on his mind. In the end, you will have control of the Masters' brand. Isn't that what you have always wanted, Mr. Latimer?"

Latimer looked at the transcripts of his phone conversations, the records of transactions from the banks, and the photos. What choice did he have, really? And he looked across the table at the thin, dangerous looking man, who had accompanied this woman into the cafe.

"I get to keep the money?"

"Of course, but the schedule needs to be kept. We're certain you can arrange everything."

"I'll need help."

She pointed to the man next to her. "Vincent will be your ally. Two snakes can get along quite well if they don't kill each other." He could sense her smile beneath the veil.

Latimer leaned back in the chair. He drummed his fingers on the table until the thin, little man reached across and laid his hand on Latimer's.

"So, where do I sign?"

The woman pushed the paper across the table and she watched as the lawyer signed.

"We will be in touch," she said standing up. "Mr. Costello will remain to fill you in on the details."

13. TWISTING TURNS OF FATE

Ben Masters sat in the subway train, his thoughts not on the clanging of the metal wheels against the steel rails, but on Lilly and Beth, locked up in Asian brothels. They were alive and he was free … at least for now.

It had been a confusing week. They'd taken him out of State prison to a safe house, supposedly for questioning, The Federal agent had let him see the folder showing, in nauseating detail, the shady deals that Brett Latimer, his designated agent, had been doing in his name while he sat locked up in State prison for Lilly and Beth's murders. He also saw evidence pointing to the fact that both women were not dead, but enslaved: Beth in Singapore somewhere; and Lilly in Thailand. When he returned to his room for the night, his door had been left unlocked and his escape had been easy. It was now clear someone had wanted him to escape.

There was a strategy in play here, but he hadn't quite figured it out. Without a live Lilly, he was still screwed. The New York DA had made too much political hay from Masters' conviction to let him go on the basis of some flimsy, almost fantastical hearsay evidence that she was alive, somewhere in a Thai brothel. No, the only choice was to mount an attempt to free her. But why him? Why wouldn't the Feds do it directly?

It was well past midnight when Ben Masters knocked at Marcia Simpson's apartment door.

"Christ, it's after midnight," Marcia Simpson yelled through the door.

Ben said softly, "it's me, Marcia; Ben Masters."

The door opened a crack, the steel security chain remaining latched. When she saw who it was, she let her old lover in.

"It's been a long time, hasn't it?" Marcia said before she realized the impossibility of him being here. She reached up and touched his cheek lightly with the palm of her hand, and led him to the couch. "Tell me what happened."

He tried to explain, but everything he told her seemed so improbable, even if it was true.

"It's too neat, Ben," she said after he got to the part about the safe house with the unlocked door, and the car outside. "Very convenient, don't you think?"

"I'm not stupid, Marcia. Of course they wanted me to skip the joint. The guy I hit practically fell down before I touched him. The question is why?" He picked up his folder from where it lay on the floor. Marcia turned on the light. She reached for the reading glasses she kept on the table next to the couch.

"Let me see the papers, Ben," she said.

"Just like old times, right?" Ben smiled.

After looking over the papers for a few minutes, she remarked. "I could go to the judge with this, you know. At minimum, it would get you a new trial, possibly even set aside the old conviction. Latimer screwed you. It's clear he benefited from having you locked in the joint."

"What do you think the chances are that I'd ever see Lilly and Beth alive if I were to do that?" Ben asked.

"I don't know."

"I know. Zero. The only choice I have is to find this place and get her the fuck out. A live Lilly is the best proof."

"Just like that? Go to Thailand, or wherever the hell they have them, bust into some well-guarded compound, and free Lilly. Who the fuck do you think you are? The goddamn Marines?"

Ben had always lived by doing the unconventional. She was right. It was a pipedream, yet given the alternative, he had little choice but to try. "I can buy muscle if I need to," he said, trying to bolster his own flagging confidence in the project at hand. "I need some walk-around money." He had funds tucked away in the Bahamas and Switzerland, but he would need some help getting access to them.

"Latimer has everything tied up in knots now," said Marcia, thinking about how much Masters' former lawyer had screwed the company. "According to Walter Haynes, who studies this crap, a hell of a lot of the real estate is underwater, given the amount of debt it raised. They sold billions in bonds backed by this property, and the banks sold many times that amount in CDSs, guaranteeing the bonds. If it comes out that these bonds are worthless, then the entire house of cards just collapses. Some people I know …" she paused, "… are scared shitless! When it goes it'll take down the commercial real-estate markets in New York, Chicago, LA, Dallas, and beyond."

"I know," Ben said, recalling how the agent had laid out the sorry state of his own empire. "I know, and I'll get our friend Brett in time. But for now, I have to go after Lilly. Without Lillian, alive, I've no proof that I was framed."

"What do you need from me?"

"Advice," he said. She had, after all, been hired as much for her brains as her looks. "Tell me what you think."

She reopened the folder the Feds had shown him. After reading the summary, she put it down. "You had a run in with this guy Costello a couple of years ago, didn't you?"

"His family tried to muscle in. I had to enlist my own help."

"Brett's become quite a good friend of Costello."

"Costello organized the kidnappings. They shipped them out like sacks of potatoes, by air freight."

Marcia shivered. Ben noted how shapely her breasts were under the thin nightgown.

"How long has it been, since, you and me …?"

"Six or seven months," Marcia said, thinking about that evening. They had made love, and he'd gone home. Then, their world had collapsed.

Ben stood up. He paced the room looking back to where Marcia Simpson sat, her legs pulled up under her nightgown. He fidgeted nervously.

She stood up. She couldn't take it anymore. She laid the folder on the coffee table and came over to him.

"Come to bed, Ben."

She undressed him and pulled back the covers. The months had been long and lonely since he'd been taken from her. They didn't make love. There was no passion left. And there was no longing, only a kind of deadly pall that hung over them both. But in the morning, when the light of day forced the gloom of the night away, Ben turned over pulling her to him. Slipping the nightgown down, around her breasts, he sucked angrily at her hardening nipples one by one.

She let him have his need, but she had no feelings for him anymore. She had loved him once, but the man who made love to her wasn't the same man who had once been her lover.

"Will you come to Thailand with me?" he asked.

"No!" Marcia had known that he would ask. Ben Masters, when he had been a multi-billionaire, a leader of New York society, the proverbial *King of the Hill*, had not been an easy man to love. He had just assumed that she would go to Thailand with him, just as he had assumed that she would sleep with him the first night he'd bought her dinner at 21. She was the hired girl, good in the docks against other legal types, and good for bed too, on demand, whenever there was a free moment.

"Why not?"

"Because this one you have to do by yourself." She didn't offer any further explanation.

"If I don't come back, you'll go to the Attorney General with the folder I gave you?"

"I'll give it to him. Yes, of course." She looked at him, suddenly realizing how vulnerable Ben was.

"There's something wrong, isn't there?"

"No!"

"What the hell happened to us, Marcia?" Ben asked.

"A lot of things, Ben, a whole lot of things happened. But what the hell do you think you'll do in Thailand? You're no James Bond. Fuck, you can't even piss straight!"

"I'm not sure what I can do, but it's better than hiding out here."

"That is, provided you can get there," she said, breaking away and looking at him, not as a lover but as his attorney. "Or that one of the Marcello brothers doesn't turn you in, or that Costello doesn't kill you first. Without money to back you up, you're human, like the rest of us."

Joseph Marcello didn't look seventy-eight years old. His hair was still dark. He kept himself trim, exercising for an hour each day. Ben showed him the folder. He needed the old man's help.

"Look at this!" Ben handed Marcello a copy of the folder. The original was with Marcia Simpson.

The Mafia boss took the report, squinted as he tried to decipher what it said, then looked up at his bodyguard.

"Bring me my glasses, Antonio."

With his reading glasses on he studied the papers again. He smiled and then laughed.

"So the Feds know that you didn't do it, Benjamin, but they kept you in there anyway. It's just like them, isn't it? Fuckers!"

"They asked a lot of questions."

"About our arrangement?" Marcello looked at Ben for the answer.

"I didn't tell them anything."

"You're lying."

"They got nothing from me. They don't really care about the bribes. They were only interested in the manipulation of my real-estate portfolio. It's leveraged to the hilt and Brett's siphoned off over $350 million in cash to shell companies. Not only has Brett borrowed from my banks, he's issued unsecured bonds so that the total debt is now around two or three times the current value of the properties. It's hanging on by a thread, and I guess the Feds are worried that it's about to be cut, and that we'll have another financial meltdown. That wouldn't be good for your business either."

"Then what can I do for you now, my friend?"

"I need to find Lilly and Beth, and then, I'm going to take down Brett."

"In that order?"

"In that order."

"Why not kill him now? It'd be easy. He's got lots of enemies, and technically, you're still up the river."

"It's not that simple. He didn't think of this on his own. I want to know who's pulling the fuckin' strings."

"Come have dinner with the family, and then we will discuss what we can do to help you."

After dinner, as he sat smoking one of Marcello's Cuban cigars, Ben told him what he needed.

"I need papers, some money, and information."

"Papers we can arrange. The money is no problem. But information, my friend … what kind of information do you want?"

"Lilly and Beth were kidnapped, Joseph. They were taken, turned into whores … worse than ending up in prison. Can you imagine if they'd turned your daughters into whores? What would you do?"

"If it were my daughters and wife, yes," Marcello said, smiling, studying his friend and business associate. "But give me a break, Masters. Your wife? Your daughter?" He started laughing, as did the others in the room. "Even Tony shagged Lillian once, and that's saying a lot about both of them."

Ben was, at first, surprised, but then he, too, started to laugh.

"That's not the point, Joseph. The bitch has now got no choice about cocks. Likely it's some slimy toad of a Chinese, Jap or Korean sticking his pecker into Lilly's pussy. Would even Tony use her after that?"

"You know, Ben," Marcello said quietly, forcing him to lean forward to hear him. "I think that you begin with Vinnie Costello. The Costellos have always run girls."

Costello stared at the gun pointed directly at his forehead.

"Your goons are gone, Vinnie," Ben said, looking back at Little John whose expertise at killing was unparalleled. "Statistics, I'm afraid."

"Who are you?" Costello asked. From the corner of his eye, he could see Jane Morgan pull the pillow back over her head.

Little John yanked him out of bed, sat him down, buck-naked, in a straight chair, then pulled his hands behind his back. Ben plastered a piece of duct tape across his mouth before he could scream.

By now, the girl had recovered from her shock. She'd been mid-orgasm when they'd stormed into the room. She tried to get up from the bed only to be shoved back down. She sat huddled against the headboard, the covers pulled up to her throat. Ben had no sympathy for the teenager. She was, like his daughter Beth, a rich, pleasure-seeking young woman, who sought out risky situations without thinking of the consequences.

"I'm getting out of here!" she screamed. He slammed her across the mouth with the back of his hand. His temper surprised him. Hitting her was like hitting Beth after having ignored her for so many years.

"Stay where you are!"

She crawled back into the bed.

"Put your face down and your arms behind your back Jane." She hesitated. Masters lashed out viciously whipsawing her arms behind her, then wrapped duct tape firmly around the wrists.

"Are you going to be quiet, or do I have to gag you as well?"

"No, I'll be quiet," she whimpered, trying hard to control her breathing and pounding heart. Her mouth was bleeding from where he'd hit her.

Masters looped piano wire around Costello's neck. He pulled it tight. Little John ripped the tape off and Costello screamed as the tape pulled at the hairs of his beard and mustache.

"Shut up!" Little John commanded. "We need to talk a bit, right Vinnie. Who buys the girls?"

"What girls?" Costello tried to play dumb.

"The fuckers you ship out to Asia. We know you snatched Lillian and Beth Masters, probably a lot more too. So who pays you?"

"All contract work."

"From who?"

"I don't know. Latimer handles the details. The jobs are easy money, no risk. They pay $10 to $20 Gs a girl, depending upon the risks."

"Who do you snatch?"

"Rich kids mainly. I get names, addresses, pictures."

"Why?"

"Fucked if I know!" Costello was telling the truth. He had no idea of the reason why, only that the money was good. "I thought for a while these rich bastards wanted to get rid of their goddamn snotty nosed kids, but fuck, that don't make sense. Who are you? Police? Government?"

Costello tried to turn around. Masters pulled the wire tighter. Costello sucked in air.

"You kill me, there's hell to pay."

"Tell me about the setup, Vinnie. How do you get them out of the country?"

"I'll talk. Just let up on that." He said, gasping for air.

Masters let up on the cord. Costello caught his breath. On the bed Jane Morgan moaned.

"Did you take Lillian Masters?"

"The Masters broad and the girl. The girl, fuck, she was a tiger, but the old lady was a piece of cake. Latimer set up both of them. Imagine waking up buff-naked in Gookland." Costello laughed at the thought, forgetting, for a moment, his own predicament. "Must have been a shocker for a classy dame like Lillian Masters." He felt the noose tighten further, and then suddenly release. Even Ben found that funny.

"Easy, easy on that. What else you want?"

"How did you get them out?"

"Air cargo, pressurized and air-conditioned, from Kennedy."

"Who set up the shipment?"

"A freight forwarder, Victory International Air Transport. My contact's a guy named Dave."

"When's the next shipment?"

"They go out on the 9 a.m. flight to Bangkok tomorrow: three kids; picked them up over the weekend."

"Get dressed." Ben Masters held the gun to Jane Morgan's temple as he released her hands. He kept the gun pointed as she dressed.

"Stand up!" Little John said to Costello after releasing the bonds. Costello stood up, and nearly collapsed.

As Costello caught his breath and shook out his hands letting the blood circulate again, Little John fired two quick shots. Vinnie collapsed.

Masters slapped a handcuff on the girl's wrist, while continuing to point the gun at her chest.

"Give me your other hand." Little John ordered her. She reached out in a daze. He squeezed her hand around the grip, removed the silencer, and then dropped the gun next to the body.

"Let's get the hell out of here now."

"My bag?" she looked over at her handbag.

"You won't need that where you're going, Jane." Said Little John with a broad grin. "Besides the cops will want some evidence besides the murder weapon."

Her stomach turned inside out, on to the floor, giving the room a sweetly odor of partially digested food and too much alcohol.

The warehouse was just at the edge of Kennedy Airport. Masters rang the doorbell and waited.

"Costello sent me. We got one more in the car," said Masters, pointing back to the car waiting just outside the door.

"Another broad?"

"This one's personal. Seems the Morgan girl's an embarrassment. Vinnie thought she might need a vacation."

"Gotcha," said Dave, opening the door. "Where is she?" He looked outside at the black car.

"In the car."

"I'll get the drugs. Wait."

They carried Jane into the large, open room filled with C-1 and C-3 air-freight containers. Dave came back with a silver gray mummy bag and opened it.

Taking his knife, he slit Jane's dress down the side, and then rolled her out of it. As he slid her into the open bag, his hands fondled each breast. Just a little extra perk of the job, he said to himself. Masters stuffed the remnants of her clothes inside the bag as a cushion. An oxygen hose was inserted into her nose and attached using a rubber band.

"They don't check registered shippers," Dave explained. "We keep a constant temperature, about 50 degrees inside, and it's fully pressurized."

"The boss appreciates the special help," Masters said as he lifted Jane into the rear compartment of the special container. He slid her into one of the three empty berths and strapped her in.

"No problem really," he laughed. "Got three in there now. One more won't be a problem."

Dave looked closely at Masters. He'd never seen him before at any of the Costello family meetings. He had acted on good faith, but now he was uncertain. He looked at the clock, realizing that the truck would be coming in less than an hour to pick up the container.

"What's your name again? I didn't get it before," Dave asked.

"Don Gallo," Masters said, grabbing the heavy wrecking iron, and crashed it into Dave's skull.

"Sorry about that, Dave," he said, reaching down to feel the unconscious man's pulse. Working quickly, he tied him up and dragged him to the far corner of the warehouse behind two C-1s. When the trucks came for that morning's shipment, Masters met the driver and showed him the pallets.

There was no problem getting a ticket on Business Class to Bangkok. Masters paid for it with the American Express Card that Marcello had arranged for him during the previous week. He had transferred funds from Switzerland into a new bank account that had been established in the name of Roger Carson. Masters also had $25,000 in cash hidden in various places in his luggage and in his money belt. Seated in the business class cabin, flying at 40,000 feet across the Pacific, Masters wondered if this were simply a fool's errand. Despite his bravado with Marcello, he was frightened. Thailand wasn't New York, he thought idly, and he didn't even speak the fucking language.

"He's off," Blackstone said, coming into Turner's office in Langley.

"What happened to the Morgan woman?"

"Missing, but the DA's got a good case against her for Costello's death. A warrant will be issued for her arrest later today."

Poor Jane, Turner thought, but then they all were pawns in a game of chess that stretched from the steamy streets of Bangkok to the cool, glass skyscrapers of Manhattan.

"Anything from Kim?"

"Nothing since that first bunch she sent last week with the Masters' broad's name."

"Get a message to her through that buffoon Marston in the Bangkok Station," said Turner reluctantly.

"I wouldn't do it," Blackstone said thinking out loud.

"Nor would I, Blackie. Still, we owe her a heads-up on Masters. Make it simple. She'll know what to do."

14. THE MAN FROM RIGA

"You're late, my friend," said Zhvikov to Livowitz, the Latvian.

"I was detained."

Zhvikov, from Moscow, motioned for the waiter to bring the drinks he'd ordered. He knew the Jew's taste for Polish vodka.

"Drink," the Russian said, watching the Latvian down the drink in a single gulp. "The last shipment was of poor quality. We were cheated!"

"Everything was checked off on the manifest."

"Twenty percent was defective, or out of date; unusable really. We pay good money; we expect products that meet our needs, not crap," Zhvikov lied. Some of the products had been older and defective, he really didn't know, but most of the products imported had met the immediate needs of filling the shops with the illusion of growth in the economy, and success in trading. But anyone knowing the price of oil and other minerals could do their own calculations about the health of the economy. The Russian bourse reflected the pessimism.

"Let me ask then, my friend," Livowitz said philosophically, "why have you come back if we give such poor service?"

"Time is short." Zhvikov didn't offer further explanation. "We simply expect you to do better."

"Give me the list," Livowitz said, pulling his wrist from Zhvikov's grip. "We value your business. Tell you what, I'll throw in a 10% discount on the next order and put 5% of the price into your bank account as well."

Zhvikov smiled. He knew they had little choice but to deal with this man. The Latvian Jew was their safest conduit for the Russian gold.

The rouble had lost 30% of its value in the last year, falling with the collapse in the gold, oil, and base-metal prices. Of greater worry was the sudden surge of Russian nationalism that was driving off private investors, both Russians and foreigners. Russia faced a liquidity crisis and a severe shortage of capital. Russian gold bullion had been sold privately, at preferential prices, to a foreign consortium in exchange for luxury goods for the elites, and the capital equipment now needed to rebuild Russia's manufacturing base. Additional funds were transferred into Central Bank coffers to prop up the rouble. Years of dependency on Western capital and supplies had left much of the core economy in ruins, and what had been rebuilt was dependent on a flow of spare parts to keep the machines running. It was a desperate gamble to keep the secret that the vast gold supplies that had been accumulated were nearly depleted.

"We'll be shipping more gold," Zhvikov said.

"The usual arrangement?" Livowitz asked.

"Yes, the usual." Zhvikov looked around. The noise, even at this hour, was great. There was a party of drunken police officers at one table, but they were in no condition to listen.

Zhvikov was a product of the Moscow bureaucracy. He had been raised to dislike and consider the Jews as money grubbers and thieves. The well-connected Jewish oligarchs had profited from the collapse of the Soviet state, buying billion-dollar companies for fractions of their true worth. The great fortunes of the Russian plutocrats had been built by bribing or stealing, or by simply outsmarting their compatriots. Jews, he thought, could make money even in hard times; especially in hard times. They were the perennial parasites, and had been living off the body of the Russian State for centuries. They had prospered while others had fallen into poverty. They had pushed and shoved their way to the top of the pyramid, grabbing the best assets, establishing a class of new, elite billionaires with close ties to the Government. Eventually, the new leadership had regained control, but by then, much of the wealth had fled to London and New York, into football franchises and high-end property in these cities. Still, Zhvikov was willing to suppress his hatred to accomplish his goals. For now, they needed the likes of Livowitz and Avramowitz, but in time, they would be expendable.

"Your country continues to amaze me, Zhvikov," Livowitz said, "You profess to be capitalist, yet if someone makes too much money, then you cut them down like a good Stalinist."

"We are, as usual, of two minds," Zhvikov explained, his tongue loosened by Polish vodka and lack of rest. "On one side, we wish to be taken care of by the State, but on the other, we wish to be rich like the Americans, or better now, the Germans. Years of excess spending on luxuries, neglect of our manufacturing sector, and too much dependence on exports of minerals, oil and gas has left us vulnerable. If the truth had come out, in this era of instant communications and social media, there would have been disastrous social unrest. And so, we have no choice but to hide the truth and sell the gold, while we rebalance our economy."

"And this Professor, this man Avramowitz with the contacts, what of him?" asked Livowitz.

"The Professor," Zhvikov sighed. "Once he's no longer of any use then he will be taken care of; him and his American spy daughter."

"And in time, you will cut off his head, right?" "Livowitz said with a laugh, "just like the Czar."

Zhvikov now handed Livowitz the next order. Each gold shipment came by truck from somewhere distant, disguised as ingots of nickel or cobalt metal.

"It'll take some time to assemble the next deliverable."

"We need a better price for the gold." Zhvikov argued. Gold had once sold, briefly, at nearly $1,800 an ounce, but it now stood at less than $550. And the Russian gold went for less than that; closer to $500 an ounce. "I don't set the international gold price, you know that. The price will be what it is," he shrugged.

"Less the special discount that you impose," Zhvikov countered.

15. MOTHERS AND DAUGHTERS

Marston reread the message from Francis Turner at Langley.

"What's wrong?" his deputy asked, seeing his boss's discomfort and sour look.

"Turner wants me to send a warning to Kim."

"Wu's been compromised," the field operative that handled Wu and other Thai conduits said with some alarm.

"What tells you he has?"

"The man's suddenly frightened by his own shadow."

"We'll have to take a chance. An order is an order."

"It'll carry risks for Wu and possibly for Kim. The boy who's the contact with Sheng's place is unreliable."

"She can damn well take care of her own butt," Marston answered. "Get this out immediately, Larry."

Wu was a fixture of the Central Bangkok Food Market. He was nearly blind, and sold used pots and pans to poor people, helped by his eldest daughter and her sons. He'd been in the same spot each day for thirty years.

"I'm certain Old Wu passed a message to one of the kitchen staff," said the old Thai fruit seller that took fresh fruits and vegetables from the market to Eden each morning. "They say he works for the Americans, passing information."

"Old Wu?" said Sheng, surprised, for he, like so many others, threw a coin in the old man's copper pot for good luck whenever he passed. "You're certain he works for the Americans?"

"Just a rumor, Sheng,"

Kim scrubbed the floor of the bathhouse. The hot, scented steam coated the floor with a thin slime that needed to be cleaned daily. Inside, she could hear the laughter of the young girls and boys cavorting in the pool area, as well as the guests' squeals and screams of pleasure.

Standing up, she let the blood flow back into her legs, wondering how much longer she could take the abuse and physical labor. She was forty-three years old, and this was a young girl's game. She had learned much already, but unless Masters showed up soon, she would not stay.

Sheng entered the bathhouse. In the weeks Kim had been at Sheng's fancy brothel, she had actively avoided letting him get close, but here, in the proximity of the Japanese style bathhouse, she couldn't avoid it. She kept her eyes down and continued to scrub the floor.

"Get out of here girl," Sheng yelled, wanting to speak to Mother Cha alone. It was the first time, however, that he had taken a look at the Amerasian girl they'd hired weeks before. Staring at her, he shook his head, for she reminded him of someone he would never forget, from long ago.

Kim ran out of the door without looking back.

"Something wrong?" Cha asked, wondering what had stirred Sheng.

"Something may be wrong, Mother Cha, something may be very, very wrong."

Wu-lin showed the cottage suite to Latimer and the woman who had come with him. Latimer had been to Eden before, but only ever alone.

"Thank you Wu-lin, it will be fine," said Latimer smiling.

Brett Latimer was a friend of Lee in Singapore, and was never charged for his stay. Lee was their main contact for procuring new high-class sex workers.

"Is there anything else, Mr. Latimer?"

"I'd like Lilly Masters," Latimer said, looking at Wu-lin.

"Of course, Mr. Latimer." Wu-lin smiled.

Beth took a sip of the wine and walked to the couch. She sat down and her dress rode up on her hips showing naked thighs. She patted the couch for Latimer to join her.

"What did you think when you found me in Singapore?"

"I thought you were lovely."

"And how much did it cost to buy my freedom, Brett?" she asked, wanting to hear the story again.

"$10,000," he said with a laugh, "in cash."

"A small price for the heiress to a fortune" Beth answered, not seeing the full picture. Once Brett was done, there would be no fortune left, except for what Brett had squirreled away in Swiss and Cayman Island banks.

"I suppose so," he smiled weakly. The Masters' fortune was lost, engineered to implode in a month or two. Sometime, perhaps in late October, the bubble would break and Humpty Dumpy would take a great fall. There was no Masters' fortune left, only massive debts.

"Why do you hate Lilly so much, Beth?" Brett asked.

"The Queen of New York?" she laughed mockingly. "Give me a break! I can't stand the bitch."

"And your father?" he asked.

"You mean Ben? The man that I am supposed to call Daddy? He's not my real father. My mother fucked so many people before she latched onto him that even she's not certain who my father is."

"How certain are you of that?"

"She told me once when I was being particularly annoying that I could be the by-product of a casual fuck with just about anyone.

Kim entered with their lunch. Noticing the woman standing next to Latimer, she did a double take, certain it was Beth Masters. The girl's picture had been included in the last packet that Turner had sent.

"Lillian Masters," Latimer asked after Kim set the tray down. "You get?"

"Yes, Lilly, I get. Right away," Kim backed out of the room. This, she thought, will be very interesting.

"Looks good," said Beth, digging into the American fare. Beth had found the travel interesting and the work little different from what she had engaged in for free in New York.

"And did you eat well while you were there?"

"I fucked a lot, so I ate a lot, but I didn't like the food; too fishy."

Kim found Lillian Masters working in the changing rooms near the pool area. Despite her legendary beauty, she remained a fifty-year-plus woman with dried-out skin. Without make-up or hair stylists to improve her looks, she was not in any demand, except as a novelty item. Asians mainly preferred the younger girls and boys. Fucking the one-time "Queen of New York" was not that interesting.

"Cottage Four," Kim said in badly accented English, pointing in the direction. "Come quick!"

Lilly put the towels down, and then ran her fingers through her hair, knowing it was a mess of tangles. Mother Cha had told her Sheng was thinking of selling her to an upcountry house, from which she knew there was no exit.

Brett finished eating, looked at his watch, and calculated the time in New York. He had left two messages on Vinnie Costello's private number, but hadn't received any reply.

Tomorrow, Brett and Beth would travel to Switzerland, where he had substantial property, and where much of his money was safely locked away in Zurich banks. He would leave the dirty work of filing the bankruptcy papers to his lawyers, sometime in October.

Kim pushed Lilly into the cottage and waited outside the door to hear the chemistry among Beth, Latimer, and Lilly Masters. Lilly, still worrying about her appearance, didn't notice who was staring at her. Not until he spoke.

"Hello, Lillian," Brett said, noting that she was hardly the beauty that she had been in New York.

"Hello, Brett." Her legs shook. She smoothed the skirt down around her hips, trying to make herself look better. Despite the effort, her breasts swelled, her nipples enlarged, as her body remembered past pleasures.

"You're looking healthy, very fit, and you've lost some weight." He circled around her studying each curve. She fidgeted nervously. "Are they treating you okay?"

She didn't respond. From those guests from New York at breakfast several weeks ago, she'd learned the truth. He was knee-deep in this shit.

"Quite a nice place, isn't it?" he suggested amiably.

"What the hell do you want, Brett?"

"What I have always wanted from you Lillian; what you gave freely in New York. Simply the pleasure of your company."

"Why did you do it, Brett?"

"To get Ben out of the way. And it worked too."

"Poor Ben," said Lilly, thinking about her husband for the first time in a long time, with almost of twinge of affection rather than the customary loathing of the past.

"I suppose you are saddened by his tragedy," Brett said, thinking about the things that Lillian Masters had often enough revealed about her husband to him, when they had made love. "But I dare say it's a little hypocritical to suggest that you cared about him?"

"What do you want?"

"I wanted to see you, Lil; all of you," he said coming close.

She reached for the single clasp that held the sarong on her shoulder. The cloth fell. Then she turned slowly.

"Nice, even attractive," he put his hand on her back, and then ran it down her back, resting it on her buttocks. She tensed under his touch.

"Very tight," he said.

"I don't want to make love, Brett," she said, regaining strength, forgetting just for a moment who she'd become, and where she was.

"I don't think it's your choice."

He tried to kiss her. She pulled away from him, but despite her best effort at self-control she still felt desire. It had been a long affair when they were in New York. Her body, despite all that had happened, still remembered his touch.

"Why did you really do it? You have plenty of money, Brett, enough to live on without working for the rest of your life."

"I didn't really have a choice. Rich, important people wanted Ben out of the way. I was more pliable than he would have been, as my name wasn't on every building."

"I don't understand."

"Ben Masters wouldn't play the game that they wanted. I proved more willing to follow orders, particularly if there were benefits for me."

"What about us?"

"What the fuck about us, Lillian?" Brett sneered. "Did you flatter yourself that it was your body, or even you that I was after? No, I enjoyed fucking the image that you'd created around yourself."

She turned bright red.

"Damn you!"

"You have to be firm with a whore, Brett," Beth Masters said, coming out from the bedroom.

Lilly stared at her daughter.

"How are you doing, Mother?" said Beth smiling. "Enjoying your stay here?"

Lilly couldn't speak. Tears streamed down her cheeks.

"The bitch is crying. How sad, Brett." Her hand lightly brushed away the hair that had fallen over her mother's eyes.

Latimer watched the chemistry between the two women.

"Are you okay, Beth?" Lilly fought to control her emotions.

"Fine, just fine, Mother," said Beth, coming up to her mother and kissing her lightly on one cheek. "Brett rescued me from Lee's place in Singapore. Life's now good."

"It wasn't charity," Lilly said with some venom.

"Whatever it was," Beth said gaily, "I'm grateful." She came over to where Latimer waited and hugged him.

Beth's had been a difficult adolescence. She had gone overnight from being a little girl to a promiscuous woman.

"Brett and I are going to Zurich. And after that, he promised me that I'll be able to return to New York."

"There would be many questions."

"Brett is good at finding proper answers." Beth smiled at him. "Aren't you, darling?"

"Yes, of course, he said convincingly.

"What about me?" asked Lilly.

"It would be inopportune for you to suddenly turn up, Lil. It would spoil too many carefully laid plans."

"You'll never get away with it."

"Won't we?"

"She'll never hold up to cross-examination. She'll break under pressure."

"That won't save you, Lillian."

"I'm not that dumb, Mother," said Beth spitefully. "I may not be as smart as you, but I know how to lie."

"That's for certain." Lilly remembered the steady lies the girl had told since the time she had become a teenager. Had she really given birth to this monster that now stood, hands on hips, glaring at her?

Kim slipped away leaving the unhappy threesome to sort out their problems, and headed to the kitchen.

Sheng was in the kitchen when she arrived. Two heavyset guards held Mai Lin.

"Who are you passing notes to?" Sheng said, striking Mai Lin hard across the face, drawing blood as she bit her tongue.

Mai Lin didn't answer. Sheng stepped back and with the heel of his foot he kicked her head, pushing her teeth into her tongue and further opening the cut on her lip. Kim winced, but the big Chinese woman didn't even whimper. This angered Sheng more.

"Who do you work for, you old tub of lard? Tell me."

"No one," she said, staring blankly at her old boss. "You, I work always for you Sheng."

"I want the truth, you fat tub of lard," he said, looking at the pot of boiling oil still cooking on the stove.

"Take her hand," he pointed to the oil. "Fry it."

One of the men pushed Mai Lin's hand down into the hot oil. She screamed.

There's no pain, Kim thought, greater than that of a good friend dying, before your eyes, to protect you. Kim added Mai Lin to the long list of victims of Hwang Sheng. Someday, she thought, that debt would be repaid.

"You work for the Americans. The boy talked. He passed messages to Wu for you. Who are you protecting here?"

Sheng motioned and the guard pushed the now blackened hand into the fat once more. Mai Lin's heart gave out the minute the flesh touched the hot oil again. Years of overeating, combined with the pain and fear had mercifully pushed her over. She shuddered, and then collapsed.

"Take her body away," Sheng ordered, upset he'd gotten nothing from her. The message that had been intercepted had meant nothing to Sheng.

Kim didn't follow the body of her friend. A shallow grave would be added to the area where some of the others were buried. Death was a common occurrence among the staff. Two girls had been beaten to death in the short time since she'd been there.

"You were friends with the fat one?" Wu-lin said, coming up to her.

"I liked her. Good cook. Nice to me. Kim added.

"You're a crazy girl." He laid his fingers gently on her shoulder. "Take towels to Cottage 4."

Holding the towels, Kim watched as the drama continued. Lilly stood, feet spread apart, her wrists strapped to the two chains that were fixed to the ceiling, just for this purpose. Beth Masters stood next to her holding one of the leather whips that lined the wall of the living room.

"Do you remember when you had Daddy whip me? I was eleven years old and it was my birthday too. Can I whip her, Brett?"

"Sure," Latimer said, finding this war between the Masters women interesting.

"Beth, please." Lilly didn't fully comprehend her daughter's anger at her.

"I would like to whip you. It would be so much fun." She spoke like a spoiled child. Beth laid the whip into Lilly lightly. "Does that hurt, Mother?"

No." Lilly gritted her teeth.

"Perhaps this will." She set the whip hard against Lilly's bare flesh, raising a welt on her buttock.

"Why are you doing this, Beth?" Lilly said, sucking in breath and holding back her scream.

"You were always so perfect, so very proper, so upper-class, so into yourself." Beth continued to strike her. "You were into giving me things, but that wasn't what I needed, or wanted." Beth laid back and struck harder drawing blood. Lilly yelped. The words cut deeper than the whip.

"We did our best, Beth."

"It wasn't enough." The whip slapped again. Beth smiled. The bitch, she thought, is crying. "I cried too, Mother. I yelled to Daddy to stop, but did you listen? And I cried afterwards too. Did you come?"

The incident wasn't memorable to Lilly. It was one of a thousand of scenes from Beth's eighteen years. They'd both been too busy for the girl. She had been too into herself to notice that the girl needed a mother, not a nanny; she needed love, not more useless objects.

"Please, Beth," Lilly said, pleading for Beth to stop, not just the whipping, but also the words, which stung more deeply. At least the isolation from New York had changed her in ways that she only now understood. She had had time to reflect on her life. What a strange journey it had been.

"Stop it now, Beth," Latimer said, getting up. Reaching up, he untied Lilly from the chains and took the straps off her wrists.

The tension dissolved. "You still look good, Lillian," he said, laying his hands gently on her sore back. He lifted her head with one hand and kissed her. At first, she didn't respond, then instinct kicked in, and she returned the kiss.

"Beth, run along and have some fun with the boys," said Latimer with a wave of his hand. "I have something to discuss with your mother."

"Can't I stay, Brett?"

"No, be a good girl and go."

Beth reached for the string bag that contained her bathing suit, and then ran out the door.

"So, Brett," Lilly asked, "what are we going to discuss?"

"You wanted to know why?" Brett said finally.

His hands played gently with her. He sat next to her on the bed, his hands lightly stroking her damaged skin. She was sweating.

"Let me explain, Lil. I did care about you, but then business is business. It's screw or be screwed."

"Okay, you're on. Tell me why the fuck you screwed me, Ben, and even stupid little Beth." Everything was too crazy to believe.

"They needed to control Ben's real estate. Self-promotion is great, but it has its downsides. Ben had acquired some of the best-known properties in Manhattan, Chicago and LA. And, of course a default with the Masters name would make headlines around the world. After I gained control, I leveraged the buildings well over their current market values. The rating agencies were quite willing to say almost anything was worth more than it really was worth if you paid them enough." Brett mused about how easy it had been, but of course, others had greased the wheels for this sleight of hand. He continued. "Then, of course, the financial intermediaries, the *Wunderkind* of Wall Street investment banking sold CDSs, insurance on default, to the hapless multitudes guaranteeing the Masters' portfolio of bonds. So much for the banking reforms. The Masters of the Universe are impervious to rules, so when the Masters' debt can't be repaid this will set off another firestorm, both in commercial real estate and also in the financial markets, similar to what happened when some banks went belly-up. It's a house of cards that will demolish the US ... no, probably the global financial system."

"You knew that both Ben and I trusted you. You knew you were the executor of our wills, guardian of our child's future. And you set us up. Great!"

"It wasn't my plan, Lilly. You must believe me when I say that I never wanted to harm you, Ben, or Beth. They had used me in the past to launder drug money, and now threatened to expose me, putting me in jail for life. I just got in over my head. You've got to believe me when I say it wasn't personal."

"You destroyed us, and you have the balls to say that?" she said, sitting up and staring at him.

"Everything, Lil," he said, "has been on their orders. It was either Ben or me going to the slammer, so you can't blame me for choosing Ben. Let's be honest. You and I know that Ben wasn't blameless. He was quite happy to break laws when it suited him."

"Go back to the story, Brett. Who asked you to do these things? Why?"

"I don't know why. I just did what they wanted. It was easy to do, quite profitable too. I rescued Beth," he said hopefully. "Shouldn't that count as a good deed? I'm taking her to Switzerland, to Zurich where I have a villa. She can stay there until things settle down."

"What about me, Brett? Are you going to just leave me here to rot? Is that your plan?"

"In time, I might rescue you too … perhaps, if you're a good girl." He reached for her, but she pulled away, sliding back across the bed as far from him as she could get.

"Come here, Lilly," he ordered. She disobeyed him. She hated him now. "No!"

"Come here now!" he demanded. She didn't move.

"Fuck you, Brett!" she said, glaring at him.

"I'll fuck you too," he said smiling.

16. The House of Easy Pleasure

Thailand was a revelation to Masters. The traffic was overwhelming, and in the end, he'd never found the cargo terminal to follow the shipment as he'd planned. He'd been lucky to even find a room. He slept for almost twenty hours the first night, or day, and when he awoke he started his search. No one had heard of a place called Eden at the hotel, nor had any of the cab drivers he tried. Searching through the folder he'd brought with him, he found the name of one place that everyone seemed to know, and went there.

The House of Easy Pleasure had moved to a more fashionable neighborhood, just outside of the old downtown. It was close to the tall, new hotels where foreigners stayed. Sheng, however, was rarely there. Eden was taking all his time and energy. He left the management to his American-educated son and American daughter-in-law.

"This is a very, very good place, Mr. Ben." The translator and guide to the underbelly of Thai nightlife he'd hired smiled, showing missing teeth, the remaining ones stained nearly black by tobacco juice. Inside, Masters could hear music playing. He caught a glimpse of gaily strung lanterns in the trees.

Ben didn't answer. The *maître d'hôtel*, a tall, thin, Chinese man with a Fu Manchu beard and his hair braided into a pigtail, rushed over, leading them to an inside table.

Sheng's son and daughter-in-law had turned the brothel into a kind of Fantasyland for adults; a sexual theme park, complete with rooms copied from American movies, and girls made up to play the part of the *femmes fatales*. The decor was straight from a 1930s movie of old Shanghai, with beautiful girls, some Russian, strolling through in silk dresses that were slit all the way up to their upper thighs and an orchestra playing 1930s' tunes slightly off-key. A man, dressed like Charlie Chan, in a white linen suit, greeted them at the door. It was a scene from an old world Hollywood movie set.

"Fantasyland, with whores?" Ben looked around, amused. If he ever recovered his empire he would think about turning one of his Nevada hotels into something along the same lines …

"Something to drink?" asked the houseboy, coming up to Masters.

"Scotch and soda," said Masters without pausing, while looking intently at the flow of women and men. His translator, a fast-talking Thai "consultant" called Duek, which Masters mispronounced as "duck," ordered a white-wine spritzer. He leaned close to Masters.

"He will want to be paid when he returns."

Ben pulled out a wad of bills. They were all American: tens and twenties. He extracted a twenty-dollar bill.

The music started again. Duek smiled, anticipating a wonderful evening, paid for compliments of Mr. Carson. "There is also a restaurant, Mr. Carson," explained Duek happily.

The boy returned with the drinks and Masters paid him, handing him the twenty without comment. Ben continued to study the women that paraded through: alone; in pairs; sometimes accompanied by a man. Once, there was a small fight between two customers obviously intent on the same young woman.

"And how are you enjoying the House of Easy Pleasure," the maître d'hôtel asked, once the drinks had arrived.

"Nice joint you got here," Ben said agreeably.

"Yes, yes, very old establishment. Go back over forty years."

"I imagine it has changed a lot since then."

"Cost more to run, make more money too," said Liu smoothly, continuing the speech he had learned in his oddly accented American accent. "Old days more authentic, like Terry and Pirates, yes? Great time during American war, lots of action."

Masters didn't catch the reference to the old comic strip, nor was he sure which war the man was referring to.

"Girls then and now," Masters asked, trying to be conversational, "do you notice any differences?"

"More experienced, but prettier now, better teeth. Now, Thai college girls fuck first, then school. Study between customers too, and we sponsor scholarships for our best performers."

"Are they healthy?"

"Checked, Mr. Carson, each month, and we are licensed and certified. All guests must use a condom, wash hands, very sanitary. Safe sex, good sex!"

"Any white meat here, Liu?" Masters asked looking around. "Europeans, Americans?"

"Russian girls are okay, but Thai women are the best!" the man answered, slightly taken aback by the idea. "Why would we import girls? Expensive, and dangerous, when lots of Thai girls happy to work. No slavery here, all voluntary employees," he answered, angry at the insinuation.

"But I have heard," Masters said, leaning towards where the Chinese sat, "there are places, in Bangkok, where foreign women are being kept against their will. It would be a special pleasure to use one of these women, because they are so rare," he said, lowering his voice as he spoke.

"I think you should try one of our women," said Liu in a conciliatorily tone. "I will pick out a good girl for you to try."

Masters pulled out a wad of bills and began peeling them off one by one. When he had reached 100 dollars, Liu reached out and took the money.

"I'll be back."

"And bring a girl for my friend also," Masters said, handing over a smaller stack of notes.

He had slept with a whore twice in his life, not counting the many young women that had willingly given him sex in return for a job or dinner. But though the girl that Liu brought back was young, willing, and beautiful, Masters had little energy for sex with a stranger, so after a few embarrassing minutes, he pulled away, leaving the girl disappointed and confused.

When they came out of the room Liu was waiting. Liu spoke in rapid-fire Thai to the woman. She shook her head and blushed, then ran off. Masters watched.

"I'm sorry, my friend," said Liu, looking about. "I will find someone else; something with more fire, more life than that shameful creature."

"It wasn't her fault. I am looking for something special, something different … something that would not be allowed back home," Masters explained.

"Here, we are intent on pleasing. It is, as my master has said 100 times, our only reason for being. This is an old establishment, an honorable place." Liu pulled the $100 bill from his pocket and handed it back to Masters.

"No, you keep it," Masters said, pushing the crumpled money into the man's hand. "The problem was mine."

"And a European girl, or an American; with such a woman you would be fulfilled?"

"I think so."

"I have heard," Liu, said thoughtfully, thinking out loud, all the while seeing a way to satisfy Sheng's perpetual need for cash, "there's a place where foreign women are being kept."

Masters at first didn't respond. He continued to look around, eying the half-dressed women.

"Are you still interested, my friend?"

"Yes," said Masters, looking surprised at the man's change of heart, "but you seemed not to know such a place before?"

"I thought that you were simply unacquainted with the skills of a Thai girl. I see now that you have particular needs. The cost is far higher, but they offer, I believe, the type that you are looking for."

"How much for a fuck?" Ben asked.

"It's a package: $2,500 a day, minimum stay of 3 days. It includes room, meals, a health spa, and of course, women. As much, and as many, as you would like, all very, very special; unique."

Masters let out his breath. He would have to be convinced. There was no reason to jump at the opportunity to blow $7,500 on a turn in the hay that might not lead to Lilly or Beth. Yet he had a hunch that he was getting close.

"That is a great deal of money for a fuck, Mr. Liu," Masters said, recalling the little bit of information he had on her location. "Have you heard of a place called Eden?"

"Yes, yes, of course," said Liu out loud. "What I have just described is Eden. The price is high, to keep out all but the richest."

"And you think that I can pay for this?"

"Perhaps you can Mr. Carson, perhaps not." Liu looked into Masters' Face. "That is for you to decide. I have much to do tonight, but I will ask Young Sheng if he can show you some pictures of Eden, and perhaps arrange your visit."

Young Sheng's office was small. It had once been his father's office, when his father only had this establishment. He was rarely in the office in the evenings, preferring to circulate among the guests. Liu, however, found him inside going over the books.

"I understand that you are interested in European and American women." Sheng stated, after Liu had left.

"I have a problem," Masters explained carefully.

"The girl was too young."

"It wasn't the reason I failed, Mr. Sheng," said Masters, easing into his story slowly. "Can I be honest with you?"

"Of course," said Sheng, leaning towards where Masters sat.

"I am having a problem back home; not a serious problem, but a problem just the same."

"With the law?" Sheng asked.

"The Feds," said Masters, suggesting that he wasn't the type who would go to the American Embassy at the first brush with something illegal.

"Drugs?"

"I don't do drugs, Mr. Sheng."

"Sorry, please continue." Sheng reached for his pipe and lit it after tamping down the loose tobacco. He puffed as Masters waited.

"I have to stay out of America for some time, until things cool down, till the heat goes away. I guess the stress was too great. I thought that I could unwind here, but ... " Ben stopped and looked up, unable to find the right words.

"I think you need Eden, Mr. Carson," Sheng said confidently, thinking about the almost ten grand that this man would bring. It was enough to give Lee some of the money for the rent on the merchandise, and also pay off some of his many creditors. Since the collapse of the Chinese economy the previous year, there were fewer people willing to pay for the exclusive services Sheng offered.

"I like to think of Eden as a retreat; a place far away from your worries Mr. Carson; a place to unwind and remain hidden too," said Sheng smoothly. "But it is not inexpensive, Mr. Carson, for such service."

"Money's not a problem, Mr. Sheng."

"Of course, of course, but for a week's stay it will cost you more than ten grand."

Ben pulled out the billfold. He peeled away $2,500 and handed it to Sheng.

"Is this enough money to convince you that I am serious?"

17. Tiger, Tiger in the Night

Jane Morgan was wet. Sweat dripped down her face, trickled between her breasts, making rivulets across her bared stomach. Her head ached, her contacts were killing her, and she smelled of feces and urine.

"Who are you?" Sheng asked, agitated. Never before had a girl come without papers or identification. The three others had been sent upcountry for training, but without papers this other one had been left on his doorstep, to do with as he liked.

"Jane, Jane Morgan," she repeated, for what seemed the tenth time.

"Who are you? Why you here? He shouted at her in English. The light from the two spotlights blinded her so that she could barely see. She only wanted to lie back down, but two straps held her upright, forcing her hands over her head with her feet barely touching the ground. If any of her friends from New York had seen Jane Morgan, daughter of a successful Connecticut developer, Vassar graduate, trade book editor, and regular of the society pages, they would not have recognized her. Her hair, once well-kept and nicely wavy, was a mass of tangles and snarls; her back was now scarred from repeated whippings.

"Maybe she is Jane Morgan?" Wu-lin suggested to Sheng.

"Why would she be here then?" Sheng asked. "No papers, no history; story is confusing. She's a spy maybe."

"We could call, Mr. Latimer?" Wu-lin suggested.

"He's in Switzerland now," Sheng said, but the idea had merit. "For now, take the girl to Mother Cha. Tell Cha to clean her up, and put her to work, cleaning toilets."

Sheng walked to where Morgan hung.

He looked her in the eyes and said in English. "Maybe you Jane Morgan, but Jane Morgan is nothing now. Do what Mother Cha wants and you eat. If not, then ..." He left the rest unsaid. Sheng ran his hands through her tangled hair.

"Shave her head. It's impossible the way it is now. Full of bugs!"

Sheng listened to the man from the trucking company that had brought the container. There had been inquiries made about the last shipment. Sheng wrote down the number nervously. The fact that someone had asked about the movement of the cargo, plus the unexplained appearance of the girl, was worrisome. To get to the bottom of this would cost more money. Was the girl who she said she was? Perhaps she was a spy, or worse, an assassin, with orders to kill one of the guests. Sheng let his imagination run wild.

"We have a problem," he said to Wu-lin.

Wu-lin had long ignored Sheng's problems. He had enough to do maintaining security at Eden, and keeping the many workers in line.

"So?"

"So we have to do something about it."

"And what do you propose?"

"The Morgan girl knows something."

"You have tried to talk to her?" Wu-lin said dryly.

"I have tried, yes, of course, but there something else."

"What?"

"An inquiry with the haulage company about the last shipment Wu-lin. Someone knew that cargo was on the way. Isn't that surprising?"

"It went to Chang Mai, to the hospital there."

"Yes, yes, of course eventually. But …" Sheng stopped. Standing in the entrance of the office was a big man, an American, wearing sports clothes.

"Roger Carson." Master's extended his hand "I have a reservation?"

"Yes, yes, of course," said Sheng, coming over with a broad smile. "We sent a car."

"Yes, thank you."

"Is this the right place?"

"Yes, please come in. Usually our guests are greeted by Mr. Wu-lin in the lobby."

"There was no one there" Ben smiled, studying the setup, "so I just wandered in here."

"Please, Mr. Carson, we are honored. I will take you on a tour."

"First, you want the money," Masters pulled out his wallet and extracted $100 bills. He handed Sheng the balance. "That's $7,500, and with the $2,500 I paid your son that should cover me for almost a week, right?"

Sheng took the money and handed it to Wu-lin. "Take care of Mr. Carson. Have we decided on the cottage?"

"Number 4 is available now that Mr. Latimer is gone," Wu-lin said in English for the benefit of their guest just in case the name Latimer might impress him.

Masters followed Wu-lin down the stairs and back to the lobby. Outside it was sunny, but the air was cool and there was little humidity.

"We have one of the largest air-conditioning units in Thailand on site here," Wu-lin said proudly.

"How big is this place?"

"It's about three acre altogether."

Masters could see the large pool. There were people splashing.

"Your bags, Mr. Carson, they in lobby?" Wu-lin asked.

"In the lobby," said Masters, looking back.

"I will see that they are moved to Cottage 4. Come." Wu-lin took Masters on the tour. He pointed out the amenities, the pool, sauna, outdoor patio bar, and food area. And he showed him the guests, and some of the young women running around, some being chased by older, graying, Asian men.

"Do any women come as guests?"

"Yes, yes, sometimes, husbands and wives; separate vices."

"I suppose that's possible."

"You would be surprised what's possible," Wu-lin said earnestly. Even after all the years of working for Sheng, he was still shocked by the requirements of guests.

Wu-lin continued the tour. They stopped at one of the two tennis courts, where Masters watched a strange tennis match between a fully clothed Japanese gentleman and a naked white girl, playing in only a pair of tennis shoes. He laughed. It was absurd.

"Is there something wrong?"

"Nothing, nothing at all," said Masters smiling. "She just looks so out of place playing tennis."

Wu-lin looked again. The girl played well, the Japanese guest was running back and forth as he chased the ball while she stood nearly stationary in the middle of the backcourt. He never could understand Western humor.

Beyond the tennis court, Wu-lin led him down the neatly manicured pathways. Several Thai workers were weeding quietly, and pruning the garden.

"Cottage 4. Very nice place. Good bed," he laughed. Wu-lin checked out the rooms before leaving. The towels had not been changed and the bathroom was filthy. He would get Kim to bring the Morgan girl to clean the toilet and bath.

"How do I get a broad?"

Wu-lin had almost forgotten that small point. He smiled, went to the side table where there was a thick loose-leaf binder.

"This is our …" he struggled for the word in English, then recalled what one guest had called it, "pillow book." Wu-lin opened it. Inside there were pictures, and underneath short biographies. "Simply call our reception desk; see if your selection is available, and if so, she will be sent immediately."

"Neat," he said in his best New York accent. "Pretty neat, Mr. Wu-lin." He smiled. Wu-lin smiled. He closed the book, walking Wu-lin to the door.

"Thank you. Thank you very much, Mr. Wu-lin."

"Just plain Wu-lin, please, Mr. Carson. Anything you need, please call. Don't worry, I send girl with towels and to clean toilet. So sorry, very dirty. Stupid girls, not clean for guests. Sorry." Wu-lin backed out and then ran down the path.

Ben watched Wu-lin go, and then went to the couch. He sat down with growing excitement. Lilly's photo was halfway into the book. It was an old photo, one taken from the pages of Harpers. She looked beautiful. How long it had been, he thought, since he had thought of his wife as beautiful, and not a bitch. A lot of tears had been shed, by both of them, since then. He continued to study the picture. The knock at the door startled him. Two women were waiting outside dressed in native sarongs and cotton blouses. He recognized one immediately. It was Jane Morgan, but with a shaved head. She didn't recognize him. The other woman, older, but still attractive, was a beautiful mix of European and Asian features.

Kim pulled Jane into the bathroom and set her to work, then returned to face Masters who was studying the book, the page open at Lilly's picture.

"You want girl?" Kim asked, looking over his shoulder at Lilly's picture in the book.

"What about this one?" He pointed to his wife's picture.

"Lilly," answered Kim, smiling at Masters. "Good girl, very good girl. I get. Yes?"

"Please." Masters was excited by the thought of seeing Lilly again.

Jane Morgan was still working in the bathroom. It should have taken no longer than a few minutes to scour the tub and toilet.

"What taking whore so long?" Kim asked, going to the door and noticing Jane staring at her face in the mirror.

Kim sent a bare foot flying, striking the Jane in the butt, who collapsed, knocking the pail over with a loud ringing sound and sending water everywhere. This brought Masters into the doorway where he stared at the two women.

"What's wrong?"

"Stupid fucker wants to be beautiful, said Kim roughly. "Toilet still dirty." Kim looked in the toilet bowl. Taking Jane roughly, she pushed her head down into the bowl till her face touched the dirty water.

"Who is she?"

"Stupid girl. Not nice like Miss Lilly" Kim assured him. "Sheng find her and let her work. Not kill her like wanted to do," said Kim after Jane had finally cleaned the bowl, and was now clutching the filthy rag in one hand and looking back at Kim for approval. As she did so, she saw Ben Masters in the doorway more clearly. Recognition dawned on her face. Kim noticed the look and it worried her.

"Fuck, it's you!" was all Jane could say, as she stared at Masters.

"What?" Masters tried hard to act surprised, but Kim wasn't fooled. So Jane's unannounced arrival, just before Masters' own appearance, was not coincidental. If Sheng learned the truth, then Masters would be dead before he could be of any use.

"Shut up!" said Kim, slapping Jane hard and sending her flying out the door.

The girl babbled on, almost sobbing. Masters reached down and gently helped her up. She let him hold her arm up.

"I will take her away. Be beaten, stupid girl" said Kim, taking her roughly and pushing her quickly out of the cottage.

"She's frightened," he said with some sympathy. He had not meant to hurt her and he seemed oblivious to the danger she posed to him.

"Yes, yes, we all are. Yes, I get Lilly right away, Mr. Carson," said Kim, pulling the still-crying Jane out of the cottage. When Kim reached Mother Cha, she explained how stupid Jane had been with a guest. Jane continued to babble in English about knowing the man in Cottage 4. Cha didn't understand what she was saying. She pointed to the huge pile of dirty dishes, pots and pans. Roughly, by the ear, she dragged her to the sink and set her to work.

"Where are you going, Kim?" Cha asked.

"Must get Lilly for Mr. Carson in Cottage 4," Kim said, running out of the door.

"Good girl," Mother Cha said. Kim was the kind of girl that she could depend upon: smart, quick, and never had to be told twice.

Ben had married Lilly just out of college. She was well-educated, ambitious and attractive, but from a dirt-poor family out of the West Virginia hills. She'd attended Smith on a full scholarship. Masters had met her at a Smith dance, fallen in love with her almost at first sight. She wasn't drop-dead beautiful, but made up for what she lacked in physical beauty with intelligence and charm. People liked her instantly when she entered any room. Deep down, he knew, she feared that someone might one day discover the truth about Lillian Lynch, of Lynch, West Virginia. That was why she had put on such an act as they had risen through the ranks of New York society.

Kim hurried Lilly along.

Since Brett had left, a week before, Lilly had been left alone by the other guests. As a result, she was hungry. The thin rations of boiled rice and fish that were served to the staff barely satisfied her craving for real food.

"Brought Lilly, Mr. Carson." Kim heard the flush of the toilet as Masters came out of the bathroom, a large towel wrapped around his waist. Half-naked, he looked huge. Kim watched as Masters stared at the broken woman squatting outside the door. "That's her," Kim said, pointing, and then she shouted a quick release command and Lilly stood up. At first, she didn't notice who the man was.

"Oh my god!" she said as Ben Masters took hold her of her, smothering her words with a kiss. He motioned for Kim to leave. Kim backed out of the cottage. She ran up the path towards the kitchen.

"I have to sit down," Lilly said, her legs shaky with a deep pain in her belly.

"Yes, please do," Ben said, helping her to sit. Despite months of near nakedness, her breasts were surprisingly firm and round. She was nut-brown from the sun, her muscles taut from work and diet.

"It's impossible," she said, finally overwhelmed by the thought.

"It's a long story." He didn't try to explain. "I'm going to try to get you out of here."

"How?" Tears were streaming down her face. She ran her finger down his face, touching to see if he was real, not a figment of her imagination.

"I don't know exactly." He forced a smile. It helped slow the rush of emotion she felt.

"I missed you, Ben, you know."

"I missed you too, Lilly."

"Isn't it funny what it takes to make you appreciate the little things?" She looked around at the room. "I wondered if I would ever see the things I thought I loved again. But I didn't think that I would see you here. They had put you out of the way, hadn't they?"

"Yes, they tried."

"How did you get out?"

"I'll explain after we get out of this joint. Tell me everything you know about this place."

"Someone told me there's a moat with crocodiles."

"No, just a security fence. At least, that's what I saw when I came in."

"Is Beth here?" Ben asked hopefully.

"That bitch?"

"What?"

"I saw her last week."

"Where?"

"Where the fuck, do you think I've been, Ben? Here, of course, and with Brett Latimer. They both came to gloat. Beth whipped me and Brett fucked me. It proves I'm no judge of character." She laughed, even as she cried inside.

"I'm sorry, Lillian." It was the name he had once used long ago, when they had been honest lovers, and the closest of friends. They had not always been rich. It had been a struggle in the beginning, as Ben had forced his way into the toughest development market in the world. And she had helped too. She had naturally good taste in buildings and furnishings. She had helped define the Masters brand.

"So am I, for a lot of things, not just that. Was it terrible in prison?" she asked, laying her hand up against his cheek and caressing it slowly.

"It was bad, but not that bad. Marcello helped me. He put out the word. It helps to be rich and connected to some of the world's less honest people."

"I guess it does."

"However, the future won't be pretty. Even if we get out of here alive, we'll be paupers by the time that bastard Brett finishes screwing us, Lilly."

"I want him dead, but before he dies, can we draw and quarter him?" she said with a smile.

"And Beth?"

"I want her back. We tried to raise her right, but something happened. She heard the shouting, saw the cheating, but she missed the fact that we stayed together despite it all."

Ben Masters hugged his wife. He held her tight, amazed by his own feelings. He understood, perhaps for the first time, what they had lost as they had climbed the social ladder.

"It was hard for both of us. We were so damn busy."

"Yes, weren't we?" She stood up and paced the floor before him. Running her fingers through his hair, she felt warmth. She'd run her hands through his thick, dark hair, and had fallen in love. "Wouldn't they be surprised to see us now?"

"Who?

"Our friends, the New York crowd, that bitchy group of women that I hung out with. What would they think about this?"

Ben felt himself grow stiff. It brought back memories from the time when they had courted. Taking her in his arms, he lifted her up. The towel around his loins dropped as he carried her towards the bedroom.

18. MOSCOW

Natalya looked out of the dirty windows at the near empty street just below. Layers of filth and dirt piled on top of more dirt. The office was dark and shabby. It was a far cry from the office she'd had as the Special Advisor to the Minister; the position she had held before going to France, before meeting Michael, before becoming suspect in the eyes of the new powers that be. If only she had listened to the warnings in her head and begged Michael to take her to America. Unfortunately she had given up her American citizenship six years before. On her return from Switzerland, the FSB had taken her Russian passport, while her activities in Switzerland were investigated.

During the weeks she'd been away, the Government had changed course. The old leader had been working to rebuild the State security apparatus, to crack down on civil discussion on the pretext that it would lead to sabotage, and to reduce the power of foreign influences. But in the end, the new powerful Security Agency had turned on him, and he had escaped the country, taking up residence in his mansion in Surrey, in southern England. The billions of dollars stashed in a Cayman Island bank account would make his life in exile comfortable, and he was rumored to have been offered a seven–figure book deal for his memoirs.

Officially, nothing had changed: Russia was open for business with the West. Secretly, though, a new economic team was developing a centrally planned economy that would further reduce Western influence. Natalya suspected her father had had a hand in these plans.

"Natalya!" She snapped into the cold reality of her present dilemma. Turning, she saw Dmitry Sokolov, her new manager in the State Audit Branch, standing in the doorway. The man, she thought, was a fool; an angry fool as well.

Two months before, she had been a Senior Advisor to the Minister of Trade and Industry: an important position with great influence, and the potential to become the natural replacement for the Minister himself. At the Minister's behest, she had intervened, and used her influence to get Russia invited to the meeting in Annecy. While Natalya was away, the

Minister had been replaced, and she had found herself under surveillance, demoted, and sent to work in the Government audit branch, far from the corridors of power in the Kremlin.

"Yes, Dmitry." She extended her hand formally. "Come in, please." He sat down on the hard chair by the window.

"Did you see the report from that factory manager about the shipment from Latvia?"

Natalya stared back, surprised that this man, this stupid man, had insisted on bringing up this idiocy to her. She had read the dispatch in the morning and ignored it as irrelevant. The report about the gold going missing from Treasury vaults was far more important.

"I saw the report, but surely there are far more pressing problems to investigate? It is either a reporting error, or at worst, some small-time contraband shipments gone astray."

"Production stopped as a result of the spare parts not being available. A small matter, but all small matters add up, Natalya. I feel in my bones that there is more to this than meets the eye. This Latvian warehouse has grown massively, outpacing the port of Petersburg. The warehouse supervisor Livowitz, who has been unhelpful in this matter, has been suggesting that if I have a problem, I should take it up with the Ministry of Trade."

"I'll need my passport," she said, looking hopeful. Latvia was no longer a vassal state.

"No, your official papers will do. I've processed a re-entry short-term visa for you with the Ministry of Internal travel." He handed her the papers. "You are still under investigation," he reminded her.

The walk to the outlying subway station had been through a dark and bitterly cold night. Moscow, once the crown jewel of the Soviet Empire, was now a city frightened of waking one morning to find that the trains from the south, carrying their precious cargo of food, had not arrived, and that there would be queues in the shops again.

The subway stopped with a sudden jerk, reminding her of just how bad things were getting in Russia. There were now breakdowns every day. There were, but few grumbles. Russians were becoming used to long lines and waiting. It was like the old days. Once again, the attitude was, "they pretend to pay us and we pretend to work."

The lights in the train flickered then suddenly died, then flashed on again. The car lurched forward. It halted almost immediately, and now, even the emergency lights, their batteries depleted and defective, didn't come on. Natalya sat quietly with the others, in the blackened car, waiting. This was the second failure in two weeks of riding the subway home.

"They say that there is not enough fuel in Moscow for the winter," one voice in the dark said. The cold weather had only just started, and already there were food and fuel shortages.

"They say gas is being shipped to Europe rather than here, to feed bank accounts in Switzerland," another voice said, the face hidden in the darkness of the stalled car.

The lights flickered on and then off. Another voice in the dark shouted out, "And they say the power authority is well run?"

There was widespread laughter. This was life in Moscow. If the trains didn't roll, or there was no gas for the trucks that moved the food to the stores, then the people suffered. But the elite never suffered, even during the worst of the Soviet days in the 1930s. But this was a different world; no longer would the Bolsheviks have to hand out pamphlets in the streets to organize the masses. Now, there was the Internet, Facebook, and Twitter to ignite a revolution. The demonstrations against the Government, in 2012, had shown the power of social media to mobilize the masses. Natalya hoped and prayed that when that day came, she would be out of the country, for people like her would be the first to be thrown to the mob.

The lights came on. The train began to move forward slowly, gathering speed. Natalya looked at her watch. It was nearly nine o'clock. The next station came into view, just four stations from her home, but she wasn't convinced the train would make it to her station. The upcoming station was close to her father's apartment. She also had need of his advice, so she decided to get off as the train pulled into the station.

Pyotr Avramowitz handed Zhvikov the glass of expensive wine. Wine this good was wasted on a man like Zhvikov.

"I know Joseph that you don't agree with at least a few of my ideas. But you will have to explain why, not just say they that our goals are impossible to achieve."

"Your policies, Comrade Professor, promote the class system. The gap between rich and poor has widened during the last twenty years, under our form of capitalism. It is worse than it was in Soviet days."

"We must get the best out of our people. Open markets and free exchange are better than planning and repression. You know that, I know that. The old leadership knew it in its heart too, but we are going back to the old ways. Why? They won't serve us any better than what we have now. We are already seeing improvements in our manufacturing sector, now that energy prices are lower, we now depend less upon exports of our raw mineral and energy wealth to solve our problems." He paused, and then answered his own question. "Or is it that our new leadership fears the people? They fear the power of social media, the connectedness of the Internet. They fear being removed from power, and possibly killed."

"We have tried that path before, Professor. It does not work. Open markets, and freedom to choose leads to social anarchy, chaos."

Pyotr thought of the students he had nurtured over the years. They had become the young reformers of the 1990s. He had known them all: Chubais, Gaidar, Kagalovsky and Aven. Some had become rich; others had fallen far. Through it all, however, he had remained the rock and anchor that held the post-Soviet State securely in the fast-flowing currents of the global market, for better or worse. He had survived by standing in the shadows, behind the curtain, pulling the strings. Would Machte be proud of what he had accomplished, or what he might soon make possible? He often wondered. The old fascist ruler of Enigen had been a strange man. The Master of Enigen haunted his dreams and his nightmares too, for he knew what was coming, and what was coming was worse than what was happening now. And yet, from out of the fire, would rise a new order, like the legend of the phoenix. There would emerge a new world, a new super economy, or at least, Pyotr thought with his native skepticism, that was the plan.

Pyotr knew full well that both he and Zhvikov were playing a risky game, where no one was to be trusted. Pyotr's retirement was likely to be a death sentence, not a house in Pasadena and a lecture tour.

"So the gold's nearly gone," Pyotr said flatly, and noticed that Zhvikov's face reddened. Then it was true: they had shipped the last of the gold from the Moscow vaults. Little more would be coming in from the Siberian mines. The miners were not stupid, and had found another channel out of the country, through the gold markets of Asia.

"We really had no choice."

"And what will you pay for the goods with now?"

"We must find a new source of hard currency. If we are to save the older companies from disaster then capital equipment and spare parts are needed. Your reforms, Professor, have made us dependent upon Germany, Japan, America, and China. The gold was the only asset that the State had that was worth anything, once the oil and mineral prices collapsed."

Pyotr stood up. He paced the room. In a way Zhvikov was right. He had pushed to remake Russia in the image of the West, but he had failed. The economy had become too dependent upon hard currency to meet basic needs. Russia's failing State enterprises had never adapted to the capitalist model. "Have you seen my latest ideas?"

"Reform is not the answer, Professor. Only a return to the discipline of the past will make us great again. Only sacrifice will recover the Russian soul from Western capitalism's false illusion."

Zhvikov looked around at the trappings of power in the apartment. The fine furnishings contrasted with the poverty of the nation. In time, these too would be gone, as would Avramowitz. Russia's history was one of a series of upheavals. "Thesis and antithesis," as Marx had written in *Das Capital.*

There was a knock at the door. Pyotr felt a moment of fleeting panic, fearing that it was the knock from which there was no escape.

"Hello, Papa," said Natalya.

"What a surprise, Natalya," Pyotr said, with only a hint of a smile. Her arrival was inopportune. Yet he didn't let her see his displeasure.

"Are you busy?" she asked.

"Joseph Zhvikov from your Ministry has stopped by for drinks. We are discussing my latest study, the one I gave you to read last week, on Social Capitalism."

He guided his daughter into the room.

"This is a pleasant surprise." Zhvikov clicked his heels.

"Please, Papa, don't let me interrupt. I was stuck on the subway. Another power failure and I panicked. I was hoping to stay here tonight, if you can't drive me home."

"I'll call a car for you," Avramowitz offered. "Have you met my daughter before, Zhvikov?"

"Once, a long time ago, in the Minister's office," he answered. "Let me suggest, however, that my driver can take her home, while we finish our discussion, Pyotr."

Pyotr studied Natalya. She didn't look healthy. Her self-confidence was visibly draining fast. Demotion and the reprimand had ruined her. He had not fought to stop her transfer. For her own safety the less she found out about the sale of the gold and the contraband purchases, the better. Stuck in the hinterland of the Investigation Secretariat, Pyotr had felt Natalya was safer than in the high-profile position she had had before going to France and Switzerland last month. "I have some more to discuss with Joseph. Are you free for dinner tomorrow night, Natalya?"

"I'll be in Riga tomorrow," she said, thinking about her early morning flight.

"Riga?" Zhvikov and Avramowitz said almost in unison.

"Yes, something to do with a shipment that went astray," she answered. "Probably nothing of any real importance I think, but my superior has demanded that I go there and get to the bottom of the mystery."

"Sokolov has sent you, am I right?" Zhvikov tried to hide his nervousness. The last thing that was needed was an official investigation into the activities at that warehouse.

"Yes."

"He's sending you to Riga? Why?"

"I have an appointment with a man called Livowitz. Sokolov believes there's something strange going on, and wants to find out who he is dealing with in Russia. It's absurd, but I was ordered to go."

"A waste," her father agreed. He knew that it would be a disaster if his daughter discovered the gold. "Natalya," Pyotr asked, making small talk with her, "have they given you back your passport?"

"No," she said worried. They'd come in to her office soon after she'd returned from Switzerland and demanded her passport. She had given it without protest, having seen other, less cooperative coworkers disappear. No one was protected; no one was safe anymore.

"The extra week with your American lover was well beyond what your assignment called for." Pyotr reminded her. "People are questioning your loyalty."

"Are we enemies or friends with the Americans? I offered to take the time as part of my vacation. There was no cost to the State."

There was a long, awkward pause as Natalya tried to understand the hidden meaning in his words. Finally, Zhvikov looked at his watch. "Let me go downstairs and see that my driver takes you home, Natalya."

Pyotr watched as Natalya looked around the room. She had her mother's grey-green eyes. He had failed her, to be sure, but sometimes a child had to be sacrificed for the greater good.

"Until we meet again, Natalya," Pyotr kissed her lightly on both cheeks at the door. He was a born charmer. People were naturally taken in by his flattery. Natalya was, however, immune to his words. She doubted his love. She knew she was expendable to him if it suited his needs. He had shipped her off to America, but had first turned her over to the State to be trained, without thinking twice about what the duplicity of purpose in her going there might do to her delicate psyche. No, she thought, he didn't love me; not now, not ever.

The three-room apartment near the Ministry of Trade and Industry had been her reward for reaching a senior position. In America it would be considered second-class housing, but it passed for privilege in the "new Russia." On a Government salary she couldn't afford the newer market rate apartments in the city's more fashionable shopping districts. Looking around in the gloom given off by the low-wattage bulbs, which were all she could buy in the stores these days, it reminded her more of a tomb than a home. Unlike her father's five rooms, with high ceilings and pre-revolutionary finishes, this flat was the by-product of seventy-five years of neglect of human individuality.

The telephone rang. At least it still worked. It was Sokolov in a panic. She listened, and then hung up the receiver. So, now he didn't want her to go to Riga. Why? He had been so insistent early that day. What had changed? Zhvikov had tensed visibly on her mention of visiting Riga. Was there a connection?

The telephone rang a second time. At first, she let it ring unanswered. Finally, she could not stand the sound of the ringing any longer. There was a long silence, some static, and then she heard his voice. She cried.

"I love you," was all she said when Michael had finished talking.

"I know."

"I will always love you, Michael," she repeated, tears rolling down her cheeks without control. She didn't trust other words. Perhaps if things had been better on her return, the lure of this American might have been less. Now, she needed the escape he might offer, but even that escape had been cut off abruptly when they took her passport. She was afraid to tell him the truth about her situation. She had no choice but to try to get out, and get out quickly. She would beg, plead for her father's help to get her passport back. First, however, she needed to go to Riga.

"What's happening? Are you okay?" asked Michael, worried by her absence at the meeting that had been held in Scotland a week before. "Why didn't you come to Scotland?"

Natalya could hear the fear and worry in his voice. He was in love with her, that much was clear, and this made her happy and sad at the same time.

"I don't know, Michael. I've been transferred to another division. It's temporary, but ..." She was afraid to say more. They were waiting for her to panic, to say something that might be taken out of context and could be used against her. She saw enemies in everyone, including her father. "Travel has been restricted. It's nothing; a misunderstanding." Natalya tried to remain upbeat, and calm, but her worry must have come through because she heard him sigh. There was a long, heavy silence. She sensed a growing barrier between them would soon be insurmountable. She felt suddenly weak and helpless. What if she couldn't get back to him? What if she was detained and sent out east? How could she live?

"I love you, Michael." Even that simple phrase, given the precarious nature of her position, could now be dangerous. Natalya felt that black cloak falling again, and she was going to be caught in the darkness. "I have to go now."

"Natalya, please." He pleaded for more news.

"Accept my love, Michael," she said through her tears. "It's all I can give you."

She hung up the receiver to stop herself from saying more. The entire conversation had left her feeling empty inside. Tomorrow, she would go to Riga despite their warnings. And after that, she would get out, with or without permission.

INTERLUDE V

The academic looked at his mentor. He'd met the industrialist almost forty years before, when he'd turned down a job at one of his companies and chosen an academic career. But his mentor had continued to look after him, financially, over all these years, and now the debt could be repaid.

"Money will be spent to ensure that the Central Committee confirms Sun-lee Hu, as Head of the Central Bank," the industrialist said, smiling.

"And, I will ensure that Sun-lee knows what he must do to save China."

"The last time it was allowed to fester," the industrialist said, thinking about the previous bust, and how it had wrecked the carefully laid plans of his enterprises. "It was a disaster. We need stability now that the economy is doing poorly. Investors and savers are losing out. Rates must be increased to show we are strong, not weak, and that we have faith in the future," he added.

"Of course, we learn from experience."

"I hope so."

"And Kenji will take over at the same moment in Japan."

"The Ministry of Finance posting is his to take."

"Excellent. They will work well together."

"You trained them well, Dr. Son, very well indeed."

"And the timetable for this?"

"It should happen at the same moment. I will inform you of the date when it is known."

"Yes, of course." He left the rest unsaid. His old friend would likely profit greatly by the advanced knowledge of the date.

"Let us go to dinner. Come." He put his arm around his younger protégé and together they walked into the shimmering hotel dining room.

19. WASHINGTON NIGHTMARES

After the election, late in 2012, Michael had been brought into the White House to head the Domestic and International Economics portfolios. His thankless job was to coordinate the efforts of the executive branch as the liaison with the Treasury, Labor, Commerce, State, the Federal Reserve, and the US International Trade Representative's office. It was a job made worse by the infighting between the senior economic policymakers in each of these fiefdoms.

The economy had been hit hard by the fiscal cliffs and subsequent sequester, in March 2013. And then there was the brinksmanship that had closed down the Government in October of that year, and led to a near default on the Federal debt, when the debt limit had been held as ransom by the opposing party. Of course, that had just been one problem among many. The economy was moving too slowly to overcome its many problems from too low salaries, too much part-time work rather than better paid full-time employment, and a continued sizable trade deficit. The sequester, and the Government shutdown had added to the gloom.

Willing to try anything, Michael's radical thoughts on US trade policy, and the importance of rebuilding the American manufacturing base, had been welcomed by the new economic team. The President, soon after the election, had become obsessed with growing the American manufacturing base, which had long been in decline since the 1990s. The brinksmanship that the opposing party had played with the Government shutdown and the raising of the debt ceiling in October of 2013, had led to losses in the House and Senate races in the mid-term elections the following year, that had made the Congress more responsive to a grand bargain. Midway through the term the Responsible Spending and Revenue Act of 2015 was passed. A Grand Bargain with some changes in the tax code, in return for entitlement reform, it was a charade, a smoke screen hiding behind creative accounting's longer-term problems of increasing health-care costs and an aging population.

The Responsible Spending and Revenue Act contained the policies that Michael had pushed for; it went aggressively after countries that had prospered through unfair trade advantage. Michael had also been able to thwart the President's plans to ask for fast-track authority, to negotiate a new Trans-Pacific Free Trade Agreement that would have likely backfired, given the ability of many of these countries to get around the seemingly ironclad provisions of fairness and equality of environmental and health standards for their traded products. This pullback by the United States from being the most open of all countries set in motion a chain of events that was unforeseen, as other countries started to impose their own trade restrictions, setting off a trade war, as governments, globally, sought to protect their home markets. The biggest loser was China, as foreign capital fled from the threat of protection, and without exports supporting growth, the house of cards, built up from years of cheap lending that had fueled real-estate boom, fell apart.

Global economic growth, once relied upon to compensate for slower domestic growth, was itself sputtering as European government policies vacillated between austerity and stimulus. Global trade slowed, and had even shifted into negative territory for the first time since the 2008–9 financial crises. Energy and minerals prices fell, while prices for agricultural commodities, in short supply because of the rolling droughts across the grain-producing regions in North and South America, Europe, and Australia, soared. The only thing that seemed immune to hard times were the corporations, with their flexibility to shift production and lay off workers. Corporate profits continued to outpace wages, and the stock market had barely fallen from the record highs in 2015, but there were persistent fears that this could crash at any time.

For Michael, returning to Washington after a week with Natalya meant facing up to the fact that he still had no silver bullet; no single solution to offer the President that could restart the global engine. Each new idea or policy that seemed to offer hope fizzled after a few years. First, there was the 2000–2001 Internet startup boom. Then, the ability to bridge distance with rapid communications, and cheaper and more frequent liner and air-freight services, mainly between Asia and North America and Europe, made longer supply chains, and complex multi-national business arrangements feasible. Then, there was China's surge, with its positive impact on other emerging markets but damaging effects on rich, industrialized countries in North America and Europe. The fracking boom, which had unlocked new, abundant American gas and oil supplies, had led to a weakening of crude oil prices. Of course, Ross thought, there was the continuing move to shift production from high-wage to low-wage countries, with little in terms of countertrend of previously outsourced production returning to America, to take advantage of the new, lower energy costs.

But none of these trends had been strong enough to keep the global economy humming. What was needed was a new model; something that united the world's economic engines in a common purpose: growth. The competitive model and the emphasis on short-term profits over long-term growth encouraged super-lean enterprises, and the outsourcing of jobs to less costly parts of the world. Further, the outsourcing of jobs had failed to add materially to the prosperity of these countries, as the governments were forced to suppress the wages of local workers, under the threat of the new jobs being moved on to even lower cost markets.

The emphasis on balancing Government finances had also become a hopeless race to the bottom, as revenues declined faster in the face of the resultant slower growth. Despite his initial optimism when the Responsive Spending and Revenue Act was first tabled, Michael now lamented that it had contributed to the global economy becoming further stuck, and that taken on the whole, Government policies were anti-growth. In his heart, Michael knew that policy would continue to fail because no government, not even the United States, could enact a solution that had the necessary global reach. Despite a multitude of G8 and G20 meetings since 2008, efforts to develop a coordinated government approach had largely failed. After years of frustrated policy, and many long evenings of contemplation, Michael thought with a certain sense of irony, as an academic and government advisor, that it was only the largest, global multinationals that had the size and necessary reach to effectively deliver a solution to these problems, and that only when the largest, most important companies worked cooperatively and at a global level, only then could the global economic engine be restarted. However, there was no way to do that in today's world. No CEO would take the chance, and only if all major companies agreed to it, which would be a clear violation of American anti-trust laws against corporate collusion, would it even have a chance of jump-starting the world economy?

"If you could change one thing, Michael," the President asked, turning from the window overlooking the Rose Garden to face his economic advisor, "what would you change?"

"Honestly, I don't know. We took some hard decisions, and they have had consequences, but eventually things will right themselves," Michael answered, without much conviction that things might ever get right again.

"What the hell should I tell them when they show up here for the free lunch tomorrow?" the President asked, thinking about the monthly meetings he had with the CEOs of the largest US companies.

"No more words," Michael said realizing he had no new ideas to offer.

"Are we really powerless?"

"No, not entirely. We can still make things worse, but we've lost our ability to make it much better. Unless businesses invest and hire, then our economy and those of our trading partners will fall back into recession, or worse."

The President grew silent. He looked out the window, noting the bright sunlight and the warmth, and wondered if he might be better off on the golf course than talking to this economist. He had just months left in his term and would be happy to return to private life after eight years in the White House.

When President Toure had been first elected, he had tried to be a conciliator, bridging the differences between the hard right, the centrists and the hard left, but he had quickly run into unreasoned hatred. Despite his middle-of-the-road policies, and even adopting some of the more progressive ideas of the other party, he was considered to be a liberal, and even a socialist, by his critics. In the space of a few years, the opposition had moved further to the right of its traditional politics. And while Toure saw Government as a solution, especially to the economic problems begot by the 2008 financial collapse, opponents saw his Government as the problem. He had wanted to solve the problems afflicting the country through cooperation, but was faced with a hostile Congress as the country moved from one budgetary crisis to another.

Despite being re-elected by a wide margin in 2012, Toure entered his second term facing an even more intransigent and downright hostile political gridlock in the Congress. Despite the intense opposition that he had faced, the fiscal crisis that had been developing was serious enough to have allowed him to broker a longer term deal on the budget impasse, and to finally pass the Responsible Spending and Revenue Act of 2015. He often sardonically mused that the only other major achievement of his second term had been to lock in place the deep political divide between the two parties. Each party now saw its role as one of saying "no" to whatever the other party proposed. The gulf had widened such that Michael, after three years of seeing little improve in the way of making the country stronger, richer, and ready for the uncertainties of the future, was frustrated and ready to leave.

"What went wrong Michael?"

"The collapse of the Internet bubble, taking with it the idea of a bulletproof economy, and replacing it with the uncertainty that came after the terrorist attacks late in 2011, which led to an economy less stable and predictable than in the past. Although attempts at stimulus were made through tax cuts and rebates, these failed to do much to restart the business cycle. The US economy also slowed as the world economy also slowed. Companies cut back on hiring and investing, or at least investing here. Although new markets, fast-growing markets, were discovered in Brazil, China, and even Russia, these markets turned out to be mirages, as their prosperity depended upon rapid growth in the global economy, which itself depended upon increasing wages and salaries and jobs, in the more advanced country markets. Although the consultants and economists were adamant that long-distance supply chains offered the best and least risky strategy for these firms, American manufacturers became mere shells, depending upon others to make the products they sold. We lost 8 million good paying manufacturing jobs between 2000 and 2010. Although profits soared and productivity was high, it was due to wages being kept low by the threat of further outsourcing.

Finally, there was the failure of the last Administration to support the banks that had become insolvent. If the Government had shown a bit more confidence in the financial superstructure, then, perhaps, the collapse of 2007 and 2008 in the financial markets might have been controlled and the damage to the economy that is still being felt today could have been reduced."

The President fidgeted, thinking about his first term. He'd come into office at the worst of all times for the economy. Political gridlock had stopped him from expanding on the stimulus that had been too little to compensate for the size of the downdraft from the financial crisis. The economy had barely recovered at the start of the next year, but when the stimulus stopped, the private sector didn't take up the slack. The recovery had been modest, and unemployment had fallen, but only because many older workers had dropped out of the labor market.

Michael continued, feeling certain that President Toure knew all of this as well as he did. "Demand drives our economy. Without people having jobs, there's no demand and no hiring; the vicious cycle repeats itself." He stopped. The President knew the story. There was no point in repeating it.

"And the companies ... did they really stop investing and hiring?" the President asked.

"They continued to invest. They simply didn't invest here. They hoarded profits, or used them to buy back stock. Our friends on the other side of the aisle refused to penalize companies for selling out the American worker, and they made much of the fact that the new health-care law could make smaller companies less willing to hire, for fear of having to provide workers' health insurance if they breached the fifty-worker barrier. Then came the brinksmanship of the Government shutdown, and the debt ceiling debates that damaged the already weak recovery, continuing the path of slow growth and limited job creation. All this added to uncertainty in the economic environment.

Although we were able to close that tax loophole with the Responsible Spending and Revenue Act, it was too late. Most of these jobs did not return, and we are now stuck with weak job growth which is barely enough to keep unemployment from increasing, and not enough to pull the long-term unemployed back into the labor force. We have gotten used to paying less for things that would cost more if made here. In the past, companies were willing to train workers for jobs, but not now. Now, they complain they can't find anyone to do the work. It's a lame excuse really. Anyone can be trained to run a computer-driven machine tool if you make the effort. Previously, companies had training programs, and paid to upgrade their workers' skills."

Michael stopped because he had no answers. There were no more quick fix policies to right the ship of State. Most of the traditional approaches had been tried by every Administration since the start of the financial crisis: quantitative easing, near-zero interest rates, financial regulation, financial deregulation, Government intervention, eliminating protection for the environment, new subsidies for small businesses, deep tax cuts, increased taxes to pay down the debt, elimination of entire government departments, cuts in Medicaid, targeted pump priming, fiscal austerity, trade controls, no trade controls ... the list of failed policies went on and on. Alternating between conservatives and liberals, between moderates or middle-of-the-road pragmatists, the American economy, the global economy was, indeed, out of steam and on the rocks. It was no wonder they were depressed.

"The problems were there before you took office," Michael tried to assure the President. "We didn't inherit the usual garden variety of fiscal imbalance. We inherited a flood of red ink, closer to Biblical proportions, and a weakening economy that couldn't be healed by oratory, only through some kind of Marshal Plan. But as you know, Mr. President, we didn't have the votes to push that one through."

There was one more theory on why they had failed that Michael was afraid to put into words. It had come to him like an epiphany when he had been listening to Walter and Katherine talk. Von Kleise had remained indifferent to what they were suggesting, as if he was in on the plot they were hatching. As he had listened, he thought about how single or multiple shocks to an unstable system—and the global economy and especially global financial and equity markets which were highly unstable— could destroy carefully worked out economic plans. You didn't have to manipulate everything, or even know the outcome in advance. You only had to make the system unstable. Once this pattern of instability was set in motion, then a trader could profit easily, gaining on both the up and down legs of the swing.

The President broke Ross's train of thought.

"Is there evidence that data has been tampered with, or are all of these errors simply random and unconnected?"

"There's evidence," Michael said, "but knowing that, and finding out who is tampering with the data, is another thing."

"It's like a goddamn puzzle isn't it?" The President went over and poured himself a glass of water. The interview was almost over. He had other fish to fry.

"Do you need more help with this, Michael?"

"Yes," Michael said, thinking about Natalya.

"Who could be helpful?" the President asked, remembering the very interesting intelligence report about the Russian girl.

"The Russian woman I met in France" said Michael quickly, without explaining.

"Why?"

"She's intelligent, brings a different point of view, and she's being sidelined by the Russians. She could be an asset for us."

The President smiled. He had read the intelligence summaries that had described Michael's weeklong absence in vulgar detail. He also had perused the thick file on Natalya Avramowitz, and on her father. An interesting family, he thought idly. He wondered if this rather mild-mannered economist was up to the challenge that someone like Natalya offered. There was a problem with her too. From Natalya's thick file it was difficult to decide where her true loyalties lay: with Russia or with America.

"Things are going from bad to worse over there, Michael" the President warned. "You had better try to get her out quickly, before they clamp down so hard no one will be able to leave." The President had made the decision in Michael's favor. It was a small thing to do. He was of the view that Natalya probably didn't even know who she was, let alone which master she really served.

"Can I ask Turner's help?"

"You can," the President said, making a note of this for his own logs, "if you think that this girl can help us," he said with a sly wink to Michael.

"Thank you, Mr. President."

As Michael was leaving, the President stopped him. He had one more question.

"What's happening to the price of gold, Michael?"

"It's up to $597 an ounce today."

"Tell me, if we are really in the middle of a bubble which many expect is going to break, and cause a market collapse, that would drive up the price of gold. Right?"

"Gold is considered a safe haven market to equities and bonds," Ross answered, "so that could happen. But it would be a disaster if too much wealth flowed into gold at the expense of equities and bonds. It's useless. It's non-productive, and costly to hold. Let's hope, Mr. President, that that doesn't happen for it could lead to deflation that would be worse than the current disease."

Michael entered his office to see the gaunt face of Francis Turner, the CIA contact for economic issues. Each week, sometimes twice a week, they reviewed the latest developments.

"The immediate worry," Turner said, "is what happens if the Masters' properties can't make their October payment to the banks and bond holders," Turner said. "The probability of a full default has risen since last week to around 70 to 75%." The total debts of Masters' company are estimated to be at least 140% of the value of its real-estate assets. And there are the CDSs on them that are multiples of the actual outstanding bonds. Rumors of an impending fire sale of Masters' assets has already created a fall in prices for commercial real estate. And if real estate was to tank, then it could take the whole economy down with it. The damage will be severe when it happens, and there's nothing we can do to stop it. We can't ask for help from Congress either."

Michael knew that, in Japan, the Government was in shock over the resignation of the Prime Minister, owing to a suggestion of financial impropriety. The Government was broke, and the country still remained mired in a slow, snail-like recovery. The green shoots of a recovery had given way, once China's economy collapsed, to extreme pessimism and collapsing business confidence. One idea that was being debated in the Diet, was to lift the quotas on rice and grain imports that had propped up Japanese agriculture for so many years, but which had limited the redevelopment of small-scale farms located in a zone close into the major cities. And if these were lifted, as appeared likely in the next few weeks, then these farms would no longer be viable, and the price for land around Tokyo and Osaka would collapse putting more pressure on the banks that financed the overpriced urban real estate.

Then, Ross thought idly, there were the continuing problems in Europe. The Italian, or in other words, non-German centric head of the European Central Bank, had saved the euro in 2012, by opening the floodgates and buying government debt, which cut borrowing costs across Europe. But after his term was up, the leadership of the ECB passed back to German hands, and the promotion of policies that emphasized austerity rather than growth. The Germans were becoming fed up with a union where the stronger were continually bailing out the weak. The fact there was a new nationalist party gaining strength was also worrisome, to say the least. And if Germany left the euro then the entire post-war European efforts to create enduring peace might be lost.

Chinese growth was now closer to 3 to 4%, well down from the 8 to 9% that Asia and the world had come to expect, and needed just to keep trade growing within the region. The result was a collapse in demand for primary products and international trade that dragged down other economies, dependent upon selling to the fast-growing Chinese market. The most important impact was on the price of commodities: oil and minerals. Australia and Indonesia suffered, as did much of Africa and Brazil, now dependent on Chinese demand for investment inflows.

"Is there any more word on the rumored port strikes in Asia?" Michael asked. He had asked Turner to look into it upon his return to Washington.

"Yes, it's definitely one more problem to add to your list," Francis Turner said. The intelligence on this had just come from Tokyo earlier in the week. It had taken time to verify its truth, but it was enough to cause anyone, understanding the complexity of the interlocked global supply chains on which global commerce and production depended, to panic.

"Should I be sitting down?" Michael quipped, looking at the picture of Milton Friedman that hung on his wall. Milton's dour smile seemed to counter the optimism that Michael had felt after the President's election. Michael was not a monetarist, but he liked to point to the man who had single-headedly caused the 2008 financial crises, even if it was after his death. The belief that markets knew best, and free markets knew better than any others, had filled past Administrations, both Democrat and Republican, with fervor for laissez-faire capitalism, and the stripping back of regulation of banks and financial institutions.

"Three days ago, in Tokyo, Atshuhi Watanabe, the head of one of the largest Japanese trading companies, a man of around seventy, a billionaire many times over, met with a union organizer, Akio Itou," Turner said with a smile, then continued, "to offer $100 million in support for the International Brotherhood of Asian Transport Workers. Akio has been organizing the workers in ports throughout the trans-Pacific region, even establishing a close link with the American west-coast dock workers' unions and crane operators. When the bottom fell out of the economy in 2014, trade collapsed. Companies running port operations reduced wages and benefits drastically, and cut hours. Now that there's been some recovery, the workers are angry, spoiling for a fight. They are planning a work action across the entire Asian region in October. Watanabe is going to fund the organization of this action, and provide financial support to the striking workers."

Michael stood up and looked at the whiteboard. He noted the convergence of dates: the likely bankruptcy of the Masters' real-estate empire; the new controls on money and debt coming out of Europe; and whatever Walter and Katherine were planning. The new Government in Japan added more uncertainty to the markets. The problems in Russia might well come to a head in late October. German regional elections were also scheduled for around that time, with the nationalists likely to take control of a number of States. As Germany turned more right wing and anti-Europe, it added to the trend already apparent in other Northern European countries of electing right of center governments. The result would be chaos ... complete and utter chaos.

All of these issues were there on the table, but the latest fear was that these factors weren't coincidental, that they may be part of some orchestrated plan. Neither man could fathom how the world economy could survive a simultaneous implosion, or who might benefit from this.

"Could we warn the markets?" Turner asked.

"That would be like putting a match to a powder keg. No, we simply have to try to ride this one out, and hope that I'm proved wrong. Or find a way to stop at least the most damaging of these events; maybe convince IFF not to make their ultimatum to the banks, or have the Fed buy up the worthless Masters' bonds before they are deemed junk."

"What have you heard from Natalya?" Turner asked casually.

"I spoke to her this morning." Michael related the conversation.

"She needs to get the hell out of there before it blows up. She'll be the first to be purged, along with her father."

There was an edge to Francis Turner's words that worried Michael. He had been lulled by Natalya's quiet assurances that she was okay. He wanted to believe in her invincibility. But seeing the expression of concern on Turner's lined face sent shivers down his spine.

"What can we do?"

Turner thought about their options. The situation was considered to be serious. The foreign policy community, centered around the Council of Foreign Relations scholars, was betting on a dissolution and breakup, possibly even a civil war, revolution, and counterrevolution. There could even be a further fracturing of Russia itself into regional conglomerates of the Old Russian State. "Someone in Moscow can try to get her out, but I can't promise anything."

"Please do what you can," Michael said, hoping this wouldn't poison the well further for Natalya with her superiors. "I don't want her to get harmed."

20. A Visit to Lenin Street

Natalya shivered in the thin prison smock. She had been arrested at the airport on returning to Moscow. Two FSB agents had stopped her just as she showed her re-entry documents. They'd driven her to the large, fortress-like building on Lenin Street that the FSB, the successor to the KGB, used to process suspects. There she'd been strip-searched and physically abused by a burly female guard. Finally, they'd thrown her into a cell, and as the steel door clanged shut, she found herself on the floor between two facing rows of steel benches.

There had been a point, before she left Latvia, when she had almost run to the American embassy to ask for help, but then she had let that thought go, and had continued on to the airport. At the time, she had reasoned that since she had given up her American citizenship, the embassy would have refused her help. However, she had lived in the States for years, had once had citizenship, and she knew that Michael could use his influence to get her a new passport. So why had she not taken that opportunity? Sitting here on this cold bench, frightened for the first time in her life by Russia, she couldn't answer that question.

The cold metal walls of the cell closed in around her like a tomb. Five women sat on the two narrow steel benches attached to the walls. The cell was entirely of steel, windowless, claustrophobic. And the smell was horrific: a heady mixture of body sweat, urine, feces, and fear. In one corner was a pail, while the door had a slot where food was pushed in twice a day. The pail was removed just once a day and now stood nearly full. Time stood still here, counted by the opening and closing of the door. The light stayed on day and night, making it difficult to track time. It might well have been hours, days, months or years. She remembered the training at Koslov for what spies should do if they were caught, but little of what the instructor had told her so long ago seemed relevant to this kind of hell; this Soviet-style hell invented as much to torment as to punish.

She had read about Stalin's purges and gulags, but she'd never believed that, in post-Soviet, democratic Russia, the new Russia, that this still happened, or could ever have happened to her. In Stalin's day, mere suspicions were enough to send a man or woman to a living death in the mines and the camps, but that was in the uncivilized past, not the present. This was the twenty-first century, not the 1930s. While the large work camps may have been turned into privately run businesses, the cells in Moscow Central on Lenin Street clearly hadn't changed.

It was officially forbidden for prisoners to speak. But humans are social creatures with an ingrained need to talk, so they did, in whispers, like co-conspirators in a spy story.

"Admit nothing, Comrade," advised one of the women. Her voice was no more than a whisper, having endured endless sessions of questioning, interspersed with sudden, unprovoked pain. The woman did not even know the crime they were accusing her of, but in time, they would make her confess. That was the goal that this place was famous for achieving, again and again.

Natalya's trip hadn't even been a success. Livowitz, who ran the warehouse, despite trying to hit on her the whole time, had told her little. He was sorry about the shipment, he said earnestly, and claimed he didn't control the goods passing through his warehouse. He had only appeared flustered when she had asked about the nickel alloy being shipped from smelters east of the Urals, on their way to Western markets. Was something hidden inside those ingots? And why had Sokolov told her not to go, barely five hours after demanding that she make the trip? Only her father and that strange man Zhvikov had known she was going to Riga. She recalled that Zhvikov seemed to have tensed when she'd mentioned the name Livowitz.

There were footsteps in the hall outside. The whispered conversation stopped, and all eyes looked towards the steel door. The sound of the metal key was amplified by fear, and the creak of the door opening sent shivers up and down Natalya's spine. No experience, not even the psychological conditioning of Koslov, had prepared her for this. The guard looked from face to face and then pointed to Natalya. With a firm hand, he pulled her out of the cell. Her thin smock caught on the edge of the lock, and she found herself gathering up the torn garment and wrapping it around her to cover up her nakedness.

She walked down the hall, trying to compose her thoughts, but nothing came. They went up one flight of stairs and down an identical hall, stopping only to open one of the identical heavy steel doors that lined the wall of the hallway. Opening it, the guard shoved her into a high-backed wooden chair. The room was almost pitch-black and it took a while for her sight to return. The guard attached thick leather straps around her chest and around the back of the chair, and then tightened them until she couldn't breathe. She gasped for breath, frantically sucking in air, until her body relaxed enough to allow circulation to return. Relax, relax, she said silently to herself, don't fight it, and let it happen.

"There are, of course, more comfortable chairs in America. Isn't that right, Comrade?" said a disembodied voice out of the darkness. Spotlights turned on suddenly, painfully bright. Natalya blinked from the shooting pain through her pupils into her brain.

"This is a mistake." She forced the words struggling to make sound. "Call Sokolov, or better still, Director Passoff in the Ministry of Trade and Industry. He'll tell you I'm working on important matters."

"Always the same: the guilty are not guilty" said another man, his voice laced with irony and sarcasm. He looked back at his associates who were only visible to him in the shadows at the back of the room. He then leant down to Natalya so he was at eye level, his face almost touching hers, and screamed at the top of his lungs. "You are a spy for the Americans! Isn't that correct? How long, Comrade? Years, yes?"

It was ridiculous. What had she done that had set them off? What secrets had she stumbled upon?

"No!" was all she could say in her defense. And yet there was a certain logic to the accusation. Why else would a person exchange a good life in America for an uncertain and risky one in her country?

"Why did you go to Riga?"

"I was on official business."

"Your superior, Dr Sokolov, did he not order you to *not* go to Riga? Yet you went? Why? Did your American paymaster demand you go there, Natalya? What did you find, and who did you meet?"

"It was my duty. I found nothing. There was nothing to find. I met no one!" she shouted.

"Is your duty, Comrade Avramowitz," he answered formally, "to disobey orders, direct orders from a superior officer? You spent a week with the American economist. What did you discuss? What secrets did you divulge? He called yesterday. Did he order you to go?"

"I …" Natalya stammered, then choked back her words.

"That's better," said the man, his face again up close. He growled, almost like an animal. "Now listen, bitch. Here, there's no one to save you. Not even your important father! Not the American economist! Not anyone! Here, you are ours to do with as we please. Here, you are alone!"

He wrenched her hair back. She screamed. He slammed his hand across her face. Her head bobbed back, wrenching her neck. She felt dizzy and in the stress she peed, the warm urine running down her legs.

When the guard returned her to the cell there was little fight left inside. They'd stripped the remnants of her torn clothes, and they'd caressed and stroked her. They had hit her with a broom handle. However, they had not raped her, for which she was grateful. She knew that despite her humiliation, far worse had been done to other prisoners. All of the other women in the cell, even the old, weathered one, had been beaten up and raped regularly.

Pyotr listened without changing his expression to the telephone call he'd received later that morning. Given Zhvikov's agitation, he should have suspected that he would have found a way to stop Natalya's investigation. When she had not obeyed Solokov instructions, Zhvikov had given the orders to isolate her. She was now in the FSB center on Lenin Street. In a civilized country, Pyotr mused, Natalya would have been merely reprimanded, but these days, Russia was far from civilized.

Later that day, Pyotr met with Yura Ionanova, a former student, now working on Security issues in the Government. Ionanova had heard around the departments that the beautiful and talented Natalya had been caught in the web. It was disturbing.

"Your daughter is crazy, you know, Pyotr. First, there was the American economist, and now this."

"She is difficult, Yura, but she's not subversive."

"And if she had discovered the shipments of gold, then what?"

"I would have made Natalya understand the importance of them to Russia."

"What if she had been pig-headed?" said Ionanova persistently. "She is your daughter, after all! What if she had refused to believe it was for the best, then what? Can you be sure she wouldn't have told the American?"

"Get her out of the clutches of the security service, Yura. That's the first step. Everything she tells them under torture will go to Zhvikov. And that will be dangerous."

If Natalya had discovered this truth, and the wrong people found out, what might have happened? It could bring down the Government, collapse the already weak ruble, and destroy any chance of the conservatives and the liberals working together, in the hope of righting the sinking ship.

Yura Ionanova suspected that despite the old man's calm demeanor, inside he was a mass of nerves. Visibly, however, his daughter's predicament barely rippled his brow. Pyotr was looking for the right solution, not simply the easy one.

"So what can we do?" Pyotr asked his friend.

"Arrange a transfer from Lenin Street. One of the new re-education camps will get her out of immediate danger. Aserkoff is on our side. Go to him. He has influence in the FSB. I do not."

"As usual, Yura, you're right. Natalya is like loose cannon on the deck of a ship. She will wreak havoc if not handled carefully. A few weeks in the camp might be best for everyone. At least, until she can leave the country."

INTERLUDE VI

Akio Itou waited patiently at the Port of Long Beach, California, for Mark Stromberg, the leader of the International Longshore and Warehouse Union. The ILWU organized the ports along the west coasts of the United States and Canada, making the union one of the most powerful in the country. More than 70% of American liner trade moved through their ports, so that any work slowdown or strike would cause great damage to the economy.

For many years, labor problems on the docks had been easily settled tiffs. The union and port operators understood they depended on each other. However, over the past decade, inflation and the weakened economy had squeezed the union workers. Increasingly, shipping conglomerates were taking over port operations, and were aware that their profits now came from moving containers efficiently on and off vessels, not from transporting them across vast distances. When world trade had collapsed in 2015, owing to the problems in China spreading throughout the rest of Asia, the west coast ports had suffered layoffs and wage cuts. Subsequently, the ILWU needed to demonstrate that it still had power, and Akio was in a perfect position to help them.

Stromberg was a big man, and when he shook Akio's hand he almost crushed it. He then stood back and studied the slight Japanese union organizer. Did he have the stomach for the trouble he would cause if a strike or even the hint of a strike, around the Pacific Rim ports was threatened?

"Well," Stromberg said, "it's a pleasure to meet the terror of Asian transportation at last."

Akio smiled. He had only recently formed the International Brotherhood of Asian Transport Workers, which aimed to prevent owners from underpaying their workers, relative to port workers in Europe and the United States. It was true, he had caused a stir, but his union wasn't powerful enough to prevent ships diverting to less unionized ports if labor problems became too difficult. Something more audacious was needed. He had the money to organize it, but he needed to enlist the help of the ILWU.

He knew about Albion Hall, the 1934 strike that had crippled America in the midst of the Great Depression: the lives lost, the fights, but the victories too.

"Thank you," Itou responded, "I have learned much from your organization, and its history. But I must ask a favor, that you join us, even if only in name. Let the port operators see us as natural allies. Although we serve the same masters, our members work for only one tenth of your wages, and have no benefits."

Stromberg smiled. There would be better leverage if trade could be brought to an immediate stop rather than a slow crawl. If Asian workers threatened to strike on their own, then the ships already on their way could still unload their cargos, and its effect would be muted, long enough for replacement workers to be sent in. If, however, there was a joint labor action, if the ILWU walked out in sympathy with their Asian brothers, then the companies, and indeed, the governments affected would have to cave.

"Of course, Akio," Stromberg said, putting his arm around the shoulders of the Japanese organizer. "Of course, we can walk out in sympathy to your cause. The cause is just, right and true, isn't it?"

"And," Akio answered, "I am sure that my union can contribute funds to support your action."

"So, when is this action planned?" Stromberg asked.

"October; the end of October, around the 25th" Akio said. "Is this a problem for you?"

"No," Stromberg answered, aware that this action would need to remain secret from both the ILWU's leadership and membership until the last moment.

21. A NEW INTERNATIONAL ORDER

Jenny fingered the gold choker that fit snugly around her neck. It had a lock for which only Carlos had the key. The necklace was a visible sign of how much she was now controlled, not only by Carlos but also by Walter and Katherine. She had lost sight of her beliefs on how best to refinance the global economy, and now agreed with most of what Walter and Katherine wanted, in the interest of harmony. Political considerations, Walter explained, were more important than technical issues that could be sorted out later.

Each night, Carlos methodically destroyed the old Jenny Bennette and transformed her into something new. Her cold, inner reserve that had always been her armor had quickly fallen away under his charm and seduction, and she was now utterly dependent upon him to satisfy her cravings. She'd initially accepted the gold choker with its miniature lock, complete with a D-ring, with a tremble of excitement as part of their sexual role play. However, Carlos never removed the choker. Now, as she was forced to wear her collar and humiliation in public, she thought that all that was now missing now was the leash!

"We need to talk, Carlos," said Jenny. She found herself drowning as new elements in their preformed plan overwhelmed her own careful reasoning. They were sitting in a small, lakeside restaurant just outside of Geneva, waiting for the English journalist to arrive.

"What's the problem, my love?" Carlos said, stroking her bare thigh. "Are you worried about meeting, Rawlston?"

"No, but I'm not sure I agree with Walter and Katherine's plan. And to sell it, I have to believe it will work. Right now, it has too many unintended consequences. Governments and private banks might agree eventually, but before any compromise can be reached, the entire global economy could well collapse, leaving an unholy mess. In Rome, the indebted Senators used the people's anger against moneylenders to call for a general cancellation of debt, hastening the fall of their own empire. What IFF is threatening may be far worse."

"Do you see any other way? Be honest, Jen, without the threat they will never negotiate in earnest. You know that to be true. All those years you traveled, did you do anything helpful, anything to set the balance sheet back to zero, so that countries could have the money to start afresh and develop properly?"

The flaw in Carlos's argument was that much of the debt had been accumulated by leaders who had stolen the borrowed money, and had done little to help the poor, or invest the funds in roads, schools, and clinics. What would actually change if their debt was forgiven, and they were allowed to start again without a change in leadership? Yet the overhang of debt, built up after the collapse of the global economy in 2008–10, and the very slow recovery since were preventing any hope of a full recovery to the world economy.

The threat of a default was always there, a threat hanging over the banks, but it damaged the countries making the threat as well. When Argentina had defaulted, and it had paid a heavy price. The Holtzs aimed to ensure that the threat of a default was seen as guaranteed, like a ticking bomb unless a compromise on the debt was reached within weeks.

Edward Rawlston was a journalist. Twice a week his "*Letter from the Continent*" was printed as a feature in the Wall Street Journal. He was one of a handful of influential financial reporters capable of moving markets, or causing the collapse of stock prices.

Rawlston was a crude man who drank too much and was never without a cigarette, ignoring the Swiss and French laws against smoking in public places. Despite his personal flaws, he was a great reporter who would go anywhere for a story. One long series for the Journal had dealt with the secret world of terrorism finance, and had taken him to many dangerous places. The global recession had offered a wealth of stories, and in turn, the means to fund his vices. He had warned, in a feature earlier in the week, that if the debt issue were not solved soon there would a global disaster, as country after country defaulted, and banks throughout the world failed.

"Mr. Rawlston," Jenny said, flashing a warm grin, extending her hand to the tall, thin man with a noticeably sallow face.

"Miss Bennette," he answered, taking her hand limply.

"You know Carlos, of course." She glanced to her side, where Carlos stood waiting to be introduced.

Carlos poured a glass of wine for Rawlston first, then Jenny, before filling his own glass. Rawlston sipped it, and then took a deep drink. He wanted a Scotch badly, but the wine would do for now.

"How are Walter and the lovely Katherine?"

"Fine, fine. They send their best wishes. They are meeting the new Secretary General of UNCTAD this evening, otherwise they would be here to join us," Carlos said, despite knowing that in truth, the Holtzs preferred the pitch to Rawlston be made by Jenny and Carlos. Limiting their involvement in such meetings would reduce their exposure if things didn't work out as planned.

"Waste of time, UNCTAD," offered Rawlston, looking at Jenny for confirmation. "All talk and no action."

"The UN is an acquired taste." Carlos said lightly. "Still, you have to work with it. Having a voice in an ineffectual organization is better than no voice at all, and it allows politicians to argue to their people that they are working through the proper channels, reducing the risk of unilateral action like expropriations."

"I don't think I've ever acquired a proper appreciation of all talk and no action."

Their conversation continued in the same vein for most of the evening, barely mentioning the question at hand. Jenny found herself appreciating Carlos's subtle method, even if bored by the time his indirect approach took. By dessert, Rawlston was well lubricated with the rich food and fine wine. It was dark outside and there were few diners left in the restaurant.

"We were to discuss debt, I think?" Rawlston asked.

"Yes, yes," Carlos said with a smile, "but I think that we should save that discussion for tomorrow. We have some new ideas that we'd like to run past you."

"New ideas?" Rawlston was a journalist at heart and was, therefore, interested by the carrot that had been dangled, even if he recognized that IFF had its own agenda. "Where and when?"

"At our offices, in town," Carlos suggested.

"And what earth-shaking news do you have to entice me to this meeting, Carlos?" Rawlston leaned towards him with a leer.

"We are in the process of negotiating a union of debtors and poor alike. Once that pact is in force, then we will negotiate with the banks and their governments, threatening a mass default if real concessions are not made on all outstanding private and public debts. Only the threat of financial Armageddon for creditors will allow for there to be reasonable negotiations on how to tackle debt." Carlos dangled the bait expertly. He let his voice fall to a whisper as he said the last part, forcing Rawlston to lean towards him.

Rawlston smiled, though his attention was less on what Carlos had just said and more on Jenny, and in particular, her quite visible cleavage.

"The threat, Mr. Rawlston, is real," she added smoothly, "but the opportunity to find a way that works for all parties is also quite extraordinary."

"You endorsing this concept seems a bit out of character, Jenny," he said. "Everyone I've talked to says that you have a history of turning coal into gold, and describe you in negotiations as being unyielding and as cold as ice."

"I've had a change of heart. The only conceivable way to solve the problem is by compromise, having a carrot and a stick. Tomorrow, we will lay out the elements for you to see, and give you an exclusive, but we need your secrecy."

The chance of a scoop on a total global default was certainly worth spending another night in Switzerland for. One had to take the Holtzs seriously, especially with their influence over the poorest countries.

"It is a threat, yes," said Jenny the next morning, choosing her words carefully, "but also an opportunity to find a solution that involves more than just simple austerity. Without strong global growth, like we had in the 1990s, there is no real way out of the crisis. So growth should be the objective, not more of the same tough medicine. It is time to rid the world of the IMF-imposed Washington Consensus. It's never worked, and the well-paid bureaucrats in Washington just won't admit it. Tough measures imposing austerity on government finance and higher taxes has never stabilized economies after they are in free fall. Everyone loses: borrowers, creditors, and the poor bastards that have to live through that hell."

Rawlston knew it would be a huge coup if he could break the story, even if the threat proved to be just a paper threat, easily defused by political and even military pressure. Still, some nagging voice inside his head warned him not to trust Jenny, Carlos, and most of all, Walter and Katherine Holtz.

"We will all benefit from the faster growth that will come from lifting the debt burden holding back development. With more money these countries can start to buy more on the world markets, adding to total demand." Jenny said this easily, having convinced herself that, at least, that statement was true.

Rawlston smiled. They were old, stale words. These countries would never develop unless they had a revolution. They were kept down by backwardness and greed. Corruption was so much a part of these cultures that it was accepted as the price of doing business there. And unequal income distribution, driven by low wages—a by-product of globalization and a reliance on export-led growth—prevented the development of the mass markets needed to sustain domestic growth.

"Why will this work when all the other efforts failed, from the Club of Paris to Bono?"

"Commitments are to be firm and binding, signed by the highest authorities in each government, allowing us to present a united front. No more cherry-picking by the rich countries offering sweet deals to some, and leaving the others exposed. It's all or nothing. One settlement, one general approach, that's the only way to solve the debt problem and get the world economy moving again."

Inside, Rawlston was excited. It would be the story of the year, and might even, if he played it right, earn him a Pulitzer.

"I trust you will keep this quiet. There are people in London, New York, and, of course, in Washington, who would like to stop this now, if they got wind of our plans."

"Of course. So when will I be able to break this story?"

"We'll tell you closer to the date, and in time for you to make the front page of the paper."

22. LITTLE JADE

Masters awoke sweating. He had been a fool to speak so openly to Lilly. Sheng would have a camera and a microphone hidden somewhere, and it wouldn't take genius to identify Roger Carson as Ben Masters.

"What's wrong, Ben?" Lilly felt him tense. She had seen it before, when a deal hadn't gone as planned, or when he was worried sick about the future of his company.

Ben smothered her question with a long, drawn-out kiss. She tried to pull away, but then gave in to the long dormant feeling of desire. The last eight months had, in a strange way, saved their marriage. It had reminded them both of what was important. They had each been pulled down from great heights to the lowest level of humanity, and in the process, had lost the ability to control their own destinies.

"I don't like the setup he whispered, softly muffling the sound in her body.

"Are you frightened?"

"A little," he smiled weakly. "Who the hell wouldn't be?" He pushed himself up on one elbow and looked around the room. Light shone in from outside from the small lights that lit the pathways between the cottages. Recordings of tropical birds and insect sounds could be heard.

"It looks like that place in Aruba," he said, forgetting the name. "You remember the one with the plastic beads for money?"

For Lilly, there was nothing of beauty in this place, only pain and humiliation. "Can we get out?" she asked in a near whisper. "Can you get me out of here, Ben?"

Nothing could have prepared him for the task ahead of them, not even his years in the rough and tumble world of New York construction. He'd come blindly, without a plan.

"I don't know. In time, yes, of course."

In New York there had been nothing that Ben couldn't do, Lilly thought, so why was he saying "in time?" Why didn't he have a plan that would allow her to escape this prison?

"What did you think you would do?" she shouted, angry and upset, forgetting that they might be heard, "get a quick fuck, and leave me to rot?"

"Stop it!" He covered her mouth with his hand. "It's fuckin' dangerous, so shut the fuck up, Lillian! Listen!" He didn't know what his next move would be. "I need time to look around, to work out a plan."

She could see his confusion. Everything was new to him. He was overwhelmed. Yet, he had come. He had come for her, and that counted. If they were to get out alive, then she would have to do the thinking. What had she noticed about Eden? She trawled through her memory, but nothing came to mind. It had been dark when she'd first arrived from the northern camps.

"What happens in the morning?" he asked, thinking about the next few hours.

"Sheng ordered that I be kept in shape. I thought he was joking, but they all take that little bastard very seriously. So Wu-lin comes each morning, before breakfast. He takes me to the center courtyard where I'm exercised like a prize horse for half an hour each day. Some guests watch and laugh too."

"And after that?" Ben felt Lilly tense. He stroked her body, but it did little to ease his agitation or her own. "What if I want you back?"

"Then Wu-lin will return me here."

Lilly reached up for him. For now, more than ever before, she needed him. How many times had she rejected him, forcing him to sleep in the guest bedroom? For the past eight years, ever since she had discovered that he was regularly screwing Marcia Simpson, she had refused to sleep with him

"Did you ever stop loving me?" She kissed him hungrily.

"Never," he admitted.

"Even when I wouldn't let you lay a hand on me, Ben? Even then?" Lilly asked, wondering if he was telling the truth.

"I never stopped loving you Lilly, not entirely."

Had she stopped loving him? Maybe she hadn't even loved him in the first place. Certainly, she had loved the power that his money and name brought her. She had gloried in the publicity, and even notoriety. But now, she needed Ben more than life itself. He was her only hope.

As Kim went to collect Lilly for her exercise, she tried to think of a plan. Three people fleeing seemed impossible. The chain-link fence surrounding Eden was ten feet high and electrified. They would need to force someone to let them out, and the only person of importance who could free them was Sheng. As she walked, the seed of a plan developed, and the more she thought about it, the more she liked it. They could escape, and Sheng would pay for his atrocities, including what he had done to Little Flower and Mai Lin.

In the kitchen, Wu-lin faced an angry Mother Cha who was holding Jane Morgan by the scruff of her tunic. In one hand, Cha held a leather whip. Jane was infuriatingly slow, indifferent to the guests' needs, and insulting too, throwing out a constant stream of French and English swear words.

"I'm done with this whore!" exclaimed Cha. She forced her foot on Jane's back, driving the girl's breasts into the pavement. Wu-lin looked down at the American girl squirming under Cha's prodigious weight.

"What's Jane done now, Cha?"

"Everything, everything wrong. Hopeless, stupid, filthy," Cha stammered in a mix of Chinese and Thai." Jane crawled to her knees, only to be sent reeling and back to the floor by Cha's hard slap across the face.

"I'll talk to her," he said, offering to solve the problem.

Cha turned and left the room, throwing up her hands. Wu-lin looked to where Jane lay on the floor crying. He reached down and helped her up with some gentleness. She was a small woman, not unattractive in that very American way, and Wu-lin towered over her. His English was reasonably good. He'd managed Sheng's establishments in the city for many years.

"Why you make Cha complain? You fed, housed, clothed, so what more you want?"

"Fuckin' woman!" Jane shouted.

"Jane, Jane," Wu-lin's tone of voice was still friendly, "Sheng let you live. Better than die? Yes?"

Her world had turned into a nightmare. Each pass by the pool showed her what had become of her beauty. Her hair, her best feature, had been shaved from her head. She wore rough black cotton pajamas two sizes too large. The language was strange and grating to her ear. If it had been sex, she would have known what to do, but she would never get the hang of cleaning toilets, washing dishes and scrubbing pots from dawn until late at night. She was tired and hungry, and fast going mad, and sensed that she would only last a few more weeks. Jane Morgan, society girl and party animal, would become a permanent wreck.

"Generosity? Fuckin' monkey-face!" she screamed, just to get the anger out.

Wu-lin ignored the slur, not entirely certain what she had called him. "Sheng let you live. Easy to kill you, Miss Jane. Easy, no one care. Who care?" He laughed.

"You have to listen," she pleaded. Her anger released, realizing that Wu-lin was her only hope.

Wu-lin took Jane and sat her down at the table. He smiled, gestured with his hands for her to begin. Perhaps there was a story worth hearing.

"The man in Cottage 4," she said, knowing she needed to make a point with this man quickly, "he was there, when Marcello was killed."

The name Marcello meant nothing to Wu-lin. But if Carson had known the Morgan woman in New York, it was worth alerting Sheng.

"Come," he smiled brightly, showing his gapped front teeth. "Perhaps you not useless after all." He guided her out of the room.

As he led her out of the room, Lilly and Kim entered. On seeing Wu with the Morgan woman, Lilly became agitated. Last night, she'd heard what had happened in New York. Jane Morgan looked at Lilly without comprehension. To Jane, Lilly was just another old whore.

"No exercises today," said Wu-lin, his hand running playfully over Lilly's now quite well-toned flesh. He laughed, and then turned her out with a pat on the backside. With one hand on Jane's tunic, he led her along. Sheng would be in the office at this time of the morning. Let him work out if Jane was telling the truth.

Kim had seen the look. Lilly Masters was nervous. She remembered Jane's look when she'd seen Masters in the room the day before. Instinct told her they had to act now. She pulled Lilly outside and hurried her down the path towards Cottage 4.

Sheng was old-fashioned, working with an abacus and recording his accounts on paper. He was behind in his payments to the bankers, to Lee for the leased women, and to the grocers and butchers too. Bookings were also down. The demand, which had once seemed unlimited, had dried up, as the Asian economy had turned from boom to bust.

He would have to cut back. He had already reduced the number of guards. He would send some of the older whores to his Bangkok establishment in an effort to get the most "bang for his buck". Sheng examined the contract that he had signed, but he couldn't see a single clause that would let him reduce his monthly rent.

"Sheng," said Wu-lin, entering the office quietly.

"What is it? Be quick Wu-lin," Sheng said, angry at being interrupted.

"This girl has a most interesting story," Wu-lin continued, despite seeing Sheng's anger increase.

"I'm busy Wu-lin, very, very busy. Please go away."

However, as Wu-lin began to leave, pushing the American in front of him, Sheng changed his mind. The numbers were not going to get better, but perhaps a bit of fun with the stupid girl might amuse him.

"What is your new story, Jane?" He squeezed her wrist, twisting her to the floor in front of him. She cried and Sheng smiled happily. "Some new farfetched tale, yes?" asked Sheng, unzipping his fly to pee on the sobbing girl on the floor. However, only a few drops came out which lightly covered her back. He scratched his balls, and then zipped up his fly.

Jane had her epiphany at that moment. She knew who Roger Carson was. The sight of Lilly Masters, the flash of a picture in a New York tableau about Masters opening another one of his monster developments in Manhattan with his glamorous wife at his side smiling, led her to the name of the man in Cottage 4. Even without the trademark hair, Masters was recognizable.

"Roger Carson is a fake."

"And who is he, if not Mr. Carson?" He had seen the man's passport, but fake passports could be manufactured easily.

"Masters, not Carson. Ben Masters," said Jane looking up from the floor at Sheng hopefully. "Lilly's husband."

If she had said he was the man from the moon it wouldn't have struck Sheng as less crazy. Could a man convicted of murder, of second-degree homicide, be out so quickly?

"And how can we be certain of this?"

There was a way to know, of course. Carson had requested Lilly last evening, and it would be on tape. She would know him, and they would have no doubt talked.

"We will watch the recording of last evening," Sheng said, as Wu-lin pulled up the video recording on the computer. As they all watched the video it became clear that Jane was not lying.

Kim knew that only surprise would save Masters. It was obvious that the Morgan girl had some knowledge of Carson's true identity. Why else would Wu-lin take her to see Sheng? It was only a matter of time before they came for Masters, so she had to strike first.

"Come, both of you," Kim said, pushing Lilly, now out of breathe, into the cottage.

"Who are you?" a startled Masters demanded. Before she had talked to them in pidgin English, but now she spoke with a fluent American accent.

"I'm on your side, but there's no time for explanations, Masters. Sheng will come for you soon unless we strike first." A confused Masters hesitated, but then followed without protest.

With Lilly between them, Kim led them down the path directly to Sheng's office.

"Get the guards and detain Masters and Lilly," Sheng ordered Wu-lin.

"Where should I take them?"

"Downstairs to the quiet rooms," said Sheng with a smile. There was some pleasure in torture, especially if it made the American talk.

Kim waited patiently beside the door as Wu-lin opened it. He didn't see the blow coming, and collapsed into Masters' waiting arms. Finding rope in one of the drawers of the desk, Kim tied him up and gagged his mouth.

If Sheng had been in the office, he might have heard the noise. Instead, he had taken Jane with him into the back bedroom. He would fuck her as a reward. There was something quite attractive about the girl despite her shaved head. He started to undress as she watched lazily from the bed.

"You have been helpful, Miss Jane," said Sheng with some kindness as he came close to her. His fingers began to unbutton the black pajamas she wore.

Kim caught Sheng with piano wire around his neck and yanked him back off the girl. She could have easily broken his neck in an instant, but he was still more valuable alive.

She jammed her knee into the small of his back forcing him to bend backwards. "A poor way to die, isn't it? They say that you turn blue first."

Sheng gasped for breath. On the bed he saw the Morgan woman staring openly at something behind him.

"You, goddamn it!" Jane flew off the bed leaping at Masters. Ben easily controlled her, sending her flying with a cuff of his hand to her head. She began to cry uncontrollably.

"Shut her up, Masters," Kim ordered, switching to American English.

"Who are you?" Sheng asked through clenched teeth.

"Can't we save the girl?" Lilly asked, still confused by the sudden turn of events.

"We're not out of here yet, Lilly," Kim answered, while tightening the grip on the wire. It would be so easy to kill Sheng. She had good reason to do so, but for now she still needed him. Sheng, now bound hand and foot, stared at Kim. Something about the girl had suggested danger when he'd first seen her, but he'd ignored it. A stupid mistake on his part, and one he was now regretting as he now remembered the identity of his captor.

Kim, noticing that Sheng had made the connection, spoke to him in Thai. "It has been many years, hasn't it? Do you remember how we parted?"

"You ran away, Little Jade," said Sheng, recalling that day when she'd left. "I still have the scar." He turned his head with some difficulty.

"Do you remember Little Flower?"

How could he forget Little Flower? She had been a young Amerasian, like Little Jade. Kim had taken a liking to the girl, like a big sister, but Little Flower had died at the hands of a sadistic German tourist.

"I was wrong to let him take her," Sheng admitted. She had died later that night from internal bleeding. Her fragile little body had been dumped in the kalong; a fitting end to a poor life.

"What do you intend to do now?" Sheng asked, curious about his fate. "Kill me and Wu-lin?"

"I don't think that would be useful." Kim said, looking around towards the papers on Sheng's desk. The files in the office could be of value to Turner, and she would need to find a weapon. So far, everything had worked far better than expected. Kim looked over the account books and smiled as she saw that Sheng was deep in debt and still losing money.

"What are we going to do now?" Ben asked, looking around.

"Get the hell out of here." Kim said, handing him a carry case with the papers and laptop. She picked up the thin trousers and tunic that Jane Morgan had been wearing and handed them to Lilly. Lilly untied her sarong and dressed quickly.

Kim walked back to where Sheng sat bound. "Order the car, and have it downstairs in ten minutes."

"If I refuse?"

She slapped Sheng hard across his face, causing the chair to fall back with a thump. He looked like an inverted insect. Kim placed her foot squarely on his windpipe and stared down at him.

"If you won't do it, then Wu-lin will."

Sheng coughed struggling for breath. "I'll call." He choked on the words. She stepped aside as he gasped for air.

"That's better." There wasn't much of his arrogance now. "You may just live long enough to explain to your creditors why Eden isn't profitable," she said with a laugh.

Lee would never understand. The struggling enterprise would plunge quickly into bankruptcy, and there would be hell to pay.

Masters lifted Sheng upright. The chair settled back on four legs. Kim held the receiver against Sheng's ear, and then dialed the main gate where the vehicles were garaged. After Sheng was finished, she hung up the phone.

"You should be able to see out from that window," Kim said, recalling that the office looked out on the front gate of the complex.

She continued to search the desk.

"You must have a weapon somewhere," Kim said.

Sheng remained silent.

The gun was hidden in the bottom drawer of the desk. She pocketed the box of extra cartridges in her tunic, and held the gun, aiming it carefully at Sheng's head for practice. She had the same smile that had intrigued him when he had first seen her as the slight, eleven-year-old, Amerasian girl that Mai Lin had found wandering the streets of Bangkok one night.

"The car is coming," Masters said, as he watched the big black limousine pull up in front of the office.

The driver fought hard and was well trained. Only the hard butt of the revolver silenced the man, but the damage caused by the resulting noise and confusion had been done.

"Are you okay?" she asked Masters, who was breathing heavily. Lilly helped him up, holding him tightly.

"I'm fine."

"Okay, we have to get Sheng downstairs without anyone seeing. Lilly, go down and see if the lobby is clear."

Lilly hesitated.

"Go!" Kim ordered roughly. "Do it quickly and quietly."

"What about the girl?" Masters asked, after Lilly had left the room.

"Leave her."

"I can't!"

"You don't have much of a choice Masters, do you?" Kim suggested. "What if she talked? Then what? That business with Costello would be front-page news. She's a liability to everyone, even to herself, given the evidence the police have against her," Kim reasoned.

"But ..." Masters protested weakly. He had thought of exactly the same points, but had not wanted to disappoint his wife.

"Besides, in time, Jane will find her way home. There are plenty more deserving victims penned up here."

Sheng's mind was engaged in trying to find a solution to his situation. He wanted desperately to survive, but as he went through the girl's motives for revenge, it became clear to him that he would likely die. He had raped her the first night that Mai Lin had brought her in. And while he'd loved her in his own way, he had found pleasure in punishing her, using a wide leather whip. There were also the deaths of Mai Lin and Little Flower to repay.

Lilly returned in a panic, out of breath from the climb. She'd seen two guards downstairs in the front room, reading Thai girlie magazines.

Kim held the revolver and eased herself quietly down the steps.

"We can leave now." Kim said, looking to where Wu-lin sat up against the wall. She helped Masters carry him to the bed. They dropped him next to the now desperate Jane Morgan.

The girl tried to talk through the gag. She looked up at Lilly Masters, appealing with her eyes to the older woman for help.

"Can't we?" Lilly asked Kim.

"No!" said Kim sternly. "Now, let's get out of here before something else happens." Sheng walked down the stairs. Masters would have to drive. She took the hat from Sheng's chauffeur.

"Pull down his trousers, Lilly."

Lilly stood silently without moving.

"Pull them down now." Kim demanded.

Lilly unzipped the fly of Sheng's trousers. The pants fell in a pile around his legs. "His drawers too," Kim ordered.

With his penis and testicles exposed, Kim took the piano wire. She needed Sheng thinking about something other than escaping. She remembered a punishment Sheng had used on a recalcitrant houseboy. He had had good fun marching the unfortunate street waif around the room on a long tether, connected by a noose around his testicles. She looped the wire around Sheng's, and pulled it tight.

"You've changed, Little Jade," said Sheng matter-of-factly, all the while sweating like a pig.

She didn't answer, but tugged the wire, causing Sheng to double up in pain.

Kim helped him stand and guided him to the car door. The car was parked in the front entrance, under a wide awning. She shoved Sheng roughly across the back seat, until he was at the far left window. She slid in next to him, her grip firm on the piano wire, the weapon hidden in her lap. Lilly sat in the front seat, next to Masters who was driving; the chauffeur's hat barely fit his head.

"Drive slowly until we reach the front gate. That's about a mile beyond here."

"And then what?"

"If Sheng knows what is good for him, he'll cooperate."

"Sounds simple enough."

"It should be, but you can never tell. You have the guard's gun, Ben. Use it on the guard and ram this car through the gate."

"How many should there be?"

"Four or five, but they're a lazy bunch and rarely patrol the perimeters. They're likely a waste of money too."

Masters approached the gates just as they were beginning to open. He slowed, and then stopped.

"Okay," Kim pulled tautly on the wire. "Do your thing."

Sheng sucked in air, and then spoke quickly, his voice choked and his words garbled. The guard looked into the car, hesitated, and then pulled out his weapon.

Kim flinched; pulled hard on the noose which caused Sheng to double over in pain as the noose slit through the sac holding his testicles. Masters pushed the accelerator to the floor. The heavy car leaped forward, tires screeching, flinging gravel everywhere.

Kim knew that somewhere at the edge of the property there was a bridge across a small tributary of the Chao Phraya River. The width of the stream was no more than eight or nine feet, but Wu-lin had pointed out that the bridge could be drawn back to keep unwanted visitors out.

"Sheng!" Kim pulled him up into a sitting position. She looked down at the open wound that the wire had inflicted. A trickle of blood covered the seat. Sheng moaned in agony.

"Go faster," said Lilly, looking back at the car which was chasing them.

The road twisted and turned through mango groves and swamps. The first shot shattered the rear window, Lilly ducked behind the front seat. Shards of glass hit Kim and Sheng in the backseat. In his desperation to get away, Sheng pulled the door handle. The door swung open wildly as the car swerved. Kim kicked Sheng half out the door, and then fired twice. With a final push, she sent him out the door and back onto the road. The car following rolled over the body, the force sending it careening into the ditch at the side of the road. That left only the bridge to negotiate.

Kim could see blood covering the front seat. One of the shots had hit Masters in the back and he was slowly losing consciousness, his foot slipping off the gas pedal just as the bridge was approaching. At the current rate, the big car would never clear the gap that was opening from the retracting bridge.

"Floor it!" she yelled, slamming her fist into his back. Involuntarily, he rammed his foot to the floor and the car surged forward, spinning gravel behind it as it gathered speed. Kim was thrown back against the rear seat, shards of glass shredding her clothing.

She could see the opening, and the sound of gravel striking the underside of the car was deafening. But then everything became quiet as the car left the ground. Finally, there came the shock as the car crashed down on the other side of the gap, wheels spinning in the loose gravel until it gained traction causing the car to shoot forward.

Kim reached over the seat sliding forward awkwardly until she could grip the wheel, pushing Masters to one side as she did. The car weaved from one side of the road to the other.

"Ben, let up on the gas," she screamed into Master's ear, but he was barely conscious.

Eventually, Masters' foot eased off the gas as he slumped to one side. However, the car only slowed, it didn't stop. Ahead the road twisted, and Kim fought to keep the car on the road, even at the slower speed.

She looked to Lilly huddled in the front passenger seat in fear. There was no help from her, so Kim shoved Masters towards his wife and climbed over the seat. She pulled the transmission lever back into neutral, and once fully in the seat, pushed her foot on the brake until the car slowed and then stopped.

Curley Marston was waiting at the private clinic when Kim pulled up. She'd called him from the car, and found her way to the clinic on the outskirts of the city.

"What the fuck took you so long?"

"Calm down," she said, looking over to where Masters sat.

He looked inside the car. He didn't recognize the wounded man or the woman. Two attendants were standing by, and with a nod from Marston they went around to the side of the car and opened the door. One attendant, obviously a paramedic, pushed Lilly away and removing the bandage made from the torn bottoms of her pants, studied Masters' wound.

"Who the fuck is that?" Marston said, looking at the wounded and unconscious man being rolled away on a stretcher.

"Don't you know, Curley?" Kim said smiling. She couldn't wait to be done with Curley Marston and Asia.

"Should I?"

"Ben Masters."

"And who the fuck is Ben Masters?"

"You, Curley," she said with a laugh, "have been in Asia far too long." Then she followed the gurney into the clinic, leaving Marston standing confused at the curb.

23. DINNER AT THE SAVOY

Moscow's Savoy Hotel had its own Japanese-made generators and imported fuel oil, shipped from Poland each month, ensuring it was well-lit and unaffected by the power shortages that plagued the capital. Its lobby was filled with Western businessmen, Russia's new millionaires, and a few mafia-types acting as "consultants." In the bars, lobby and upstairs bedrooms, semi-professional Russian girls in hot pants and miniskirts plied their trade at night, working as secretaries and shop clerks in the day, accepting dollars or euros for their services.

The Savoy was full of Russians spending their money before the entire economy collapsed, and it became worthless. The Russian miracle was over, and peaceful protests were giving way to dangerous riots, as stores closed from a lack of goods to sell. The streets were becoming unsafe and Internet chat rooms and social media were talking openly about revolution.

Pyotr Avramowitz was seated in the grand ballroom waiting for his guest. He looked around at his fellow diners and thought, ruefully, that they were rats waiting to flee from the sinking ship.

"You look tired," said Aserkoff as he hugged Pyotr warmly.

"Too much to do, so little time to do it," Pyotr answered, ushering Aserkoff to the chair opposite his. "Your family, are they well?"

"They're happy to be out of Moscow and in a civilized place like Washington."

Aserkoff's son-in-law was the second deputy at the Russian embassy in Washington, a plum position that Pyotr had helped him get.

"Nicki was one of my best students. It was a pleasure to help in any way I could," Pyotr said, reminding Aserkoff of his past favor.

Pyotr knew that Aserkoff was well aware of Natalya's situation. He was depending upon the younger man for many things, not the least of which was Natalya's freedom. Despite his fears for his daughter, he also had other business with this man that must come first. For a liberal revolution to succeed, then they must be sure of the military, or at least those in the military who saw Russia's path as one of cooperation with the West, rather than one of confrontation; and ensuring that those officers, who had profited from liberalization and had adapted to the more open, freewheeling, Russia, were on their side. But which of the units would be loyal to which generals remained a great uncertainty. Pyotr depended upon men like Aserkoff— a friend to both the liberal wing and the new, more conservative leadership—who had taken charge since the old government had decamped with their millions for greener pastures in the West, to bridge the gap between intellectuals like Pyotr, and the more conservative members of the military establishment. As to Aserkoff's true loyalties, Pyotr suspected, even Aserkoff didn't know. He was, like Avramowitz, a survivor and survivors tend to go with the winner irrespective of ideology.

"As you requested," Aserkoff answered, looking around nervously, "I've spoken to others in the Senior Directorate about what may be planned for October. There are only a few that we can trust. We have to be careful. The *Pamyat* has infiltrated the Senior Directorates and are gaining strength." He referred to the neo-Nazi conservatives with their racist hatred of the Jews and Muslims. Right now, the Government was balanced on a knife-edge between quasi-liberals, outright conservatives, and the resurgent Communist Party that now controlled, at least tacitly, some of the more far-flung provinces.

"Once we commit on the 24th, we must quickly gain control, or everything will be lost. Can we rely on Brusiloff?" he asked, referring to the right-wing general.

"Brusiloff will jump at the opportunity to outrank Konetief, and he is approachable. Do you know the man? But Dubinsky controls the more powerful Northern Army Group and its commander, General Lopatin."

"Yes, of the two, he is the one we should put our faith in. I will find a way to approach him."

Aserkoff furtively removed a sheaf of papers from his coat pocket. He handed them to Avramowitz.

"Is this the list of units that will support Brusiloff?" Pyotr asked, studying the names.

"Yes," was Aserkoff's response, while looking around. He noted that Pyotr shared his nervousness.

"Are we certain of these?"

"They have much to fear from Konetief, given that they have a large number of soldiers from the east under their command."

"They are all some distance from Moscow." He tried to measure the names with miles of distance.

"If you can guarantee that the railways will not be sabotaged by the workers, they will get here in time."

"The railway workers have been briefed," Pyotr said, without as much confidence as he would have liked. The old unionists, long banned, were quietly re-establishing influence. Without the trains bringing food from the south and coal from the east, Moscow and St Petersburg would fall into complete anarchy. Of the two choices, Pyotr thought, it would have to be Brusiloff who would be called upon to quell the unrest. He commanded the Moscow Military District. It would take money, but he could be bought. Pyotr knew at least one good source of funds that could be called upon for this purpose.

"Now, onto the other matter: my crazy daughter," he sighed.

"You're worried about Natalya." Aserkoff struggled to find the right words. He had finished his plate of food quickly. It had been good, finely prepared with quality meats and vegetables, but sadly there had been not enough. He had eaten all the bread that had been provided, and Pyotr with a wave of his hand had ordered another basket halfway through the meal.

"What father wouldn't be? She doesn't belong in the camp."

"Why did she disobey Sokolov orders?"

"She's crazy," Pyotr suggested, and smiled weakly.

"The young are always crazy," the FSB man agreed.

"Very bright, very foolish too," her father said with a sigh. "And we have to get her out of there immediately, and well before the 25th."

The FSB man reached into his coat pocket and pulled out a folded document. He had had the 5th Secretariat, in charge of the re-education effort, process the release papers earlier that afternoon. He handed them to Pyotr.

"There's also an exit visa signed and dated, too. Get Natalya out of the country before she is swept away by history."

"I thank you." Pyotr didn't look at the official documents. He knew they would be in order. He simply put them in his inner pocket along with the lists. He would pass the intelligence about the units that would refuse to follow the government to those who would need to know. And then he would take his official car and drive north to where they were holding his daughter. It would take until morning to reach the camp, hidden away northeast of Moscow, and then most of the day to reach St Petersburg from the camp.

"She should go out through St Petersburg." Aserkoff suggested. "There's a train each evening to Helsinki."

Later that evening, sitting alone in the back of the big Ziv sedan that had been assigned to him when he became Special Advisor to the President, Pyotr worried about all that was set to happen at the end of October. He was playing a friend to those in leadership, whilst being a friend to the democratic opposition. It was a dangerous game.

He thought back to Machte and Enigen. It was fifty years since he had been selected by Machte. It had been a great honor given to only a few, and one kept secret from all others. From that day forward, it had become his responsibility as much as his destiny to change the world. Pyotr, however, was a realist. The calm he had displayed with Aserkoff had been an act to boost the FSB Director's morale. Pyotr knew the chances of success were far less than those of failure.

The transition from planned economy to market economy had been rocky and uneven. For Russia to avoid revolution from the millions of poor who had been helped by the State during the Communist years, it had to find new wealth. For a time, this wealth had come from oil and minerals, but the collapse of the Chinese growth engine, that began in 2014, had robbed the Government of the money power to maintain the status quo. The unproductive factories, a relic of the Soviet system, had never been reformed, as raw materials replaced domestic manufacturing as the source of wealth, products to fill the newly opened stores had to be imported. Wealth from oil and minerals had created a temporary boom, but that had now disappeared. And the opportunities for making money, which had once given people hope, now fuelled resentment. New homes with their manicured yards coexisted with rundown hovels, and decaying, Soviet-era, high-rise apartments. There was no longer money to import the luxury goods to which the new middle class had grown accustomed, and the lower classes aspired to own. The result was dissatisfaction and rioting. The response from the Government was new restrictions on public meetings, and show trials of members of offending rock bands.

Despite years of freedom, the Russian soul remained fearful. There was no real tradition of democracy or free expression. If they admitted it, most Russians would have accepted the return of strong autocratic leadership. It remained a one-party state even if the name of the parties changed. Since the departure of the last government, the State had slid towards collapse. If Russia went back to Communism, then a lifetime of Pyotr's work and sacrifice would be lost.

Pyotr looked at his watch, having dozed off. It was nearly five o'clock in the morning. Light had started to show in the eastern sky.

"Would you like to stop and rest, Dmitri?" he asked the driver, leaning forward to speak through the small opening in the glass partition.

"I'm okay, Professor."

"Good," Pyotr said, studying the landscape that raced past. "How far have we come?"

"We have about four hours to go. The roads are worse than when there were Czars." The car bumped along, its speed slowed by the condition of the roads.

"If you come to a good-sized town we will stop and find some place to eat."

"If they have food," the driver responded, thinking about how bare the shelves had been in the local markets of late.

"If they have food, yes!"

"We are all waiting for the 25th October, Professor," the driver said with a sigh. "Perhaps after that, things will change."

Change, yes, Pyotr thought, but change to what? The date had become a kind of underground slogan. Who had leaked the date? But October, Pyotr thought idly, is always a revolutionary month in Russia. And this October *would* be another October of turmoil.

24. THE ROAD TO FINLANDIA STATION

Four guards stood, joking crudely about their sexual prowess, as they watched the group of female prisoners, including Natalya, digging a new garbage pit. With only shovels to break the hard, rocky ground, the work was back-breaking. The week before, the guards had chosen a big-boned Slav for their fun, unbuttoned the girl's old, Soviet style, men's wool pants and had their way with her. In return, she had been excused from doing the hard work of recovering the camp refuse.

"You're a pretty one," one of the men said, coming close to where Natalya was working. She ignored him, driving the shovel into the hard ground without looking up. The man lifted her head with his hand, forcing her to stare into his wide, flat face. She tried to turn away, only to have her head wrenched back. He squeezed his fingers against her cheeks, forcing her mouth to pucker.

"Don't be a fool," Natalya said, trying to back away. "Fuck me and you'll pay."

"Don't bother with that one, Dimitri," one of the other men advised. "She'll eat your balls."

"Panov, you worry too much. She's a whore with a flat chest and smelly pussy. And what can they do anyway? Tell the Commandant?" He didn't let go, but instead kicked out her legs, sending her backwards onto the ground.

The guard pounced on Natalya, his hands working at the buttons on her trousers. Other guards pulled her pants off as she struggled, but any real fight that she had, had been beaten out of her during the last weeks. Natalya didn't hear the shot, but felt the weight of the man on her chest, and the sickly smell of blood.

"Release her," ordered the officer, "before I shoot the lot of you."

One man pulled off the lifeless body of Dimitri, and helped Natalya up. She could barely process what had happened. The weeks in the camp had sapped her strength, destroyed her ego, and forced her into survival mode. She stared at the officer, perplexed and frightened.

"They'll be punished," the officer said, holstering his revolver as other soldiers shoved the guards aside.

Natalya struggled to stay on her feet. Her legs felt like rubber. She looked around almost in a daze, but then she noticed that her pants were still on the ground along with her torn underwear. With as much dignity as she could, she picked them up and put them on.

"Which of you is Natalya Avramowitz?" asked the officer, once Natalya was back in the pit with the others.

"I'm Natalya Avramowitz," she answered. The fear of the rape gave way to a greater fright. For whatever the guards were, their brutality was nothing compared to the terror of the Little Fortress, with its ice-cold isolation cells, where those deemed irredeemable were sent.

"Then I arrived just in time," he said with some relief. "You're wanted in the Camp Commandant's office."

She didn't speak on the short ride back. The pleasant banter of the young officer did nothing to ease her fears. Natalya noticed the Government plates on the big Ziv automobile that was parked in front of the Commandant's office. She remembered the beady-eyed Government bureaucrat, Zhvikov, who she had met that night before going to Latvia. She remembered how he had reacted to her announcement that she was going to investigate the shipment that had gone awry, and she also recalled the way he had touched her as he had announced that the car was ready downstairs. She would rather die than be his mistress.

"Come this way," he said, leading her into the building. He knocked before entering the Commandant's office.

"Your daughter is here, Comrade Professor," the Commandant said with a smile.

"Thank you, Joseph, for your help." Pyotr took a last sip from the near-empty glass of vodka and stood up. He extended his arm and shook the Commandant's hand warmly.

"It was nothing. Are you sure you won't remain here, as our guest, for the night? It will soon be dark, and the roads leave much to be desired."

"I'm certain. My driver has rested, and we have many miles to cover tonight."

"And how is it in Moscow? What's the atmosphere like now? We hear rumors …" He stopped mid-sentence, letting Avramowitz fill in the rest.

"Not as cold as here," Pyotr said dryly.

"Of course, the weather," said Joseph Rostov with a laugh, "is drier in Moscow, and warmer too."

Pyotr looked towards his daughter and immediately saw the change in Natalya. Her hair had been cut short and hidden by a scarf; her expression was sullen, distant. She avoided glancing directly at him, and her hand shook as she stood passively to one side, barely raising her head. He led her out of the building to his car.

Father and daughter sat in the back seat of the car, lost in their thoughts. Natalya watched warily as the camp gates swung open, letting the big car out. The drive was bumpy and noisy from the sound of gravel hitting the side of the car. She stared out the window, watching the rows of tall birch trees, almost afraid to look to where Pyotr sat. Finally, gathering up her courage, Natalya looked to where her father sat brooding, deep in thought. She felt ashamed.

"I'm sorry, Papa." It was the voice of a child, not a grown woman.

"Who should be sorry, you or I?" said Pyotr, for once his voice showing emotion. "I was the one who forced you to come back to this country, and to face this outrage."

"I should have listened to Sokolov. I should have ..." She broke down losing all her self-control. At this moment all she really wanted was her father to hug her and say he loved her, but Pyotr Avramowitz had never shown affection.

"We are living in difficult times, Natalya," Pyotr answered, looking at his watch. It was close to three in the afternoon. With luck, they might be in Petersburg by nine or ten o'clock in the evening. Enough time for Natalya to catch the midnight train from Finlandia Station to Helsinki.

"I was so stupid you know. It was all around me. Why didn't I see it?"

Pyotr sighed. Should he explain how he had used her to cover for his own actions?

"You visited Enigen when you were in Switzerland, Natalya?"

"Yes," she said, looking at him as the pleasant memories of her time with Michael flooded her conscience.

"I know Carl Strauss told you about Thomas Machte, and his vision for the remaking of the world torn apart by the World War. Did he explain how selected members of each class were pledged to that goal?"

"An obligation not taken lightly," she said, remembering the words of the elderly man.

"Not an easy burden for an eighteen year old to face, nor even for someone at my age," Pyotr said, leaning back against the thick cushions, picturing that dark night when he had been tapped and pledged to that purpose.

"You set out to change Russia by working within the system, by conforming, didn't you, Papa?"

Pyotr looked at his daughter. Perhaps he could hazard some explanation that she would accept. "After the fall of the Soviet Union, we believed our salvation would come through unfettered capitalism. This allowed a small group to take all of the State's wealth. The Government was forced to take back these outsized gains, but at the cost of violating the rule of law and trust. We replaced poorly made Soviet goods with better made products from Western companies. Virgin and Apple stores replaced the GUM department store. And the Internet made it impossible to manage the flow of information. Yes, each advance brings its cost. When the prices of oil and minerals collapsed in 2014, the Government was left with a difficult choice."

"You chose to sell the gold," Natalya said, now understanding the dilemma, "but you couldn't broadcast that to the world. So, it was done quietly through a middle man in Riga?"

"Yes, you were getting too close to the truth," Pyotr said. "Zhvikov was afraid. He turned you in."

"What happens now?" she asked. "People will die," she added, thinking how hard it was for so many here just to survive the winter. "If food doesn't continue to come into the cities, there will be starvation. We can't afford revolution, Papa."

"Anything is preferable to a slow death," Pyotr answered coldly. "We are falling further behind. In ten years, we will be a runner-up, a backwater. Only the historians will recall that we were once a great power. The world is passing us by unless we change, and change radically. We must repudiate more than 100 years of our past. The old order must die, once and for all. It is time to see if we can hold together, because it is the only way we can all survive the harshness of our winters, and the shortness of our summers. Real progress only comes with self-sacrifice. War is coming, and who will win and who lose is still unknown. And you must now leave. This is no longer your fight."

Natalya had listened to Pyotr in a dream. Her bowels ached, her bladder was stretched, and her stomach shrunken from weeks of deprivation. She yearned for food.

"We must stop soon, Papa. I must eat and go to the bathroom."

Pyotr looked out the window. There were forests along both sides of the roadway. The shortage of gas left the road almost deserted. The official automobile had been fitted with long-range tanks. Without these they would have been stranded by the inefficiencies of the distribution system.

"We can stop at the side of the road. Afterwards, we will see if some kindly peasant can spare some bread."

Later, as Natalya dozed, her head pressed against the leather seat of the car, she dreamed of food, remembering the hunger of the camp. They had been fed twice a day, supplemented with scraps of meat and fish. Food had never seemed important before. But there, she had dreamed of milkshakes and hamburgers.

"And what is to become of me, Papa?"

"You will leave Russia. Did you enjoy the camp, Natalya?" There was a hint of anger, mixed with irony in his question. "There will be more camps. Times are perilous, and it's dangerous for anyone under suspicion; especially dangerous for someone who is Jewish and with foreign connections. Your destiny was never here."

Natalya didn't protest. "I'm tired, Papa," she said, resting her head on his broad shoulder.

"Rest now," he placed his arm around her and she snuggled against him, as she had done when she had been a motherless child.

"Thank you for coming for me," she said, like a little girl, happy for the love and attention of a parent. "I don't know how much longer I could have survived."

He didn't answer. His daughter, this woman, was broken. It had not taken long for the old Russia, the Russia of gulags and camps and solid steel prison cells, to break her spirit. He was not even certain that she would recover, even in America, but it was their only hope. He watched as she fell asleep. He then stared out the window, his mind was racing ahead to what came next. There was so much to do and so little time left to do it in. The detour to save Natalya had been necessary, yet it had set his carefully planned agenda back a full two days.

She awoke just as they neared the outskirts of St Petersburg. It was time to tell her the truth, or at least some version of the truth.

"Have you ever wondered, Natalya," Pyotr began, "about your mother?"

"Yes, Papa."

"I will tell you the truth; not the fairy tale that I told you when you were very young. I first met your mother in New York when I was working for the United Nations. She was only eighteen years old, fresh out of high school, and working for an NGO lobbying the UN on social issues. She had come from a good family, but this was her first experience away from home. I had found her fascinating in many ways, not least because of her energy and strength. She had lived a privileged life up to that time. Although I was in my late thirties, twice her age, I guess she found that the difference in our ages made me more attractive to her."

"Were you in love?" asked Natalya.

"I suppose I was. She was quite beautiful, and there was competition for her affections. She chose me as her lover. I was flattered, amused really, finding it interesting to teach this innocent American girl lessons about the world. I became her mentor, her teacher, as well as her lover. Six months after we met, she was pregnant."

"Did you marry her?"

"I offered, but she refused."

"Tell me her name, Papa," Natalya asked. "I deserve to know who my mother was."

"Katherine Martin," Pyotr answered, "She came from somewhere in California, I think."

"What happened next?"

"Katherine lost interest. A child was a problem for her. She wanted a future, to go to college, and raising a young daughter or son was not in her plan. She wanted to go to a private doctor to end it, but I refused. At the hospital, she turned you over to my care, barely looking at the baby she had carried and given birth to. I don't think you'll find any love from her, Natalya."

"What did you do, Papa?"

"I went home soon after, taking the position as Professor of American Economic Studies at Moscow State University. And Katherine disappeared from our lives, Natalya."

"Then I was born in America? There should be records?"

"In New York, yes," he answered, thinking back to that time with some remembered fondness.

The car slowed as they entered St Petersburg. Pyotr looked out the window at the once brightly lit buildings, now just darkened forms, as street lighting had been switched off to conserve power. They would be at the station in time. He looked to where Natalya was deep in thought. Was she thinking about the United States and Michael Ross, or trying to understand exactly who she was, and to what nation she owed her loyalties?

"There's twenty-two hundred dollars in cash in the envelope. It's the most I could raise quickly, but it should be enough to get you to Washington." He handed her an envelope with the Russian passport and a signed exit visa. "The Americans are aware you are coming. Strings have been pulled and there will be a new American passport waiting for you there. Someone is looking out for you there; your American economist friend perhaps. You will be met at the train in Helsinki by someone from the American embassy, to make sure you get through Finnish customs and are on the next flight to Washington."

"Thank you." She leaned over and kissed her father. She was crying.

"Remember who you are, Natalya," he said sternly, looking at her as he had so long ago, when he last sent her off to Americ. "You are Pyotr Avramowitz's daughter; you are trained to think and also to fight. You are unique. Take it as my gift to you."

"Let me stay," she said, not really meaning it, "to help you."

"Your destiny is elsewhere, Natalya."

25. GENEVA

Masters stared at the small garden just outside the door to his room at the private Clinique Bois Gentil, in Geneva. The first bullet from his shoulder was removed in Thailand, but Turner had thought it best to get Ben and Lilly out of Thailand altogether, and so he was recuperating at the clinic. It had taken a skilled Swiss surgeon to extract the second bullet that had impacted his collar bone. However, in a week, he would be well enough to exercise his arm.

Lilly was bored with sitting in the room, listening to Ben complain. Tired of the very limited wardrobe she had hurriedly purchased when they first arrived, she was keen to go into the city. It had been years since they'd last been in Geneva. "I'm going downtown to do some shopping. I'll be back in a few hours." She saw the sour expression on his face, but ignored it. She would never again be dependent upon Ben's approval. Thailand had taught her that, at least.

Ben was lonely and bored. They were stuck there in diplomatic limbo, without passports. Little of the money Ben had brought to Thailand remained; most of it was in the safe back at Eden. And they were still didn't know where Brett Latimer had taken Beth.

"Any news from that private dick we hired?"

"I told you yesterday," she said, annoyed by the same question. "Not yet."

"Christ, Lilly, it's been over three weeks. Switzerland is a small country; it's not fuckin' China."

"Who knows, Ben, maybe I got it wrong. Maybe Brett didn't come here after all."

"Well," Masters said, his voice trembling with suppressed anger and emotion after so much waiting, first in prison, and now here, "he sure isn't in fucking New York, minding the damn store!" The news from the States was alarming. Everything they had worked so long and hard for was now about to go down the drain. Someone, probably Brett, had destroyed the business and the brand. For Ben Masters, he'd rather be dead than destroyed and destitute.

"It's no use thinking about it now, dear," Lilly suggested sweetly, coming over to the bed. She placed her hand gently on his broad forehead and stroked his head, ruffling his hair playfully. He looked up at her. She was still beautiful. The weeks here, isolated in this clinic, had reinvigorated her.

"In some ways, you know, I think what happened was for the best," said Lilly "I was talking to Marie-Eve last evening," she said. "You know Ben, she's an extraordinary person." Marie-Eve was their old French-Swiss nurse, and a strong believer in karma.

"What did Marie-Eve say?"

"She believes we're alive on Earth to learn lessons. Sometimes, you learn more from disasters than triumphs."

"I've heard that bull before."

"She thought you would say that, but some of what she says makes sense. We were self-absorbed in New York; just caricatures of what rich people should be. Beth was raised on MTV and indifference. She had money, but not love and support. We had to have everything: the ugly, impractical antiques; the yacht; and the all the houses. And don't forget our lovers. One was not enough." Her hand caressed his. "I don't care about the empire, the house, car, and the jet. They don't matter. We have experienced the lowest depths that humans can reach over the past year, but it brought us back together. If pain is what it takes to rekindle love, then I can bear it. I want you with me at my side again."

He looked at his wife, and remembered her as he had seen her for the first time, walking down the road, trying to make it back to the dorm before curfew. He'd picked her up in his old Ford and driven her back to Smith. "You're right; I wouldn't change a minute if it's brought us to this."

Brett was annoyed. They were already two hours late to the Holtzs' house, and Beth appeared to be in no hurry. She was spoilt, and he regretted taking her out of the brothel, but for now' he had to keep her out of trouble and out of the news. The clothes had cost a grand, and now she wanted luggage. Lunch had had been expensive too, and had left him famished, even as she'd raved about the cuisine. She insisted on speaking French, which despite her expensive private school education, was lousy. He could believe her stories about how all she'd done in school was give blowjobs to the faculty.

Lilly caught a glimpse of Beth and Brett as they entered the small leather goods shop on the Place de Molard by the lake front, and even from a distance she could see that Brett was annoyed. Lilly followed the unhappy couple into the department store where Beth proceeded to examine fine Swiss pottery.

They eventually emerged from the store, and grabbed a cab from the stand. Lilly took the next cab, planning to follow them back to their hotel, before going back to get Ben and confronting them.

"Where is she?" Walter Holtz asked Fritz Weber. Weber handled security. He'd called Walter out of the room, where he was entertaining his guests.

"In the study," he answered.

"Do you know who she is? Was she armed?"

"No, an amateur, most likely a journalist," he suggested.

He didn't recognize her. She did bear, however, a striking resemblance to Latimer's girl.

"Walter Holtz." Holtz extended his hand. "This is my house. Were you lost?"

"I'm a close friend of Brett Latimer's," she said, trying to peer into the next room where she'd heard voices. "He said to meet him here, but the gate was locked."

"Who were you meeting?"

"Brett Latimer. He's with my daughter. We haven't seen each other for a while," she stammered, not quite knowing what to tell this man.

"Mr. Latimer is not here, nor is he expected," he said. "I didn't get your name."

"Lillian Masters," she said, without hesitation. She'd been given a new name on entry into Switzerland, but that name was still foreign to her ears.

Fritz Weber had exited the room ahead of Holtz. He hurried into the sunroom where Latimer and the others were still talking. He ushered Latimer and Beth out the side entrance.

"You'd better leave now. Mr. Holtz will call you at your hotel in town when we are certain that Mrs. Masters has left," Weber explained.

Holtz then led Lilly out of the sunroom, insisting that they look in each room, including the children's rooms, for these mysterious guests. He seemed far too slick, and she didn't like him. Even as she followed him into each room of the house, she knew that Brett and Beth would have already left.

"Perhaps you would like to have some wine?" Holtz asked Lilly. They had returned to the sunroom. Another couple had just arrived, a tall, handsome Latino and a woman, obviously older than him, wearing clothes that, in Lilly's mind, she seemed uncomfortable in; more suited to a whore than the businesswoman she seemed to be.

"I must be going now. I'm sorry for interrupting your day, Mr. Holtz." Lilly said, walking towards the front entrance.

"Fritz can drive you back to town," said Walter with a slight smile.

Katherine greeted him when he re-entered the sunroom. "That was close, Walter. If the Masters woman had met Latimer, it would have led to too many complications, and far too much attention."

"I was surprised to see her here. According to Brett, the last time he saw her she was plying the sex trade in an Asian brothel."

Later, at dinner, Jenny asked Katherine what had happened. Who was the mysterious woman Walter had taken around? And why had Latimer and the girl left so quickly?

"Just an uninvited guest," she explained, "who thought she knew one of our guests."

"She looked familiar. Do you know her name?"

"No," Katherine lied. "Perhaps Walter remembers."

Katherine sat down on a chair and looked at Jenny. So far their program of remaking the American banker had been a brilliant success.

"And what about our friend Rawlston?" Katherine looked to Jenny for an answer. "Is he all primed?"

"Jenny," Carlos replied his hand possessively on Jenny's knee "did an excellent job. Jenny played Mr. Rawlston well." He smiled sweetly.

Jenny sensed that there was more to their plan than helping poor countries survive in a globalized world. She was being played like a chess piece. She felt Carlos's hands touch her shoulders, and the D-ring on the back of the necklace. She pulled away, but not before seeing the look of pleasure on the Holtzs' faces. Still, she couldn't fight the feeling that, after so many years alone, having such a handsome man in her life was extremely pleasurable.

"I think," Carlos added, thinking about the English journalist, "that Rawlston wants to see all his warnings come true. It was a master stroke, Walter, really, to choose Rawlston and the *Journal* as the messengers of doom and gloom."

"My wife's idea," he smiled, and held up his hands playfully.

"I had an email," Walter said later that night, "from our associate in Washington,

He rose from the computer. "Apparently, Michael has reconnected with the Russian woman we met at your father's. He was seen at Dulles airport meeting her flight. He is now living openly with her. Not surprisingly, it has caused a small scandal, with some people in Washington suspicious of her true allegiance."

Katherine lost color momentarily. She had not yet explained to Walter who Natalya was, but given the visit from her father's lawyers on Friday, she would have to reveal the truth to him. She had not liked the strong, self-willed woman she had met at her father's, even if it was her daughter by Pyotr, and realized that all their plans were now being held to ransom by this woman.

"Is there a problem?" Walter asked, seeing the worry on his wife's face.

"Yes," said Katherine, slowly sipping the cognac as she thought about what to say. "Walter, before you, I worked in New York. I had a lover. And Natalya is the product of that union."

"Natalya is your daughter?"

"Yes," she said, looking at her husband of thirty years. "I gave her up soon after she was born. Less than a year later, she returned to Russia with her father, Pyotr Avramowitz."

The thought suddenly struck him hard. "Which also makes her Heinrich's granddaughter."

My father's lawyers came last Friday asking that I sign some papers relating to his will."

"What papers?"

"Additional funds are being placed in Trust funds that have been set up for our children and for me, but ..."

"But what?"

"I am no longer the primary beneficiary of the estate."

Walter saw clearly the problem that Katherine had identified.

"I see the problem we have."

"I thought you would, Walter, but what can we do?"

"I will talk to Carlos," suggested Walter, recalling that Montoya had hinted that he knew people who could take the necessary actions to make problems like this go away.

"I would feel easier, Walter," Katherine touched her husband's hand, "if these problems were taken care of quickly, and it must look accidental or Papa will know it was us."

"You have nothing to worry about. It is as good as done."

"Thank you." Katherine said with some relief. "Thank you very much, Walter."

INTERLUDE VII

"And the money," the young politician asked, "where will it come from?"

"Private funds, but sufficient. The party is in a good position to take over the Federal Government when the next general election is held in 2017. But there are State elections that will test the power of the Social Democrats, and other more liberal parties, earlier than that."

"Marcus, our party leader, is not terribly fond of me, you know. He won't give up the leadership that easily."

"Marcus will not be a problem," his godfather said, as they walked in the garden of his country estate. "He will find it useful to turn over the leadership to someone younger and more charismatic. You will be elected the next Chancellor once the new parliament is installed, but before that, you will become the most talked about politician short of the Chancellor. Funds are being placed in the party treasury, to ensure that the New Deutschland Nationalist party wins enough seats to open the door for you becoming Chancellor, once the General Election is held. And we will force that to be held at the earliest possible date, in 2017."

"I've studied his speeches." Willie had spent hours listening to the cadence and rhythm of Hitler's addresses to the massed crowds, before and during the war. "His timing, choice of words, with double and triple meanings, and the pitch."

"We are confident that you can whip them up. The young are restless for change. And the people are angry that German money continues to be thrown at the wasteful European south. The time is ripe for a new all-German party to take control of the Reich."

The younger man looked at his godfather. His real father had long been out of his life. This man had been his friend and confidant throughout university, and now he was asking a favor. How could he refuse? Besides, he was ambitious enough to know that he craved the power that their money could bring him.

"Germany will recover, Hans."

"And be a great nation. It is time we loosened the shackles that the French and left-wing German intellectuals have made for us, in this infernal, bureaucratic union of Europe. It's filled with outsiders who don't share our ideals, and wish to take our jobs and control our destiny."

"With your money, it will be done."

26. OBERSCHLOSS

Von Kleise sat in the semi-darkened room, staring out of the window, thinking. He could just make out, in the dying rays of the setting sun, the peaks of the Jungfrau range. Even from this great height, it would have taken supernatural sight to see his schoolmates; those joined by the solemn promise they had made so long ago.

If he had had that sight, and had looked east towards Russia, he would have seen Pyotr Avramowitz struggling against the odds, to fulfil his promise to reform the Russian bear. Von Kleise knew that his chances were slim, and his risks greatest. Revolutions were dangerous and unpredictable.

Looking to the northwest he might have seen Klaus Werner, in close discussion with his bankers and advisors, getting everything ready before the mayhem of October 25th. With the euro likely to fail as a stable currency, with Germany's threat to withdraw coming from the old-line parties, and the new upstart New Deutschland Nationalists growing in influence and controlling now two of the largest State governments, he would need more cash in reserve to keep his companies solvent. Further north, he might have spied Steen Larsen walking the high, windswept, sea-misted catwalks that skirted the icy, black rocks of the fjord at his Northbroden estate. He was worried he had done the right thing, committing his family name and fortune to this purpose. His ships were all at sea, but the seas themselves would be roiled once the trans-Pacific ports closed down, and the euro went into free fall.

Further to the west, he might have observed the elegantly appointed London drawing room, where a British Lord and Cambridge Economics don spoke earnestly to the Prime Minister about the urgency of the economic situation faced by Britain, and the need for drastic action to stem the decline of British industry, and to shore up stock values on the collapsing London Stock Exchange.

Then, he might have leapt the cold Atlantic, where the senior partners of the great Wall Street firms nervously pondered their private intelligence reports, that suggested that a financial tsunami was about to strike the markets. The eminent default of the Masters' real-estate empire was the catalyst, but there were other signs that the markets were heading for a steep decline in the near future. Turning south, bypassing Washington with its myopia and inertia, he would have reached an estate set in the rolling Virginia countryside. There, Richard Kahn was saddling up his favorite horse to go riding with his young trophy wife. His brilliant trader's mind continued to work through the right trades to make in the days that would follow, in the initial crisis.

Turning further south, crossing the Equator, he might have observed the elder Montoya, relaxing with his young mistress, in the house he had built for her on the heights above Santiago. Earlier, he'd met with his advisors and his heir apparent, Diego, and started positioning his great fortune to survive the fallout from collapsing commodity prices, devaluing exchange rates, and surging interest rates. While fearing the chaos of another Latin American crisis, he also knew that, without change, there would be no real progress in alleviating the grinding poverty that afflicted most of the continent. Only by turning greed on its head might companies spanning the globe achieve good, rather than perpetrate oppression and exploitation.

If he could have let his eye wander further to the west, across the broad Pacific, he might have seen his old friend Atshuhi Wanatabe, in Japan, who had not gone to Enigen, but who had agreed with the Plan nonetheless, thinking about how best to position his assets in his globe-spanning trading company, to minimize the damage, and to be in the best position to profit from the chaos that would soon come. He had worked with Akio Itou to accomplish the strike that would cripple world commerce, at least until he was positioned, and ready to take advantage of eventual negotiations and compromise.

It had been fifty years since they had graduated, when Machte with his stern, unsmiling visage and his iron will still had stared down at each of them, demanding that they meet the greater test of the Phoenix vision. It was his vision that drove them even now. By uniting these men so long ago, a new force had entered the world.

"Dr Von Kleise," Eva Bundt interrupted her boss, "an urgent call for you."

Von Kleise listened to the voice on the other end. Despite the news he was receiving, he did not panic. After asking several brief questions, he immediately formed a plan and issued a few hurried words of instruction before hanging up the phone. The whole process had only taken a few minutes. He then called for Michelle and Victoria to join him in his study.

A few minutes later, Victoria entered with a smile. She came over to where Von Kleise sat and kissed him lightly on the cheek. He pointed to the comfortable chair to one side of the desk. She was a beautiful woman, a prize worthy of any man. Michelle then entered the room, repeating the ritual kiss on the cheek of the old man before taking her seat.

"Ola will be jealous," Michelle said lightly.

"She's busy." Von Kleise knew well enough that success, in the end, would depend upon Ola's ability to develop the programmed trading system.

He looked at where Victoria Carter, née Capolita, was sitting. He could tell she was nervous, hiding a secret from him; a secret he now knew.

"Latimer is a problem for us now. He must be dealt with, Victoria."

She had known that Heinrich would eventually learn the truth. Both Masters' women were now missing, and Latimer was hiding in Switzerland with one of them. This could complicate their plans. However, she hadn't been certain that the information was accurate until two days before. Her informant at the Holtz's had confirmed that both Beth and Lilly were now in Switzerland.

"Victoria?" Von Kleise asked, his tone of voice even and without emotion.

"Some of our rental property has been misplaced." Victoria used real-estate terms for the women that had been kidnapped, because any other term upset Von Kleise. Victoria had established the operation to collect and distribute the young women, working through Lee in Singapore and the Marcellos in New York. Rental income collected from the brothel operators throughout Asia made it a marginally profitable business. More impressively, it had given Victoria a degree of coercion and a flow of information. The Phoenix Trust, a network of high net worth individuals and hedge funds, were profiting from this information, and were now reliant upon it. Victoria liked to think of these individuals, who knowingly traded upon inside information, as pigs awaiting the final slaughter.

"In two weeks, the usefulness of this network will be at an end," suggested Von Kleise, still not letting Victoria understand how much he knew of her problem.

"What about our property?"

"See that as many as possible are returned to their proper places. They have served our purposes well. We entered this part of the plan knowing the damage we were doing, but believing that the greater good justified the damage. But where we can undo the damage, we should." Pausing, he looked towards the towering peaks of Kandersteg massif. "I would like to think we fulfilled our part of the bargain to our friends in Government and industry, whose property we borrowed in exchange for their cooperation and information."

"We will do our best, Heinrich," she assured the old man, knowing full well that some of the girls would be lost souls, unable to escape the damage that had been inflicted upon them.

Von Kleise could sense Victoria's discomfort with this subject. Taking these young women had not been an easy decision, but there had been no other way to ensure compliance. Business and political leaders had to be compromised: for some, this was done by digging up dirt; and for others, by controlling their loved ones, with a promise to only return them if they accomplished some task, such as altering an investment plan, reporting an unexpected loss in a subsidiary, or announcing a new discovery that later turned out to be worthless. No task was, by itself, obvious. It was the mosaic of events that mattered. The result of all this obstruction was an economy that was on a roller-coaster ride, as economic indicators were no longer considered to be reliable.

Over the past year, these private investors had been led into the market, benefiting from the insider tips offered, but now these "bets" would be reversed. Once hooked on inside information, these clients were no longer in a position to make their own decisions. At the same time, the METIS stock risk system, with more than $11 trillion dollars under direct or indirect management, had been gamed. The cascade of events would overwhelm it's logic, freeze it's program trading programs, leading to a sell off of massive proportions that once started could not be stopped.

"Should we be concerned, Victoria?"

She fidgeted. Looking to her right, she could see Michelle Rochard, her rival for Von Kleise's attention and love, smiling. Michelle, of course, would be pleased at her discomfort.

"One of our leaseholders, Hwang Sheng, in Bangkok, has died. One of the girls escaped, along with a client."

"Who?" Von Kleise asked knowing the answer already. "Was it our most valuable prize, Lillian Masters?"

"I have a complete report." She reached for her file folder, and removed a two-page document that she had prepared when she was certain of the facts.

"Thank you." He took it, glanced at it for a moment, and then looked back at her.

Eight years before, Victoria Carter had been at the top of the world, a star on Wall Street, and a *Wunderkind* who, at the age of twenty-seven, had been featured in *Money Magazine* as the new genius of M&A. Then the vicious media had turned on her, lured by the whiff of scandal and envy of her success. It had started with rumors that she had passed on inside information about the mergers she had worked on.

And as they dug deeper, they discovered more. The truth of her past could not be hidden under the glare of lights. Soon the headlines screamed with details of her past: "Vicky's Dad Did Time; Hard Time" or "Vicky's Pop Secret Mob Capo". It was true that he had done time in prison for fraud and fencing, but Antonio Capolita had never been a big fish. He was small fry, a petty criminal, on the edge of the mob; a loser by all accounts. And she had distanced herself from her father, by changing her name from Capolita to Carter, and working her way through college and graduate school. But he was still her father.

Then, the media discovered that she had paid for college and graduate school by turning $100 tricks for *Uptown Girl*; a call-girl outfit that serviced New York hotels. When that final bit of gossip was discovered, disclosed in 5-inch headlines splayed across both of the evening tabloids, Victoria Carter fled New York. She hid for a while, in Europe, spending the money that she had saved. At twenty-nine years old she had fallen from a high place to near the bottom. In Amsterdam, she had been arrested for turning tricks without a Dutch work permit. The police had taken her to the airport. The next flight leaving was to Geneva, so she had gone there and onto the path of working for Von Kleise.

Although, ultimately, the SEC and the Federal Attorney both concluded that Victoria hadn't done anything wrong, by that time, the damage had been well and truly done.

"It appears that Lillian Masters, and perhaps her husband too, are now in Geneva. I am also surprised to learn that our Mr. Latimer has appropriated Beth Masters, their daughter. They were both at my daughter's house this weekend. I see a problem in all of this, don't you?"

She didn't respond. Her mind wandered. She had a hundred other things to worry about, without trying to discover where Lillian or Beth Masters had ended up.

Von Kleise sensed, as he usually did, that he should not press Victoria. She was focused on revenge; on making her former friends from New York pay dearly for throwing her to the dogs.

"Can you please take care of this, Victoria? But they should not be harmed. We have enough death and misery on our hands already. Perhaps they could help the guards downstairs with their chores, until everything is over? Thank you."

She stood up, came towards him, and kissed his cheek. He watched her leave, waiting for the door to close, then turned to Michelle Rochard. He knew she would have enjoyed witnessing Victoria's discomfort.

"Would you care for a glass of wine, Michelle?"

"That would be pleasant, Heinrich. It's been a very hectic day so far."

"And it isn't over."

Von Kleise walked to the bar at one side of the office, removed two long-stemmed goblets from a small wooden holder, and selected a bottle of Agile; a tart white from the east end of Lac Leman. Opening it with some care, he poured two glasses, and handed one glass to Michelle while he continued to stand, his eyes focused on the mountains outside that were just fading in the late afternoon light.

"To your health," she said, raising her glass to touch Von Kleise's.

Von Kleise moved back onto business. "Do you think that Avramowitz will be successful?"

"The probabilities are against his success," she said dryly.

"What do your models suggest? What impact will these disturbances have on the global system?"

Michelle reached for her portfolio on the couch next to her. Removing several sheets of paper she studied each in turn, then looked up.

"Even if Avramowitz is successful, and there is a peaceful change of government on the 25th, which from a moral perspective is our preference, then there will still be a substantial increase in volatility. Any change of government, especially in a country with a track record for instability, adds risks for investors worldwide. If it turns into a civil war, with the army disintegrating, then from a financial perspective, we hit the jackpot, as market volatility and price instability will explode."

Michelle had explained years before how her political-economic models worked. The mathematics was beyond Heinrich's grasp, but he recognized that psychology played as large a role in determining market prices as supply and demand.

Pyotr had been critical of the plan, having organized the massive sale of Russian gold, on a private basis, to Von Kleise, which was now stored in vaults at Oberschloss. Now, with so much global economic and political uncertainty, the price of the metal was starting to appreciate and would soon move towards its old high, and no doubt, well beyond once events unfolded as expected.

Still, Von Kleise worried about his old friend's safety. Of all the conspirators, he was risking his life, not just his fortune. Pyotr's goal had been to rebuild Russia into a free and open society; a democratic country with a capitalist economy. It was a task that had proved to be well beyond even a man with his talents. Avramowitz, however, would not listen to Von Kleise's advice to get out before the collapse of the government. Von Kleise was at least grateful that Natalya had managed to get out.

They'd spent nearly fifty million to bribe Japanese legislators to pass a bill authorizing the free import of foreign rice, and the Bank of Japan was due to raise interest rates. The combination of these events would lead to a drop in Japanese property prices, and again, both were timed for the end of October.

"And finally, there's Mr. Latimer. When will the papers on the Masters' properties will be filed?"

"We can get our best impact by staging this in just over a week's time. The first default on the notes will occur when the balloon payments are due on Thursday, or four days before the markets open on Monday, the 31st. Declining property values will force investors using real estate for collateral to try raise cash, by selling stocks which will further add to the selling pressure."

The elaboration of the elements in the plan continued, all neatly mapped out in a timeline. The Holtzs' debt-rescheduling ultimatum would be the final straw. It had taken little to get the Holtzs to think in bigger terms, and the timing was to coincide with a string of orchestrated financial panics near the end of October.

"Montoya reports that there is some waffling among the Latinos," Von Kleise said, looking at Michelle.

"Our sources suggest that this is a smoke screen."

"It will add to the disturbance. The Federal Reserve will worry about overextending itself, and creating too much liquidity. The new Vice Chair, Fred Schurz, was hand-picked by Richard Kahn to be dogmatic and overly conservative and with the vacancy at the top due to the untimely death of the last Chairman and with no time to appoint a replacement; Schurz was the top man there. He was very much like the German and Dutch Central Bankers. He'll caution against flooding the market with money to stop the slide." It had cost less than $10 million to select new heads of the Central Banks in the US, China and Japan: all of them conservative graduates of the University of Chicago; and all more worried about managing potential inflation related risks at the expense of all else.

"Michael Ross then is the wildcard."

"You have too much faith in Ross's creativity. We've created the greatest challenge to open markets ever faced. Even Ross could not find a way to limit the damage, and certainly not in the limited time he will have, or with Congress out of session until well after the election," Michelle assured him.

"He could convince the President that he has nothing to lose and everything to gain by selling the gold, and using the proceeds to buy into the markets openly, and placing the shares in trust for the American people. I've heard him suggest this before. That might break the speculation in gold, stabilize the markets, but it will add instability to the dollar, as the financial press questions the backing of the American currency."

"Ross could still be a problem for us then," said Heinrich. "If he was out of the way, they'd be unlikely to act in any way that's insightful or forceful."

"He will be in Europe for the G8 coordinating meeting in Paris. If you invited him as your special guest to the Phoenixjahr ceremony, in Kandersteg, he could be detained here until all the damage was done."

As Michelle continued to explain the timeline, Von Kleise thought back on how he had found her. Like Victoria, she had fallen as far and as fast as any intelligent human being could fall. She had been a child prodigy: graduating from the finest preparatory school in France at thirteen; enrolled in the Sorbonne at fourteen, where she matriculated with high honors at seventeen; and attained her Ph.D. in political economics and mathematics at twenty-one. Forced to be grown-up too young, she had rebelled against the rigors of schooling in little ways. Her appetite for sex, drugs, and gambling was huge. Eventually, she had to sell both drugs and sex to feed her habits. By twenty-five, she was burned out. She lost her university posting, and was convicted and sentenced to six months in prison for dealing drugs to fellow faculty members. On her release, her family disowned her.

Von Kleise sent his agents to Paris with orders to retrieve her. He placed her in an exclusive rehabilitation center near Zurich. After nearly a year, she'd regained her health and also her courage to face the world. Von Kleise had removed her, like Victoria, to the privacy of the retreat he'd built at the top of the Bluemlisalpenhorn. At the Oberschloss she had learned obedience, and in return, had found love for the first time. Although Victoria was the genius behind the market manipulations, it was Michelle's genius to develop mathematical models for predicting the amplitudes of the resulting disturbances that would ensure the success of the automatic trading programs.

He came over to where she sat, laid his hand on her head and stroked her silken, dark brown hair. He was old, to be sure, thought Michelle, but far from infirm. No other lover had ever satisfied her like this man did, because he understood her needs better than any other man or woman she had previously known.

Later that evening, Von Kleise watched as Ola entered his bedchamber. She walked forward nervously, a tall awkward girl, her face framed by perfectly straight, long blond hair. Attractive, but not beautiful, the Swedish programmer was interesting in her own way. She was like a child: too naïve to survive in the world outside. When he made love to her, it was tenderly, barely touching, rarely entering her, but rather comforting and reassuring her until she fell asleep. There was no comparison to the sensual eroticism of Michelle, or the striking Roman features of Victoria.

"Are you facing a problem that cannot be solved? Tell me the truth!" he demanded.

"I am having difficulties," she admitted.

"Is there anything that we can do to help you?"

"I'm not certain," she stammered.

"There are programmers at the Foundation in Kandersteg that could be possibly be used."

"Our security would be breached. No, Herr Von Kleise," Ola said. She rarely called him Heinrich. "I can solve these problems."

"I will not have this fail because of you, Ola!" he said sternly.

She felt the cold in his voice. Ola began to shake. Then, with a gentleness that surprised her, he took her in his arms and held her. She pressed herself against his chest. He could smell the handcrafted perfume, blended perfectly for her body scent, and sighed.

"Come," he said, taking her hand lightly, "I am certain you will be successful."

"I will not fail you, Herr Von Kleise," Ola said, suddenly seeing the solution to the problem that had vexed her for hours earlier.

"I know, Ola, I know." He stroked her hair, his hand spotted by age, through the clean, smooth skin of her young back. He covered her with kisses, marveling at the fact that he was still, even at age, virile and excited by a woman.

27. QUEEN OF NEW YORK

Lilly Masters had been gone for four hours. Ben paced the garden, his fear and anger growing as each minute passed. He was worried about Lilly, and he feared the worst. His state of mind was worsened by the stories coming out of the US papers, talking about the inevitable collapse of the Masters' real-estate empire.

He was still pacing the garden when Kim came out. At first, he didn't recognize her in her business suit, with her hair tied in a neat French braid. Kim had returned to DC after getting them settled in the clinic, but had now returned at Turner's suggestion, to make sure things were okay.

"Boy, have you changed." He opened his arms to give her a hug.

"Where's your wife?" Kim asked, brushing off Ben's offered embrace.

"I don't know. She went into Geneva hours ago, to meet with a private detective and do some shopping. She never made it to their meeting." He slammed his fist on the table upsetting the phone.

Kim watched as Ben stormed around the room.

"Why?" he demanded, looking at Kim for an answer.

"That's a good question." She pointed for him to sit in a chair. "Sit down, take some deep breaths, and we'll try to figure it out. Start from the beginning, please."

"It's about time you woke up, Mother," Beth said, coming over to the bed where her mother had been sleeping, and gently stroked her hair.

Lilly's focus was blurred, but she recognized the familiar high-pitched, nasal voice. That voice, common among the rich, upper Eastside girls Beth had grown up with, had always grated on her. "How?" She looked at her daughter with some wonder. Where was she? She remembered the two men that had surrounded her; being pushed into the back seat of a car at Place de Molard; and then this. Her two shopping bags were sitting in the corner of the room.

"They brought you in about two hours ago, drugged, I think." Her own experience had been somewhat different. She had been bundled up by two armed men from Latimer's house in Zurich, and flown by helicopter. She had been blindfolded with plugs in her ears, tape over her mouth, and her hands tied tightly behind her back, like a criminal.

Lilly sat up in the bed. She looked around the room. There was a second bed next to the one she was sitting on. A small table with a lamp separated them. Aside from the beds, there was little else in the room. There was no window, and the room was silent except from the sound of moving air from the overhead venting.

"Don't start lecturing me, Lillian," Beth said, "I'm beyond that."

"You're a damn bitch. To think we gave you everything," she shouted, remembering the last time they had met, and what the girl had done to her.

"You're one to talk," Beth answered, remaining calm. The fight had gone out of her. They were both victims. What was past was now firmly in the past.

"Is there a bathroom?" Lilly asked.

"Over there." She said pointing to a basic shower and toilet.

Lilly stood up but almost collapsed. Beth watched her mother struggle, and reluctantly, helped her across the room.

She washed her face, brushed her teeth and combed her hair. Beth sat up on her bed reading a French fashion magazine.

"This is cozy at least." Lilly said, looking around the bare room.

Beth didn't answer. She looked up, and then returned to studying the latest in Paris fashion, in the French edition of Vogue.

"Can we have a truce?" Lilly asked finally.

"Okay," her daughter answered, curious as to how her mother had gotten away from Sheng. "Tell me about your escape."

Lilly sat down opposite Beth and began the tale. She emphasized how heroic Ben had been.

"Is it true that he isn't really my father?" The girl asked at last, seeing the opportunity for the two of them to finally tell the truth to each other.

"That's a lie," Lilly answered, smoothing out the wrinkle on her skirt nervously, "a fiction that people made up to be mean. I met your father at Smith. We married after I graduated. By then he was working for his old man, renting apartments in the South Bronx. The family was well-off, but not rich. Ben, your father, had ideas, good ones. He saw the potential of all those properties just across the Harlem River from Manhattan in the South Bronx, if the neighborhood could be made safe. He bought up empty lots, tore down the unrented buildings they owned, and made a safe, gated, middle-class community of town homes and apartments, with its own security and buses running into and out of the village, to the nearest subway stations. When you were first born, Beth, we were living in a small house in Islip, and," she added wistfully under her breath, "we were happy."

"The little house," Beth said with some nostalgia. "I remember it. Didn't it have a picket fence? And there was another little girl next door?"

"Yes, Mary Ann Reilly." Lilly was surprised that she could recall that name.

"She had golden hair, didn't she?"

"I think so," said Lilly. Trying to picture her daughter with her dark hair and olive-colored skin, playing with the little pale-faced Irish girl.

"Your father had plans for how to take the unused, nearly useless, empty, warehouses and long-shuttered old factories that his family owned in Brooklyn, close to the waterfront, and turn it into rental property for the young professionals working in Manhattan. Those nice, affordable condos and apartments filled quickly. He lured people back to Brooklyn from Jersey and Long Island. And so, we moved up in the world. Then something terrible happened." Lilly struggled to explain.

"What?"

"We became not just rich, but super-rich. It was a very long way from the hard scrabble town in the mountains of West Virginia, where I grew up." She saw the shock on her daughter's face. It was secret that she had never revealed to anyone but Ben.

An image of rolling green mountains, weathered wooden shacks with twisted stovepipes, and barefoot children, still wearing homespun or inexpensive hand-me-downs given out by wealthier church groups, crossed Lilly's mind, as she thought of where she had come from. "Often as not, we ate beans for dinner four nights a week, and oatmeal and grits for breakfast and lunch. There was an old outhouse in the back with spiders that often bit, and we had lice, Beth; awful creatures. At ten, I was working, doing odd jobs for people to pay for food for the family. My Ma, a bitter woman, worked at the coal company cleaning offices. My Dad died when I was five, of overwork, black lung, tobacco, and whiskey. All of my sisters died young, or had too many kids to feed. One of my brothers is still in prison; the other died in an accident deep underground. I was the last Lynch in a town that had been founded by Lynchs. All I wanted was to get the hell out of there. I wanted to be someone. I went to Smith on a full scholarship, and spent hours working to rid myself of my twang. And so, when they called me Princess, then *Queen* of New York, I worried about what they would think if they knew the truth about me. So, your father and I spent a fortune expunging every last trace of Lillian Lynch, of Lynch, West Virginia, from the public record."

Beth stared at her mother. "I never knew." She felt terrible. She had been awful to Lilly as a teenager. She had resented her mother's friends, lovers; the way she handled herself in public; everything about her. She had never imagined that Lilly Masters was really Lilly Lynch from a small town in West Virginia.

"I've never faced my past, Beth, but being ripped away from one life and transported into another world has made me realize what's important." Lilly reached out her hand to her daughter. "Can we be friends?"

"Friends!" Beth extended her hand, but then feeling overcome with her own guilt, she reached for her mother and hugged her. Between sobs, she tried to explain her own anger.

Frau Bundt observed this mother-daughter reunion silently. She had entered the room just as they were about reconciled. She looked at her watch. It was close to ten and Von Kleise's orders had been to bring the older woman to his study. She was also to provide clean clothes and insist that she bath or shower.

"You're wanted," said Frau Bundt with a heavy accent, interrupting the reunion.

Lilly broke away and looked up. The woman's face was stern, and there was a harsh edge that suggested she would use force if needed. She had had her taste of freedom, and now she was back in purgatory. Feeling as if she was back in Sheng's brothel, she felt obliged to try to please, in order to survive.

Standing up, she looked down towards the floor. Beth stared openly and defiantly at the heavyset Swiss woman. Bundt could sense the younger woman's anger. She took three quick strides and, with a strong, firm hand, pulled Beth away from her mother.

"You will shower and change now! Clothes in the closet on the left are for you; the ones on the right are for your daughter. I will return in half an hour." She released Beth, and then left the room.

Frau Bundt opened the door to the study and ushered in Lilly Masters. The faint ring of far-off peaks could be seen from the window, illuminated by the nearly full moon. Lilly stood quietly as the old woman withdrew.

Without realizing it, she bowed her head and held her hands in front of her dress.

"Come closer so that I can see you," Von Kleise ordered.

She walked closer. He was older—possibly seventy or more by the liver spots—and she could see a shock of white hair. However, it was the intensity of his eyes that held her frozen in one place.

"There are two glasses on the bar over in the corner. Pour yourself a cognac, and one for me. At my age, it's good for the heart; at yours, it will lighten the spirit." He continued to study her movement thoughtfully, as she went to the bar.

She returned and handed him the glass. He continued to stand, staring at her, then he reached out, and touching her cheek tenderly, pushed back a strand of stray hair. It was like fine-spun gold.

"Did you find the clothes I have chosen for you satisfactory, Lilly?"

"Yes," she said softly.

Taking her hand lightly, he led her to the couch. She sat down, turning to face him.

"I am certain that you would like to know why this has happened. Why your little world was torn apart so completely."

Hours later, she returned to the room. Beth was fast asleep, but sleep was the farthest thing from her mind. She lay in bed thinking about what the old man had told her. He had explained far more to her than she had understood. She did recall his touch. He had kissed her lightly on her cheek, and had held her tightly in his arms when she started to cry uncontrollably. He had said good-bye after calling for Frau Bundt to return her to the room. Lilly liked how she had felt when she was in his arms, happy to be so protected, away from all the chaos that was Ben, her old life, and the uncertainty that the next days or months might bring. But now, hours later, she knew the truth; she would never get out of this place alive because now, she knew too much.

28. On the Shores of the Potomac

Natalya had arrived a week earlier, a bundle of nerves and half-starved. Michael had met her at the airport. In Switzerland, she had been firmly in charge, but here, she was a mere shell, unable to decide even the simplest things for herself. Of what had happened, she had volunteered little: all her images of the time at Lenin Street and in the camp were superimposed one upon another, until they formed a single, indescribable nightmare.

Natalya should have found the small house in green, sunny Glen Echo just outside of Washington, like a dream, but she was confused. She hardly knew Michael, and was now dependent upon him. Their time together in Switzerland had been so brief, and the pain of the intervening three months so great, that she no longer knew how she really felt about him.

Michael was struggling with his own problems, mired in the world and the American economy, but his time was short. There would a new occupant of the White House in a few months; it would be their problem, not his. The signs of some kind of global economic tsunami breaking within the next few weeks were everywhere, and there was little that anyone could do to stop it. He knew Natalya needed help, but he was too busy with work to take her to a doctor, or to even convince her that she should go. He had put the country's wellbeing ahead of hers, leaving her alone to sort out the many issues that confronted her.

Natalya took Michael's lack of time for her as indifference. She felt like a burden to him, and couldn't see the obvious signs of his affection: the fresh flowers; the trips to the store to buy clothes; the small talk he tried to make to help her through the nights. The prison and the camp had destroyed the very essence of her being that made her special. Every little bit of her courage and independence had been systematically reduced, and then eliminated: firstly, by the cold steel of the prison cell with its terror and its smells—human feces, urine and fear; and finally, by the discipline and humiliation of the labor camp. At thirty-three, she was alone, an orphan, without a real country or purpose in life. Her father had made it clear to her on the drive to St Petersburg that Russia was no longer her country.

For most of the day, she wandered around in his pajamas, watching endless reruns of *Friends* and *Seinfeld,* hungry for distraction. Gradually, she began to sink into the narcotic embrace of television. The TV or radio had to be switched on all day to block out the memory of the Lenin Street prison and the forest camp. Most nights, Michael came home late, so they ordered pizza, Chinese, or Thai. Michael knew so little about Natalya that he wondered if she even knew how to cook. Eating in silence, punctuated only by perfunctory talk about the weather, they were each mired in a personal hell. For Natalya, the poorly prepared "fast food," combined with daytime meals of soda, and chips, further depleted her already overtaxed reserves of energy. She was always tired. Her beauty was slipping away. Sleep came only with a Valium, combined with a shot of cognac, which she took after Michael was asleep. She found the nights most terrifying because all the harrowing details of the last months would return to her in a series of nightmares.

As the days passed, what little she had said to him earlier in the week, became even less. She listened, but rarely spoke. She knew he was becoming frustrated, even angry, but nothing could shake her melancholy. Natalya's depression was mirrored by Michael's own depression. The future for both of them looked dismal.

It was Wednesday, a week after she had arrived, when the rains cleared and the sun came out, both literally and metaphorically. It was eleven o'clock, with most of the day remaining, and Natalya, having exhausted all other avenues of diversion, decided to take a walk. She hoped that a walk might dispel the gloom that hung over her. She dressed in her one pair of blue jeans, and strolled down the path towards the C&O Canal, that ran along the river from Washington, to Cumberland in Maryland.

Perhaps it was the bright autumn sun that brought her strength, or simply the time that had passed, but she felt stronger as she walked in the brisk air. She could forget the past for minutes at a time. When she did, Natalya noticed the brilliant colors of the trees, turning from green to autumnal reds and oranges. And as she continued to walk, the realization that she was finally free and no longer had to live in fear, increasingly dawned upon her. On one side of the path was the river, still raging from the heavy rains of the week before; on the other, the near-stagnant waters of the old canal, whose waters rippled only from an occasional turtle sunning on the rocks in the middle of the water.

Ahead of her, there was a group of school children. She listened to the children's laughter and petty bickering. It was so unlike her childhood, with its careful regiment of work and study. Her upbringing had been scientific, and her childhood had been a solitary and lonely existence, best forgotten.

Natalya followed the children, though she wasn't sure why. They led her back, away from the canal, and up a long hill, along a path that passed through a neighborhood hidden by tall trees, before finally reaching a school. The name was familiar, but she was unsure where she had heard it before. Otherwise, it was an ordinary old red-brick building from the 1950s. Still, the landscaping suggested that building housed something far more lovingly cared for than institutional.

"Can I help you?" an elderly woman asked, coming out from the building when she saw Natalya staring at the entrance. She had watched Natalya for more than five minutes from inside, and determined that the young woman didn't look like a troublemaker, but only a lost soul, decided to approach her.

"The name is familiar," Natalya stammered.

"Have you visited other schools like this one?" asked the woman, speaking slowly, each syllable distinctly accented, giving the speech a kind of sing-song cadence. "In America, they are mainly called Waldorf schools, but in many parts of the world they are called Steiner schools."

"I visited a Steiner school several months ago, in Switzerland, called Enigen, near Kandersteg."

"I don't know Enigen, but there are more than 1,000 schools worldwide today." She led Natalya into the old school building. While it was ordinary from the outside, the inside shimmered with radiance and color. The walls were almost luminescent, a product of layering veils of color on white walls. The colorful pictures also reminded her of the pictures and bulletin boards on the walls of Enigen. As they walked through the corridors she could hear the sound of strings playing Mozart in one classroom, and in another, singing, accompanied by a wooden flute.

The woman, who was also a former teacher, explained that Steiner had created a curriculum to support a child's development. Each block of lessons was designed to speak to the emerging consciousness of the child, and to educate the emerging consciousness to self-awareness and freedom. The class teacher in a school started with a group of children in first grade, and ended with the group at the eighth grade. For the teacher the eight years was a learning experience as well. Steiner's educational methods were designed to enable a child to think creatively and independently.

"If we are successful," the teacher said slowly, "then our students will go forth into the world and make it better, not worse."

The image of Enigen returned as she listened. How much, she wondered, of the old Enigen—the Enigen of Thomas Machte—had followed these principles? It, too, had started out as a Steiner school, but with a difference. What was that difference? Why had Machte rebelled against the ideas of Steiner? Like this school, the purpose of the old Enigen was to shape the child into seeing the world differently. And like this school's mission, Enigen's mission was to educate its students to make the world a better place. But there was a world of difference between the way each school taught its students to accomplish that task.

After spending over an hour with the older woman, Natalya walked out of the school. For whatever reason, the realization of her freedom as she walked along the canal path, the cheerfulness of the children, the colors in the school's hallway, or the reassuring and kind manner of the woman, Natalya felt better. The ordeals she had been through, as terrible as they were, were meant to teach her lessons. Although she knew that the nightmares would remain for some time, some of Natalya's inner strength had been restored. The rest of the healing would come in time.

It was now time for her to get on with her life.

It was close to three o'clock when she called Michael. He wasn't in, but was expected back soon. She caught the bus that stopped near the front of the school to the subway. From Bethesda it was a short ride on the Metro Red Line to Michael's office in the Old Executive office building next to the White House.

"I thought I would see how you are doing," she announced with far more cheerfulness than he had recently come to expect from her.

"Busy, hectic, the usual day." He laughed. He motioned her into the office and quickly closed the door. When it slammed shut he took her in his arms and hugged her, uncertain with what had changed.

"I'm getting better, Michael," Natalya said, pulling away with a laugh, before adding with a knowing smile. "So tonight, I'm going to show you a bit more of the old me, but here isn't the right place."

The phone rang. While Michael talked, she looked at his crowded desk, piled high with papers. She knew a crisis was coming soon; her father had hinted it would be the end of October.

After the call, Michael asked his assistant to hold further calls, and returned to where Natalya sat on the small couch.

"I'm sorry. That'll be the last of the calls for a while."

"I'm interrupting your day," she said, trying to remember why she had come so suddenly and without warning. "I was just feeling excited. I almost feel normal. I just wanted you to know." She stood up and looked towards the door.

"It is good that you're here. That was Turner on the phone, who has given you top-secret clearance to study our files on what we're up against."

The idea of enlisting Natalya's help had been Michael's. He had been heartbroken by the change in Natalya since he had last seen her in Switzerland, back in July. It had taken him all week to convince Turner and the FBI that she wasn't a security risk.

"I've been trying to get ready for next week's meetings in Basel and Paris. And tomorrow, there's a cabinet meeting on the Asian trade problem."

"The trip is next week?"

"It's just from Thursday through Tuesday, with Thursday and Friday at the Bank of International Settlements in Basel, and Monday and Tuesday in Paris, at the OECD. Heinrich has invited me to spend the weekend, and to be his guest at the Phoenixjahr ceremony at Enigen. So I won't be bored, but I'm worried about you. Why don't you come with me?"

Natalya smiled. She took Michael's hand warmly and squeezed it. "Don't worry about me; I'll be busy at work deciphering Turner's files. You have work to do, and when you come home again, we can talk. I need to tell you what happened in Russia."

"You don't have to explain. I know whatever happened was bad, and talking about it will only make it real again."

"No," she said firmly, "before we can move on, I have to explain everything, even the things I'm ashamed of. It is the only way that we can make our relationship work." Natalya stopped and looked earnestly at Michael. She hardly knew him and yet she felt safe with him. He had taken her in when all seemed lost, had saved her, and she had to find a way to repay him.

"Michael, we met in a hurry, we barely knew each other, but there was something there, I was sure of it in Switzerland. But I think, like you darling, I couldn't put what I felt into words, because I'd never felt that way before. And then I disappeared for three months before suddenly being dropped back into your life … for better or worse. So we need time to talk, to ensure that what we think and feel for each other is real. I don't want you to love me because you feel obliged to look after me."

Michael held her tight, more certain of this being right than at any time in the past months since they'd met.

"You have nothing to fear on my part. You came back to me and that's all that matters," he said, stroking her hair. "But I'm pleased you are up to working for a living again" he said as he let go. "I have a file that Katherine Grant on my staff put together. You might start to look over it and see if you can come up with anything from the seemingly random numbers."

She nodded.

Ross went to the door, opened it and called to his administrative assistant. A few minutes later, she came into the room with a file and handed it to Michael, which he in turn gave to Natalya.

"There's a spare office across the hall. It's quieter there."

As she read through the thick file, filled with notes and computer printouts, she began to grow tired. There was little of interest in these statistical correlations. However, there was one anomaly that she thought could be important. In recent months, there had been a significant increase in the number and size of stock tender offers by various private companies and individuals. All were offered at prices well below current market valuations of these companies. All had been rejected overwhelmingly by the companies' Boards of Directors, but they remained open. There was no unusual activity in these stocks, nor so many outstanding "shorts," by speculators expecting the price of the stock to decrease. Instead, there were just these stock tenders that had been ignored, laughed at, given they were valued at; sometimes as low as 10 to 15 per cent of the current stock price. Michael's researcher had suggested this was simply an indicator of the expected underlying weakness in the future market.

Natalya's mind, however, began to move towards a far different conclusion. She wanted to find out more details, but it would have to probably wait until Michael had left for Europe.

"Ready to go?" Michael asked a few hours later.

"Just a second," Natalya said studying one final printout in the pile. She closed the file and handed it back to Michael.

"Did you find anything interesting?" Michael asked, noting Natalya's concentration on one paper before she returned the file.

"Some things are of interest," she answered, without offering further explanation.

"Cathy worked for about a month on that, but she didn't find out anything except that Wall Street is a crap shoot, and not for the faint-hearted."

"Don't tell that to the pensioner depending upon the market to fund a comfy retirement. If the stock market collapses, then wealth disappears, and everyone's poorer: people and nations alike."

"Spoken like a true member of the establishment."

"Or a Harvard MBA! But you know it's true." She smiled brightly. "Now, come and buy this girl a real dinner. I'm done with junk food and take-out." Natalya took his hand, "I'm in the mood for the Old Ebbit Grill. It will cost you, but I promise to make it well worth the price when we get home afterwards."

On Saturday, both Michael and Natalya went to the office. The Congressional Budget Office had come up with lower estimated tax receipts for next year, which put into doubt the viability of the President's planned budget. Things were changing so fast that the new President, whoever it would be, would have to submit another budget soon after their inauguration. Given that advising the President was part of his job, Michael spent the morning going over the figures.

Natalya worked through the pile of CIA papers that, like most intelligence reports, failed to prove or disprove any theory. The data, most of it gathered from public sources, she had seen or heard about before.

"Did you get anything accomplished?" Natalya asked, as they walked downstairs to the underground garage.

"I'm not certain I ever do. What about you?"

"There's, I'm afraid, very little here that's of any use." She looked down at the pile of papers that Turner had sent over "Their agenda, whoever they are, is like a mirage: you think you see it, but then when you get close, it disappears entirely. The confluence of events could lead to a financial Armageddon, a tsunami of staggering proportions, but who wins from that? There doesn't even appear to be any indication that short sales are ticking up. It just doesn't make sense," she added with a sigh.

The litany of problems facing the world, even if he would not have to deal with them once a new President had been elected, turned Michael's stomach. He was as powerless to stop the trains heading towards a collision as anyone else in Government. The wreckage from these events would be far greater than any the world had ever known; even the Great Depression might be considered to be a blip compared to what would happen if almost all forms of wealth suddenly lost value on the same day.

"If I had to guess," Natalya said, thinking aloud, "I would say someone wants to destabilize the financial markets. The question is how do you gain from that instability? Of course, you might make some money by buying puts at some price below the current price, but the options markets are simply not that large."

Michael had no answer to her question, but Natalya was on a roll. She continued along this line of reasoning.

"What if the purpose of all this is to simply sensitize markets to the slightest negative news?"

"Why?"

"Traders are herd animals; they'll follow each other off a cliff. And then there's the private clubs or funds that have proliferated of late. One word to these hair-trigger traders to sell and they'll unload trillions of dollars of assets onto the markets instantaneously by computer program. Since 2008 there's been a proliferation of risk management programs, like METIS out in New Mexico, that are supposed to guard against making mistakes, but would be sensitive to so many negative data points coming in simultaneously. With no bottom, the market will crash through past bottoms. Automated trading systems have made this disaster possible. It will only take a spark to set off the inferno. Too dramatic, darling?" she asked.

"No," he agreed, smiling, "not really."

Carlos had left Jenny standing in the visitors lounge at Cointrin, in Geneva. She had not pried, but rather had simply waved good-bye. He had flown BA to Washington through Heathrow, arriving late Friday evening. Walter's instructions were to find Natalya, and when the opportunity presented itself, do what needed to be done. Carlos had not liked the Russian woman when they had met briefly months before. There was something dangerous about her.

He was now feeling bored. He had been watching the house in Glen Echo from his car for hours. Finally, a car pulled up and he saw the couple get out and go into the house. Half an hour later, they emerged in sports clothes, with Ross holding a camera.

"What about the Great Falls of the Potomac?" Michael suggested, thinking that the exercise would be nice on this crisp sunny fall day.

At the Great Falls of the Potomac, the river descended through Mather's Gorge, dropping a hundred feet in just a few miles. Over time, the waters had cut a deep gash through the Appalachian green stone, leaving a rocky stretch of palisades, punctuated by a few sandy beaches, which were used by kayakers to put their boats in the water to challenge the falls. The Billy Goat Trail ran along this rocky palisade, but was dangerous. Most weekends in summer saw at least one death caused by falling or drowning.

"You haven't been here before?" Michael asked Natalya, as they stood looking out across the river towards the Virginia shoreline, from the overlook at the end of a long series of bridges over cascading smaller water falls. As this point, the river was its widest, with the Virginia shore more than 300 feet or more in the distance. The roar could be heard from nearly a mile away.

"No, we only lived here for about a year, when I was fifteen or sixteen." They had moved to Miami when her uncle's teaching position was terminated at American University. He had never been able to make the transition from the Russian method of teaching science and engineering, to that which was required for teaching American students, who had been taught less mathematics in school. She had lived in Miami for only one year before graduating high school and entering Harvard. Her uncle's second career, as a hotel manager, had been more successful. Thinking about her uncle, aunt and cousins for the first time since returning to the States, she supposed that by now there was a large, extended Avramowitz family here.

Michael found it hard to keep up with Natalya in the dimming light on the trail. It was almost six, and was starting to get dark. Natalya, exhilarated by the freedom of her surroundings, was oblivious to the dangers, and Michael fell farther behind her. Concentrating on his footing, he didn't hear the footsteps behind him until he felt the hands at his back. With a shove, he dropped feet first, down a steep incline.

Everything seemed to be in slow motion until his foot touched the outcropping that defined a narrow ledge. Michael twisted around and grabbed the outcropping of rock as he landed. The ledge was barely ten feet above the river and he could feel the cold spray on his back. Looking up towards the darkening sky, there was no easy or even safe way to climb out without help. He called out for Natalya, but she was too far away to hear him above the din of the icy Potomac. All he could do was cling to this place and hope that she soon would find him.

Carlos had sensed the opportunity when he had seen Ross and the Russian woman enter the trail. He was familiar enough with the perils of the Great Falls. As a student he'd attended Georgetown's School of Foreign Policy, and had hiked there often.

Natalya had not slowed since starting along the trail. Rock-climbing was a passion, for she had climbed on weekends while at Harvard. Heights didn't bother her, and she was technically proficient, having climbed a few peaks in the Alps and North America. She'd even once climbed Half Dome in Yosemite. Distracted by focusing on following the twisting route safely along the ridge, she didn't see Carlos. He hammered his shoulder into her side, slamming her against the rock wall, tearing her lightweight pullover against the sharp rocks. Momentarily stunned, Natalya turned to face her assailant. Her first thought was that it was an accident, but that view changed when Carlos lunged at her again, trying to throw her over the edge of the trail, on to the rocks below. She twisted away and then kicked him hard with her foot near his groin. He doubled over in pain as she slid sideways along the ledge, her back pressed against the rock wall, her feet searching for footing on the narrowing rock ledge.

"Who are you?" Natalya shouted as she clambered up to a higher ledge. "What do you want?" A stupid question, she thought. He wants me dead. There was also something familiar about him. She had seen him before.

"Natalya," he shouted, as he climbed to the higher ledge, following her up.

"Who are you?" she demanded again.

Carlos didn't answer, but used the distraction, to lunge for her again. She moved further back, warily, until she couldn't go any further as the trail was too narrow. Her teachers at Koslov had hammered home that in a fight to the death, the one with the greater will to survive, will win. And she had everything to live for: her new life in Washington and Michael. Carlos reached for her again, this time catching hold of her wrist, and pushed her towards the edge. Natalya could feel the cold wind coming straight up the cliff face from the roaring river below.

Carlos was exhausted. It had been years since he had exercised seriously, and his grip was weak, his hands sweaty. Natalya quickly twisted her wrist free and slid behind him, her back against the rock wall. She didn't wait for him to react to this change in position, but rather kicked out with both legs, striking him in the groin and sending him flying on to the rocks and river below. Natalya slid down along the rock wall until she was on the ground, her legs hanging over the edge, trying hard to slow her rapid breathing, and catch her breath. She had watched him fall, almost in slow motion, her heart pounding as she gasped for air. She stared down at the lifeless body being rolled around the rocks by the relentless, pounding the river.

'Where was Michael?' She had not thought of him in her panic to stay alive, but now she retraced her steps calling to him as she went. There was a faint call, from somewhere ahead and below, growing louder as she approached. Looking over the edge she could just make a man's shape hidden in the shadows. It was now dark and cold.

"I'm going for help," she yelled, waving. Relieved, Michael waved back. Then, standing up, she raced the remaining distance down the trail, to the Park Ranger station.

Francis Turner came to debrief Michael and Natalya. So far the police hadn't found the body, but they would continue to look in the morning. Because of Michael's position in the Government, the official report just mentioned that a hiker had slipped and the body was still missing.

"I'd have to guess that Natalya was the real target, and that Michael was simply incidental damage. You're certain it was Montoya, Natalya?"

"No, not really. He only looked like the man we met in Kandersteg. He called me by name too. But his accent was definitely Spanish."

"Carlos Montoya's father is one of the richest men in Latin America. He's a respected industrialist, mine owner, and humanist."

"Carlos works for IFF," Michael pointed out.

"The Holtzs are committed to helping the world," Turner reminded Michael. "Why would Montoya Junior try to attack you and Natalya?"

Turner reached for his pipe. He didn't light it, but rather fondled its smooth leather surface. If it was Carlos, and he suspected it was, then there was an obvious reason why he had been sent to Washington. "Did your father tell you anything about your mother, Natalya?"

"She was an American; that he met her in New York; that she had abandoned me at birth."

"Did he tell you her name?"

She tried to recall the name her father had told her. "Martin I think. Yes, Katherine Martin."

Turner knew the truth for he had been there when Katherine Von Kleise Martin had given birth to the girl who now stood before him. He had been a young intelligence officer, assigned to the US Mission, to the UN in New York, at the time. He had been vying for Katherine's attention, but Pyotr had won that battle. The Russian had been two years older and far more of a lady's man. It was easy to see how she had fallen in love with him, despite his reputation in the UN. Francis Turner had been relegated to the unenviable position of just being her friend. Like the Russian, Turner had attended Enigen when his father, a diplomat, had been stationed in Switzerland. They had not been classmates, Turner was younger, but they knew each other.

"Why would Carlos have done it, Francis?"

"How do I know? Perhaps it wasn't Carlos. People die there all the time. There are crazies everywhere."

"You're supposed to know these things. Isn't that your job? *Intelligence?*"

"I don't know everything," Turner added, wondering if Katherine was really so heartless as to order her own daughter's death, to protect her inheritance. It bothered him. It ruined the memories of that springtime so long ago, when he'd been younger, and she'd been the object of his affections.

"Is Natalya in danger? Am I in danger?" Michael asked, worried and perplexed. Within the past four months, he had now been attacked twice.

Natalya clasped Michael's hand tightly, trying desperately to calm him. The ordeal had shaken him more than the attack in France. "Let's wait until they find the body. Isn't that the right thing to do, Francis?"

"You're a sensible woman, Natalya," Turner responded, "and personally, I don't think either of you are in any immediate danger."

Michael left on Wednesday evening from Dulles. Natalya drove him to the airport, and then returned to the house in Glen Echo. She wandered around the empty house, trying to sort out the past few days in her mind. Something in Turner's look and his questions about her mother bothered her. She would have to go to New York and find out why. On an impulse, she called her Harvard classmate, Marcia Simpson, in New York.

"When did you come back?" Marcia asked.

"Two weeks ago" she answered, relieved to be able to say it. She shivered remembering her last days in Russia.

"What happened?"

"It's a long story," she answered. "A very typically Russian story too, I'm afraid."

"Tell me about it. Please, Natalya?"

"Are you free for lunch tomorrow," Natalya asked.

"I'll make sure I'm free. Will you be staying over?"

"Not this time, I have a lot of work to do here."

Marcia Simpson noticed how much thinner Natalya was since they had last seen each other. She looked like she'd been wrung through a roller, physically and mentally.

"It's been too long," Marcia said, hugging her warmly.

"At least eight years, I think. The last time was just before I went to Russia with Goldman's."

"And now, are you back with Goldman's?"

"No, I'm doing a bit of consulting. And you, still with the firm?"

"Yes, but sometimes," Marcia said, thinking about the upcoming Masters' bankruptcy, "I wonder why I ever wanted to become a lawyer."

"Not going as well as you thought?"

"There are problems with some of the properties." That was a grand understatement. The Masters' fortune had been squandered in a series of bad deals and outright frauds. They'd filed preliminary motions for protection earlier in the week, and word had leaked out. The property market was collapsing as prices went into free fall upon the expectation that the huge Masters' portfolio of commercial real estate would be liquidated, at fire-sale prices.

It was almost two thirty when Natalya left Marcia Simpson. What she had learned was informative; it confirmed what she had suspected, that the bankruptcy was part of the broader scenario that was playing out. Legal papers would be filed formally on October 24th. There would be, as Marcia explained, consequences for the financial markets, as many New York investors were heavily invested into real estate, and leveraged beyond the current worth of many of the properties. When the banks called in the loans—as they would—this would force a number of these investors to sell stocks to raise cash, and to avoid default.

Marcia gave Natalya back the safety deposit box key that she had looked after since Natalya had left New York. She went straight to the bank, getting there just before closing time. Inside her box, she found $4,000 in travelers checks, her now expired driver's license, a copy of her naturalization papers, and what, if she believed her father, was a false Russian birth certificate. On leaving the bank, she hailed a cab and after more than an hour in traffic, made it to Brooklyn, to the New York City Vital Records Office, just before it also closed. It was late in the afternoon and there was no line.

She read the name on the certificate carefully. Under her mother's alias was listed "Katherine Von Kleise," not Katherine Martin. It wasn't until she was in the cab on the way back to Penn Station to catch the express to Washington that Natalya asked the other question. Would a mother try to kill her own daughter? She would, Natalya reasoned, if a great fortune were at stake.

"Natalya," Michael said with some relief later that evening. "I was worried. Where have you been? I've been calling for hours. You need to get a cell phone so we can stay in touch."

"I went to New York to see an old friend." She looked at her watch. It was seven-thirty in Washington, 1:30 a.m. in Switzerland.

"Why?"

"Loose ends, darling. Don't worry about me. I'm fine. I doubt if the viper of a mother I have will send another assassin."

"Your mother?" he asked confused by the outburst.

"Yes, Katherine Holtz is my mother, can you believe that? I'm sure it was Carlos who tried to kill us."

"Why?"

"Money! Once she realized that Von Kleise had met me, she also saw that the inheritance might not automatically flow in their direction while I was alive."

"Turner's been trying to find you. Give him a call, will you?"

"Turner?"

"They need you to identify the man who tried to kill you."

"I'll call him," she said distracted. "How are the meetings?"

"Extremely boring, given how little time I have left. I should have stayed home. I did see your old friend, the Italian, I forget his name, but he wanted to know what had happened to that beautiful Russian girl."

"Tell him she's okay, and now a 100% red-blooded American. I was born in New York, not Kiev." She looked at her watch, it was now nearly 2 a.m. in Switzerland. "You'd better get some sleep, love, or you'll fall apart tomorrow."

"I miss you," said Michael in a whisper.

"I miss you too," she whispered back. "Now, go to sleep. I'll talk to you tomorrow evening."

He was about to hang up, but then remembered why he had called. "I just wanted to remind you that Heinrich has invited me to Kandersteg for the Phoenixjahr ceremony on Saturday. I'll drive to Paris on Sunday the 25th. So you won't be able to get me at the hotel that's on the itinerary. Try the cell phone if you want me. I'll be the only outsider at the ceremony who didn't go to Enigen. It'll be fascinating. Some of the world's most powerful men will be in the same room."

"Give Heinrich my regards," she said, wondering exactly why her grandfather had never said anything during the three days they had been there. "Go to sleep," she commanded, before hanging up.

After putting the receiver down she stood by the phone thinking. She had not told Michael her fears about the significance of the 25th. The Phoenixjahr ceremony scheduled for that weekend now seemed to be more than a coincidence. Natalya had not told Michael her evolving theory that whoever was behind this was someone wealthy, and committed to changing the world in a significant way, a man perhaps like Von Kleise, who was meeting with his fellow Machte prodigies that weekend. A man whose vision of the evils of the world, and his will to change the world to make it better, was as strong, or stronger, than even the overly sanctimonious Holtzs. Michael's invitation to Kanderschloss did not surprise her. It was clear Von Kleise liked and respected him, but could there be another reason too? If Von Kleise was the puppet master behind all that was happening, then getting Michael out of the way at this juncture of potentially market-shaking events was critical for ensuring maximum market chaos.

Ross had already told her that the Secretary of the Treasury, the Chairman of the Council of Economic Advisors, and the Federal Reserve Board Chairman had all voiced their concerns at taking unconventional action in response to the potential financial and economic disaster, at meetings during the previous week.

Natalya went to where the mail lay. She picked up the bundle from the State Department. Opening it, she removed her new passport. She toyed with the idea of calling Michael back and demanding that they meet, not in Kandersteg, but in Paris. Then the phone rang again forcing her back into the real world.

"Avramowitz,"

"Natalya, did you talk to Michael?" Francis Turner asked her.

"I just hung up."

"Can you come and look at the body?"

"If you want me to, but I think it was Carlos Montoya."

"I can't break away just yet, but I'll give you the address. They're expecting you.

She recognized the man's face immediately. What had been not obvious during the fight was clear now. It was Carlos Montoya … and he worked for the Holtzs.

"I don't know him," she lied to the policeman at the morgue, looking at the body again, and then turning away.

"But wasn't he the one who attacked you?"

"Yes, but I don't know him."

She sipped the wine. Kicking off her shoes, she pulled her feet up underneath her and stared at Turner who had come over. She thought that he knew more than he let on.

"You knew the man?"

"It was Carlos Montoya. Michael and I met him at Kanderschloss. He works with the Holtzs." She said dryly, watching Turner carefully.

"Montoya," said Turner trying to seem surprised by the connection. At Enigen, he had also known Carlos's father who was a classmate of Von Kleise.

"Do you know him?"

"I know his father, or at least I knew him once."

She was surprised. This American intelligence official was well known to have circulated in rich company, but Montoya had a fortune in the billions, and businesses scattered throughout the length and breadth of South America.

"Do you have any idea why he might have attacked you and Michael?"

"You're the senior director at the CIA, you tell me."

"Don't give me that crap. There's a file this thick," he showed her a two-inch gap between his thumb and forefinger, "on your training. There are some who still think that you are working for Russia, for the FSB."

"I never worked for the FSB. Besides, I spent a week in a six by five steel cell at Lenin Street, and a month in a re-education camp, so cut the crap, Francis. I'm not FSB and never have been. Besides, I'm as American as you, or Michael." Turner didn't look surprised at all by the last comment.

"You were in New York today."

"Vital Records, City of New York," she said, looking at him. "I discovered something extremely interesting about myself."

"That you were born in New York City, not Kiev?" he said.

"Yes. You seem to know all about this, Mr. Turner. How is that? Is that in my file?"

"No," he sighed, thinking back to how Katherine Holtz had looked back then. "I knew your mother and your father a long time ago, in New York." He remembered Katherine as a young woman, pregnant and frightened too. "I was present at your birth."

"Is that another mystery for me to unravel?"

Turner sighed again. He was getting too old for this business. "Your father was two years ahead of me at Enigen, along with the elder Montoya. Your mother was the daughter of another upper classmate."

"Heinrich Von Kleise, yes," Natalya replied. "Katherine didn't want me so she left it to Pyotr to raise me in his own way, didn't she? Were you in love with her too, Francis?"

"Both your father and I were involved with Katherine, when she worked that year in New York."

"And now, thirty-three years after I was born, here we are, both of us adults, again discussing the various interests at play when I was born. Doesn't that make you wonder about Fate?"

She waited for him to answer, but he didn't. She was angry. He had known who she was and to whom she was related all this time, and had not told her. So she continued, if only to drive home the point to Turner that Katherine Von Kleise was not the paragon of virtue that she might have been, when he and her father had fought for her attention so long ago in New York.

"Let's lay the facts in order, Francis. First, there's Carlos, yes? Why would Carlos come here? Carlos is a creature of the Holtzs. Was it Walter's or was it my mother's orders that sent Carlos to kill me? It wasn't Michael who was the target, was it? And you knew that last week. You knew I was the one they wanted face down in the Potomac." She stood up and paced the room.

Again, he remained silent, watching her. She went on.

"Perhaps, Francis, it's all about money. There's a fortune at stake now that Von Kleise has met me. And with Michael as my lover, there's all the more reason to change the will."

"Isn't there enough money for both of you?"

"Not if you have to support the great causes of the world, as Walter and Katherine do. Without me in the picture, then the whole fortune will go to Katherine."

"I suppose that's reason enough for trying to kill you, but don't you think that Von Kleise would learn the truth?"

"Perhaps, perhaps not, especially if he was told it was an accident, a slip on the rocks, a terrible tragedy. I think it was a chance that they could afford to take, because they had no other options. I was an unpleasant memory that came suddenly back into her life at an inconvenient time. I risked all their plans, and given their zealous views, removing me, in their minds, assisted them in their cause of serving the greater good. Isn't that right?"

Natalya paused. She looked at Turner wondering with which group his loyalties lay: to Enigen or to America?

"But killing me, or even Michael, is a side show; something important for Walter and Katherine, but not the main event."

"What's the main event?"

"A collapse of the financial markets, timed precisely to occur simultaneously across all markets, one that will burn all investors, big and small."

It had not taken his analysts long to come to the same conclusion months before. Questions remained to be answered: who and why, but not how. Terrorists were the logical conclusion, yet even the most dedicated Al-Qaeda cells were hardly sophisticated, or well-connected enough to have conceived and executed half of what had occurred so far.

"That isn't anything new, Natalya."

"Of course, of course. We all believed in our hearts something like this could happen. But I know the date when it will all hit."

He looked up, surprised.

She pulled out the notepad and showed him the series of coincidences that would be laid one upon another, until they sent the waters crashing down around them all. It was barely sixty hours away.

"An interesting theory," he said, without committing to anything.

"I saw in your reports a reference to *Tycoon*. Perhaps you can explain that code name."

Turner remained silent.

"I know who Tycoon is Turner," Natalya continued, when she was not given an answer. "Marcia Simpson told me that she was handling Brett Latimer's legal work, and she referred to Ben Masters by the same name: Tycoon. It was the title of his bestselling book wasn't it?"

"Yes," Turner admitted.

"And Masters is free, isn't he?"

"He's in Switzerland with his wife."

"Another of your strategies, Francis, but it didn't work. You didn't reveal that Lilly was alive and well, did you? Why?" She paused, thinking about the benefits, as well as the costs of that strategy. When Turner didn't answer, she continued.

"Why not let Masters emerge now? If he surfaces, maybe he could possibly save his little empire from collapse, or at least throw a monkey wrench into the timing of the bankruptcy filing. And if it didn't collapse, as they expected it to, then at least one event could be avoided. What's holding you up? Embarrassment or is it something else?"

"Lilly and Beth have since disappeared, and it might not have stopped the inevitable, but simply turned it into a media circus that no one wanted to face, given we were the ones who busted him out of State prison. Without a live Lilly or Beth, we would spend the rest of our lives in court, or before some Congressional Committee." He felt very tired now. He wanted to get away from this difficult questioning. And he didn't owe Natalya any answers.

"It could help."

"Or it could hasten the collapse. Even Masters couldn't save his fortune now."

"Tell me about the Phoenixjahr," said Natalya, abruptly changing the subject. "Michael is going to Kanderschloss this weekend, to observe the ceremony."

"I don't know," Turner admitted. "Machte died the year that Von Kleise and your father graduated. A select few of their class were the last ones to be initiated into the Society. And after Machte died, the traditions changed, as did Enigen."

She didn't say anything more to Turner, but instead, finished the wine. She yawned audibly and Turner, taking the hint, stood up.

"Will you be okay?" he asked.

"I will be, so long as Carlos's name can be kept from the papers."

"Your identification wasn't positive."

"I told them it was the man who attacked me, that's all."

"Then, I think you'll be safe for a while."

"Someday, not now, I'll have to have a talk with Katherine."

"They may try again."

She stood up. "I'm not afraid."

"I didn't think you were."

"I can take care of myself."

Natalya walked him to the door. She watched as he got into his battered automobile. Despite the fact that he was two years younger than her father, he was not in as good a shape. Where Pyotr looked robust even when exhausted, Turner looked worn and tired.

It was three o'clock that morning when Natalya awoke with a start and sat up in bed sweating. It had been a dream, but as realistic and frightening as if she were awake. Climbing out of the warm bed, she went into the cold study of the house. She riffled through the printouts and then, turning on the computer, she connected into the White House's unclassified system, where Michael's staff had coded into the computer the financial data that she had asked for. It didn't take long, no more than an hour and a half, and she had the answers.

Natalya next placed a long distance call to Dr Grunlian at Enigen. He promised to call her back when he had the lists in hand. She waited a tense thirty-five minutes before the phone rang. Grunlian read her the list of classmates who would be celebrating their Phoenixjahr on Saturday.

She returned to the computer and searched the Internet for details on each of the names. While for most of the people the estimates were sketchy, she was astonished by the wealth that that group had amassed.

Of the twenty classmates inducted into the Phoenix Society that year, twelve were still alive today. Of those twelve, six could reasonably be considered billionaires. Some had managed to amass great fortunes outside of public scrutiny. There were a few who had remained in the academic and governmental ranks for their entire careers, but even they were considered to be independently wealthy, but not with fortunes as large as the others.

She now knew for certain that Kandersteg was the center of all that was happening, and she had to be there. She booked a seat on that evening's flight from Dulles to Switzerland via London, which was scheduled to get her to Geneva at around eleven on Saturday morning.

With a few hours to spare, Natalya decided to return to the Steiner school near her house. Grunlian had no idea what Machte might have told the students, but perhaps there might be clues in the historical records at the Washington school.

"You look better," the old teacher said to Natalya when she entered the school that morning. "You are ready to take on the world. I can see it in your eyes."

"Thank you for helping me."

"We didn't help. You did it all yourself."

"I have a question."

"Ask away," the woman said, with a wave and a smile.

"I told you that I visited a school in Switzerland that was like this," she said.

"Yes, I recall, but I forgot the name of the school you mentioned."

"It was Enigen." "Let me see." She went to a bookcase in the school office and pulled down a thin directory. She reached for her glasses that were hanging from a chain around her neck, and taking these up, she studied the listing. Then turning the page she read.

"It is now a Steiner school, but before it was not."

"The founder, Thomas Machte had some connection to Waldorf schools. That was what we were told in Switzerland."

"Perhaps we have a book that can help you," she said looking towards the door. "It's in the library, in German, of course, but I can translate it if you can't read that language."

Natalya followed her into the library, and waited while a thick book, obviously old, and quite dusty, was taken down from a high shelf.

"Followers of Steiner are into writing books. Perhaps your Machte is mentioned. Of course, it stops in 1933, when Hitler closed the German branch of the schools, and threw the teachers into labor camps. Hitler denounced Steiner and Anthroposophy as early as the mid-1920s. He, with Himmler, had delved into a far darker and dangerous version of the secret wisdom, or as Steiner called it 'Occult Science.' New members of the SS were inducted in secret rites at Wewelsberg Castle. You might say that Anthroposophy, with its emphasis on the conscious soul and the goodness of man, and Nazism, were mirror opposites. Closing the schools was one of the Nazi's first acts when they took power in 1933."

Natalya was surprised. "And after the war?"

"After the war, the schools in Germany were reopened by the Allies. And when Eastern Europe was finally free, the first schools that the new governments opened were Waldorf or Steiner schools. Steiner himself developed Waldorf educational methods in 1919, in an effort to rebuild the German soul and free it from nationalism. He believed you needed to re-educate the German *Volk*, or people, into a new language that was based on heart, not will alone."

Natalya wondered if it would ever be successful. She had read the report on Wilhelm Brantheim his New Deutschland Nationalist Party, and its message that promoted a radical form of German nationalism, with its growing influence in the various German states.

After ten minutes of reading, the old woman looked up. "Would you like to read this in German yourself?" she said, pointing to the passage in the book.

"I'm out of practice," Natalya admitted. She had learned it poorly in Russian schools, where their concentration was on teaching English. At Koslov, they had taught her enough to travel and make conversation, but not to read well.

"Then I will tell you what I get from this. Machte did, indeed, teach in the Stuttgart school that Steiner set up at the Waldorf Astoria cigarette company. But in 1928, after Steiner had died, there was a rift in the faculty. Followers of Steiner and followers of Machte warred. Steiner had believed that each human consciousness should be educated to make free choices about good and evil. The image he chose was that of Lucifer, the light-giver, the angel that had given humans free will, making us all custodians of our evolving souls. Machte, in contrast, chose Ariman, the embodiment of soul-less, mechanistic materialism as his guiding light. He felt that the schools must stress moral imperatives. Only through material wealth could social objectives be achieved, such as solving the problems of poverty and hunger. So Dr Machte left the Stuttgart school and founded Enigen at Kandersteg, where he worked on strengthening and reinforcing the students' *will forces* rather than the *heart forces*. He believed in the power of the individual to make the world a better place, through the accumulation of power, influence, and wealth."

"Is there any more?"

"I'm afraid that we have nothing else here, but perhaps in Dornach, where the Anthroposophical Society is based, there is more."

"You've given me what I need. Thank you."

Natalya left the school and went home as quickly as she could. Taking her passport, the credit card that Michael had given her and the money from the safety deposit box, she packed a small suitcase, with her laptop, a few items of clothing, including her hiking shoes and ski parka, and drove to the airport.

On the flight to London she typed everything into the computer. It took most of the six hours to finish the report. Breakfast was being served when she reread it for the last time.

When the aircraft landed at Heathrow, Natalya went to a pay phone and called Turner's home number. She woke the old man from a deep slumber.

"Where are you, Natalya?"

"I'm in London, on my way to Switzerland. I'm emailing you a file."

"You're where?" he asked, suddenly waking.

"Heathrow, with a connecting flight to Geneva in about an hour, and I'm sending a file by email to your private account. You decide if I'm crazy, but I think Michael's in grave danger now. No one is going to save him if I don't."

"He's supposed to be in Kandersteg with Von Kleise. How grave a danger does that present, Natalya?"

"According to his office," she said, having checked with Michael's Assistant before leaving on Friday afternoon, "he changed his plans. He was going to go directly to Paris to meet with some of the other economists before the meetings on Monday, and decided not to make the detour to Kandersteg. I called the hotel in Paris, but he hasn't checked in. My grandfather, your old friend, is at the center of the plot. He's the anchor on which all these different wheels turn. Von Kleise will want Michael out of the way, incommunicado for the next few days. All the President's other economic advisors are creatures of the men behind the plot. My grandfather has too much faith in Michael, so he will not want him there to disagree with the advice of the status quo, and let the markets determine the fate of the planet."

"I'll read what you wrote," Turner said, "but I think Michael will be at that meeting at the OECD in Paris, on Monday."

Turner was now wide awake. He looked at his watch. It was four-fifty in the morning.

"Send it to the secure account. I'll check it from home."

After hanging up, she opened the computer, logged on to Michael's account and sent the report to Turner. She suspected he would never agree with her conclusions. It was, she admitted, too farfetched for him to buy into. And, she thought suddenly, he could be in on the conspiracy. He had, after all, attended Enigen, and the conspiracy definitely centered on some of the group who had pledged their honor to Machte's vision of a new world order.

Was it an irrational panic she felt now? She called Kandersteg. No, Herr Von Kleise couldn't come to the phone. He was not at home. She had not expected to reach Von Kleise. She checked Michael's hotel in Paris again. Again, he was not there.

The flight to Switzerland was on its final call so she ran for the plane.

29. A NEW UNDERSTANDING

"Where's Carlos, Jenny?" Rawlston asked.

"In the States," she answered, knowing that it had been almost five days since he'd last called. It was good, however, that he was away, for she had had time to finish her work. Carlos was like a drug. The more she had, the more she needed. Tomorrow, October 24th, she'd present the final draft to the ministers gathered for the announcement the terms of the debt compact. On Saturday night, it would be announced to the world.

"I'd have thought that he'd be back by now," Rawlston said, his hand idly touching her wrist. She pulled back, but he persisted and she relented.

"So would I," she said dryly, wondering why Katherine and Walter had insisted that he make the trip.

"I take it that you are not amused?" Rawlston asked.

"Apparently, there was something he needed to do for the Holtzs that was more important."

"What?" Rawlston asked surprised. Most of the world's senior economic ministers were gathered in Basel, prior to the G8 meetings that were scheduled for the following week in Paris.

"Ask Katherine or Walter, I really don't know." She tried to walk away, but Rawlston reached for the D-ring on the golden choker chain she wore around her neck. She halted short of breath as the metal cut into her windpipe.

"I see you are attached." Rawlston continued to finger the choker. Jenny shivered.

"One of his jokes," she suggested. "He has the key as well."

"And does he have the leash, and of course, the whip? Boys must have their fun."

"Yes," she said, without thinking, remembering back to the week before, and how humiliated she had been. They had gone to a reception for bankers at the DeBergue. Half of the men and women in the room were her friends from the international banking circuit. In the middle of the party, as she was speaking to a group of New York investment bankers, Carlos had whispered in her ear that they must be going. She had ignored him, pushing him away with a slight pat. He had come back moments later, and snapping on the leash, had led her out of the room.

Katherine came up to where Jenny stood talking to the *Journal* reporter. She was wearing one of her designer gowns, and looked ten years younger than her mid-fifties. Rawlston stopped speaking to Jenny and snapped to attention, and leaning down, kissed her outstretched hand.

"Edward, as usual, it's so good that you could fly in for this."

"I wouldn't miss it for the world, Katherine." He looked around. There were Finance Ministers and Central Bankers from nine of the twenty countries that would make up the Pact of the Andes. The original compact had been signed in draft in Quito, Ecuador, a week earlier.

"Did you see today's edition?" he asked.

"Fabulous article," Katherine agreed, "and I am looking forward to the second part that you promised for Monday's edition."

Seeing Walter motion her, Katherine drifted off, leaving Jenny alone with the Englishman.

"What do you think of Katherine?" he asked.

"She's a woman with a mission. It's more than I can say for myself really."

"And you Jenny Bennette—turncoat and traitor—what can be said about you? After all, that will be written immediately and long into the future. What will they say about Jenny Bennette except that she betrayed her class, her people, for a warm cock and a good fuck?"

"Vulgar as usual, Rawlston. No, I think if they write anything it will be that she was committed to her vices." She laughed self-consciously. Inside, she felt suddenly quite hollow. All of her self-respect had disappeared over the months she had been working at IFF.

"There's a difference between succeeding at something and having a success," observed Rawlston, with a certain amount of tact. "They could succeed, cancel the debt, but the fallout will be worse than the overhang of debt could ever have been."

Jenny didn't respond. She thought about what she had done. The plan had several phases. The first was the announcement of a debt moratorium: no more money would be paid back to the major American, European and Japanese banks, until there was a negotiated settlement on the debt outstanding that was to the benefit of the borrowers. The negotiated settlement called for the oldest fifty percent of the debt to be completely forgiven: that was approximately $800 billion dollars. Twenty-five percent of the newest debt would be repackaged as equity, using collateral in the form of a pool of government and some foreign-owned companies, where each piece of equity carried with it a randomly drawn collection of shares of these enterprises, from all member states. The final twenty-five percent would continue to be paid at existing interest rates. The order of precedent would be based on the age of the outstanding debt. The newest debt would be repaid first.

It was likely that a secondary market would be developed, and the banks would sell the equity stakes to private investors. Despite her optimism that this was the best that could be achieved, she secretly harbored a great deal of doubt about its viability. Nor, she thought, was it certain that all the countries signing this pact with the devil would remain inside the compact. There were already rumblings that some of these governments were on shaky ground, and would be replaced either by military interventions or new elections. Was the plan nothing more than a ploy to rile markets, and send the global economy into a tailspin?

"Have you decided, Edward, if I will succeed or be a success?"

"I think the verdict is out," he said smoothly, taking a last sip from his glass, and putting it down on the table next to him. "It's already late," he looked at his watch, "and you have an important day tomorrow."

"Are you suggesting that I leave with you now?"

"My hotel is near, the night is cold, and Carlos is away," he said with a grin.

"I'm not that kind of woman," she said

Rawlston didn't speak, but taking his left hand he touched the collar she wore. "I think it has already been established the kind of woman you now are, Jenny."

She had little shame left and no pride. Where Carlos had been gentle, Rawlston was rough, but the effect on Jenny was the same.

"Turn over," he ordered, his hands massaging her half-turned ass, his fingers probing deep inside. She turned over like a good slave. She was not prepared for what came next. With both hands prying her buttocks apart, he pushed in making her gasp, choking back a shout. There was no afterglow with Edward Rawlston. She had been used, and used badly. Before the morning light, he threw off the covers and forced her out of his bed.

"What's wrong?" she asked in a daze, standing in the half shadows from the light in the bathroom. She shivered from the cold, still naked, smelling of sex.

"I'm done with you. Now it's time for you to go home, and for me to get some sleep."

Jenny looked at the clock on the side table. It was four-thirty, hardly the time to be waiting in a hotel lobby for a cab.

"Damn it, Edward, it's four-thirty in the morning."

"Get dressed, go home, love. Be a good girl now, and don't make a scene. It's time to go home, Jenny."

She was still half-asleep when he forced her out of the room with half her clothes in her arms. She finished dressing in the dimly lit hall.

On returning to her apartment, she showered, but the stench from the decay she felt inside wouldn't leave her. When she went to the bathroom, there was blood, reminding her of how far she had fallen.

30. THE ROAD TO KANDERSTEG

In Thailand she had felt at home, even if uncomfortable in the heat, but Switzerland was too neat and tidy for Kim's liking. It was two weeks since Lilly had disappeared. There had been no communication, no ransom note, and no demands. The Cantonal police and the Federal police had been polite, but they were not interested in finding Lilly. Officially, she wasn't in Switzerland. Officially, she was dead.

Ben Masters stared through the binoculars at the house that Latimer rented. There were few windows, and only a single heavy front door. Latimer also traveled with bodyguards.

"What do you suggest?"

"Hard to tell what to do really. You could be bold and walk up to that door and knock?"

"Goddamn it, Kim. Suggest something sensible."

Kim, for her part, was tired of babysitting Masters. When he had been the talk of New York, she had hated him. Any man, who demanded that his name be plastered on every building he owned, must be some kind of sociopath. She was tired of his obsessions, his constant chatter, his worries, his angst, and his conceit. He was obsessed with regaining his fortune, his wife, sometimes, and his daughter. The order of these three goals was often different, but more often than not, the fortune came first.

"Okay, if not the direct route, then perhaps some tact with Latimer."

"Like what?"

"Latimer is able to stay here only because the Swiss allow him to stay. He has to be careful. He can't really go back to the States: too many questions; and there are possibly some creditors who would want to kill him. You're both stuck here, and your empire is hanging in the balance. Perhaps it's time to make a deal with Latimer. Here's his private phone number. Call him." She handed him her cell phone.

The Odeon was a Zurich landmark. Lenin had passed many of his years of exile there, penning his revolutionary articles, while sipping coffee and arguing with both followers and critics alike.

"Do you think he'll come?" Ben Masters asked nervously.

He looked around again, while strumming the table nervously. He hated waiting.

"Fuckin' piss eater," he cussed. Latimer was ten minutes late.

"Calm down, Ben," Kim cautioned.

"What the hell is keeping that bastard?"

"I'm over here, Ben," said Latimer, coming in the door.

Masters looked back, watching Brett swagger into the room. Ben started to stand up, but Kim put her hand on his shoulder and sat him down. Behind Latimer two thin, dark men stood watching. Kim noted that each had reached for hidden weapons at the same moment that Masters had stood up.

"We are all here to discuss the same thing," Kim said, pointing to the empty chair. "Sit down, Mr. Latimer. Your guards can see you from over there."

Latimer smoothed out his hair after sitting down, and looked at Ben, smiling brightly.

"You're looking well, Ben."

"You're dead meat," Masters hissed.

"Perhaps a drink might help?" Kim suggested.

"Without Lilly or Beth you're buried," said Latimer, while he looked back at his two bodyguards, who had taken seats at an adjoining table.

Masters quietened down. He stared at Latimer, and wondered how he had been so blind to the man's true colors. He was like a snake; all charm and guile. Once, long before, Marcia Simpson had warned him, but he had dismissed her warnings as sour grapes, given that he had used Latimer for his personal legal business, and not her firm.

"Where's Beth?" Kim asked.

"I don't know. She disappeared."

Masters leaned forward, and Kim watched the bodyguards tense.

"That isn't an answer, Brett." He tried to reach Latimer, to physically pull him towards him, but again, Kim intervened.

"It's unfortunately the only answer you're going to get."

"What did you do to her?"

"I didn't do anything." He held up his hands in defense. "It's a mystery to me too, Ben."

"Perhaps," said Kim trying to be reasonable, "you can clarify for Mr. Masters what happened."

"You want the whole truth? I'll tell you the whole truth. We were coming back from town. A car cut us off, two cars really, pointed a whole mess of guns at my friends over there and at me, and took Beth."

"Do you know who? Why?"

"I have an idea, but I've been warned not to say anything."

"Warned? Give us a name, Latimer?"

"The people who set you up set me up too." He looked at his old friend. "You think I wanted to do this to you, Ben? You think I liked destroying Lilly, and the kid? I got into it too far. Playing with the Mafia's business was exciting, just like some of your deals, but then I was hooked, and couldn't refuse what they wanted. That's not to say it was a bad deal for me. I was able to keep some of the money I raised by leveraging your properties, but most went somewhere else. And, pal, I liked the feeling of being the one calling the shots. I liked it too that you were upriver, and out of sight and out of mind."

"You said you have an idea of who took, Beth?" Kim said, trying to get the conversation back on track, before Masters could respond.

"I think I know the guy who was directing the heist. I met him once before."

"What's his name?" she asked calmly.

"What's in it for me?"

"Perhaps your life," Kim said in a quiet, but threatening manner.

Latimer stood up, pushing back his chair. Kim continued to sit, but Masters jumped up.

"If I were you, Latimer, I would sit back down," she said in the same quiet voice. "Look behind you at your men. They're not dead, just drugged," she said with a smile. Earlier, she'd paid off the waiter to doctor whatever the men ordered with a sedative. "Now, look closely at the newspaper on the table." She directed his gaze to the paper that hid her right hand. Lifting one corner, she showed him the gun complete with silencer that was pointed at his chest. "And now, I think we will have a long and productive talk. There are a number of things that Washington needs to know, and also some things that Ben Masters would like answers too, as well."

"Who are you?"

"I work for a government agency," she smiled. "That's all I will say, except that the Swiss Government has given me sanction to take you out if I decide it's needed," she lied.

Latimer edged back. Kim looked to Masters who reached across the table and pulled Latimer back, slamming his chest into the heavy wood of the table top. "I'm not going to let Ben kill you, not yet," Kim remarked flatly, looking at Latimer and then at Masters. "We want to know who it was that took Beth. If you tell us a name, if the story is convincing, if you can repeat it three, four times in a row, then you'll walk out of here alive. If you don't, then I'll let Ben finish you outside, behind the cafe. As I said, the Swiss don't care; they want you gone. There won't be an investigation and your assets here will be quietly liquidated. It's a win-win for everyone."

She could sense Latimer's discomfort. He looked around. The room was now almost empty.

"There's no help coming, Latimer. So, let's begin again," Kim said.

"This Brunner, where do we find him?" Ben asked Kim after they finally left Latimer an hour later.

"We'll go to Bern tonight. We have contacts who can locate Brunner for us."

"And then?"

"And then we talk to Brunner."

31. THE HERMIT

Paul Thommen's official position was Senior Advisor for Counterespionage and Counterterrorism in the Swiss Federal Government. Thommen was a man whose life was shrouded in the deepest mystery. He was the keeper of the secrets in a country of secrets. He worked alone, usually without backup or direction from superiors. The fewer people who knew who he was or what he did, the better, and he liked the nickname that he had earned: 'The Hermit.'

"I am surprised you came back, Natalya," Thommen said, fondly remembering the hours they had spent together, before he had escorted her out of the country over a misunderstanding about Swiss banking laws. "I'm impressed too that you have the ability to change nationalities at the drop of a hat. I hear that you now are a full-blooded American. Yes?"

Natalya smiled, ignoring Thommen's sarcasm. "I couldn't get enough of Switzerland," she answered. "It's so beautiful here."

"I will pass your comments on to the Swiss National Tourist Office," Thommen said dryly. "Now, tell me the truth. Perhaps you suddenly realized that you missed me?" He smiled showing the small gap between his front teeth.

She laughed, and sat down on the chair opposite his desk.

"There are no secrets that the Hermit doesn't know," Natalya said lowering her voice, "are there?"

She looked around the small, spare office he kept in Bern. She found her eyes wandering as fatigue finally overcame her adrenalin. She was tired, bone-tired, but there was no time to rest, not yet. She'd taken the noon train from Geneva, and now, close to two o'clock, she was sitting in Thommen's office in a nondescript building overlooking the famed bear pit.

"So what brings you to Switzerland?"

"Michael Ross," she answered, yawning as she spoke.

"The American who, if I understand correctly, you've given your heart to? That's too bad, you know."

"Too bad that I didn't accept your kind offer to screw you before you kicked me out of the country? Is that what's bothering you, Paul? The truth," she paused, "was that I was somewhat tempted by your offer."

"We are a perfect match, Natalya," he said quite seriously. "Let's be honest, this American simply reminds you of your father, nothing more," he added with a grin. "You and I, however, Natalya, we are cut from the same cloth."

"Blackmail was your tactic with me, not psychoanalysis." She leaned back in the chair, relaxing and recalling that day. It had not been entirely unpleasant: the lunch, at least, had been excellent. "Besides, you advised me that leaving quietly was a far more efficient way to solve the problem than a long stay in a dark and rat-infested cell, in a country without the right of habeas corpus."

"Contravention of Swiss banking laws is a terrible crime in this country: far, far worse than murder really."

She didn't reply.

"Tell me ..." he took a cigarette and started to light it, but then thought better of this and stubbed it out. "Trying to stop. Stupid, isn't it?" Instead, he picked up a pencil nervously. "Are you in love with him?"

"Yes" she admitted.

When Thommen had first met her during the interrogation, her beauty and her calm had affected him. Here was a woman his equal in nerve and in intelligence. When the banks had withdrawn their case against her and the Ministry that she worked for, Thommen had, with some reluctance, escorted her to the airport in Zurich, taking a side trip to Montreaux for lunch. She had politely declined his suggestion of being desert.

"And why has this American economist brought you here?"

"He's missing."

"And you are certain of that?"

With a minimum of detail Natalya related to Thommen everything that had happened during the last months. He listened dispassionately to her story, and without interruption. She handed him a copy of the report she'd prepared on the airplane.

"And have you called Von Kleise?"

"He's not taking phone calls today," she reported.

"Perhaps he's quite busy. It is, after all, an important day for his Enigen class. I will check with my man in Kandersteg."

The Hermit had arranged a small security detail for the reception at Kanderschloss on the Friday night, and at Enigen, for the ceremony on the Saturday.

Thommen picked up the phone. She couldn't understand what he said in Schweizerdeutsch, the seventeenth-century German dialect that was still spoken in the German cantons.

"Ross did visit Von Kleise. He attended the reception held on Friday night, and was there at Enigen for the ceremony the next morning. He then left for Paris from there. He didn't return to the house."

Thommen paused, mentally calculating the time needed to drive to Paris. It could be eight hours, even ten, before Ross arrived there. "He will be there by nine or ten at the latest," he suggested. "You see there is nothing sinister about this." He looked at the report she had handed him. He read it quickly, and glancing up, showed his surprise at what he read. When he had finished it, he didn't speak for a few minutes, and then he smiled.

"An interesting thesis, but hardly convincing evidence don't you think? And quite imaginative too, placing your own grandfather in the middle of the thick of it. It would make a good story, yes?"

She felt let down, deflated by his distrust and criticism. She had tried Michael on his cell phone, but it was either broken or not turned on. It was highly unlikely that Michael on a long drive, on unfamiliar roads, would turn it off. Paul Thommen continued, adding more salt to Natalya's already significant wounds. "I'm afraid I find it farfetched to believe that some of the wealthiest individuals in the world, including Herr Von Kleise, who are all quite honorable men, would do what you've described. A financial meltdown must impact their fortunes even more than yours or mine. Don't you even at least find that out of character?"

"Believe what you want, Paul," Natalya said standing up angrily. "I'm going to Kandersteg to try to see Von Kleise."

"And what of your economist?"

"If he is in Paris, which I doubt, then I will be able to reach him there, but if he is being held somewhere by Von Kleise, then I will find him. He is reachable by cell phone almost anywhere in the world, but his phone is not working. Doesn't that seem strange to you, Paul?"

"Perhaps I could go to Kandersteg with you," Thommen suggested. "Just to ensure that your theory isn't correct," he suggested.

"There's no chance between us, Thommen." Natalya could almost feel the man's eyes undressing her.

"I know," he said quite carefully. "Still, I have some time, and if Ross turns up in Paris while you are in Kandersteg, then I'm sure we can enjoy each other's company. If I recall, you're an accomplished alpinist in your own right. We might be able to do a bit of climbing there."

This would not be an official investigation for Thommen. To touch a man like Heinrich Von Kleise, even the Hermit would need the approval of the Council of State. Still, if after hours of climbing they reached the Oberschloss, then the rules of hospitality alone might allow them to look around.

"So, are you a believer now?"

"No, but I am a cautious man, and if Von Kleise has Doctor Ross hidden away and out of touch with his government, he will be at the Oberschloss. To reach that retreat, it takes even an experienced climber eight or nine hours. Are you prepared for that?"

Natalya was surprised that Thommen had changed suddenly from skeptic to possible ally. She stood up and extended her hand. Thommen took it, squeezed lightly, and then let go.

"When do we leave?"

"Now. But first, we need to gather some climbing gear. I suppose you didn't plan for that, but I have some spare equipment."

It was close to 5 p.m. when they rounded the last hairpin turn leading to Kandersteg. A Cantonal police vehicle stood at one side, its lights flashing. Thommen stopped the car.

"Should we take a look?"

"What do you think it is?"

"They were looking over the side at something."

A cold, unspeakable fear gripped Natalya.

"I don't think they would kill him, Natalya" Paul said, sensing her panic.

She opened the car door and they walked back to where the police car was parked. Two officers were looking down below. Off to the side of the road there was a sheer drop of about 200 feet. At the bottom of the cliff there was a car lying on its side, with wisps of smoke coming out of its engine compartment. Natalya listened while the officer explained to Thommen what had happened. She couldn't understand the language, but from the hand motions she understood pretty much what had happened.

"Some tourists stopped here to take a picture when they saw that the siding was sheared off, as if something had gone over the cliff. There's a small car down below."

"Is it Michael's car?" Natalya asked.

"I don't know. Highly unlikely, but since you won't relax until we know, I'll go down to investigate. They certainly won't. They'll wait for the emergency response team to come." Thommen took one of the nylon climbing ropes from the car. "Any idea what kind of car Michael rented?"

"I insisted he give me the details: a small Fiat with Basel plates. Here's the plate number," she said, handing him a slip of paper. He looked at it, then handed it back.

Natalya watched as he worked his way carefully down the sheer rock face. Thommen was an expert climber so it didn't take him long to reach the car. Kicking out to get a better view of the back, he read the license plate, and peered into the car. He drove his metal reinforced climbing boots through the already damaged front window and looked inside, using his head lamp.

A few minutes later, he climbed over the top, scrambling to his feet as he did so. Natalya was there to greet him.

"Tell me the truth," she demanded, her voice cracking. "I need to know."

"No one's in the car, but it's his car. Don't say anything," he said, touching her arm, "but perhaps there is more to this than I had first guessed."

He'd agreed to take her to Kandersteg expecting to bed her. The last thing he expected was that her theories might actually be correct.

It was late October, and only a few tourists were staying in the Victoria Hotel on the square that was the center of the village of Kandersteg. Natalya insisted on separate rooms, but Thommen managed to ensure they had an adjoining, shared bathroom.

"Give me an hour," she said, looking at her watch. It was dinnertime and she'd not eaten since early in the morning. "I'll meet you downstairs."

She put her hand to the door to open it, but Thommen stopped her. His touch was firm as he turned her.

"Don't be frightened."

"Do I look frightened, Paul?"

"Yes," he said, seeing how her pupils dilated.

"It's just the jet lag," she said. "I'll be better in the morning."

"Good, because in the morning we have a tough climb up to near the top of the Bluemlisalpenhorn, where your grandfather has his retreat. It snowed last week and the drifts and services will be hard to see, and are very dangerous."

"I'm not afraid."

He held her hand, but she didn't pull back. She needed Paul's help, but she didn't love him. "I must get changed." She pulled away, fumbling with her key.

"Of course," Paul said, watching her open the door to the room. Then he turned and went to his room.

"Feeling better?" Thommen asked as Natalya came down to the bar with a smile

"Yes, much" she said relieved that Michael had not been in the car, but now worried more than ever about where he could be.

"There was something on the news that might interest you," he said, looking at the television hanging over the bar. It was tuned to Radio Télévision Suisse, the local French station.

"What?"

"IFF has successfully concluded their Treaty of the Andes between twenty major Third-World and European debtors and private banks: a kind of *über* Club of Paris. These countries will refuse to service their debt until it is restructured."

"That should send tremors through the markets on Monday," Natalya said dryly. There was no "shock value" in the announcement for her. She had predicted just that in her report.

Thommen looked as another couple came into the darkened Gastrube in the old hotel. They were an odd-looking pair: a middle-aged American man with a strikingly beautiful Eurasian woman. They sat a table at one end of the room, where the American spread a topographical map over the table.

Thommen recognized the map for it was the same one he had brought, covering the area from the edge of the Oeschinensee, and going to the 14,000-foot summit of the Bluemlisalpenhorn. The Oberschloss, at just over 11,000 feet, perched on the Blumlisalp Rothorn. It was a difficult climb even for an experienced mountaineer. On one side there was a 1,000-foot near-vertical cliff, and on the other, a difficult traverse that even the most experienced climber might find impossible. They watched as the two Americans huddled with a Swiss guide, mapping out a route.

"Who are they?" Natalya finally asked. The man's face seemed familiar. She was sure that she had seen his face somewhere.

"The man is Ben Masters, traveling in Switzerland, under US government sanction. He's using the name Bernard Rogers, and the woman is an American intelligence operative, Kim Donovan."

"Why are they here?"

"That is an interesting question. Perhaps your theories are not as crazy as I first believed."

"You believe me?"

"Possibly. Masters' wife and daughter are both missing. Based on your rather," he paused and smiled warmly at her, "inspired theories, then they could well be at the Oberschloss until Mr. Masters' little real-estate empire takes down the entire commercial real-estate market within the next few days."

"Then you'll call for help, Paul?" Natalya asked.

He laughed. "No, no. The Hermit works alone." He knew that no Swiss Government official would sanction what he was about to try. A man like Heinrich Von Kleise was untouchable.

She said good night to Thommen at her door. It was early, not later than nine-thirty. Inside, she locked the door and opened the door to the bathroom. It took her no time to wash her face and brush her teeth. On leaving the bathroom she locked the bolt from the outside, changed into a short nightshirt and collapsed in the bed.

Natalya was awoken by a light, insistent rap on the connecting door. She listened, and then buried her head under the eiderdown cover. The room was cold. The tapping started again; this time, more insistent. She sat up in bed, and then quietly went to the bathroom door.

"Is that you, Paul?" she asked, knowing the answer.

"Open the door, Natalya."

"I don't want to," she explained. "Go back to sleep. I need sleep, not sex."

"I want to talk."

"Just talk?" She looked at her watch. It was close to three in the morning. It was hardly the time to discuss business.

"I need to rest," she insisted.

"Open the door, Natalya," he said firmly.

She slid open the bolt. He walked into the room closing the door behind him. He was wearing short pajamas and a cotton top. The cold didn't bother him. Natalya ran back to her bed and slid under the covers. He continued to stand watching her.

"I couldn't sleep." He seemed much less like a Titan now. "I was thinking of you."

"Has it been that long since you have slept with a woman?" she asked, patting the bed next to her, but keeping the comforter between them.

"It has been years."

"Are there no Swiss girls that you can attack?"

"None as beautiful as you, Natalya," he complimented her.

"Aren't you cold?" Natalya asked. "You should go back to sleep. We have a long day ahead of us."

"Sensible, but I can't sleep alone."

"I don't want to have sex," she stated firmly.

"We must talk about tomorrow," he said seriously. "Perhaps I could climb under the covers just to stay warm," he suggested.

She lifted the comforter and let him slide in next to her. He pushed in close, and she pulled back until she was at the edge of the bed. She then pushed him towards the edge of the bed.

"Just to stay warm," she said, with a finality that Thommen accepted.

"We must be out of here early, by six at the latest. I propose we hike halfway around the lake and make our way up by the shorter route. We will reach the glacier just below the Oberschloss from the southeasterly direction," Thommen explained, thinking about the difficulty of the ascent. "It's steeper, but faster than the more obvious route of using the well-marked hiking path number 23, that leads to the Blumlisalpenhutte at over 7,500 feet, but would put the climber too far to the east to reach the more difficult, but lesser peak of the Rothorn. That will be the one that I expect Masters to use, but he'll have to leave it around halfway up, and cross a difficult stretch of rock and glacier. Even if they reach the glacier just below the house, they'll find that the way from there isn't as simple as knocking on the door. Von Kleise has a small contingent of guards, mainly Valaisan mountain boys, to shoo off any uninvited guests."

"How technical is the climb?" Natalya asked, studying the elevation markings on the map for clues.

"It shouldn't be that technically difficult." Despite his bravado, he had little idea what they faced once they started the climb. There was little honor in going after the lesser peaks of the range, so he knew less about the routes to the Rothorn, except that it was mainly across rock, not glacier.

She had watched him pack the backpacks in the Bern apartment. He'd taken ice picks, pitons, and a two-person climber's tent. He had insisted that she take a sweater and long underwear. The hiking shoes just fit once she added a second pair of socks. There were crampons; ice cleats that attached to the hiking boots that Thommen had in his gear that just barely fit her foot. She wondered if Ben Masters and the American agent were as prepared for the journey as they were.

"Why do you think that Masters is here?" she asked Thommen, changing the subject.

"His wife's disappeared. It's a confusing story of kidnap, rape, sex, violence, Asian brothels, but then perhaps your wild imagination will find an explanation for that as well. Of course, in Switzerland we think of Herr Von Kleise as a saint, not a trafficker in stolen women."

Natalya tried to understand why Lillian Master's reappearance might be a risk to the plan. She guessed it was simply a precaution. Why take a chance? Why keep her alive and not simply dispose of her? At least they were not shooting people randomly, and for that, she was pleased. She would hate to think of her own grandfather as being that callous with life.

She felt Paul come closer to her, but this time she didn't pull away. He leaned towards her and kissed her lightly. When she didn't pull back, he was surprised.

"This means nothing, Thommen," she said out loud. "You understand I love Michael."

"Of course," he said, as he quietly caressed her breasts.

She spread her legs to hurry him along. He came too quickly. She was happy for it satisfied him, and repaid him for the favor of his help.

"It's time to get up," Natalya shook Thommen. It was five-thirty.

Thommen opened his eyes and turned and looked. She was sitting up in bed. He pushed himself up so that he might reach for her, and pull her down and back towards him.

"It's over. Don't try again."

He stood up, pulling the covers from her and looking directly at her nakedness. Natalya pulled them back, remaining in bed.

"Get dressed," he ordered.

"You get out and I will."

"As you like it, as you like it."

She didn't answer, but watched him leave. When he was gone she stood up, stretched carefully, and followed him through to the bathroom locking the door to his room from the inside. Natalya showered, scrubbing his smell from her body. When she was satisfied, she dressed carefully. The insulated underwear, thick socks, woolen hiking knickers, and heavy turtlenecks and rag sweater made her sweat. She removed the sweater and added it to her pack. When she was dressed and ready, she looked around the room, smoothed out the bed sheets and pulled the eiderdown cover back into place. Then she opened the door and went down to breakfast.

32. LIES AND HALF-TRUTHS

Jenny felt no elation at the celebratory dinner that the Holtzs had arranged in the Richemond's gilded private dining room, on the second floor.

"You look worried," a smiling Walter Holtz said, as she stood looking out at the lighted promenade across the street along the lakefront.

"Do I?"

"Since the press briefing, you've been very quiet, withdrawn. We're worried about you." He touched her arm. She pulled away.

"I'll be okay, really." She knew, however, that she would never be the same. She was, after all, a traitor to those people and institutions to whom she had given the best years of her life. As she had defended herself and her plan from the press, the reality of what she had started began to sink in. She was frightened of what would come next. The markets almost collapsed every time Greece sneezed. What IFF had just proposed would be far worse.

Walter went back to where Katherine was holding court. He noted that his wife was in her best form: charming, smiling, and confident of success.

Jenny saw Edward Rawlston walk towards her, obviously quite drunk. Taking her arm roughly, he pulled her away from the others.

"I have to speak to you," he said, slurring his words, "in private."

They walked over towards the open bar, on the other side of the room from where the Holtzs were holding court.

"And how are the King and Queen doing tonight, Jenny?" Rawlston's tone was mocking and insulting. "Of course, I could do with a drink, a stiff one; perhaps two under the circumstance." He walked her to the bar, ordered a drink for him and one for Jenny without asking her. "Don't worry, Jenny, you'll need the fortification." She had a vague premonition of the disaster that was about to ruin her life.

"What are you talking about, Edward?"

"Those shits over there, the Holtzs, used you and me badly. I will certainly lose my job, and it could mean jail time too, though I doubt if they can prove I profited from this disaster."

"I still don't see it."

"Let me put it clearly, Jen. Shorts have been taken in the name of W&K Trading, which is a holding company owned entirely by Walter and Katherine, has taken short positions in more than twenty major bank stocks, ahead of Monday's opening of the markets. I was on the line to my editor an hour ago about it. He's furious at my involvement. When the market opens, the world's financial system will collapse. Bank stocks will plummet, and our friends will make a fortune."

"But," Jenny said, struggling, "why would the Holtzs do this? It's if not illegal, highly unethical."

"For money, that's why. Do they need any other reasons? Did you think it was for the downtrodden and the poor? They're human like the rest of us, just a bit more greedy than most."

"It isn't insider information," she said, trying to figure out the legal issues involved. "At least, not technically speaking."

"No, not really, but the effect is the same, as they knew the banks would lose money. And we destroyed our reputations playing up the compact. My exclusive has been updated to include that the Holtzs are shorting the market: that may give them some heartburn, but not change the result." He took the drink and poured it down his throat in one long, terrible gulp, followed by a hiccup. "That's better now," he said with a drunken grin.

"What can we do?"

"I don't know. We can hardly bury ourselves any deeper. Suppose we go to a desert island, you and I, have sex all day long, and eat coconuts at night." His hand brushed openly at her breasts and he cupped each in turn. She pushed him away, sensing the others around them watching.

"Let's go, Edward."

Instead, Rawlston pulled her across the room to where Katherine was holding court.

"Miss Bennette," he said with a drunken grin, "has a few questions for Herr Holtz and Frau Holtz." He bowed, and then faltering, he fell to the floor in a howl of laughter. People began to pull back. Jenny, on one knee, reached for Rawlston, and helped him up. She looked at the Holtzs, who were now staring at her with some wonder.

"Do you have a question, Jenny?" Katherine asked, in her most condescending voice.

"I'll get him home," she said, helping Rawlston up. She guided him out of the room. In the lobby she retrieved her coat, then led Rawlston, stumbling drunk, out of the hotel into the cold night air.

She took him to her apartment, where she helped him out of his clothes and into her bed. When she was certain that he was asleep, Jenny drove the red Porsche that she had leased, across the Pont du Mont-Blanc to where the Holtzs had their villa on the south side of the lake. She arrived just as the Holtzs were arriving home.

"I thought you and Ed were off to Never-never Land," Walter said with a smile.

"I wanted to clear up some things, Walter. Can we go inside?"

"If you like," he said laughing. "Come." He guided her into the house. Katherine was already warming her hands by the roaring fire in the stone hearth.

"So you have some questions, Jenny?"

"A few." Jenny suddenly felt weak.

"Perhaps Walter you should pour all of us another drink?"

"Yes, yes, of course. You will take a nice cognac, Jenny?"

She nodded, but continued to stare at Katherine.

"Such a look; so much anger. Why, Jenny? Tonight, we triumphed."

"Did we?"

"Don't you think we did? You were brilliant at the press conference. Those reporters didn't lay a glove on you. It was a great performance, Jen. Don't you think so, Walter? Don't you think that our Jenny did very, very well?"

"Of course, of course. You were very, very good, my dear."

A performance, she thought, that was what it was: not the truth that what they were doing would collapse the global economy as surely as if they started a war. A sudden collapse in confidence, a withdrawal of credit, would likely cause more harm than good to the countries she had thought she was going to help. She had been played, and played badly, and Rawlston was right: they both had nowhere to hide. She looked at one Holtz, then at the other, and wondered how she had been so blind before. They were like strutting peacocks. All the sugar-sweet words they used, all the compliments … everything was a show.

"Edward found out that you've been short-selling bank shares ahead of Monday."

"Honestly, Jen. It's an opportunity to capture at least some of the ill-gotten gains of the market for the poor."

"You've traded in your names, not even IFF's." Jenny reported.

"IFF is the embodiment of Katherine and me. We have given

everything to this organization: our fortune, our reputations, everything, and for years."

She didn't answer. They had a way of manipulating and spinning facts that left her confused.

"Where's Carlos?" Jenny asked, suddenly changing the subject. "Where did you send him?"

"Carlos is dead. I'm sorry," said Katherine, approaching Jenny. She laid one of her hands on Jenny's. "We found out this morning, but Walter didn't wish to upset you."

"How did he die?"

"He fell into a river, drowned. They found his body only a few days ago."

"Why was he in Washington?"

She sensed their unease at the question. She repeated it, her voice showing the anger she felt. Finally, Walter answered, after looking at Katherine and then back to Jenny.

"There was something that Katherine and I needed to have accomplished. Carlos loved danger and we warned him, time and time again, not to push Fate, but …" he sighed, "he apparently did just that. The accident happened at a place called Great Falls. I've been told that this is a terribly dangerous stretch of river near Washington."

It wasn't enough of an explanation. Jenny was losing her grip on what mattered. She felt used, abused, and lost. Everything that had once been important to her, was now lost. She had no honor left.

"You will find someone else. There are many men that will be happy to give you a good workout from time to time, Jenny. I will even volunteer Walter for that duty if you'd like."

What did they think she was? Jenny thought. An animal to be exercised? She was a human being, a woman with feelings. She had loved Carlos, or at least, had told herself that she did. Yet Walter was right about one thing: there were many men who might do as well. Once started, the sex had become like heroin; and she had to have a fix.

Edward Rawlston awoke when Jenny returned. She looked at this angular Englishman lying under the covers in her bed. She had stripped away all his clothes, throwing them in one corner as she did. Now, she stripped off her clothes. After tonight, there would be no turning back. She had no bitterness towards Walter or Katherine. They were family now, the only family she had left.

Katherine was right. She wouldn't miss Carlos, and there were others who would give her a workout from time to time.

When she was naked she stood, legs spread apart, hands on her hips, and waited. Rawlston looked up; he lifted his hand and pulled back the covers.

"Where have you been?"

"Out," she said, without offering further explanation.

"Then come on in."

She climbed into the bed, pressing her body next to his, and he used her, leaving the once-proud Jenny Bennette with no self-respect, but fully satisfied.

33. THE LAST REDOUBT

When Michael had left after the ceremony at Enigen, intent on getting to Paris by Saturday night, he had been met by one of Von Kleise's assistants, who had begged him to spend another night with Von Kleise at his private retreat, the Oberschloss. An airplane from a private field near Interlaken would fly him the next day to Paris, thus saving him the long drive. He would be Von Kleise's first visitor to the Oberschloss: it was an honor he couldn't turn down.

The Oberschloss had been carefully sited. It was not at the top of the highest peak in the Bluemlisalpenhorn massif, but on a false summit that carried the weighty name Bleumlisalp Rothorn; a promontory point standing some 1,000 feet below the highest peak of the mountain chain. Few climbers wasted time on the lesser challenge of trying to scale this peak. It was also less accessible and harder to reach, protected by sheer walls of rock and a crevice-filled glacier. The Oberschloss was itself a fortress, self-contained, with its own power generators and communication links: a redoubt, a typically Swiss bastion set in a high alp.

Von Kleise handed Michael a glass of sixty-year-old scotch. "You are depressed, I can see it. You need something more challenging to do than trying to push policy through a recalcitrant Congress. You are worn-out by Washington's inability to do the right things for those not at the top of the pyramid. I know that with my money, I can get anything through your government, any government in fact, democratic or autocratic."

"You're right, of course, but what can I do? I promised the President to at least commit to finish out the term. By 2017, it will be someone else's problem. Every initiative we have tried has been stopped by greed, jealousy or simple spite. And the private sector didn't help matters," he said, looking directly at Von Kleise. "Companies would rather buy stock or hide money under the mattress than invest and hire new workers, or raise wages. They have made it the role of government to try to get stop incomes from falling by cutting taxes, or paying out new benefits. It's no wonder that the economy, American and others, have just limped along since 2008."

"Nonsense, Michael. With the right resources and with your creativity you could fashion policies that could help. It's the conventional wisdom that needs to be changed. We have to stop rejecting all ideas that are out of the ordinary. Your problem, my friend, is that you have been trying to change thinking from the wrong power base. Only the private sector can solve the economic problems brought on by laissez-faire government policies. Believe me, with enough resources and the right leadership, not from government, but from men of good will, then the world can be changed for the better. There are good solutions to all problems, from climate change to creating enough jobs for anyone willing to work."

Michael had heard this before from Von Kleise. How could private companies serve the interest of the public, as well as their shareholders? Even if a few companies did truly commit to such ideals, it would be dependent upon private deals to divide up markets, or by gentlemen's agreements about turf, or through technology-sharing and licensing arrangements. However, competition would always reassert itself once the market shrank, or new products or innovation were developed by new companies, making sharing unsustainable.

"You think the world can be made better simply by turning over the government to the private sector, where we must depend upon the good will of the wealthy to do what is right for their employees, and for the economy as a whole."

"I'm not that radical. There is a role for government, but also a role for well-meaning capitalists with the skills and finances to make things happen. Government alone can't keep an economy growing, or ensure that everyone who wants to work can work."

"Describe this new man; this well-meaning capitalist," Michael demanded, showing his own cynicism about businessmen in general. Too often he'd seen them act in the interests of themselves, rather than society, company employees or even the shareholders. Cutting jobs often profited them more than growth, and those profits relied on government assistance and subsidies. These captains of industry would then yell and scream that the government had to bring its accounts into balance.

"Only men who own companies outright are true capitalists. I own my companies, which means that I can take chances and forgo short-term profits, in order to get growth and stability for the workers who make my firms successful. The same can't be said for someone hired by a team of outsiders, who may be only there for a year or two before they are gone, but who, in that period, may do damage to the company's reputation and its workforce. It's simple arithmetic: the circular flow of money has to be maintained; and productivity gains have to be shared with the ultimate consumers. Henry Ford saw that. He paid workers enough so they could buy Ford automobiles. I would say that your current version of capitalism is broken, Michael. For the past thirty years, ever since economists got into their head that globalization was the answer to all problems, rich and advanced countries' workers have been in a race to the bottom. Wages have barely increased, and in many cases, have fallen. Don't you see? It is time for something different; something noble and good; for both the owners and the workers."

Von Kleise stood up and walked towards the plate-glass window. The mountains spread out before him. "You see, Michael, I have a longer time horizon than most of my competitors. I can accept a smaller profit. I can be paternalistic to my workers by paying them a living wage and training younger workers rather than depending on government to do the training or, as in your country, complaining that there are no workers that can do the job, or don't have the right skills immediately. I can ignore the popular trends, and not strip my companies to their bare essentials, in the interests of a few pennies here or there. I invest in new ideas. I don't skimp on research and development, but benefit from the long-term benefits they bring, even if my short-term profits are less. Yes, of course, I am still a capitalist: I put up money that is my own, and I risk it on new products and new ideas. But without other companies doing the same, the world economy performs at well under its true potential." He didn't look at Michael, but stared out into the space that spread out before him, the endless range of high mountains, capped by dwindling glaciers and lesser snow packs. "Unfortunately, there are too few men of wealth *and* character left in the world."

He continued. "Have you ever wondered if this world, as we know it, can go on as it has forever?" He didn't wait for Michael to answer. "We have created great wealth, but also great inequality. We are choking on our own excesses from income inequality that robs economies of demand for ordinary things, to the pollution that overconsumption and limited regulations has unleashed on our planet. Billions of people will be without water or food in the future, as floods and droughts afflict rich and poor alike. Free enterprise has created a paradox: greater abundance and even greater poverty. Markets are not self-correcting, nor fair. Rarely do they produce results that are even approximately optimal. We are at a point, Michael, that without some higher authority stepping in, our world will self-destruct, choke on its on excesses, and billions will die. It is the economist's delusion that free markets work best."

Von Kleise passed Michael a goblet filled with red wine, and told him to drink from it. The wine tasted bitter, too tannic for his tastes. It was old, likely very expensive. He put the glass down, without taking more than a sip.

"You don't like it, yet it's very expensive. The price of that bottle alone would feed a family in India for a year. Isn't that absurd, Michael? We value it for its cost, not its taste."

"There's no comparison." Michael answered. "Besides if the world's poor were to become even modestly rich, the resources of the world would be taxed to breaking point."

"So, you are against development because it will interfere with your lifestyle? That is what you believe. But perhaps innovation might make it possible to stretch our resources, or new resources might well be discovered, if we searched more diligently. Today, there's no incentive to do that. You and I pay lip service to the notion that the world's poor will, one day, through hard work and diligence become like us. But we fear that day, for all its unintended consequences."

Turning, Von Kleise looked intently at Michael. Did Michael have the courage to accept that the old economy had to be extinguished, destroyed, before its successor could emerge? Was he the right person to see this grand experiment through to its logical conclusion? Michelle, always a good judge of people, had believed he wasn't the right one to carry on. He wondered too, and yet there was no one else. He was dying, if not this year, then in a few more. The doctors had told him that much. He saw the turmoil in Michael's eyes. He had accomplished his goal. He had reminded Ross of how he had once burned with indignation rather than resignation.

"You can do better, Michael. If you believe in yourself, if you trust your better instincts, then great things can be accomplished."

He left Michael alone with his own inner turmoil. To seize the day you had to be bold. Von Kleise had always been bold, and willing to challenge convention in his drive to succeed.

The housekeeper, Frau Bundt, entered with a tray of food and a bottle of white wine. Victoria and Michelle followed her into the room. Michael could see by the way he treated them, and the way they responded to Von Kleise that they were far more than employees, more like mistresses.

Michelle poured the wine. Handing a glass to Heinrich, she watched as he took one of Frau Bundt's pastry shells filled with a fatty goose rillette, and ate it quickly.

"I saw that," she said, stopping the old man from taking another pastry shell like a protective mother. "Remember what the doctor said. It will stop your heart for sure if you eat too many of those."

"Doctors know so much, but also so little." He looked at Michael and smiled, "Isn't that right, Michael?"

Michael sat, staring openly at Michelle, but his thoughts were of Natalya and what she might think, given that he'd changed his plans and had not informed anyone. She would be worried.

"Michelle, go and get me something healthy, because I have not eaten since two, and even then, there were so many guests to entertain, that I barely took a bite to eat. Go now!" He chuckled as he watched her rush out of the room in search of healthier food.

"She was a find, a real find, Michael." Von Kleise looked at Ross and smiled. "Perhaps you would like to sample her delights tonight?"

"I … I…" Michael stammered.

"Perhaps someone else then" he said with a laugh.

"You have quite a harem here, Heinrich."

"Yes, yes," Von Kleise laughed. "Even if they are beautiful Michael, they are also intelligent, uniquely qualified for their work. Michelle has a Ph.D. from the Sorbonne, and is an expert on game theory; Victoria was once a well-known Wall Street investment banker; and little Ola is a computer genius."

"Where are you, Michelle?" Von Kleise called out, breaking the spell by changing the subject.

"Here," said Michelle.

"Frau Bundt is having her usual problems in the kitchen, Heinrich, but I managed to prepare some sliced apples, pears, and hard cheeses."

"I prefer the rillettes," Von Kleise said, reaching for another one of the forbidden pastries, and popping it into his mouth. "Is it time yet?"

"In a minute," Michelle said, looking at her watch.

"Then, turn on the television, and let us see if Hans Joseph has succeeded."

Michelle went to the wall. Touching a hidden switch a large flat-panel TV built into one side of the huge living space was revealed. It came on instantly.

"It is set on the German cable, but for Michael's sake we'd best get the BBC feed," he said, motioning for her to switch the cable feed.

There were a few minutes of fumbling, and then he heard a BBC announcer and saw a picture of the City Hall in Berlin.

"...Wilhelm Brantheim's New Deutschland Nationalist Party has won control of the Bavarian Government in a special election, placing his party in a good position to take control of the Federal Government in the elections that will be held in 2017. Bavaria, with its more than 12 million people, is the largest and most important state in the German Federal Republic. He is about to address a cheering crowd. The emotion of this crowd is unbelievable as they wait for their new hero. The torch has been passed to the young, and they feel empowered by the rhetoric of this new German leader, whose party triumphed in both the national and regional elections held this week. There are nearly half a million people, young and old, standing heel to toe, in the middle of the large square, and millions more throughout Europe tonight, listening for clues to understand what his radically different policies will mean for their lives, and the lives of others in Europe. The new President of Bavaria, and a member of the Federal Council, was elected on a platform of restoring German greatness, by throwing off the legacy of sixty years of self-effacement and apology to nearly all nations. He will speak first in German, and then immediately in English. From the advanced information we've received, this speech may start the process of the dissolution of the European Union, and the withdrawal of Germany from the euro."

The crowd scene faded, and the picture resumed with a larger-than-life image of the young Wilhelm Brantheim. His New Deutschland Nationalist Party had defeated both the Christian Democrats and the Social Democrats, to gain control of the Bavarian State Government. Michael had not been paying close attention to German politics. He had had enough to worry about without adding this to his agenda, but from the looks of the crowd he could see that this man might well be a problem. He was a man in his early forties, of medium build, and with a shock of blond hair that he was forever pushing back and away from his eyes. Brantheim had tapped into the Germans' deep desire for prosperity, after more than ten years of slow, or even negative economic growth. And he had found a scapegoat in the European Union policies that limited German economic policy prescriptions, and tied them to the failing economies of Southern and Eastern Europe, and burdened Germans with paying for the proliferate ways of Greeks, Spaniards, and Italians. "Do you see Hans yet?" Von Kleise tried to see, but his eyes were not that good. Victoria noted he was squinting. She went to the side table, found his glasses, and handed them to him.

"Ja, there," she pointed. "Behind Willie. Do you see him?"

The speech began like any other speech by a winning candidate. The voice was calm, the cadence measured, and there were compliments to the losers in the other parties for running a clean campaign. Then suddenly, Brantheim paused, the pitch of his voice rose almost an octave, and he increased his tempo. The language became harsher, more guttural, as the speed increased.

The mass of people standing in the cold seemed to rise with the quality of the address. The camera focused on his face. He was mesmerizing, his words strong and appealing, playing to their fears and their hopes. He was to be the new savior of the German soul, liberating Germany from the guilt of the past, and leading it into a new, better tomorrow.

"He's good. Hans was right; a natural actor. Look at their faces, good! Not that bright, our Wilhelm, quite pliable and a bit naïve, but he has a natural talent as an actor. But he has studied the cadence and inflections. A natural actor, yes," Von Kleise added, looking over at Michelle, who was smiling. But Michael was worried. Add the uncertainty of what Germany, the banker for most of the European Union, would do, and the markets would collapse. But Germany was only one element in the plan; not even the most important one.

Von Kleise looked over at Michael. He could see the worry in his eyes. "He simply called for Germans everywhere to reassume their world leadership in culture, politics and economics that they had given up long ago: to the faceless bureaucrats of Brussels; to the weak-kneed and lazy French; or to the spendthrift Southern Europeans."

It was starting, Michael thought, just like it had started before. Hitler had called for nothing more than that when he had started by rejecting the restrictions imposed by the Allies, at the end of the First World War.

Brantheim called for a new path; a German path. One that was independent of kowtowing to Brussels to be sure. Michael recognized the impact would be felt, at least for now, in the financial markets in Europe. There would be a massive sell-off of sovereign debt. The ECB-backed bonds that had underpinned the recovery would quickly become worthless if Germany pulled out of the EU. The value of European companies was based largely on their access to the European marketplace, which would be put in doubt by the dissolution of the Common Market. Tariff walls would go up, and trade would grind to a halt. Germany would lose along with everyone else. The euro had been good for German trade, especially German trade into the rest of Europe. In 1990, Germany had held a 54%

share of the European market, but by 2000, just as the single currency was coming into effect in the core countries initially within the currency, it had fallen to under 40%, as a result of the Deutschmark's strength against the other countries' currencies. But by 2015, it was likely to be in the 45% range. So, pulling out of the euro made no sense for Germany. It made more sense for countries like Greece, Portugal and Spain, which would benefit from more German tourists spending euros.

"They're in a frenzy, aren't they? You can see it in their faces, Michael. Germany rising again, united and powerful … it's frightening, isn't it? But it's an illusion, you know. Still the Americans might find it good if Germany took a stronger role in helping to govern the world, rather than hiding behind post-World War II pacifism."

Michael didn't answer. Although there were few Jews left in Germany, there were millions of Turks, Slavs, and other refugees from poverty stricken countries, who had lived in Germany for generations. He didn't need a full translation to get the point. For the first time since arriving at the Oberschloss, he was frightened. Everything he saw was designed to panic already frightened financial and stock markets.

"He didn't say anything more than he had said before, but it was the way he put it this time that will shake them, especially the English and the French. He's an actor our Willie. Yes, Michelle, a great actor really, not a politician. But, of course, in your country, actors are often politicians, Michael."

Brantheim stopped speaking in German, and switched to English. He was, after all, the product of an American education: University of Chicago and then a Masters from Harvard University.

"... To America and the West, our long-time friends and allies, we say it is time that we Germans again played our historic role in the world at large. To the Russians, and those countries to our East, we offer our hand in friendship. Let us forge a new unity of purpose, to make our part of Europe the most prosperous and peaceful part of our troubled globe. To our partners in Europe, let me say that we have lived within the straitjacket of our own making. It is time to return power and responsibility to where it should rightfully and totally reside; in the sovereign governments of each and every nation on the Continent. My party's goal is to make Germany the force that it once was in the world; a force for good in the world. The world need not fear a Greater Germany, but welcome the firm hand we offer in friendship; to all who seek our help: prosperity for those nations willing to accept the German way—hard work, sacrifice, education, saving for things we want and need, rather than borrowing without hope of repayment. These are German virtues, and they have made us one of the wealthiest nations on the earth."

"You see," said Von Kleise, excited and pleased, "that is what Hans inserted in the text; the phrase," he spewed it out in German, then looked at Michael and smiled. "Greater Germany. That will scare them in Paris and London. But, Michael, don't worry. Willie is a good boy, and Germany will remain Germany, not revert to its dark past."

"When he spoke German, was the speech the same?" asked Michael.

"Yes, it was how he said it, his choice of words, and his repetition of phrases that set the crowd cheering."

Michael felt his stomach churn. Despite Von Kleise's assurances, he found the words and the picture from Berlin frightening. In little more than a week, the world had been turned upside-down. Earlier, he had learned about the Holtzs' declaration. But this change in Germany would, if unchecked, lead to the dissolution of the European Union, and the collapse of the euro. Trillions of euros and dollars would be bet on the future by hedge-fund managers, adding to global instability. Rumors of a shift in monetary policy in China and Japan had been circulating for weeks, with expectations that interest rates would rise. This, along with the Masters' Property empire woes, had led to a sudden fall in prices of homes and offices in America and Asia. Margin calls would exacerbate the sell-off in equity markets throughout the world.

Victoria turned off the set.

"Are you tired, Michael? Hungry?" Von Kleise asked him.

"More tired than hungry" Michael said, feeling very fatigued and very worried too.

"Then, perhaps we can continue our discussion tomorrow. I have some things that I would like to discuss before you leave for Paris."

"I would like that." He nodded to Von Kleise, and then followed Victoria towards the bedroom, where his bags had been placed.

"I think you will find this comfortable Dr. Ross," she suggested, showing him the room for the first time. "If you want anything, the intercom connects to Frau Bundt's room. Food is served until eleven. Good night."

Michelle waited until Ross was gone before speaking. She had her doubts about his commitment, or even willingness to take over once Heinrich was gone.

"You look worried, my dear," Von Kleise asked, noticing her look. He had seen it before, when she was displeased or worried.

"It's Michael Ross," she said, looking at her friend and lover; at the man who had rescued her, and given her purpose again. "Heinrich, he will not carry through with the plan. He'll sabotage it because he's more afraid of censure from his peers, than of doing what is right."

"What would you have me do?"

"Make Victoria and I your heirs. You don't know this girl, or what she stands for, except that she's Pyotr's daughter with your daughter Katherine. You can't trust Ross's judgment, and you don't know Natalya. He made it clear that he didn't think the status quo could be changed, or that he had any answers to the problems that have come from the gulf between vast wealth and utter poverty."

He had thought about making the girls his inheritors, but the others had balked. They no more trusted Michelle Rochard than they trusted Michael Ross, but only someone with Michael's standing and political connections could make the plan work once it began. Besides, he had at least a year before the death that had been foretold by the doctors; time enough to guide them both down the path that he and the others in the Society had chosen.

"Come," he said; standing up and reaching out his hand for her. "It's time for bed. It has been a long day and tomorrow will be longer still."

The three-room cabin had been built on the plateau, 150 feet below the main complex, to house the guards Von Kleise employed year-round to keep people away from his retreat. They were drawn from the hidden villages high in the mountains of the Swiss Valais, on the other side of the mountains from Kandersteg.

Lilly looked out from behind the bubbling pot of thick stew which she had just finished preparing. It reminded her, in many ways, of the wooden cabin where she had been born and raised. Like the Lynches of the West Virginia mountains, these men were rough, hardened by the life that they had been born into. They barely spoke, even to each other, and when they did, it was in a language all their own; Schweizerdeutsch, a dialect of old German that distinguished the Swiss Germans. She understood little, but they made their needs known using a mix of English, German and sign language.

"Beer," one of the men shouted, and glared at her while holding up his empty glass. Lilly lifted her hands from the dirty dishwater, wiped them on the grimy apron she wore from the moment that she woke up in the

meter detail was not fine enough to allow him to select the best route. He cross-checked the map with the hand-drawn diagram that the two mountain guides at the Hotel Victoria had prepared for him. Despite his bravura performance with Kim, he wasn't certain that this would be an easy climb. He had left the trail too soon in his impatience to strike out for the distant peak of the Rothorn, rather than take the longer route across the Bluemlisalpengletscher that was likely dangerous at this time of year, after a warm summer thaw, and filled with hidden crevasses. Instead, he had chosen to use the rockier outcropping that the map showed went nearly to the hanging glacier that surrounded the smaller, or lesser peak of the Rothorn, where Von Kleise had his retreat. Nor were his wounds fully healed. He felt his age of over fifty for almost the first time in his life, but he was determined to save his wife and daughter. It was the least he could do for them.

By his own calculations, they might well reach their destination by four or five o'clock in the afternoon. By that time, the sun would be starting to set, hidden behind the wall of the French and Italian Alps to the West. It would become colder, icier, and the rock walls that lay ahead would be impossible to climb without more equipment. He had scoured the shops in Bern, and in Kandersteg, but he was worried about the limited number of cams, pins, and pitons he'd managed to secure. At least, they had seat and chest harnesses, and what he judged to be enough high-tensile rope, as well as jumars and daisy chains for each of them. So, Ben reasoned, they had to hurry before the darkness and cold set in. If they didn't make it to the shelter of Von Kleise's retreat they would be forced to endure the bitter cold of the mountain. Ben had purchased lightweight, down sleeping bags and a small two-man tent at the shop in Kandersteg, but they would be a last resort. Dehydration was also a concern. They each carried two liters of water, but there was melting snow and ice that could be used if need be. But all that equipment was heavy and slowed their ascent. More people had died of dehydration, made worse by altitude, than from falling off the side of a cliff, or missing a foothold.

Kim tried to piece together the last few days as she climbed. Everything had accelerated once they had caught up with Brunner in Geneva. Masters had had to beat Brunner to within an inch of his life, but eventually, he had been willing to talk. Still, Brunner had only been able to say where he had left Beth: at Simental, in an abandoned automobile that had been conveniently left parked beside the road. At that point, Kim had had to step in to stop Masters from killing the man outright.

Then, a day later, a message had come from Turner. It had been imprecise, but had hinted that the plot itself might be directed from Switzerland. He had mentioned Von Kleise by name. Although Turner had initially laughed at Natalya's theory, when he added it all up—Latimer's meeting with Holtz; Brunner's relationship to the Von Kleise Foundation at Kandersteg; the location of the drop-off of Lilly and the girl near Kandersteg—everything pointed to Heinrich Von Kleise.

So, if Lilly and her daughter were to be found alive, then they would likely be at the Oberschloss. Where else would they have been taken, and hidden way at such short notice? She had told Turner that she was going to help Masters. Turner refused her request to participate in any rescue attempt. However, after a sleepless night, her mind was made up. She would go with Masters, even if it meant destroying her career.

"Look up there," said Ben, pointing towards what seemed to Kim an impossible distance above them. "That's where we're heading."

"Are you sure?" she asked, staring up towards the barely visible destination, already nearly exhausted from the climb up and down rocks to reach this point. They were squeezed along a narrow rock shelf. An hour before, they had jettisoned the frame pack and transferred the minimum they needed to daypacks. Masters had stashed the tent and sleeping bags in a place he assured her they could find again if they had to retreat, but she was certain it was more hope than certainty. But even this smaller pack was weighing her down. She didn't have the stamina and balance for this type of steady, uphill climbing, and it was getting progressively colder too.

Was this the place where her luck ran out? Not in a rain of bullets, but from frostbite or losing her footing and falling a hundred or a thousand feet to the icy, rocky ground below? After so many close calls, and so many people wanting her dead over the past twenty years, to die here would be ironic. Kim pushed that thought out of her mind and pressed her fingers into the small cracks along the rock face, inching her feet along the narrow, icy ledge. She could feel the steady drips of cold water that bounced off her jacket, and sometimes, fell directly on her face. Looking up momentarily, she lost her concentration and began to slip backwards, until instinct took over, and she caught herself, jamming her right hand into a small opening, and spreading her fingers to stop the fall. Her breathing peaked, and then slowed as she recovered.

"Where did you learn to climb, Ben?" she asked, finding a better hold and a wider ledge to rest on after a short, vertical climb up a mildly sloped incline. Talking, she thought, might just calm her enough to go on. She watched as he selected a flat piton from his rack of tools.

"I climbed when I was in prep school, and then in college," Masters explained. "I liked it; a kind of challenge that didn't require teamwork; just me against the rocks and heights. So, with my father's money I came to Europe, and spent several summers near Grindelwald, at the Swiss Climbing School. After Lilly and I were married, and before I became overworked, I would go climbing a couple of times a year in the west, trying my hand at the big walls in Yosemite and the Rockies."

Looking up, Kim asked, "How much further?"

"We should be close; an hour perhaps." He continued to study the objective, but there was a rocky outcropping that obstructed his view, making judging distance difficult. With great care, Ben inched forward. His eyes searched for a crack in the rock just above. He found a space just large enough to push in one of the three small, camming devices he'd purchased in Bern. Kim watched him squeeze the metal cam into the hole, lock it in place, then slip a carabineer through the wire. He snaked the rope through the carabineer and tested the small cam, which he hoped would hold him if he fell, by leaning back on the rope attached to his harness. The fixed point held. If he was lucky he could use the belay rope to allow a traverse across the rock face, by placing the soles of his boots flat on the rock, and leaning back as he tried to walk, crab-like, across the rock, until he could snag the next handhold he'd spotted, nearly ten feet to the right and slightly higher.

The boots he'd purchased for them in Bern were not the best choice for this type of wall-climbing. For the most part, the Alps were a mix of difficult-to-cross features in the rock face, with long stretches of easily traversed rock or glacier, using crampons, attachments to the boots that gripped the ice, in between. On Alpine peaks, you could be freezing cold in an instant, and then cross into open, sunny glaciers, where thermal clothing could cause heat exhaustion. They were a mix of rock, snow and ice that made choosing clothing and accessories difficult, especially as the winter months approached. But he hoped he would have enough equipment to reach his objective. Despite what he'd told Kim, he knew retreat was not a real option.

As he moved out sideways, without much support except for the tension on the line that Kim controlled from twenty feet below, he shouted commands to her. He eyed a small crack or fissure in the rock slightly to the right and a few feet higher. He wished he had taught the girl more techniques before entering this more difficult part of the ascent, for much would depend upon her concentration and skills in tightening and loosening the belay rope. Ben grabbed the rock outcropping. He'd cut the tops off the climbing gloves so he could get a good grip, but the rock was ice-cold and stung. He held tight.

Taking a lost arrow piton from his diminishing kit that hung from the harness, he hammered it into the narrow opening in the rock. Then, taking a daisy chain, a series of flat webbing footholds from his kit, he hooked a carabineer to the piton he'd just hammered in, followed by the webbing, and stepped on the lower rung to test its hold. He climbed to the top, and seeing a point to further to the right where he could place a protection, he reached for it and hammered in a copper-headed steel loop into the small fissure, hoping it would hold. Hooking one more carabineer he looked back to where Kim waited, tied in by a three-point anchor on the ledge, now nearly thirty feet below and twenty to the left of where he hung.

However, before he could get to the next wide ledge that lay just below the last seventy-five-feet ascent to the Rothorn glacier that surrounded the Oberschloss, there was a nearly vertical rock wall, thirty feet to the right and twenty feet up, that had to be crossed somehow. There was no sense in worrying about that now. He had little choice but to continue as best he could.

Ben was still standing at the top of the daisy chain, a set of webbing with foot holds in the double chains that were higher than the next. He ran the belay rope up to the newly placed protection just at the end of his reach and over to his right. When that was done, he let go of the lower protection and started to walk crab-like across the wall, using the rope to provide tension for the traverse. He shouted to Kim down below, to loosen and then tighten the belay rope to keep the tension, so he could get traction on the nearly smooth rock face. At the end of the extension, he noticed another fissure in the rock and reaching for it, he flattened his body against the rock, handing precariously from the rope while he placed a knife blade in the hard, granite of the mountain. On his traverse, Ben had noticed that she'd let the tension lapse for a bit. He suspected she'd not locked the braking device she wore on her belt. "Kim," he shouted, looking back to where she was far to the left and below. "Make sure you're anchored, and that the rope is through the brake. You can lock and unlock it to keep it taut. I'm going to have to try a pendulum to get across the next bit of rock."

Kim could sense his nervousness. "Worried?" she called up to him, trying to penetrate the incessant whine of the wind that almost howled as it vibrated on passing across the rocky inclines of the mountain.

"I'm not worried," he said, but without much confidence as he reached towards a small crack a few feet to his right. He saw two free moves after which he would be in a good place to hammer in another piton, before attempting the pendulum that might get him into a position to free-climb towards the broader ledge he'd spied from down below.

"You're watching where I'm stepping?" he asked, looking back down to where Kim waited nervously, even as he realized that she would likely have to follow the fixed rope up, if she had any chance of making it to where he ultimately wanted to be. The equipment would have to be left as he didn't expect a novice to clean the pitch as she ascended, using the two jumar devices he'd been able to procure in Bern.

Where there had once been a ledge, there was now a flat wall, about thirty feet across rising towards a ledge at least fifteen or twenty feet higher up. He could just make out a narrow chimney in the dimming light, for the sun had dipped behind the mountains in the western sky. Ben hoped this might allow a faster route up to the hanging glacier that surrounded the Oberschloss, perched as it was at the top of the Rothorn. Wind and water had carved the rock face smooth, with few obvious toe holes or handholds. Even in his prime, Masters thought, this traverse across a nearly vertical hard rock wall would have been difficult, but he had little choice but to try or to retreat down the mountain, which might be equally dangerous.

Kim, holding the belay rope, played it out through the braking device she wore on her climbing harness. If Ben fell, it would be her job to break his fall. She could hear his heavy breathing and it worried her. He was in his mid-fifties, but while the time in prison had given him time to work out, gaining upper body strength, the prison food had not appealed to him, and he'd lost more than thirty pounds in the months he'd been inside. And it had been twenty years since he'd last climbed.

Kim noticed Masters' shaking hands and that his breathing was strained; a combination of being out of shape and altitude. He was having problems, and if he had problems then so did she. If he fell or died here, then she knew, instinctively, she was lost as well. Finding her way down the mountain, in the dark, would be impossible. She would freeze to death before she made it out.

He reached a point, about twenty feet across the cliff, where there were no obvious breaks in the rock wall. He moved his free right hand, feeling for something that could hold a cam. There was a small, but seemingly solid crack that one of the last cams might fit into, and provide a firm hold for the next maneuver; a pendulum swing to the more obvious protrusions that he could see in the light of his helmet, about ten feet from where he rested. Ben placed the cam at a height at arm's length to his right. He tested the cam, depending on it to hold him as he ran back and forth across the rock face to gain height and distance out. It was another dangerous move after a series of dangerous moves, and he wondered how long his luck would last. It would be a difficult traverse, even for a more experienced and younger climber.

Kim lowered him ten feet below the anchor point, and he held onto the rope with his left hand while he ran, feet perpendicular to the rock, back and forth across the rock face. He reached for the small opening in the rock with his right hand. Finding it, he pushed the small piton he had in his hand into the crack. Then with each succeeding swing, he hammered it into the rock further. Each swing allowed only one firm blow.

On the third swing, he hooked a carabineer as he hung on the small metal pin momentarily. On the fourth, as the safety wobbled in its hole, weakened by the violent pendulum-like swings, he was able to attach the etrier to the carabineer. With a final swing, he placed his right foot into the loop of the etrier. Now, he pulled the rope through the carabineer. He was breathing very heavily.

"Once we have this thing licked, Kim" he called to her below, "there are free moves further up to the ledge." Ben said, trying to catch his breath, and maintain his confidence. The cold wind was blowing hard, adding to his fears. It would be dark soon and they needed to get to shelter before that happened.

"Do you have enough pitons?" Kim asked, staring up at Ben still hanging precariously above her. She looked back, from where they had come, and wished he would call a retreat. She watched as he pulled out two of the pitons leaving, him only one secure point on which to support his nearly 200-pound frame.

"Should be okay," he answered, looking down at the nearly empty rack on his belt where he had hung his tools. He had cleaned out the shop in Kandersteg, but he didn't know if it would be enough. He had not tried to get Kim to clean the rock face as they ascended, so it would be close. He would have her follow the fixed rope up using the jumars and daisy chains, once he was firmly in place on the higher ledge. She looked down momentarily, and then suddenly, felt the rope lurch. She tightened the rope instinctively, but six or seven feet had played out before she stopped Masters falling further. The last safety he had placed held, and he dangled precariously above her. It wasn't a long fall, and a good climber accepts falls as part of the game, but the shock had wrenched his wounded shoulder, and the shooting pain blinded him momentarily. He let out a scream. Kim's heart skipped a beat.

"Are you okay?" She tried to look up, but was afraid to move. The thin nylon cord cut into her gloves as she struggled to hold his weight.

Masters didn't answer at first. All he could hear was his own heart pounding in his chest, and the sound of his lungs sucking in air. His breathing was labored and rapid. He was too old for this nonsense, and yet had little choice now but to continue. Lilly was right: who did he think he was? Rambo?

"Let me rest a minute" Ben said finally, shoving his boot into a crack and taking some of the weight off Kim, who was struggling to hold him up.

"Take your time" she shouted through gritted teeth, as the doubts that they would survive the ordeal started to filter into her mind. However, she managed to drive those thoughts away. So much of her life had been a risk, and yet she had made it to her forties; an accomplishment that as a homeless eleven year old on the streets of Bangkok, had seemed far, far away.

"Stupid mistake, stupid mistake" she heard Masters mumbling, over and over again.

Michael looked at his watch. It was Sunday, four o'clock in the afternoon.

"I think I should be leaving," Michael said, wondering how he might make it to Paris in time to get some sleep. They had spent the day discussing the issues that plagued the world. Michael was tired of hearing the repetition of the litany of problems: from the poverty of nearly five billion humans, to the deteriorating environment and global political paralysis that made it impossible to do anything about stopping further deterioration.

"I can't let you go just yet."

"But I have to be in Paris by tomorrow morning."

"There are things that we still must talk about," said Von Kleise.

"What more can I say? I can't solve the world's problems. No one can. God knows I've tried, but damn it; it's beyond what anyone, or any country can do alone."

"We have other things to discuss." Von Kleise said, and then added as an afterthought. "The meetings you are going to will likely be cancelled. By tomorrow, the world's economists will have far more on their plate than simply another discussion of a forecast that will, by then, be out of date. I suggest that you listen carefully to what I now say." There was ice in his tone of voice. The kind, grandfatherly presence that Michael knew had evaporated, and he was left with the cold, hard business executive, intent on making his captive listen closely to what he was offering. Michael was a mass of nerves, realizing that not only was he at the epicenter of the problem, but that he was also powerless to stop the inevitable. The long-awaited crash of the financial markets was about to begin. It was Sunday evening here, but already Monday in Asia, and the resultant panic was setting in motion a chain of events that no one nation, government or institution could avert.

"Did you fully understand the significance of the Phoenixjahr pledge, Michael?"

"I think I did. You were pledged to change the world. There's nothing unique about that, Heinrich. The only difference I can see is that you and your classmates actually set out to do just that. But do you fully understand what you've started, and can you be sure that you can make this disaster for the world economy turn out to be something positive?"

"You see, Steiner believed in the goodness of man, and naively assumed that humans are free of greed. Machte, on the other hand, was a realist, and recognized that to achieve harmony, a few good young men of ability should enter into a compact to do good with their lives. But in order to accomplish this, they had to first achieve great wealth and power. His charge then to our group was not the usual valedictory speech: not to sacrifice all at the start for humankind, but rather to become wealthy and powerful, so that when society faced its greatest challenges, our great wealth and position could be put to use for the greater good.

"Machte recognized that the competitive model would be stretched to breaking point by changes in human productivity, that made much of what passed for physical labor obsolete, thus fewer jobs and less pay would lead to the demise of the capitalist system, in much the same way that Marx had envisioned that capitalism, or better called human greed, sowed the seeds of its own destruction. On the night of our induction into the Society of the Phoenix, he told us what would happen over the next fifty years. He was a visionary." Von Kleise paused, remembering the dim light of that ceremony, held in the ancient ruins of an old tomb from ages past.

"Millions of jobs would be lost, replaced by technology, and third-world labor would be exploited only for its low cost and willingness to endure poor conditions, with no real prospect of advancement from poverty. Unless countries and companies could learn to cooperate and manage this transformation, then the global economy would slow to a crawl and everyone would lose. However, in a way, he had absorbed Steiner's thinking, because Steiner believed that only through the strength of the community working together could mankind prosper, and survive the disasters that were coming in the next millennium.

"You know, as well as I do, that without cooperation, economies will collapse under the weight of the mistakes that markets make, in the allocation of income and wealth. With so much wealth concentrated in the wrong hands—those without a shred of social decency—the global economy can no longer prosper and grow."

"And what will replace competition?"

"A new model, Michael; one built on cooperation rather than competition, where profits and shareholder value are less important than social stability and steady employment. A world where companies do useful things, and governments have compassion and help those left behind by the pace of technological change; where companies can do well at the same time. The goal must be full employment of all human potential, not just those smarter or better connected than others. If we are successful, then this model will ensure continuous and balanced growth, without destroying the world on which we all depend. There are enough resources to meet the challenge of poverty and the rising middle class in developing nations, but we must be creative; we must invest in new materials and new modalities; we must not be wedded to the next quarter's results, but to the longer-term health of the company, and the global super-economy in which it operates."

"What of the shareholders? Won't they be upset?"

"Stock markets are no longer the efficient places to raise capital for industry; rather they have become a new form of gambling. They draw in the middle class, promising ever-greater wealth from markets that never retreat or falter. Wealth is not created that rapidly. The best the world economy can grow at is about 3%, and that growth rate is rarely achieved. And those self-proclaimed Masters of the Universe, the Wall Street traders and mutual fund managers, are like vampires, living off the ebb and flow of the market, but contributing little to the welfare of the world at large. It was easy to harness their greed, by providing them with inside information, which they are now dependent on." Von Kleise smiled, thinking about how those sheep were being led to their own slaughter. "Tomorrow, you'll see the result. Cut loose from having to think for themselves, they will be impotent in the face of a tectonic shift in the way markets work. They'll panic and sell. The sell orders are piling up now on the basis of our last email to our loyal members of the Phoenix Group. And their paper fortunes will evaporate."

He paused, studying Michael's face for clues as to how these arguments were being received. He knew that deep down in Michael's soul these radical ideas were also his own, long suppressed by a more conventional route to the top of his profession, but they were there all the same. Somewhere, there was the young man that Heinrich had known, who had once preached the idea of cooperative growth rather than competitive destruction, to promote economic growth.

He had moved on in his thinking, putting that thought of cooperation away for some time. It was the dream of an idealist, but Michael had lost his idealism once he had started to move up through academic ranks, and later, into the highest reaches of government. He had become stuck in the conventional wisdom that saw government as helping the people, and the private sector as unable to separate its own need for profits from doing the greater good for its employees, or the country as a whole.

"No one will win if we let it all unravel. Everyone loses: the rich, the poor, and especially the middle class. You're playing with fire."

Michael felt under attack, and yet the ideas were not foreign to his ears. He had often, in the quiet of his office, had these same thoughts, but had feared voicing them. It was a brave economist that argued against the conventional wisdom of the profession. But it was true that the greater problems of the world would never be solved, so long as the competitive model that revered profits and penalized companies for doing what was right for broader society, continued.

"Have you ever wondered, Michael, why I have cultivated your friendship over the years?"

"I have wondered, Heinrich." In truth, it had flattered his ego when he was a younger man, while also making him question whether he deserved the attention.

"You had ideas, new ways of thinking about the world back then. It was refreshing. A rich man always gets people who hang on him. You didn't behave like that. And when you showed up with my granddaughter, then I knew for certain that you and Natalya were the natural heirs to my legacy."

"Natalya? Your granddaughter? Katherine's child," Michael said surprised.

"Natalya is Pyotr's daughter by my daughter Katherine. Hardly the most responsible mother to the girl, wouldn't you say?"

"Then Natalya doesn't know?" Ross asked.

"No, at least she didn't when you came to Kandersteg in the summer. But now, perhaps she does know. Francis Turner certainly knows. Pyotr always believed it was better to tell her that her mother had died."

"Didn't you want to meet your granddaughter before now?"

"Of course, but I understood that Natalya needed to develop her own life, without being burdened with a rich relative. She has made her own way in the world. And now, Natalya is one of a kind: intelligent, resourceful, trained in business, statecraft and war, and with a will of iron. You are a lucky man, Michael."

There were footsteps in the hall. Michael looked, as did Von Kleise, to the door where Victoria Carter stood silently watching.

"Is it time?"

"It's five o'clock," she said softly.

"Come, Michael" Von Kleise said, reaching down and helping Ross up. "It's time that you met the real members of the Society of the Phoenix, not the ceremony of Machte, although a few were from my class and the one before, but the others who have pledged an equal devotion to doing what's right for the world, rather than what is profitable, or in the interests of a small collection of already super-wealthy individuals."

So, Michael thought, not everyone who was at the formal ceremony that had been performed with great pomp and circumstance earlier, were the true members of the group, responsible for the mayhem that was about to be unleashed on the world.

Paul Thommen handed Natalya the night-vision glasses, and he pointed further up the sheer rock face ahead and above them.

"Up there. Do you see him?"

She could just make out a man looking down at them.

"Who is he?"

"One of the farmers from the Valais that Von Kleise has paid to guard the approaches to the Oberschloss. They're armed and I suspect they'll attack us if we get too close."

"How much longer to go, Paul?" She looked up at the rock face that still had to be scaled.

"We have an hour, perhaps less, to go."

"It's getting dark." She could hardly see the variation in the rock face in the dimming light.

"Are you afraid?" he asked, then added under his breath, "because you should be." They were getting into the most dangerous part of the ascent when their bodies were at their weakest, and the darkness and the cold were setting in.

All day, as they had climbed, Thommen had become increasingly infatuated with Natalya. She was a natural climber with no uncertainty in her choice of handholds and her placement of safeties. They had chosen a less-used route up the Blumlisalp Rothorn, and although steeper, it was more direct.

Thommen traversed the nearly vertical rock face, with Natalya acting as his safety. He looked back and watched her pick her own way following his lead, cleaning the unneeded tools from the rock, even before he'd stopped placing safeties further up the route, in a show of speed-climbing that even impressed him. Stopping before a difficult pitch, he pulled out the map and studied it. He'd marked their path up the mountain in red. From where they rested, there remained 1,000 feet of altitude and about a half mile of distance, before they reached the tongue of the glacier that lay just below the final rock pinnacle, where the Oberschloss was sited.

"We have to hurry." Natalya said, as she reached the ledge where he stood. "I don't like the look of those clouds." The storm clouds were coming in from the south, over the Italian Alps. The wind was already picking up.

"We will be there before it gets too dark," Thommen promised. Natalya could tell though by the tone of his voice that he was worried.

She was thinking about the Swiss guards. "What if they shoot?" she asked.

"You've used a gun, correct?" he asked. "So I assume you know how to use it." Thommen the reached up, finding a fingerhold, and pulling himself up sent cascades of smaller stones down the side. Finding his footing again, he caught his breath. His breathing was noisy and uneven, and his arms felt like rubber. He let the lactic acid drain out and waited for his muscles to recover. Natalya waited below, anxious to follow, and getting colder by the minute in the icy wind.

Ben almost puked as he finally pulled himself over the ledge. The final climb from where he'd fallen, the replacement of safeties, and the ensuing series of traverses, using tension moves and shorter, less dangerous pendulums up a slightly different pitch than he'd tried before, had taken everything out of him. Still, he was pleased that he had done it, despite the odds. They had been climbing now for nearly nine hours: four since leaving the well-used trail to the Blumlisalpenhutte. But now he sat, his back against the cold, wet rock, heaving, but satisfied. These last two traverses had been the most difficult ones, and he doubted looking around at the rock wall that lay just behind him, that there was anything like that up ahead. There was a narrow chimney rose almost 100 feet to another ledge closer to the glacier that could be easily climbed.

However, it was nearly all vertical and he was at the end of his endurance. His arm, not fully healed from the bullet wound, was killing him, but they had no choice but to continue on, and hope that once they were over the top, there would be some shelter against a rock where they could rest for the night.

"Are you okay, Ben?"

He didn't answer, not at first. She waited while trying to see if she could duplicate his feat. She doubted she could. He looked down to where Kim waited anxiously. In a daze, he watched as she began to cross.

"As you pass, try to clean the face. We may need those pitons and carabineers further up." Ben called down.

"I'm ..." She choked on the next words, and looked down. Below, there seemed an endless drop. One foot slipped free and she panicked. It took a moment to control her foot and find the toe hold again.

"Push the jumar up along the rope, and pull it down to lock and get a handhold," Ben explained as she made the ascent. "You can do it."

"My arms, Ben, they're ..." She stopped, unable to cough out the words.

"We have to keep going, Kim, or we'll die here, so crank!"

She cranked the jumar along the rope, using it as the handhold, as her feet fought for tiny imperfections in the rock for support. Slowly, she threaded her way across the rock face, suspended only by steel and nylon roping, with her legs most of the time fighting to find even miniscule placements.

"I hope you did a good job of getting these into the rock," she said, suddenly realizing that her life was tied to each of these steel nails hammered into the hard rock.

"Not a single Masters building has ever collapsed. Think of that, Kim," he said, as she approached the ledge. He reached down and pulled her up. She lay prone for what seemed hours, but it was only minutes.

"Let's have something to eat and drink. We deserve that at least."

"I can't," she said, and still breathing hard, looked up at the fading light above.

"It'll be easy from here. The chimney's narrow, but passable." Ben said, looking over to where there was a narrow opening in the wall.

"Don't tell me about it now."

There was something wrong. Lilly sensed it in Urs's voice. One of the guards had come back, said something in Swiss German, and Urs had tensed. When the man left, Urs had pushed back his chair roughly. Standing with a grunt, he looked around. Earlier, she had taken food into Beth, whose fever had returned. She had pleaded with Urs to leave her daughter alone, but to no avail.

"Is there trouble?" Lilly asked.

"No," Urs said standing up suddenly. "Climbers. Too close."

"Climbers, here?" asked Lilly surprised, but hopeful too.

"Post signs, but foreigners not read German, get lost, and some die. Mountains dangerous."

"Are you going?" she asked.

"There's time. Still far away," said Urs coming closer, unbuttoning his shirt as he approached her. She backed away, almost touching the hot soup pot on the stove. He reached and pulled her close.

"Maybe husband coming for you?" he laughed.

Urs touched her face, pushing back her golden hair, lifting her chin so that her mouth opened instinctively.

"Maybe I kill him. You like that? Yes?"

Lilly felt for the knife on the table behind her. Urs tried to kiss her. His breath was foul, a mixture of sharp cheese, potatoes, onions, and gherkins. She gagged. He slid his hands possessively down her back.

"I kill you one day?" he joked as he reached his hand under her skirt. His hand, used to getting exactly what he wanted, cradled her, and then he shoved two thick fingers inside her. The attack startled her. She pushed against his chest with her hands, but to no avail. He pulled her closer, almost suffocating her. Lilly reached for the knife, then without thinking about the consequences, she slid it up underneath his ribs. The sharp, long, blade cut easily through the soft tissue piercing the diaphragm, and she didn't stop until it reached his heart.

Urs didn't react at first. He then shoved her away, but the knife remained embedded in him. She watched, in a dream, as he weakened, collapsing onto both knees blood coming out of his mouth, and then fell with a thud to the floor, driving the knife even deeper into his body.

The sound of Urs's fall woke old Hans who came running out the room. He looked at them both and screamed at her. Instinctively Lilly knelt down next to where Urs lay, pulled the revolver from his belt and fired three shots into the old man. He fell next to Urs.

Lilly now went to where Beth lay. Her daughter was burning up with fever, and was delirious.

As she sat there, trying to remember what she could do to bring the fever down, memories of Beth as a child dominated her thoughts. She recalled, with tears running down her face, the child's first steps, her first words. How had the sweet little girl turned into the out of control teenager with a foul mouth and a bitter hatred for them.

Thommen and Natalya had reached a narrow ledge about six feet below the glacier that surrounded the Blumlisalpen Rothorn. The guard's hut sat on the glacier, back towards the rocky outcrop where the Oberschloss had been built 100 feet higher up. Thommen pulled himself up carefully over the top only to drop back down, almost falling off the ledge as two gunshots pierced the eerie grey of the late afternoon with its swirling clouds of light snow.

The rock shattered just above Natalya's head, sending shards of stone and ice flying over them. Two more shots followed from a different direction, but the second guard was well out of range.

"There are two of them," Thommen said, pressing himself against the rock wall. He pulled out a flexible night scope, snaked it up over the top, and studied the image in the small eyepiece. Natalya looked up. She couldn't see anything but the grey clouds.

"Did you hear that?" Natalya asked, hearing three muffled gunshots in the distance coming from a different direction.

Thommen nodded. He had not expected the guards to shoot to kill. He opened his pack and removed the two disassembled marksman's rifles. He screwed the barrels to the carefully machined gunstocks, and checked that the ten rounds were properly loaded. Finally, he snapped the night-vision telescopic scopes into place, complete with their laser range and target finders.

He handed her the first rifle.

"Good luck, Paul. Be careful."

"A kiss for good luck?" he smiled hopefully. Despite his bravado, he was scared.

Natalya leaned towards him, kissing him lightly on the cheek.

"I'm, of course, disappointed," he said smiling.

"Go!"

Thommen didn't waste a moment. Pulling himself up over the top, he rolled away and flattened his body against the ice. Another volley of shots hammered the rock just above Natalya's head, forcing her back to the lower shelf. She took a second clip from the pack, and shoved it into the outside pocket of her coat, before hooking the sling around her left arm, and pulling herself up over the top. Rolling away in an opposite direction from which Thommen had rolled, she saw a small, low outcropping of rocks, twenty feet away. Standing up in a low crouch, she ran towards the rocks as a hail of bullets hit the ice all around her.

The Hermit slid out further onto the ice of the glacier, breathing a sigh of relief when he'd heard no shots fired in his direction. Unlike Natalya, who was safely behind a rock outcropping, Thommen had no cover, and continued to press his body flat against the ice. Turning his head slightly, he could see Natalya trading shots with one of the guards hidden behind a cable-car pylon.

The bullet that drove Thommen back came from another direction. It sliced through his shoulder, shattering the bone. There was little blood, only pain. Thommen was spun around on the ice, shouting "Natalya" loudly, before collapsing with his back pressed against the hard-packed ice.

The cold dulled the throb in his shoulder. He pointed the rifle and fired towards where the shot had come from. There was an immediate return of fire. A second shot hit him in the leg. He saw a glint of metal in the distance, another flash, and then the sound. The sniper was behind another one of the pylons. It would be a difficult shot even if he were not wounded. But he was fading fast. The sensation of pain added a new dimension to the challenge. But before he could fire, he saw Natalya stand up, oblivious to the danger, and fire two quick, accurate shots at the guard on the pylon, her angle better than his. The Hermit watched as the man fell twenty feet to the rocky surface below the tower.

Still standing, she ran, zigzagging, towards where Thommen lay, almost motionless on the ice. Two more shots bracketed her as she ran. The Koslov training overcame her fear, and dropping to her knees, she steadied the rifle wrapping the grip around her forearm, and sighted it in the direction the other shots had come from. I came this far, she thought, as she waited for the man to show himself. I'm not destined to die here. She fired, now spreading her shots slightly. The first missed, but the second yielded a short yell, and then the body fell ten feet to the snow below, at a distance of around 300 feet from where she had fired.

"You're badly hurt," Natalya said, studying Thommen's wounds.

"Leg's not bad; the shoulder's a mess," he reported, as pain shot up from the damaged knee, causing him to nearly double over. "I'll be okay, Natalya," he said through gritted teeth. He was bleeding, the stain coloring the icy snow that lay on top of the glacier.

"Not unless I get you help."

He smiled weakly, knowing there was nothing she could do to get him help.

In the distance, Natalya saw the cabin. It was only about a half a kilometer away, across a relatively flat stretch of snowy ground. Before she could move him, however, she had to stop the bleeding. Below, with the packs, was the first-aid kit that Thommen had packed.

"I'm going to go back down for the kit."

"Don't leave, Natalya." Thommen said, his strength fading. He reached out for her, but she moved away.

"I'll be back." She backed over the edge, and missing the first toe hold she fell almost five feet, her hands fighting for grips as she slid on the icy rock wall. When her foot touched the ledge, she realized that she was more than ten feet from where they had left the packs and the rock here was crumbly and icy. Slowly and deliberately, she inched along the narrow ledge towards the packs.

"There's someone up there, Ben," said Kim. She'd seen a face stare down at them and then move away and she'd heard the rifle shots some distance away. There was only twenty-five feet left to climb before reaching the plateau.

"I don't see anyone."

"I saw a face up there." She pointed towards where the ice hung over the edge of the rock face.

"There's no going back," Ben said, looking back at Kim. She was uncharacteristically frightened, but what choice had they but to go on?

She tried to concentrate, but her mind pictured death in this cold place, hanging from a rope, freezing to death, unable even to cut the rope and die quickly.

Urs had placed Yan at the Eastern approach to the Oberschloss, because the route up to the plateau was almost impossible. Only an experienced and well-prepared climber could traverse the gap and reach the glacier from that side. In the six years that Urs had been in charge of the defense of the Oberschloss, no one had arrived from the east side. Most had simply followed the glacier up, and then had been shooed away by the signs, and occasionally, by the guards. Most of the climbers were just lost, having missed the route that led up to the true summit of the Blumlisalp.

Yan was the youngest and least experienced of the men. Thus when he had seen someone just down below, he had hesitated to shoot. He had skied back in the direction of the cabin, but had stopped when he saw Detter coming towards him in a rush.

"There's someone below," yelled Yan as he approached.

"On the eastern side?" said Detter, amazed. "You're imagining things."

Detter heard shots coming from the cabin. He looked towards the house, a half kilometer away with surprise. Then there was the sound of a second set of shots coming from the western approach. He could see the other guard shooting towards the rocky ledges below. It was a moment of crisis.

"If anyone comes out of that hole," he pointed to where the chimney opened onto the hanging glacier where the house stood, they are likely to be armed and dangerous. Shoot them!"

A cold wind blew down the valley of the Kander from the north. Yan shivered. Far off in the distance he could see heavy storm clouds coming in from the west. The first snow had arrived early this year, leaving the glacier covered with a thick snow blanket.

Yan hefted the rifle over his shoulder, and with a quick kick, freed his skis that had frozen in icy snow. He looked towards the eastern side of the plateau, back towards where the rock chimney lay partially hidden, and he waited.

Thommen now pressed his wounded shoulder against the ice, letting the cold slow the blood and ease the pain. He looked back to where Natalya had disappeared. Twisting around, he looked up towards the Oberschloss, which lay up another almost vertical incline of rock and ice. With his wounds, a climb would be impossible. Two guards had been killed, or badly wounded, but there would be others waiting. He held the rifle in both hands, but found it difficult to focus.

"Should I kill you now or later?" said Detter in Swiss German. Thommen felt the rifle against the base of his skull.

"Why kill me?" Thommen answered in. "I'll die from the cold anyway. Leave me. Why add my blood to your sins."

"You came alone?"

"Yes," Thommen lied, trying to turn over to see who was there.

"You're lying. I heard two shots from different directions."

"Prove it." Thommen twisted around, a shooting pain in his arm causing him to gasp for breath, but at last, he could see the man's face.

Detter stood back. Still pointing his weapon at the wounded man, he moved around so that he could face him and see what he was hiding. He had seen no weapon.

"You have a weapon?"

Thommen pushed the rifle way. It slid across a patch of ice.

"Any others?" Detter asked, looking towards where the rifle waited.

"Are you going to kill me, or help me?"

Detter was in a quandary. Herr Von Kleise would not be pleased by the visitor, but none of Urs's men were natural killers. He could rationalize killing an injured man, and yet, if left alive, he would tell tales. He thought of the women in the hut. What they would say? No, this man could not be allowed to live.

"I'm not going to help you or kill you," he stated "but accidents happen." Thommen felt the boot against his shoulder. He winced in pain, but found himself helpless to stop sliding on the icy surface back towards the rim. The edge was close. Dropping his weapon, Detter began to push Thommen towards the cliff.

Natalya heaved herself over the edge. She didn't see Thommen at first, but heard the thump of a boot against a solid object. She was thirty feet from where Thommen lay in obvious distress. Natalya watched in horror as a man stood over him, and then reached down and rolled him towards the edge. Twisting the rifle off her shoulder, Natalya fired three carefully aimed shots. Detter spun around and fell back. As he dropped, he knocked into Thommen, causing the agent's body to slide over the edge as Natalya ran towards him. In a rage, Natalya kicked the wounded Detter over the edge after him. Sobbing, she knelt looking down, at the two broken bodies barely visible in the snow below.

Wiping away her tears, she stood up, and looking towards the house, shouldered her weapon and started towards the cabin.

Yan pressed his sight almost against his eye and waited. He was cold, shivering in his thin coat, and his bladder was full. How many were there? He had seen one, but there could be an army waiting. He had heard shots from the other side, but in the gathering darkness and the swirling, wind-driven snow, he saw nothing.

The hat came first, and then the head, but it quickly disappeared. Yan drew the rifle up to his eye and sighted on the spot. He had two magazines, twenty shots. He fired two shots. They'd been warned, he thought. Let them go back down.

"There's someone up there" Masters said pulling back. "Not too friendly either."

"Damn!"

"You have a weapon?"

"In my backpack if I can get to it." She slid down a few feet, freed the pack, and removed the Uzi submachine gun that the guards at the Embassy in Bern had reluctantly lent her. It was only effective at a short distance.

"You stay down there," he ordered, taking the protective role.

"I'll think about it." She waited a minute more, before swinging herself up over the top, and rolling away. Three more shots rang out, each one missing. Kim could hear the bullets ping against the rocks, giving her the direction of the guard. As she was moving, she saw Masters climb over the top, then roll to the other side. Two more shots were fired in quick succession, but these were aimed at Masters.

"Keep him busy." Kim yelled, as she zigzagged towards the sniper.

Yan had seen two people come over the top, but now he could only see one. He kept firing, but in his panic, his aim was off, and he missed what should have been an easy shot. He was just starting to reload when Kim suddenly came up on him. She didn't give him the option of surrender, unloading the entire magazine into the boy's body. He was dead almost immediately, his head having been blown clear off his body by the force of the shells.

"There could be others," Masters warned.

"Perhaps." Kim looked towards where there was smoke in the distance as she reloaded. "But we'll have to take our chances. We'd better find some shelter. It's beginning to snow, and I'm fuckin' freezing."

Lilly dragged the bed to the main room, setting it before the fire. Beth's fits and shivering were worse. She was frightened the girl would die. She added logs, pushing up the temperature in the drafty hut, but still the girl shivered. Taking a wash rag, she bathed Beth's head and body, desperate to bring her temperature down.

Holding Beth to her, feeling the heat through her cloths, she wondered what dreams her daughter was she having. It was a nightmare for them both. She smoothed her daughter's hair back, while trying to remember a song from her childhood. She heard the door open and felt the immediate draft of the cold outside air on her back. Her immediate reaction was to reach for the Urs' gun, but it was across the room, on the table where she had dropped it.

"Who are you?" Lilly looked up and stared. But it wasn't one of the returning guards. It was a woman.

"Natalya Avramowitz," she answered, pushing back the hood and shaking out her dark hair.

Lilly could see the rifle against her back, a coiled climbing rope lay across her chest, and her jacket ripped on one side with the insulation hanging loosely. She watched, almost detached from the scene, as the woman stripped off the coat.

"Your name?" asked Natalya sharply, as she set her the pack down. She was tired and upset by Paul's death. She recognized the woman from the pictures she had seen in the press, and from what Paul had told her.

"Lillian Masters."

"Ben Masters' wife?"

"Yes."

Lilly stood up, letting go of her daughter. She tried to smooth down her skirt, but then gave up. Pushing her hair away from her face, she stared at Natalya.

"And the girl?" asked Natalya looking at the young woman, who was obviously very sick, lying on the bed set in front of the fire.

"My daughter," answered Lilly, looking over at Beth and wondering if she would live. She was sick from the cold and the sores, the beatings that Urs and the others had administered.

"She's ill?"

"She has a high fever." Lilly looked at Beth who suddenly let out a short scream as if some demon had attacked her in her delirium.

"There must be medicine for a fever. Did you look for a first-aid kit?"

"I didn't look," said Lilly ashamed. Of course, there would be something for a fever. "I've been bathing her head."

Natalya walked out of the room and over towards the kitchen area. Behind a counter she found a small first-aid kit. Opening it up, there were vials of penicillin, and the high strength aspirin suppositories favored by Swiss doctors. Taking the penicillin and the suppositories, she went back to where the woman sat next to the girl.

"Turn her over," she ordered, coming closer and taking a good look at the girl. She was sick and damaged. Whatever they had done to her had not been nice or kind. She had been used, that was clear. Natalya tore open the heavy aluminum wrapping of the suppository as Lilly turned her daughter over. Pushing back the blanket, she saw the damage that the week had done. Beth's backside was bruised and swollen. Her anus had puss and blood oozing out. She emitted a putrid odor, and her skin was hot to the touch. She would need help soon if she were to live.

"This is a suppository. It should bring down the fever. You can use one every three or four hours."

She inserted the small, white pellet until she was certain that it was in. Then carefully she helped Lilly turn Beth back over.

"You've been giving her water?"

Lilly nodded. She had been trying, but Beth had spit out half of what she took in.

"These are penicillin tablets. Give her three now. In four hours, give her two more. Then again, four hours later." She handed Lilly the tablets. Looking at her watch, she saw that it was now close to eight o'clock. It was dark, and the snow was getting heavier, and the wind more intense.

"She'll need help."

"She needs to be in a hospital." Lilly said, looking at this savior with a strange sense that she, like the woman who had rescued them in Thailand, was an angel.

"I'll try to climb to the Oberschloss. From there, we can get back down to Kandersteg and a hospital." Natalya went to the door.

There was a blank look on Lillian Master's face.

"Keep her as cool as you can. I'll be right back." Natalya grimaced as she pulled on the jacket. She had hurt her arm when she had rolled away from the gunshots and now, freed from the constraints of the coat, it throbbed. Lifting the rope and shouldering her pack, she went out into the cold.

The narrow beam of light from her headlamp was reflected back by the falling snow. She had gone only about 30 feet when the hopelessness of attempting the climb now, in this weather, and in the darkness, overcame her urgency to get the girl help. It would be suicide to attempt the climb until morning. She turned back, reaching the hut with some difficulty. Natalya pushed open the door, and then slammed it shut behind her.

"We'll have to pray for your daughter," she said to Lilly, "and hope she'll last until morning."

Standing by the open fire, she looked at this shell of what had once been a great woman. Whatever the altruistic motives of her grandfather, the destruction of a human being, even one as vain as Lillian Masters, was unforgivable.

The storm, by the standards of ones later in the season, was a small one, but for Masters and Kim, now roped together, it was frightening. The cold, blowing snow limited visibility to no more than a few feet, and the hut they had seen before the snow started was completely obscured. It had seemed like they had been walking for hours. All Kim could think about was how many people had died on Everest in weather like this, often only feet from their tents. She was frightened that if they didn't find the cabin, they would either freeze to death, or be buried in the snow until the spring thaw, or fall over the edge of the glaciered plateau.

"Are you certain of the direction, Ben?"

"Fuck, I'm not certain of anything."

"Great!"

"If you know so damn much then why don't you take the lead."

"I don't have the foggiest idea where we're going."

"Shut the flashlight off." Once, in a fog, she'd found it easier to drive with the low lights than the high. "We may be better off without it."

Masters looked at the compass, shining the light on it to check the reading. He had taken a reading before it became too dark and the storm too violent. They were roughly heading in the right direction, but how far they were from the cabin was anyone's guess.

"We should be close" he said, more to buck up his failing courage than anything else.

"Let's keep going," she suggested, as she stamped her feet and hugged her torso. She started to walk, and Ben caught up, and then forged ahead of her.

He looked down at the compass again. He pointed. Taking a few steps forward, he rammed into a wall. He fell backwards. Kim jumped out of the way.

Masters, laughing, almost crying, lay on the ground.

"Close the damn door," Natalya ordered looking up at Masters and the CIA agent. They stood in the doorway, shaking the snow from their clothes, thankful to be alive. Then, almost as an aside, she added, "What took you so long?"

35. 1600 PENNSYLVANIA AVENUE

The President slipped into the chair, stretched out his legs, and listened to the end of Harley Mumford's long-winded reply to a simple "yes or no" question from the Secretary of the Treasury. To the President's eyes, Mumford looked like an overstuffed pig. The Chairman of the Council for Economic Advisers was hardly the smartest guy in Washington, but with Michael Ross out of contact, the President needed all the help he could get.

"Thought I'd come over and see what you have has come up with," the President said, with some irony. He didn't really have much trust that they could find a path through the minefield. From the CEA Chairman's window, the President could see the White House bathed in lights.

"We were just discussing how best to handle Monday morning, Mr. President," a flustered Mumford said, hating informal discussions with the President.

"Go on, go on," said the President, motioning with his hands as he looked around the room.

Fritz Schurz, the acting Chairman of the Federal Reserve Board, was the youngest in the room at just thirty-eight. He had been recommended by one of the President's key political contributors, Richard Kahn. Kahn was a "trader" with a trader's instinct about how markets moved. He'd made a fortune buying low and selling high; everything from hogbacks to entire companies. Seated next to Schurz, was the Treasury Secretary Bradford Stevens. He was a solid performer, but lacked vision. The CIA Director had also been invited. He fidgeted nervously, as if he'd rather be thinking of his lakeside retirement in Minnesota than the impending collapse of the global economy. Francis Turner, the Special Deputy Director for Economic Intelligence, sat next to the Director feeding him advice.

The only one missing was Michael Ross. They'd been trying to contact him since Friday, and it was now Sunday. He had never reached his hotel in Paris on Saturday evening. The FBI had contacted the Swiss and French intelligence agencies, but so far neither had a clue as to his whereabouts.

By Saturday, after the Masters bankruptcy papers had been filed late on Friday, there were fears that property values on commercial real estate would collapse. The banks would be screwed as collapsing real-estate prices would put their commercial loans underwater. And with the cancellation of the developing world debt, there was no hope for the economy, without a miracle. Another 2007–8 type bailout was impossible given the fiscally conservative Congress. Then, in Germany, Brantheim's speech had set off alarm bells, particularly throughout Europe. No one was quite sure what he had meant by the term "Greater Germany," but it was eerily similar to the one that Hitler had used in 1933, before seizing the government and disbanding the parliament. The President doubted that Brantheim was a Nazi or another Hitler, but he had not voiced much confidence in the euro, or in remaining in the European Union. With German support for the euro in doubt, there would be panic on European markets when they opened later that evening. Oil prices had jumped, as the less secure Arab states teetered on the brink of a second "Spring" revolution. The final straw was the walkout in Asian and US West coast ports, which had now stopped global trade physically in its tracks.

"This is the one-way elevator to the basement, Mr. President," the CEA Chairman answered, with the dramatic flair of the one-time thespian he had been at Yale. "I've gotten five calls today from the CEOs of the largest banks, asking if we were prepared to bail them out. I don't think we can avoid another credit crunch."

"Brad and I are in agreement, Mr. President," Schurz said, his voice honey smooth as he tried to dissuade the President from action. A graduate of the Chicago School of Economics, along with the new Chinese Central Bank Chairman and the new Minister of Finance in Japan, he saw inflation and the devaluation of currency as worse than the lack of economic growth and joblessness. He had not supported Bernanke's quantitative easing, and had voiced concerns about the Fed's nearly three-trillion-dollar balance sheet. "It'd be a waste to pump too much money into the economy, until we see what falls out from these disturbances. It's too early to tell if this won't correct itself once the dust clears, and markets have a chance to reflect."

"And why the hell not pump in some liquidity, if only to show our support for the US economy? If what Brad says is right, then we'll need it to keep the economy running," the President asked, looking squarely at the Fed Vice Chairman.

"Because it would send a signal to the financial markets that we are giving in to short-term pessimism. It'd be counterproductive," Schurz answered, looking directly at the President. "And it'd be too much money chasing too few goods."

The President shook his head in wonder at this economic gibberish. The last time he'd checked, US manufacturing capacity utilization was just 70%. And then there were the shuttered factories in China, India, and elsewhere in Asia, that were happy to ramp up again if this were true. There was a hell of a lot of room for growth without inflation. And there were millions of unemployed, poorly educated workers that could be employed if the private sector got off its ass and trained them, rather than complained and blamed Government.

"I don't believe this is all coincidence. Any idea who's behind this and why?" the President asked, turning to look at the Director of the Central Intelligence Agency, in order to get away from more economic gibberish.

"I think we have covered these points in briefings over the past year and a half. They're not new and they don't require a conspiracy to explain. The Chinese economy needed some discipline in its lending practices. We've been pushing to sell grain to the Japanese market for years. The third-world debt question has been ignored for so long that it's hardly surprising that it's come to a head just now. And in Russia, the reemergence of the factions, once the long-term leader had left the country, was also expected. As for the Germans, it's more surprising that they put up with kowtowing to that cabal of thieves in Brussels for so long. The only thing that has really come as a shock to me, and which worries me the most, is the trans-Pac dock strike. That will send tremors through more than one market, you can count on that, Mr. President."

The President was impressed. He thought the Director had been napping. As it was, he spoke with his eyes partially closed. Looking at his watch, the President stifled a yawn. It was late, and none of them were likely to get much sleep.

"What about Germany?" the Secretary of State asked. "Doesn't that frighten the piss out of you, John?"

"I've met Willie twice: a fine young man, a good heart, hardly the stuff of horror stories. And he's no Hitler, Mr. President, be assured of that."

"Germany's been barely growing for years, tied as it is to the rest of Europe," Francis Turner answered. "They need new blood and new thinking, too, for their export-led growth is failing now that more countries are moving to protect their dwindling manufacturing sectors. Despite the hype about German workers being the best, and their middle-sized companies being the rock on which the German miracle is built, they have an underlying problem of inequality. They hate the euro bailouts, and Willie simply channeled that into a massive victory. But the real problem is the timing. All the shit is hitting the proverbial fan on the same weekend. I believe it's a conspiracy. The connections between some of those involved are too close to ignore." He looked directly at Fritz Schurz, the Federal Reserve Vice Chairman.

The President deftly changed the subject. "If there's weakness in equities and bonds can't be trusted, what's the likely winner?"

"Gold is the safe haven of choice." Brad Steavens answered, "and it closed Friday at just over $1,650 an ounce, but in Asia, where it's Monday morning, it's already over $2,135."

Despite the good fight that the CEA chairman put up for supporting the banks before the start of the week, the President's idea of announcing a massive fund to support private financial firms was ripped apart in the usual Washington fashion. In the end, nothing was decided and the meeting was adjourned.

The President walked out of the room first. He stopped, and then motioned for Francis Turner to join him.

"I've been trying to reach Mike in Switzerland all weekend. Do you have any ideas, Turner?"

"He went to a meeting with Heinrich Von Kleise, at a school near Kandersteg, but he was supposed to drive back to Paris on Saturday. They found the car, in a ravine, just outside Kandersteg. Ross wasn't in it, thank God, and our key contact in Swiss Counter-intelligence, Paul Thommen, has also gone missing, and none of his associates have a clue where he's gone."

Francis Turner didn't tell the President that he suspected Michael was being held hostage by one of the richest men on the planet. Turner was starting to believe Natalya's crazy theories. And where was Natalya? Or Kim? Had she ignored his explicit order not to help Masters? He suspected that she had. What they were proposing was dangerous. He had climbed in those same mountains as a high-school student when he was at Enigen, and the weather reports on the Kander valley were for snow and dropping temperatures. He was worried about her.

36. THE ANCIENT AND HONORABLE SOCIETY OF THE PHOENIX

The hallway ended at a spiral stairway, which descended three levels to a windowless chamber that had been cut out from the mountain. In the middle, was a round, polished, rosewood table, twenty feet in diameter.

"Michael, please sit over there," Michelle said, pointing to a chair.

There were only a few chairs, with the rest of the spaces around the round table indicated by a small marker, and an electronic node in the ceiling above. The room itself was bathed in semi-darkness, but where Michael and Von Kleise were seated small spotlights were positioned to make the area around them as light as day.

"Holographic projections," Von Kleise said when he saw Michael's confusion.

"Who are the members? Not all were in your class, I gather."

"No, Michael, some were. Not everyone attended the ceremony, and others have been recruited as they have the same wish, to make the world better; to change the dynamics that have moved us to this point—open markets and seemingly free markets—but also ever widening gaps between the top 2% and the remaining 98%.

"We can begin, Herr Von Kleise," said Ola, looking at her panel with its blinking lights and array of three-inch monitors, showing images from fourteen other locations. "We have synchronization with all signals."

Heinrich smiled at the American. Their earlier argument had upset him. Had he made the right choice bringing him here at this time? Michelle was not sure, and without Michelle on his side after he was dead, the plan might never move forward as they had planned. He looked around the slowly darkening room with a sense of wonder, as one by one, faint outlines of men appeared around the table, each in his own place. After a minute, these images solidified as flickering, ghost-like images appeared at all the places around the round table. Through the wonders of holography the *Ancient and Honorable Society of the Phoenix* convened.

"My friends," Von Kleise said, looking around the room at the flickering images. "We begin. Time is short, and there is much to accomplish."

"Why let this outsider in now, Heinrich?" said one of the flickering images. Michael looked to where the sound had come from. He spoke in English, but his accent suggested that his native language was likely German.

"Michael is our witness and my heir. Long ago, he laid out his vision of a new economic model, a new form of capitalism, where companies forwent profits for growth, where they both competed and cooperated to restart the business cycle when it failed, as was the case in 2008. He understood that advanced economies could no longer afford to throw millions into poverty rather than working together to insure a full recovery. Without any social safety nets, the task of fighting recessions passed from companies to governments. He proposed that, in the future, we may be forced towards this private sector synthesis of corporations working together for the good of the common rather than passing on these costs to others So, my friends, our goals, and his are the same: to transform the old into something new; something better that can endure. The old system of capitalism will not survive beyond tomorrow. It is time to bring new, younger blood, and new ideas into our Society."

"Why now, Heinrich?" said another of the flickering images. He was younger, in his fifties. He looked familiar and had an American accent.

"There was no other choice, Richard. Michelle will explain why Michael has to be here, and not in Washington.

"We felt that there was a significant risk that Michael could influence American response to the crisis in a way that would reduce the benefits we gain from the panic. For example, he has long advocated selling the American gold, and using the funds to buy the assets of American companies, to support social security and Medicare trust funds. Had America chosen to do this—selling its gold—not only would the panic have been shortened, but our gains from the sale of the gold would have been greatly reduced."

Michael looked towards Von Kleise. He was confused. *Who were these people?*

"I can see by your look, Dr. Ross," said a well-dressed older man with a clipped English accent, "that you wish to know who we are." He paused, took a sip of what was obviously not water, but an aged Scotch that he savored before continuing. "Long ago, in fifteenth century Paris, there existed a group of rich and scholarly men, dedicated to restoring to the world the knowledge that had been lost during the long period of darkness, after the fall of Rome. These men formed a secret society that they called *L'ancienne Sociétié de la Phénix*. The society had died out by the middle of the eighteenth century, but its existence was discovered by Machte, when he was researching French history to teach a block at the school. He decided to resurrect the society, and to select some students to join it. I, along with Von Kleise, was among the last to be asked to join. Of the numbers in the Society there were never more than twenty or thirty, who remained loyal to the goal. Others have been added to the group from outside, who share these same goals. "

"And your goals?" asked Michael, understanding for the first time that these rich men, all seemingly responsible leaders in their own right, might well destroy the careful edifice of the world economy, in the hope that out of that wreckage might come something that would serve "the greater good." Lord, he thought, spare us from do-gooders, who know not what they are doing.

"Our goal is to change the world in a way that will provide, not delay, the needed remedies, so the human race can survive the coming catastrophes. For too long, economic actors, private companies and governments have pursued short-term goals or solutions. Pursuing short-term economic gain has been the excuse for failing to do the right things, with respect to the environment, or society as a whole. We've suffered for too long, waiting for the market to solve the pressing problems of our times, only to see the inequality become entrenched and accepted as 'normal.' Political systems have become gridlocked, unable to solve problems, and more prone to make things worse rather than better, by their convoluted efforts at compromise and appeasement of small factions. We can't afford to wait any longer. The ice caps are melting, the droughts are becoming longer and more prolonged, the storms more destructive, and the gap between the richest and the poorest grows wider, even in the more socially and economically advanced countries."

"And to reach these goals you have murdered, kidnapped and blackmailed many innocents. Can you justify that?" Michael demanded, looking directly at his old friend, Von Kleise.

"We did what needed to be done," Heinrich answered, understanding that he bore the guilt of those who had been hurt, whose lives had been destroyed in the process. "Even out of great evil, good can come. Now, Michael, it is time that you listen."

37. SECRET TREASURE

"Who are you?" Kim asked as they entered the room.

"Natalya Avramowitz."

"The Russian?" said Kim. "Turner told me a little about you and Michael Ross."

"Then you know why I am here."

"No, not really, I'm not even sure why I'm here." She laughed nervously, if only to break the ice that had formed between the two women. Masters had been brusque, even unfriendly, and Kim wanted to dispel that image, at least on her part.

"Because this is the place where the conspiracy started. It's from here that the strings were pulled, that sent Lilly and Beth Masters to Asia. Tomorrow, when the markets open, there will be a bloodbath and there's nothing we can do to stop it, Kim, absolutely nothing. Up there, Heinrich Von Kleise is playing with the fate of nations, and the livelihoods of billions of people caught up in this maelstrom he has unleashed." It was heart-wrenching for her. She had hoped to find another close relative her whole life, and now, upon finding one, she discovered that he was not a loving grandparent, but a monster.

"Can it be stopped?"

"I don't think so. Tomorrow, we will find out the truth one way or the other, but for now, I need rest. It has been a very, very long day."

"And tomorrow, what happens?"

"Tomorrow, we climb a bit further, to the Oberschloss, and confront the puppet master himself: Von Kleise … my grandfather."

A very tired Ben Masters came out of the room where Beth Masters lay sleeping, leaving Lilly still beside her bed. The fever had abated somewhat, but it was still high, and she was drifting in and out of consciousness. She would need help and better medicines to live.

"There's food on the stove, Mr. Masters." Natalya offered, pointing to the kitchen area.

"I'm not hungry."

"Eat," she ordered. "You need your strength."

"Who are you?" Masters said, his voice heavy with repressed anger.

"She's okay, Ben," Kim tried to diffuse the quite obvious tension.

"I didn't ask you," he snarled.

"Natalya Avramowitz." She extended her hand only to have Masters ignore the gesture.

He went to the soup pot, and ladled a bowl of the thick soup that Lilly had fixed earlier in the day.

"I'll be back," he said gruffly, taking two bowls back to the room where his wife and daughter were.

A minute later, he reemerged. He walked over to where Natalya sat and pushed back a chair. "Okay, talk, and no crap. The truth. Who the hell are you, and why are you here?"

"Why are you here?"

"I asked first," growled Masters, becoming angry.

"I don't like your attitude," said Natalya staring back at him. "I was climbing with my friend Paul Thommen, a Swiss Government official, when two men started shooting at us. They killed my friend. I killed them both."

"That's crap, and you know it. I want the truth," he reached across the table and gripped Natalya's collar pulling her towards him. She resisted.

"Let go of me!"

"No, not until you answer some questions."

"Like what?"

"Like what the fuck you were doing on this mountain? How did you get here?"

When Masters didn't let go, Natalya slammed her fist into his solar plexus. Masters keeled over, wind knocked out, and then backed away.

"The next time you do that I'll kill you, Masters."

He looked surprised, but he sensed that the threat was real.

"I just want the truth, nothing more, nothing less." He smiled his best boyish grin. "You're a pretty woman, Natalya, or maybe that isn't your name." He looked to Kim for confirmation.

"It's Natalya," Natalya answered. "Tomorrow, when we get up to the Oberschloss, then perhaps you will find out the answer to the mystery." She stood up, attached a new strap to her pack, and then walked slowly to the bedroom, taking the rifle with her.

"Wait!" Masters grabbed Natalya's arm. She pulled away easily.

"I want to get some rest."

"What happens tomorrow?"

"We get the truth," she said, pulling away, and continued to walk towards the room with the bunks. Natalya lay down. She was exhausted, but also frightened. What if Michael wasn't there? What if he was dead? Pulling the thick blanket around her, she dozed. She heard the door open, and looked up to see Kim and then Masters find free bunks. A few minutes later, Lilly Masters came into the room. She spoke to her husband for a minute, and then taking his hand, she led him back to the room that she had shared with Urs.

Natalya woke at first light. She looked at her watch, it was just on five in the morning. Kim was still sleeping.

Taking her pack she went out into the main room. Passing the room where Ben and Lilly Masters slept, she could hear the big man snoring. There were still hot coals in the fireplace, but no heat. She placed a fresh log from the wood stand, adding it to the embers from the last fire, and waited until it caught alight. When she was warm, she went to the kitchen and taking the day old bread from the pantry ate it.

It was still very cold outside, but the storm had died down during the night. She studied the remaining cliff to be scaled. The wall was a 150 feet, but there were many easy holds visible, suggesting a relative easy climb.

Natalya climbed steadily, her rhythm constant, as she found the next hold easily. She feared Masters reaching Von Kleise before she did. He would kill the man without thinking, though not without cause.

When she was close to the top, near where the cableway entered the mountain, she stopped and looked down. She could see two small figures far below, pointing up at her. Reaching for the next handhold, a big stretch for her five foot six inch frame, she gasped for breath. Ten feet into the traverse, she nearly fell as rocks flew, chips cascading on her head. She looked back to see Masters firing Kim's weapon, but the Uzi was not accurate at that distance and the shots missed her.

With four strong moves she crossed the distance to the top and with one final push, she was over the lip of rock. She had finally reached the Oberschloss.

"Damn you, Kim," Masters said. His last two shots missed because Kim had pushed his arm up at the last minute. "I'm going to kill you." He pointed the weapon at her, but when she rolled away, he didn't fire. Then taking his pack, his rope and the weapon, he ran towards the rock wall.

Standing up, Natalya looked around the upper station of the Kanderschloss-Oberschloss cableway. At one side, there was a small open lift that was used to take supplies down to the hut below. The control room was behind a heavy sheet of armored glass, but there was no one inside. There stood a steel door leading into the main complex. The door was locked from inside.

From her backpack she removed the small kit that Thommen had added at the last minute. Inside, along with some plastic explosives, there was a type of plastic that could cut through steel plate. She squeezed it around the two heavy hinges on the door and lit it, watching as it cut through the heavy steel of the door hinges. After being forced back by the acrid smoke, she peered over the ledge to see where Masters was. He was taking almost the same route up the wall that she had taken. He was a strong a climber. For a second she thought it might be best to kill him before he reached the top, but that would be murder. Still, she knew he would be a problem. She had been appalled by what the men in the hut had done to both Lilly and Beth, and that was Von Kleise's doing. Added to that, Masters would understand that it had been Von Kleise who had destroyed his family and his business empire, and it would be a toxic mix. Still, she couldn't kill him, but would rather allow events to unfold, and then act as needed. She looked back at the door. It continued to glow red in places, but the flame had died. Standing up wearily, Natalya walked back to her pack, and removed her climbing gloves.

The plastic had cut through the two heavy steel hinges, but the door was still jammed into the frame. She looked around for something to pry it open with. Finding a steel rod, she levered the door open just enough to slip through, hoping that Masters would find the fit too tight.

Natalya saw that behind the door was a long corridor cut into the granite of the mountain. Taking her flashlight from the pack, she studied what lay ahead. The corridor ran for more than 100 feet before branching off, with stairs leading up, presumably to the main living quarters above, while another corridor continued deeper into the mountain. Curiosity made her take that path. Not far down, a heavy steel grill blocked the entrance to the first of many chambers. Shining the light inside, she stepped back in amazement. The room was filled to the top with ingots of gold. On the side of each ingot, the imprint of the Russian Government was clearly visible.

She counted the chambers, each filled with gold bullion. It was likely the greatest hoard of gold in the world. So, this was Pyotr's contribution, she thought, and wondered to what purpose it was to be put. That was a question she intended to put to her grandfather.

She stopped exploring the tunnels that continued on for what seemed like hundreds of feet further into the mountain, when she heard the steel door squeak and then make a loud booming noise as it fell to the ground. Running back up the tunnel, she caught a glimpse of Ben Masters climbing the stairs towards the living quarters of the Oberschloss.

38. THE PHOENIX CONSPIRACY

He was a prisoner, admittedly a very well looked after one, but unable to leave. The strange conclave he'd attended with the ghostly images haunted him. Their words had once been his own, but he had long since given up on that dream as being unachievable.

"Did you have a good evening?" Von Kleise asked, when Michael came into the brightly lit breakfast room. One of the Swiss girls, who worked in the kitchen, came in quickly and brought him juice, and filled his coffee cup.

"When can I leave, Heinrich?"

Von Kleise studied the American, and wondered if he'd made the right choice to leave the Trust to him once he was dead. "You can't leave today," he answered finally.

"I'll be missed."

"Undoubtedly, yes."

"And what will be my excuse? I was kidnapped by a man seemingly above reproach? Should I say that?"

"You took a holiday. You visited your old friend, didn't feel well, and slept the night. There are many suitable excuses, Michael. That isn't the problem at all, is it?"

"I don't want an excuse to stay. I want to leave. Can I leave now?"

"Sit down!" said Von Kleise, his voice firm and commanding. "You must eat," he continued in a gentler tone, once Michael sat down again. He touched a remote control device and a large-screen television came on.

"Stock prices on the Tokyo exchange began the day with a massive sell-off, falling almost twenty-five percent before trading was halted at noon, Tokyo time..."

"So it's beginning," said Michael, staring dumbly at Von Kleise who continued to butter his toast.

"Yes, it's the start, but not the end. I suspect it will be up to you and Natalya to find the right end for this story."

Michelle, Victoria and Ola came into the room, and Victoria flashed a V for victory to Von Kleise. He stood up and waited as each woman approached him in turn, and kissed him lightly on the cheek. He pointed to chairs around the table.

On the giant television screen there was a picture of Red Square in Moscow filled with a sea of people. The scene switched to a close-up shot of riot police and demonstrators clashing.

"... In Russia this morning, nearly a million people jammed into Red Square in front of the Kremlin, to demand a change in leadership, a return to democracy, and for the economy to be freed from the tyranny of the Government. A spokesman for the movement, Nobel Prize-winning poet Sakharov, called for a return of the basic freedoms lost during the last ten years. Led by the Committee for Russian Freedom—an ad hoc group of bureaucrats, professors, intellectuals, and factory workers—this upheaval has come on the anniversary of the Bolshevik revolution some ..."

"London gold-fixing is in two hours, but in Hong Kong, it closed at over $2,800 an ounce," Victoria reported, after studying the screen at one end of the room that showed a continuous stream of market data. "We can expect about a 25% increase from there when London opens. The reports suggest that demand is overwhelming the quite limited supply." She smiled. They had played the market well, driving down the price to less than $500 for a few months, before buying up large quantities, using the leveraged buying power of fifteen of the richest men in the world. And they had then drained the Russian gold supply, along with some of the reserves of several other countries. "Oil prices spiked in Asia at over $70 a barrel, up $20. We expect them to reach over $100, making our options bought at $50 worth more than $7 billion."

Victoria looked towards Ola.

"You're ready?" she asked the Swedish programmer.

"Yes." Ola pushed her bright gold hair away from her eyes. "We have confirmation and interface, but of course, we will wait until the markets reach near bottom to act. It may be days before we have to enter and buy."

"And the banks, the contracts, are in hand?" Von Kleise looked at Victoria.

"They're all ready. Spot contracts will be executed, the transfers made electronically, the gold transferred at a later date."

Why had he been so blind? To take advantage of market weakness, something was needed that would not be deflated in a collapsing market: either currency or gold. Gold would be best, as it often as not appreciated as stock prices fell: the perfect hedge for blindly collapsing equity markets. Many investors selling off stocks would seek refuge in the metal. The goal, as Michael had learned, was financial control of the 200 to 300 most important international companies, for less than 10% of their prior market capitalizations. These purchases, in addition to their already sizable personal holdings, and the consortium, would have effective control of the world economy. These global companies, with businesses spread across the rich and poor countries alike, from finished goods to raw materials to services, could then drive demand for intermediates from smaller companies, and by this means, force a recovery that had strength and staying power, rather than anything governments could do in the short-run with their stimulus and tax cuts.

"When you showed up with Natalya," Von Kleise said, looking directly at Michael, "I knew what I had to do. The bulk of the estate passes to the Trust when I die. The control of the Trust will be the joint responsibility of you and Natalya. My will was signed and registered in Zurich two weeks ago. The terms are strict, and, of course, the responsibilities are immense. The future of the world economy will be in your hands."

"And Walter and Katherine? What of their claims on your fortune, Heinrich? Won't they protest?" Michael asked, knowing in his heart that a man like Von Kleise would have considered that possibility, and countered it.

"My daughter and son-in-law have a dream, Michael, but it is quite different from my own. They will protest, but they know that they know they won't win."

"And what of the others in the Society? Don't they have a say?" Michael asked, confused.

"We agreed that the ownership rights are shared, but that the strategy for our work will be decided here within the Von Kleise Foundation offices, and you will control that unless there is a vote of the shareholders to change that direction. You will have to work with them to make this work. They are all good men, committed and honest."

"But will their heirs believe the same things as they do? What if they don't have the same ideas and commitments? Then what?"

"There are protocols to cover that eventuality."

There was another question that Michael had to ask, but it was obscured by the idea of changing the world, of having great economic power, not the power of governments, that was diffused, confused and more often than not, diluted by compromise. But the power of corporations, committed to a different world in which cooperation rather than competition was the primary organizing principle.

"And what is the work that you will be entrusting to Natalya and me?" Michael finally asked.

"To do what's right for the most people; to make the global economy strong and healthy, and sane enough to solve problems of poverty and climate change, before these two unmet challenges lead to chaos, and millions, possibly billions of people dying needlessly. Solving these challenges should be seen as an opportunity to strengthen the global whole, not as costs to be borne or problems to be ignored, until they consume even the best fortified nations. Ignoring or denying these problems has been what we have done for the past fifty or more years. We can't afford to wait any longer. So, Michael, you and my granddaughter are my legacy, and in your hands will be placed great power to do good. Commit to finding solutions rather than ignoring problems."

"You speak as if you will not be around to help, Heinrich," Michael said, worried by the tone of Von Kleise's voice. It was as if he knew he was to not live beyond this day, or the next.

Von Kleise looked at the younger man, his eyes tearing up as he imagined the world he was leaving for them to create. The last scan had confirmed he had less than three months to live before the brain cancer killed him.

"The Foundation's purpose is to create new wealth, not distribute it." Von Kleise studied his disciple. Could he withstand what would come naturally, once the dust cleared and the players realized they had been had? "You must not tie up capital in unproductive uses. Use it to create jobs and opportunities, and to solve problems. I am giving you the gift to change the world for the better; to force the only true actors in the economic sphere, the major globe-spanning companies to do what is right for the true stakeholders and for the economies that depend upon their continued growth and health."

If I were King, Michael thought, this is how I would make the world whole. That was why he had become an economist. But he wasn't king, and questioned whether even the Foundation's wealth would be sufficient to achieve their lofty objectives.

"I will not live out the year, Michael. Death will take me in an hour, a day, months perhaps, if I am lucky. The doctors are uncertain. I have an embolism that is hanging by a mere thread, poised to strike deep inside me, that could stop my heart or destroy my brain. And there is a small cancer growing inside my brain that may do the trick before the embolism strikes. Neither one is accessible through surgery nor drugs. I'm not afraid of death, only of having died without passing on my hope for a better world, to someone who is capable of carrying it on."

Michael's anger at what Von Kleise and the others had done started to fade. "I'm glad that we have had this time together."

"Good. I hope in time you will forgive me for what I have done. We made some difficult choices. We have harmed many innocents in the process. For that I'm ashamed, but it was done for the greater good."

"I can't promise that your plan will succeed. But I know that hating you, or refusing to carry on your legacy will not undo the damage that has happened, and is about to occur."

Before Von Kleise could respond, Victoria Carter walked back into the room. "The European markets have opened on schedule." She handed him a sheet of paper summarizing the opening stock prices. "Gold in Zurich will open near $2,900 an ounce."

"It will go higher," Von Kleise said, smiling.

"Ola reports that the sell orders are flooding into the automated trading system in New York, in advance of the opening."

"Does Michelle have any estimates of the impact of the fighting in Russia?"

"She's working on that now."

Michael remembered the question that he'd failed to ask now. "Heinrich," he said, looking up as a man charged into the room. "I will need a list of who controls the other assets. It's important."

Masters burst into the room full of rage. He stopped and looked towards the far end of the room where two men and a woman were watching a wall-size television screen. He fired two shots at the screen, shattering the picture. The sound startled Michael who looked up to see a huge, bear of a man, pointing a rifle at him. He dived under the table for cover.

Von Kleise stood up and faced Masters. He didn't flinch, but stared him down.

Masters knew instinctively that this man was the enemy. Yet something in this old man's eyes, the way he stood ramrod straight, staring at him, prevented him from firing immediately.

"Who ... who are you?" Masters stammered.

"Heinrich Von Kleise. This is my home."

"The men, the guards on the glacier ... they're your men?"

"They guard this plateau against terrorists and intruders, yes."

Masters growled, "And screwed my wife and daughter." He fingered the weapon nervously.

"Put down your weapon, Mr. Masters."

"So you know who I am?"

"Of course," Von Kleise said. His voice was icy and without compassion, but also was without hate or anger. "Who doesn't know of Master town and Master City: pleasure palaces for the rich and famous, all with your name alongside faux art and atrocious architecture?" He paused, taking a sip of water, then resumed speaking. His eyes zeroed in on Masters' eyes, adding to the American's nervousness. His calm compounded Master's anger.

"You were driven by an overpowering self-love, an ego that was larger than even New York itself. What a soaring vision you had! Did you give away any of your large fortune to worthy causes? No. Rather you simply spent it on yachts, houses, aircraft, things … not people. In fact, Masters, it was your success in making your name synonymous with wealth and power that made you and your lovely wife perfect candidates for what we had planned."

Master's rage had been building as the old man talked. Here was the puppet master who had ruined his life, and that of his family.

"You screwed me, my wife, and my daughter. Tell me why the fuck I shouldn't kill you?"

Von Kleise sat down. He waited, allowing Masters to regain his composure so that he could listen. "None of this was personal. You were a well-known womanizer, making it easy to frame you for your wife's disappearance and likely death. And Latimer was easily coerced. It was simply convenient to use you. Your real-estate holdings were critical to the success of the plan too. They are being sold off, or will be sold off at bargain basement prices after this is all done, and I think the names changed too, given your failed empire, which weighed down by billions in unsecured debt, will be one of the root causes of what is about to transpire."

Michael was prepared to drop to the floor expecting a hail of bullets, but instead stood transfixed by the drama unfolding. Von Kleise was goading Masters, almost willing him to use the weapon

"Before Asia, your wife, Lillian—yes, Lillian—played the whore many times with many men. And your daughter had slept with everyone from the cook's helper at the Mansion, to her English professor at school."

Ben finally exploded, squeezing the trigger, and sending a burst of gunfire just as Von Kleise lifted the table, hurling it with an almost superhuman strength at Masters. Michael dived to the floor, as the room seemed to reverberate with the sound of bullets and shrapnel flying everywhere.

And then it suddenly stopped.

He opened his eyes, lifted himself from the ground, and saw Natalya running towards him, stepping over Masters' collapsed body. She helped the still shaking, but unhurt Michael to stand up.

He looked down. Von Kleise lay next to Victoria Carter in a pool of blood. Natalya checked the woman's pulse first. She could feel nothing. Von Kleise was alive, and just able to speak in a whisper.

"Help me up," he asked, struggling to lift himself off the floor.

They propped him up against the back of the table. Blood poured from several large wounds. He was dying, but still hung onto life by the strength of his will.

"Is that you, Natalya?" He blinked several times, the pain worse than he had imagined it might be.

"Yes," she answered, coming closer so that he could look into her face. He reached up his hand, missed, and then touched her cheek. She was crying.

With a supreme effort, Von Kleise looked first at Natalya and then at Michael. Yes, he thought, they would be a formidable couple, and he smiled weakly at the thought, knowing he would not be there to see that thought come true.

"Michael knows the truth," he struggled, the energy draining from his body.

"Don't talk, please," she pleaded, trying in vain to stem the tide of blood with the tablecloth. The cotton quickly became red. Michael looked up in time to see Frau Bundt along with the two Swiss women who helped her. He wondered where Ola and Michelle were. Bundt looked at the damage, screamed, and then taking each girl's hand, turned and ran out of the room.

Von Kleise reached up and pulled Michael close to him, using the last of his strength, and said, "Use the wealth to do what's right for the world. There is no other way ..."

Slowly, Natalya let her grandfather down on to the blood-stained carpet. She looked at Michael and saw the doubt in his eyes. Could the good that might come from Phoenix outweigh the damage that had been done?

"Masters' wife is down below. The daughter needs to be taken to a hospital immediately," Natalya said, thinking practically about what needed to be done.

"It's started, you know," Michael said, struggling for words, all the while looking at this woman who had rescued him, "Markets are in chaos.

Your father's leading a revolution in Russia, but it's likely to lead to civil war and total collapse."

"I know."

"Did you see the gold?"

"Yes, some of it; mainly the haul taken from Russia," she answered. "It's a huge amount of bullion, likely to be more than there is at Fort Knox, or anywhere else in one place."

Natalya saw two women close the door to the cable car as she approached. Then, the car began its descent. She entered the control room, but was unable to stop it.

"Look down there," Natalya pointed. She looked over the side and saw Kim making the final effort to cross the open space just below them. Taking the rope, Natalya let it fall to where Kim waited on a narrow ledge.

"Masters' is dead," Natalya said, as Kim slid over the top.

"Beth needs help. The fever's broken, but she's dehydrated."

"We'll get them down to Kanderschloss. There's a lift over there that we can use to bring them up from the glacier."

"What happened?"

"Masters shot Von Kleise. He was going to kill Michael, so I shot him."

Kim didn't respond. Looking to one side, she noticed Michael standing there, seemingly unharmed.

"Are you alright, Dr. Ross?"

"I'm fine," Michael answered, his mind still distracted.

"He's figuring out the odds of saving the world. How's it looking, love?" she asked playfully.

"Not great," he laughed. "Really not great."

As the cable car descended towards Von Kleise's Kanderschloss estate, Michael looked over at Lillian Masters and her daughter Beth. They sat huddled together in one corner of the car, wrapped in a blanket against the biting cold. He looked towards the green of the valley below, but his mind was wandering far away from there. It was now close to two o'clock. All eyes would be fixed on the opening of the market in New York. He could imagine that sell orders were flooding in, encouraged by Von Kleise's network of newsletters. As the market fell, then brokers would be obliged to call in loans, forcing further sales of stocks to repay margin accounts. Each hour would add fuel to the fire.

"What was their plan?" Natalya asked, as the car approached the Kanderschloss station. "They didn't simply wish to destroy without rebuilding, did they?"

Before leaving they had searched the Oberscholoss. Victoria was dead, but Michelle and Ola, the Swedish programmer, were missing. They were likely the two women Natalya had seen entering the cable car. In one of the rooms there was a bank of computers and servers. The screens were blank, but the computers were on, humming and showing activity, but when they tried to access the system, it could only be accessed via a password.

"There was a plan, but I am worried that Michelle and Ola might have sabotaged it by leaving." Michael had spent more than an hour trying to get onto the computers, while Kim and Natalya retrieved Lilly and Beth from below. Computers controlled from the Oberschloss were needed to execute the complex series of trades in equities and gold. Without access to the computers, it was likely that all of the detailed analysis for executing the necessary buy and sell orders would be for nothing. "There's a group, they call themselves the Society of the Phoenix, who worked with Heinrich on this. I didn't recognize all of them, but some were familiar faces. One, at least, was Richard Kahn, a personal friend of the President.

"The politicians and Central Bankers will be timid," Michael said, thinking about the likely discussions now going on in Washington, London, Brussels, Tokyo, and Beijing. "They'll discuss the options, but by nature, governments are conservative. I wouldn't put it past them to have compromised the governors of both the Japanese and Chinese banks too. None of the current Central Bank governors are contrarians; they don't think outside of the box. And in Washington, without my voice, with barely a week before the election, no one will offer any radical solutions. They'll just let the storm take its natural course."

"Then perhaps we should trust in Von Kleise's plan working?" Natalya suggested.

"No," said Michael. "It depended upon a schedule and the automatic trades that Ola programmed. If, as I think we both believe, the system is locked down, then these will not take place. The gold will remain locked in the vaults up there, and the world will crash around us."

Michael suddenly looked at Natalya in wonderment, wondering how this incredible woman could love him. She had climbed the Blumlisalp, and against all odds of survival, saved him from certain death. "Did I tell you that I love you?"

"No," she said, kissing him lightly on the cheek. All the uncertainty was gone. Michael was the man she had been waiting for, but he needed her help. Pyotr would know what to do, but Ross might not, without prodding or support. She could give him the backbone that he sometimes lacked. Was it love, or simply that they were pieces of the same puzzle that were meant to fit together.

The car came into the lower station and lurched to a stop.

Inside the main house, the housekeeper showed Lilly and Beth to one of the many bedrooms and called for the doctor to come immediately. Leaving the housekeeper to make the two women comfortable, Michael, Natalya and Kim went into the living room. They had explained to the housekeeper that Von Kleise was remaining in the Oberschloss, but that he had asked that they be given all the help they needed here.

Michael went to make one phone to call Washington, while Kim found a second line to update Turner, and Natalya caught up with the latest market news.

"Come. Have some food," Natalya said several hours later, as Michael put the telephone receiver down. He had reached the Secretary of the Treasury at his office, and had tried to convince him that the President needed to act forcefully, to prop up the markets. Although they had been allies in the past, all of Michael's pleading on the matter had been to no avail.

"You're overreacting, Mike," the Secretary had said. "This thing will blow over like all the other panics."

Michael felt disgusted, and glad he was in Switzerland and not Washington, where he might have killed the lot of them.

"Washington aren't going to be any help. They think that everything will calm down on its own."

"And what do you think, Michael?"

"Von Kleise knew what he was doing. Without intervention from the Fed or the Government, share prices will stay very low for weeks, if not months, and tens of trillions in wealth will be lost. The natural reaction of companies will be to freeze hiring and lay off workers, expecting the worse, not the best as the outcome. And who would blame them? They'll be egged on by governments trying to close budget gaps rather than simulate the economy. And the last years have shown that monetary stimulus is a weak cousin compared with private industry hiring."

They ate a late lunch mostly in silence. Michael kept a wary eye on the television set tuned to the financial channel. Natalya took a call from the Swiss police. They would send a team to bring down the bodies, and protect the gold stocks.

"How will they respond to his death and the fortune?" Michael asked Kim, thinking about how many lives had been ruined, and how many laws had been broken to accomplish their goals.

"The Swiss prefer to keep these things private. As to the fortune … from what you've told me, it's now yours. His personal lawyer is in Zurich, and is on his way here now. Mr. Turner has asked Interpol to put out an alert for both Ola and Michelle," Kim answered.

"What about Lilly Masters and her daughter?"

"I've also been discussing that with Turner," said Kim, rising from the table. She walked stiffly; every muscle was beyond sore from the climb the day before.

"And what does he think?" asked Michael.

"He suggested that it would be complicated if Lilly were to return to America right now. The State of New York could claim she staged her disappearance to frame her husband. It's best that they remain here, at Kanderschloss; at least, until we can develop a new identity for her and Beth."

"What about Masters?" Michael asked, wondering how they might cover that up.

"The body will be flown back to New York, and there will be a quick cremation at the prison. Officially, he will have died in a prison fight. No one will be charged."

"And Latimer?"

"He's already fled. Likely he's in Rio, but I doubt that he has too many friends there, and has at least a million people who would like to wring his neck. So I doubt we will hear much from Mr. Latimer in the near future."

The doctor rolled Beth Masters over. The girl's temperature had shot up again, and her breathing was irregular. Filling a syringe with Keflex, he brushed one side of her buttocks with a disinfectant pad, and injected the antibiotic.

"Her temperature should be under control, but some fever is good for fighting the disease. Use these to bring it down if it gets above 38 degrees centigrade, and give her a sponge bath if it's over 39."

"And her lungs, Doctor?" Lilly asked, having listened to Beth's shallow breathing and worried about the risks of pneumonia.

"She's young, and will get better, but it will be a slow recovery. She must drink too; broth is good, or tea, but nothing heavy. Do you understand?"

Lilly nodded, but it had been a long, long time since she had taken care of her daughter all on her own.

"I will come tomorrow morning to check over her again. My number." he said, handing her a card as he packed up his bag. "If there's a problem, of course, we can move her to the hospital in Thune. But for now, it is better she stays here where it is quiet." He looked around. He had always wanted to see the inside of the Kanderschloss. He wondered where Herr Von Kleise was.

He walked towards the door to the room and Lilly followed him. Outside, she saw the American economist whose name she had forgotten.

"What did the doctor say, Lilly?"

"That she will be better if she rests and follows my instructions," answered the doctor. "I would like to pay my respects to the master of the house, if you please," said the Doctor very formally, in English.

"Herr Von Kleise is indisposed at the moment. He's at the Oberschloss," which strictly speaking, was not a lie.

"Then you will tell him that Doctor Fritz Nagale pays his respects, please?"

"Yes, of course" Michael said. He watched as the doctor left the room.

Michael looked at his watch. The markets in New York had opened on time, then closed for two hours, and then reopened, under rules designed to prevent markets overreacting and becoming disorderly. Turning the television on, he sat down to watch. He didn't see Natalya come and sit next to him. After a half hour, he stood up and turned off the television.

"That bad?" she said, noticing the look of worry on his face.

"Worse, far, far worse. They are about to close the market again until two o'clock, so that they can try to process all the sell orders."

"Where's Kim?"

"The Swiss police arrived and she's being debriefed. We'll take them up to the Oberschloss after that's done."

"What about Ola and Michelle?"

"Turner knows the importance of finding them," she said, seeing the stress in his face. He looked exhausted, as much from the tension as from the lack of sleep.

Michael leaned back letting the soft cushions of the couch surround him. He was physically drained. He closed his eyes and as Natalya watched, he fell asleep.

Standing up, Natalya went to the window. She looked up at the mountain that was passing in and out of low clouds. It was beautiful here, with no hint of the storm that had been unleashed outside, on the world at large.

It was dark when Michael awoke. Natalya handed him a coffee.

"I slept?"

"For hours," she said, looking at her watch. Three or four hours had passed.

"You went to the Oberschloss?"

"The computers are working. That's obvious by the way the hard drives are acting, but they are probably not trading, given the current price of gold and the movement in stocks. To get them started, we need the password. The expert that was sent believes they are still receiving and processing data, but the outbound feeds are silent. He was worried that any attempt to tamper with the computers would shut down the program completely. We need Ola!"

"Where's Kim?"

"Sleeping. She's exhausted."

"And Lilly?"

"Collapsed on the bed, next to her daughter," reported Natalya. "I gave the girl another dose of the medicine. Her temperature is close to normal for now."

"So that only leaves you to worry about." Michael said, touching her hand. How could he exist without her strength? "Aren't you tired?"

Natalya pressed her body against his, turning to look directly at his face. She ran her fingers through his hair playfully in answer.

"What happens now?" she asked.

"I guess it depends upon what happened in New York. They were closed earlier, before I fell asleep. Did they reopen?" he asked as she nodded. "How bad was it?"

"You don't want to know," she said, pulling him to her and kissing his lips. "You don't want to know," she said again, coming up for air. Then she stood up, reached for his hand, and guided him to bed.

39. THE CLEANSING FIRE

Pyotr Avramowitz stood to one side of the polished wood desk that had, at one time, been Lenin's. The desk was huge, and far more solid, Pyotr thought, than this government. It would be a cold, hard winter. Millions would starve or be killed by neighbors. Without organized trade in goods and services, few people could survive for long in cities such as Moscow or St Petersburg. To run skyscrapers you needed energy, which would be in short supply, as would affordable food.

The Prime Minister had fled, along with more conservative cabinet ministers and some of the members of the Duma. They had regrouped and re-established Government in Saint Petersburg, supported by the Russian North Army Group and the formidable naval forces, with their strategic punch that made their headquarters along the shores of the Baltic Sea and Gulf of Finland. This meant that Russia was being one side holding Moscow and the South, and the other, Saint Petersburg and the north. No one knew what was happening across the far-flung empire that stretched across nine time zones. So far, at least, the gas continued to flow from Siberia, but he wondered how long that would last.

"There's still fighting?" Sakharov asked Colonel General Brusiloff, the newly appointed, stern-faced military commander. How much of the military General Brusiloff commanded remained to be seen. Old scores would be settled one way or another. Units were changing positions by the minute. Pyotr didn't doubt that some were now planning pogroms against the new upper class, who were cowering in their mansions and luxury high-rises. Some of the anger would be directed against plutocrats, but many of these men and their families were well away by now, staying in their New York or London houses.

Brusiloff wished to deploy the army immediately, to regain the control from the mob that was growing outside and to protect Moscow from the Northern Group units that were closer to Moscow than their units were to St. Petersburg. He jabbed his finger towards where Sakharov sat. "We must regain the initiative, Mr. President. We must send the people home, so that order can be restored. Units will only remain loyal if we show strength. I have several battalions that could march towards St Petersburg at this moment."

"And start a civil war, General? No, we need the people on our side."

The General scowled. He hated politicians, but for now, he needed what little legitimacy this new government had, to maintain the fiction that there was someone in charge.

"War is with us. It is only a question of time before that mob decides you are the problem, not the solution, Sakharov. And someone else will be put in charge." Brusiloff looked at Pyotr. There, he thought, was the real power behind the figurehead of the President.

Sakharov stood up. His hands shook, his legs were weak, and his bowels were loose. He was not the man to rule this country, Pyotr thought. He lacked the skill, and possibly the political intelligence to navigate the dangerous waters. He was too intellectual to win the hearts and minds of the people, and he was not ruthless enough to survive the inevitable solution to the problem of there being too many mouths to feed, and not enough coal for the furnaces.

"Brusiloff is right, Sakharov," Pyotr said. "Order must be restored. Russia must be made whole again. Deploy your units. Strike before they strike us. We may be able to get some money too, to bribe the Generals of the North Army Group to come over to our side. Civil war must be avoided if possible."

Sakharov sat down weakly. He was exhausted and worried. He looked at Pyotr, then at Brusiloff.

"Do what you need to do, General," he said, falling back into the oversized chair.

After Brusiloff left, the two, old friends sat silently. Pyotr stood and walked to the two-story window that overlooked the square. The crowd was growing. The shouting was loud and the chants dangerous. There were reports of looting and deaths. There was no comfort in quoting Lenin or Trotsky on revolution. Death was death; it was always painful.

"Do you think that we will make it? Or are we simply deluding ourselves?" Sakharov asked without much hope. Outside, there was a jumble of barricades and patrolling troops. They watched as the armored personnel carriers and the tanks entered the square, pushing the crowd back by force. It was growing dark, but there were no lights except in the Kremlin, where generators supplied electricity.

"I don't know." Pyotr was in despair.

It was Wednesday morning in New York. The President stood on the balcony of the New York Stock Exchange, with the Chairman of the Council for Economic Affairs, Harley Mumford, watching the mayhem taking place below in the "pits." He was standing at the epicenter of capitalism, and what he saw frightened him. The only market where prices hadn't fallen was precious metals: gold, platinum, and silver. Gold had hit a record $3,500 an ounce, before a small sell-off drove it down to just under $3,100. Mumford had explained that there was almost no supply being released into the market, so the price could go higher than that. Lifetimes of hard work evaporated in minutes as 401K retirement accounts were worth less than a fraction of what they had been. The Federal Reserve had reluctantly offered credit to the banks, insurance companies, and private investment banks on Tuesday. It was too early to tell if this confidence-building measure would help at all. And it was too early to tell what companies might do: whether they would lay off workers in anticipation of zero or negative growth.

"What's going on down there?"

"It's quiet now. Not much activity" said the President of the New York Stock Exchange, looking at the relative calm below. The tape was moving slower. The market had not yet, however, hit rock bottom. But the panic, induced by the programmed trading algorithms, had subsided. He had been up all night, watching as the markets had opened one by one on Tuesday morning. Losers outnumbered gainers by 10 to 1.

"A lot of the money is now sitting in gold, isn't it?" the President asked.

"There are outstanding orders for gold, but not much available for sale."

The President had noted that the interest rate on Government debt was a bargain, with the short-term yield now below 1%. The deficit, however, would be staggering, as the losses would cause tax revenue to fall, as automatic countercyclical government spending on unemployment and other welfare programs increased.

After leaving the Exchange, they went across the street to the New York Federal Reserve Bank. Inside the lobby they posed for a photo with the acting Chairman of the Federal Reserve Board, the President of the New York Federal Reserve Bank, and the Secretary of the Treasury. The President took a few questions from the waiting press, and then they all went into a private meeting room. Once inside the office of the President of the Bank, the United States President kicked off his shoes and leaned back in the chair.

"Okay, I want the goddamn honest truth on this one. How bad is it? What do we do to stop this destruction? And when the hell is it going to get better?"

"Bad," answered the President of the New York Federal Reserve Bank. "The one bit of good news is that the short-term rate on Treasuries has dropped by more than two percent, and is near zero now. It is basically free for the Government to borrow money. People are looking for quality, but the real-estate market's a disaster. About a third of the expensive stuff is deep underwater. There's also been a lot of selling of mortgage-backed security paper and the worthless Masters' bonds are depressing the market. Some of the big banks will go belly-up if we can't step in with some much needed capital."

The Treasury Secretary took up the story, providing additional details about the disaster unfolding in markets across the world, "Some money is coming into the country from abroad, as US Treasuries are viewed as a safe haven and all, but more money is going out to prop up overseas accounts. The good news is that this disturbance may be limited to financials, or at least until the strike along the Pacific Rim causes factories to shutter, and stores in the US have nothing to sell."

"And your opinion, Dr Mumford?" the President stared angrily at what was left of his economic brain trust, now that Ross was seemingly out of touch and unreachable. He knew Harley to be indecisive, academic in his thinking, and conservative in his approach to problems, so he didn't expect much in the way of advice. He was also angry with Michael Ross. He had point-blank refused to return from Switzerland, saying he needed to rest and recuperate from his ordeal.

"We can't stop this by anything we do, nor by anything we say. We simply have to let it run its course. In time, it will correct itself."

"That's rubbish," the President replied. "We are in a crisis. The world's waiting for some action, not more mumbo-jumbo economist talk about invisible hands and moral hazard. Brad, are there options we can use to reduce the impact on the economy as a whole?"

"We've been studying our options, Mr. President," the Secretary of the Treasury said, pulling out a thick briefing paper that he had asked his staff to prepare. "We need to ask for emergency funding from Congress, and begin to funnel credit direct to companies if the banks won't do it. But that can't happen until after the election next week. We expect money to be very tight with so much wealth lost, some of it possibly for good. Keeping lines of credit open is our only chance to stop companies laying off workers. We lost nearly 8 million jobs in the first two years of the 2008 crisis, and that collapse was tame compared to this one."

"So," the President said, looking at Fred Schurz, "will the Fed step in?"

"As a lender, yes, but not as a bankruptcy trustee, Mr. President," Fred Schurz said smugly. "Bradley's right, it's a Government responsibility to make good on the FDIC, to rebuild the banks, and there's a precedent for direct loans and restructuring. We will look at Bernanke's notes on what to do, but we already have so much bad paper on our books that I hesitate to be more *creative*. I was never really impressed by the way he expanded our balance sheet. And it's proven impossible to stop the bond-buying, given the panic selling that comes whenever we try to retreat from expansionary monetary policy."

"Who the fuckin' hell do you represent, Fred? God?" The President had a visceral hatred of this smug young Boston banker. Out of all the men in the room, only Schurz looked rested. At least the others had that desperate, haggard look of men afraid of what would come next.

"I represent the future trust of the world in the credit of the United States of America, Mr. President. We are the bulwark against runaway inflation, and the reckless endangerment of the economy. Let me tell you, printing more money and throwing it at this problem won't solve a thing. There are a lot of studies that show quantitative easing didn't do anything, except increase risk-taking, without solving the underlying problems of business confidence."

"That's bullshit, and you sure as hell know it," responded the President.

As his advisors entered into heated argument, the President retreated into his own thoughts. None of them understood that this crisis could well lead to a revolution, or a major depression like the 1930s. And they were so wedded to old ideas, so protective of their turf, that they wouldn't do anything imaginative or unexpected. Yet could he go against his advisors? To do so would be risky. The press would find out; one of these guys would leak it, and it would make things worse, not better. And it was almost time to pass the torch on to whomever won the election.

"Shut up!" the President yelled, breaking up the chorus of discord. "I want solutions, not arguments. I'm leaving. I'm addressing the American people at eight o'clock tonight. I want words, and also a set of actions to announce. Let's not posture too much. No half-baked ideas either. Just the facts point by point, and then what we are doing about them, one by one.

Do you understand what I am asking Brad, Harley, and Fred? Whatever I say, it has to be good, and sound uplifting. We can't seem to be panicked by this. And I'll expect all of you to be there to answer questions from the press after the address."

He looked around the room. He could see the shock on each face. Good, he thought, they got the point. "You call me when you have something. Send the key points by five so I can have Tom Simon craft it into something I can give, without choking. Now, get to work!"

Walter Holtz raised the glass and looked at Jenny. "To Jenny, with much thanks." He then continued, "And yes, there is further good news! I have had calls from six G8 Finance Ministers, as well as the Secretary of the Treasury. All have agreed to a meeting at the end of the week, to discuss our plan. They are frightened and in a mood to compromise, I am certain."

"They have little choice really. The markets are in free fall. They need to show that they are willing to act, but the negotiations will be difficult. What we did alone would have set the markets off for a day, but with everything else happening, it's anyone's guess if even God could save the world economy now," Jenny replied.

She stood up. It was late. Now that Carlos was dead and Rawlston back in London, she was lonely.

"There's a spare bedroom here, Jenny," Walter said, looking towards where Jenny waited.

"I'm quite alright, Walter, really."

"It is no trouble for you to sleep here, and we'll celebrate with a huge breakfast feast."

"Thank you, but no." Jenny went towards the door. Walter took her hands in his, leaned towards her and kissed each cheek in turn. Then he reached for the door, opened it, and watched her leave.

Returning to where Katherine waited, he leaned down and kissed his wife, letting his hand stray to brush her breast. After nearly thirty years he still found her desirable.

"What are you thinking about, Katherine?" asked Walter, sitting down and pulling her back towards him. She fit neatly against his chest, but continued to stare out the window at the brightly lit city across the lake.

"I've spoken to the lawyers in both in Basel and Zurich, Walter. Given the language of Papa's will, the fact that most of the money is left in the Foundations hands, and that Natalya is closely related to the old man, it will be hard to get at it fairly."

"What about gaining control of the Foundation?"

"Papa expected we would try, and the wording is ironclad. They won't go against his words, and he mentions you and me in his will as being specifically barred from having anything to do with the Foundation, or the Von Kleise Trust."

"We will survive, my Katherine," he said, clipping each syllable. In the last few days, their carefully placed puts had yielded them close to $25 million dollars in their personal accounts.

"Listen, Brad, you have to move on this. You can't sit on the sidelines and wait it out" said Michael, almost shouting into the phone at the Treasury Secretary.

"This will pass, Mike, believe me. The markets will calm down in a week or two. It's not World War III, just a financial crisis. What did the *New York Times* call it? Oh yes, '*a global psychosis of negative expectations*'."

"That's good to hear," said Michael sarcastically.

"Now, I have been hearing some ugly rumors, Mike that you're holed up with that Russian whore, fucking while Rome burns. You best get back here and reclaim your territory, or that dumbass CEA we have, Harley Mumford, will take over." Then Bradford's voice dipped to a low rumble, and he said, "You know that the President likes you, Mike, and he wants you back here. He needs you."

"He'll be out of office before you know it," Michael answered, almost hanging up after what he had just said about Natalya, "and I have some things that I still need to do. Besides, you're all convinced it will pass, and things will get better."

"If you did come back, what would you tell the President?"

"Sell the gold, all of it, and break the speculation. There's probably close to a trillion dollars locked in the vaults in New York and Fort Knox. Take the money, buy into the markets and distribute the shares into a true Social Security trust fund, backed by real American assets, not some paper fund." Michael knew someone as conservative as Brad Stevens would see the idea as a radical solution, bordering on State socialism.

"You've been listening to the Brits and the French too much. But have you seen them sell one ounce of their precious gold, Mike? They haven't sold an ounce."

"Gold can't buy jobs. It soaks up wealth. Sell it, save the markets and replenish the Social Security trust funds," Michael repeated.

The Secretary of the Treasury didn't like being lectured. What Michael suggested was, as far as he was concerned, a nonstarter.

The conversation ended with Michael realizing just how desperately they needed to find Ola, and soon.

"We're getting nowhere. If they don't act, then it may take years to regain confidence in the markets," he complained to Natalya.

"I warned you not to call," Natalya said. "You need to resign, you know that." She came over and gently massaged his neck and back muscles that were tensed like steel cables in a storm. "Think of it from their point of view. They're in a storm, the ships are tossing and turning, the waves are rising all around, and they have no idea except one: eventually, the sea must calm because it always has before. They have limited vision, and can only see this as a disaster, not an opportunity for change; meaningful change."

He looked up at her, his head resting on her lap, seeing in her eyes something more than love. She had a confidence in him that he didn't have in himself. To manage what Von Kleise had left them would take the skills of a businessman, not a dreamer or an economist. And yet she felt that they would succeed.

"The men behind Phoenix, Von Kleise and the others, were morally wrong in what they did. Still, they did these things because they wanted to make the world a better place. They sinned, they transgressed, they assumed that they could control human destiny, and in the process, created a monster. However, it will all have been for nothing, Michael, if we don't use this opportunity. But remember this," she looked at him, "that we carry none of their guilt. Our task must be to turn their evil into good."

She reached down, lifted his head, and kissed him deeply. "Come to bed now. It's late."

"I can't sleep. It will be Friday tomorrow. Almost a week." Michael paced the room, frustrated by their inability to do anything. Only Ola mattered now. Without her, the entire system would collapse, and they would be left with the world's greatest private hoard of gold, and nothing they could do with it. And if that happened, then all this destruction of wealth would have been for nothing.

"I want you to stop worrying," she said, turning him around to face her.

Michael smiled. She was right. There wasn't a damn thing that could be done now.

"You want to go for a hike tomorrow?" he suggested, after pulling away. "The exercise will do both of us good, and as you say, we can't do anything but worry here." It seemed weeks since they had both been in Washington, but in fact, it had barely been in a week.

"Where will we go?"

"I'd like to learn how to climb." Kim's heroic climb had had an impact on him. If she could do it, he should try to learn; at least the rudimentary steps even if he was an out of shape, mid-forty year old.

"Thommen told me of a place on the other side of the mountains from Kandersteg, the Gasterntal Valley, that's good for rock-climbing."

"Good. Then we'll go there. And perhaps we can have a breakfast out as well. I have a hankering for eggs, rosti, and lots of coffee." Michael laughed.

The Gasterntal valley lay hidden between two ranges of mountains. On the south side were the peaks separating the Canton of Bern from the Valais. Early traders had crossed through the Lötschepass to reach the Valais, and then Italy. On the northern side were the towering heights of Bluemlisalpenhorn, and the Jungfrau glacier. The tiny village of Selden, inaccessible during winter, lay at the end of the road from Kandersteg. Few Swiss and even fewer tourists ever made it to this savagely beautiful place. The road that ran alongside the fast-moving Kander, was partially covered at spots where the river spilled over its banks. At the end of the road was the isolated village of Selden, and a small guest house-hostel that catered to the many hikers and climbers hiking the Kanderfirn glacier, that lay on the southern flanks of the Blumlisalp massif.

"Where are we going?" Michael asked, looking at the road that seemed to stretch on until it reached the solid white of the glacier ahead.

"A little further," she said, studying the map. In a few minutes they came to a long, flat straightaway. The valley narrowed, with the mountains now coming down close on either side.

"Are you hungry, Michael?" Natalya asked, knowing there was but one hotel at the very end of the road at Selden.

"Let's climb first, and then we can eat," Michael said, hoping that exercise would take his mind off the impossible problems at hand.

The rock wall rose at a slight incline for about 300 feet. It was high enough to make the climb just a little dangerous, yet it had numerous handholds and cracks that allowed for an easy climb without needing to use cams, pitons and etriers.

By nine-thirty Michael was exhausted. His hands were cut from scrambling for holds on icy walls, and while Natalya was a good teacher, forcing him to climb even when frightened, Michael's mind was elsewhere. She stopped him from trying to go up again, using a different route. Perhaps, she thought, another time, when the fate of the world was not resting on their shoulders, they might have the time to truly learn and enjoy the challenge.

About three miles further up the road they reached the Hotel Gasterntal in Selden. It had private rooms, as well as a hostel-style dormitory, catering to climbers looking to explore the Kanderfirn glacier, and the hikers who used the passes through the mountains. Once a day, the Swiss postal bus delivered the mail, and brought visitors in and out of the area. But it was now out of season, and the town empty of tourists. Soon, the hotel would close for the winter until the spring thaw.

"Good morning," said the old woman just inside the door to the restaurant. She was dressed as in a postcard, wearing a white, embroidered blouse, blue peasant skirt, and an embroidered apron. The couple ordered eggs and rosti, plus plenty of coffee with warm milk.

"Want to do that again sometime?" Natalya, asked wondering if Michael had enjoyed the morning climb. Michael didn't answer. He was staring out the window, at the waterfall that was visible in the distance. "You can't take on the world's troubles. You have to let it go, even if just for an hour," she said, reaching across the table and taking his hand.

"What happens if we can't unlock the computers, and start the process?"

"We'll find Ola," she said as brightly as possible, while trying to suppress her own growing doubts.

Ola Durenberger had been sleeping when Frau Frunzell, the hotelkeeper, had come to her room. Earlier in the week, she had arrived in this hidden valley after fleeing Kanderschloss. Michelle had suggested it as a place to hide out, pointing out that hardly anyone knew its existence. Ola did not have a valid passport, and was a virtual prisoner in Switzerland. And, in the eyes of the Swedes, she was still a fugitive.

She had arrived on the postal bus with only the clothes on her back. It was near the end of the season, and Frau Frunzell was glad to have the extra help from the girl.

"Hanalei, get dressed," Frau Frunzell said, waking the sleeping girl. "We have guests for breakfast. Hurry now." Frunzell kicked the bed to make her point, rousing Ola from the dreamy world in which she mainly lived.

When Frau Frunzell had left, Ola quickly dropped her nightdress on to the floor of the small back room where she slept. She took the borrowed dress, and slid it over her head. Passing a comb through her long hair, she tied it tightly in a bun. Most of the week before she had been cleaning the floors and doing washing, in preparation for the winter closing of the hotel. These were the first guests to come since she'd arrived. The hotel was closing in a few weeks for the winter and Ola hoped that Frau Frunzell would allow her to stay, in return for doing chores around the small farmstead.

Michael looked directly into her eyes when she set down the two cups for the coffee. They had both noticed the girl because she bore such a striking resemblance, at least in body shape and hair color, to the missing programmer. When she returned with the eggs and rosti, he was certain that she was the same woman he'd met at the Oberschloss the week before.

"I think we've found her," he said quietly, once she'd returned to the kitchen.

"Are you certain?"

"Yes," said Michael, looking back towards the kitchen.

Natalya stood up. Quiet as a cat she inched towards the swinging doors that opened onto the kitchen. She could see the girl arguing with Frau Frunzell, then, pulling away, the girl ran from the room. Natalya tore after her, through the kitchen, past the startled Swiss innkeeper.

"Ola," Natalya shouted as she pushed her way outside. "Stop!"

Ola hesitated.

"We're not going to hurt you." Natalya covered the distance to the open space in the front of the hotel where Ola waited. She put her arm protectively around her. "We're going to take you home now. Okay?"

Ola nodded. She was very tired and confused. This woman was like Herr Von Kleise, she thought. She is strong. She will protect me.

Michael drove the car back to Kanderschloss, as Natalya sat next to the girl in the backseat, holding her hand. Ola was like a young child, and the most important thing to do was to re-establish trust.

For Ola, the Oberschloss had been a refuge, not a prison. She knew she could not survive in the frightening outside world. Her troubles in Sweden had come from being impressionable and young. Jan had been the first man who had paid attention to the awkward, possibly mildly autistic, little girl in a woman's body. In return, she had given him her skills and intelligence, which he had used to hack the networks of some of Sweden's largest companies, and steal their technical secrets. For more than a year, they had sold technical drawings and plans to the highest bidders, living well on the proceeds. Then, one of these "buyers" had turned out to be a private detective, hired by a large Swedish electronics firm, and their little empire crumbled. The result was a ten-year sentence at Gothenburg prison, for both Jan and her.

Michelle had read about the case at the time. Ola had fit their needs: a brilliant programmer with a sordid past that could be used to control her. Some carefully placed bribes had ensured her quick release into a rehabilitation program, funded by the Von Kleise Foundation. At the Oberschloss, and safely protected from the outside world, she had transferred her love from Jan to the stern, but indulgent Von Kleise.

Michael parked the car and Natalya led Ola into the house. It was nearly eleven in the morning. The markets had been open for almost two hours in Europe.

"Ola, when you left with Michelle, what did you do to the computers?" asked Michael on the way up to the Oberschloss.

"We switched the computers to hold."

"Why not let them work?" Michael asked.

"Michelle was frightened and angry," said Ola, remembering Michelle's look as she had come into the room just in time to see Masters shoot Von Kleise.

"But they can be started again?" Natalya asked.

"Yes." Ola's face lit up now for the first time in hours. "Still, perhaps it is not so much a problem," she said, looking far away and thinking. "The programs are self-adjusting: the probabilities are being monitored, using selective news feeds, allowing the buy and sell orders to be changed as needed."

"Herr Von Kleise was my grandfather, Ola," Natalya explained. "Michael and I are named in his will as his heirs."

"And after I fix the programs, where will I go?"

"You will have a place with us as long as you wish." Natalya reached out and held her hand. Ola moved closer, and Natalya put her arm around her, and held her tight against her, feeling the Swedish girl relax. Then Ola thought and pulled away, and looked at them both as the cable car slowed as it reached the upper station of the lift.

"And you will not turn me back in to the authorities in Sweden?" She looked worried, "They would send me to a disciplinary camp in the Arctic this time."

"We will protect you," Natalya agreed, considering that the fate of the future world economy rested on Ola's abilities.

Ola relaxed and smiled, pleased to be home again.

Natalya led Ola into the living room of the Oberschloss. Frau Bundt, along with the two Swiss women who helped her, had returned earlier in the week, and had cleaned up the rooms. A faint smell of cordite still hung in the air. A smaller, temporary television had been set up, to allow them to keep up with the world news.

They followed Ola into the room filled with banks of servers and communications links. Ola went to the console, typed several commands, grimaced, and then repeated the sequence. After a minute, she looked up and smiled. She pointed to the screen.

"You see, the computers are still monitoring the markets." Ola pointed at the screen. "There is the current gold price out of Zurich for spot sales, and the London fixing is there." A few more key strokes and the entire display of market data was pulled up, filling the three screens that were grouped around her desk. Another key stroke and the information was displayed on the plasma screen that covered one wall of her office.

Michael noted that gold was now trading at close to $3,500 an ounce. Ola showed them the open orders to buy at that price.

"A sequence of commands will begin the trading. We will sell at least some of the gold; just enough, to partially satisfy the demand." She typed a few more commands. Then she looked at the calendar on the wall. It was Friday, nearly a week after the start. She ran an estimate of the future size of the portfolio. The delay had added at least 20% to the value expected at the end of the play.

"Victoria's design takes advantage of Herr Von Kleise's existing open-market positions. Many of these have been already executed, as our offer prices were more than current prices. When orders in Zurich are great enough to dispose completely of a portion of our gold, then we sell. This ensures that we get good prices." Ola pointed to the debit side of the neatly printed ledger. "And there are the purchases on our credit balances in New York, London, Paris, Frankfurt and Tokyo, Hong Kong, Singapore, Rio, and a half a dozen others. The program, in real time, recalculates probabilities and market elasticity, modifies positions, and then trades accordingly."

"What determines the buy points?"

"Michelle and Victoria worked out a program that predicts the likely lows that shares will reach, at different points in the new cycle, based on preexisting market psychologies, and the current patterns. Victoria supplied the market knowledge, Michelle the trader psychology. You see that list of stocks?" She pointed to a long list of stock symbols, with two columns of figures next to them. "We will concentrate our buying in mainly these companies, but to make it work, will spread buying and selling in many, many others, in markets everywhere."

"This column" Natalya asked, pointing at the screen, "what does that represent?"

"These are existing orders to buy at a fixed price. Herr Von Kleise had a term for it..." The Swedish girl struggled with trying to recall the exact technical term.

"Tender offers?" Natalya filled in.

"Yes, yes, tenders outstanding," she said, recalling the explanation that Herr Von Kleise had offered her when she had first asked. "Just like tender nipples, yes?" Ola smiled, thinking about how the old man had touched her breasts lightly when he'd explained it to her.

Michael looked puzzled, but Natalya laughed, thinking how Von Kleise might well have explained this concept to Ola.

"And these have been fulfilled?" Michael asked.

"I will bring up our current position in terms of percentages. We are not allowed to buy more than the preset regulatory limits." She pulled up a second screen, sent it to the printer and handed it to Michael. Michael studied it. It read like the International Fortune 500.

The first part of the plan, to gain effective control, was obvious. But to use that control effectively, a group of people would have to be put in charge, with the same basic business philosophy. Governments would consider any cooperation between companies as collusion and an anti-trust violation, so everything would have to be done secretly. Human greed would also get in the way, and undoubtedly, there would be complications, including massive legal battles tying up the stock for years, even decades. To work then, the Society of the Phoenix would have to remain a closely held secret group, using its power to control the activities of these companies in the background. Managing this size of portfolio would be nearly impossible, let alone changing the culture of the management and employees.

"Is this entirely for Von Kleise's account?" Natalya asked.

"I don't know. These stocks are the ones we have been allocated. This list is of our primary targets. This, Herr Ross, is the list of secondary companies we will buy, if there are sufficient funds."

A few moments later, Ola smiled, and told them, "The first sale of gold has been executed. We have sent orders to the automated systems in London, Paris, Frankfurt, and have placed orders in New York for the opening in a few hours."

"What's our position now?" Natalya asked.

"I'll put it up on the screen," she said, switching on the overhead monitor. "We will trade the commodity markets in the US when they open. Oil is far higher than we expected, but metal and food grains are lower. We will buy futures contracts at these low prices, and then later, add demand in the spot markets. This will allow prices to rise, and we will sell these at a profit."

Ola chattered on happily explaining how the programs worked. "We pause now and let the markets settle. If a rally begins, then we will sell some of the shares. It will take not much selling; not more than three percent of our existing portfolio—half a billion dollars—to panic the markets again. And after the weekend, we will begin again. Victoria called it 'milking the market.'"

"And if I want to buy in the afternoon?"

"You mean override the computer?" She looked surprised. "Why, Herr Ross? We have tested the algorithms thoroughly."

As they listened to Ola's dispassionate explanation, the hours passed and stocks were bought and sold by machine intervention communicating with other machines, asking for confirmations, and relaying this back to the human inhabitants of the room.

"When do we have to physically move the gold?" Michael asked thinking about the problems of that transfer.

"We had deposits of about 10% in the SBS vaults at Zurich, but the bulk is here. The first sales were thus made out of our stocks held in Zurich. The remainder will come from these stocks. However, gold is rarely shipped. So, as we sell our gold from our vaults, it will remain here, and we will charge storage costs to the purchaser."

According to Ola, the Society owned some 5,000 tons of gold, which, if sold carefully, could bring in half a trillion dollars. The list of target companies that Ola showed had been worth close to 4 trillion dollars before the market crash, but had now fallen to be worth less than 1 trillion dollars. Given their existing holdings, and the fact that these companies had diverse ownership, they would only needed to purchase about 40% of each company, to effectively gain control of the Board of Directors. In the end, if Ola's calculations were correct, they would end up controlling all of the most important global multinationals in the world!

Michael took Natalya out of the room. "What do you think?" he asked her, wondering if they were making the problem worse.

"We have no other choice, but to let Ola do her magic, Michael. We don't know enough to make strategic buys. Let the programs work. Then we can decide what to do next."

"But the money was ill-gotten. We've now violated a hundred different laws in a hundred different countries."

"Perhaps," she said, thinking about the likelihood of legal actions succeeding, "but it would be difficult to prove in court." In the end, they were merely the inheritors of the Trust, and not really responsible for setting the collapse in motion. "Apparently, they will file all the needed papers to make this legal. As Ola reported, as they buy more than 5% of a company's shares, they will file the necessary forms. Victoria was careful to follow the appropriate laws. In the confusion of the last week, there will be few analysts studying these reports. No, they will prefer to see this as simply the interplay of markets, not some global conspiracy." Secretly though, she knew that, in time, there would be many people who would want to take them to court, once the truth started to come out.

Natalya saw the continuing turmoil in Michael's eyes. The Dow Index had stood at close to 13,000 before the sell-off. The low had been reached within a week, hitting just over 2,540, and rivaling the 1929 market collapse in sheer percentage drop. There was no choice but to execute the automatic trading programs, before there was nothing left but jetsam and flotsam in the market. There was just no one buying stocks. Early indications from private surveys suggested that companies were cancelling investments, and hiring plans and layoffs were already starting in the retail and construction industries. The world economy was collapsing, and unless they allowed Ola to act, the long-term fallout would be catastrophic.

Natalya tried one final time to get Michael to see the broader picture. "Heinrich has given us a gift. We must use it wisely, as he asked. It's the only solution. You said yourself there's paralysis in the markets, and that governments will not act, at least, not until all the damage is done, and then it will be too late. This is the only solution."

"At the end of next week, Natalya, where will we be?"

"Where's your vision, Michael?" she said sternly.

"I'm trying to think about what we have to do after the smoke clears. The other members of the group may not be so kindly disposed towards our leadership from here on, now that Heinrich is dead. And who are they really? We know so few of the names of the members: Carlos's father is one, Richard Kahn another, but that's all I have at the moment." He paused, the worry showing on his deeply lined face. He was exhausted. "How do we even contact them?"

Natalya sat down next to him. He was, she thought, so like her father. Now, he too carried the weight of the world on his shoulders.

"The world is changing. It's a new playing field, and we have no choice but to play the game until it ends. The important point is that we are in this together."

"If we sold the gold now, dumped it, and bought into the market, choosing stocks at random, and started a rally, then we might well break the speculative bubble, Natalya."

"Then, we let the same greedy players prosper. No, my love, it is time for change. Let's make it a change for the better, not worse. To do that, we must have enough control of global economic power to influence the direction of change."

She had to reach him, and make him see that he was not alone in this, that she was with him. "I saw your face when Von Kleise laid out his vision that day atop Ob Barglvi. I saw that you believed, as he believed, that the problems can be solved, but that they will not solve themselves; that the invisible hand of Adam Smith is fallible."

He closed his eyes, lying back against the cushions of the couch. He didn't see the Shining City on a Hill of Ronald Reagan. Instead, he saw a squatter's town just below a high-rise apartment in Sao Paulo, the slums of Calcutta, and the shanty towns of Southern Africa. She was right. The only model for the modern age was one that was cooperative and holistic in scope, that would create a sustainable path where all people could flourish. Socialism repressed individuals and prevented them from achieving their potential, but the free market, if left to itself, would eventually lead to social revolution.

"Perhaps, Natalya," he said, when he opened his eyes, "I lack the vision."

"I'm here to help," she said, quietly reaching for him and pulling him close to her bosom as a mother cradles a child.

They didn't speak for some time.

"I need to resign, and the sooner the better," said Michael eventually, pulling himself away from Natalya.

"They won't be happy."

"They're not happy now." He had already had a series of heated telephone calls with Washington. The week abroad had seemed like a lifetime, and the separation from his colleagues' opinions had made the gulf wider than normal.

"Type it out and you can email it to them. They will still be at work."

Michael nodded and stood up. He went to the computer and composed his short letter of resignation. He felt a pang of conscience, but Natalya was right. He could do far more good from here.

"There, it's done," he said when he had sent it. "Now, we're both free."

Ola stood up when they entered the room. She had hardly eaten at all, taking only a bite of the sandwich that Natalya had brought her earlier.

"How has it being going?"

"Well, very well, I think." She handed Michael a two-page table, detailing the day's activities. He studied the numbers, and then handed the paper to Natalya who smiled. Ola felt contented too. She felt at home again.

"The market, did we have an effect?" he asked.

"The Dow is up ten per cent from its low. The NASDAQ is still below yesterday, but we've slowed the rate of decline. We are letting techs slide a little more before starting to buy aggressively. We will need to acquire a lot of tech companies, so we need them to stay cheap."

"And gold? Have we sold any, and at what price?"

"We've lost about 12% off the high. Still, we are ahead as the price is about 40% above our estimated sell points. We have sold about 7% less than had been budgeted for, but we will sell more next week."

Frau Bundt entered the room carrying a tray of drinks and hors d'oeurves as the phone rang. Michael picked it up, grimaced, and then leaning against the couch, listened as the President of the United States chewed him out for quitting while the battle raged.

"You can't just quit, Mike! The press is already having a field day, wondering where you are, and why you're not here to fight the good fight."

"I have too much to do here. And then there's the problem of a conflict of interest."

"What are you doing there? They tell me you and the girl are holed up there like two cats in heat."

Michael didn't answer. It was no use arguing.

"I gave Brad my best advice, Mr. President: to sell the gold and put the funds into buying stocks and bonds, to shore up the market."

"They'd scream bloody murder if I tried that, Mike. I'd be impeached. I'm not even sure that I have the authority to sell the goddamn stuff either. Nor is there time, no precedent for it. And who would do the selling? I'm a lame duck, or will be next Tuesday, so that is a nonstarter."

"It's my best advice, Mr. President." Michael repeated.

"Not one of the others agree. Even if I had the authority, it would smack of State socialism," the President pointed out. "And Brad tells me the market had a small rally this afternoon."

"You see, it's going to be okay, even if you don't have me there."

The President looked up as Brad Stevens followed by Harley Mumford entered the room. Both men were smiling, obviously pleased with the improvement in the New York stock market over the last few hours of the trading day.

"Just a second, Mike. I got Harley and Brad here with me. Let me put you on the speaker, okay?"

Michael waited, the quality of the sound changed as the microphone picked up everything going on within the Oval office. He could imagine the President, slumped back against the big, red leather recliner. The others, Michael knew, would be sitting on the edge of the other overstuffed leather chairs that were spread around the big desk in the Oval Office.

"You still there, Mike? I got Brad and Harley here."

"Yes, Mr. President."

"Hi, Mike," Brad Stevens said in his most boisterous tone of voice. Then there was a kind of low rumble, which was Harley Mumford chiming in.

"I was just telling Mike that he can't quit. I won't let him, not now anyway."

"And I was just telling the President," Michael said, realizing that he had some control over his own destiny too, "that I can't come back just yet. And besides, you won't take my advice."

"Rather strange advice, Mike," Harley Mumford said with a laugh "Did you really tell Brad that we should dispose of the gold at Fort Knox to break the speculation, and then buy into the equity markets directly? That's a very un-American solution, bordering on socialism."

Michael decided not to correct Harley. "But I see things are improving. I'm certain things will get better without you adopting my radical solution. You made any progress on settling the labor dispute in the Trans-Pac?"

"A little. At least the two sides are talking."

"Ride this out and it'll all turn out well," Michael said, looking at Natalya. "I'm sure the market will respond once the shock is over, and some of the unknowns are sorted out."

"What do you think we should do about the third-world debt? Seems to me that …" the President fumbled for the piece of paper that he had been handed by Fred Schurz, "that the IFF proposal could cost the US government and our banks around $300 billion."

"I think that we can strike a deal with IFF," Michael said, thinking about the frantic calls he'd received from Walter earlier in the week. "Let me call the Holtzs and see if we can get some kind of compromise. What Walter and Katherine really want is to be recognized as major players at any meeting between borrowers and lenders."

"Great idea, Michael!" Brad Stevens chimed in, feeling almost happy at the prospect of turning that can of worms over to Michael for his attention. "I was thinking about that option."

"I'll give them a call after I hang up."

"Must be late there, Mike," the President said feigning consideration.

"It's close to ten."

"We'll talk tomorrow. I'll call you, and Brad will be in touch to see what you can get out of our friends in Geneva."

Michael put the phone down. His offer to call the Holtzs had been meant as a gesture only. He doubted it would stop them from moving forward. And he hadn't told the President what he wanted to say.

Michael sat up against the cushioned headboard and watched Natalya get ready for bed. Despite everything that had happened, he was finally beginning to feel happy.

"What are you thinking about?" asked Natalya, sliding down next to him.

"How safe I feel with you beside me." He pulled her close to him. "I don't know how I could function without you."

"You don't have to now." She nuzzled closer.

As he reached for Natalya, he was interrupted by the ringing of the phone. Michael picked it up. He immediately knew who it was.

"Is it too late for you, Mike?"

"No, Mr. President," Michael let his hand lie on one of Natalya's breasts as she squeezed close to him to hear what was being said. Playfully, he rolled his finger around her nipple has he talked, and she tried to suppress a giggle.

"I just thought we could have a private talk, just you and I, without the others."

"That would be good, Mr. President."

"You're really intent on resigning?"

"Yes, I really have no choice now."

"I talked to Turner," said the President, thinking about what he had been told. "He said you inherited Von Kleise's fortune. I can see why you wouldn't want to come home."

"Not exactly, Mr. President. Natalya and I are trustees of the Foundation."

"I can understand that, but, Mike, is it more important than the future of your country?"

"America will be still there long after I'm old and gray. You can count on that."

"To quote an old expression, it looks like the world's gone rather quickly to hell in a hand basket. The election's coming up, and it's thrown the race into a kind of dogfight as to who can do the best job of fixing the mess. But in truth, I think the candidates are scared more of winning than losing. Whoever takes office will face a problem larger than the one I faced back in 2009. Frankly, I can't blame them either." Michael continued to listen quietly to this soliloquy of woes.

"I can't tell where things will end up. We have problems on all fronts. Asia's in crisis, the Germans seem bent on destroying seventy years of European integration, and the private sector is already sending signals that that they will be like turtles when it comes to investing and hiring. Worst yet, there's a whole bunch of Islamic clerics that are pointing to the markets' collapse as a sign from Allah of the impending destruction of the Western materialist and secular model." Then pausing, almost as an aside, "And on Tuesday, the American people will go to the polls."

"Make selling the gold your last act, Mr. President, and buy into the market in a big way. They can't impeach you if you're not President next term. Tell the American people that you have faith in the future. Put the Government's money where it has faith in American companies. There's enough money from selling the gold, combined with the growth we would get over the next twenty to thirty years in share prices and company revenues, to close the gaps we have in the Medicare and the Social Security trust funds."

The President was silent. "You'll have to convince Brad Stevens and Fred Schurz. I'm going to get them on a plane to Switzerland this evening."

Michael put the receiver down. He looked towards where Natalya waited.

"What did he say?"

"He's thinking about it. He's sending Brad Stevens and Fred Schurz to talk it over with me."

"Do you think that you can convince them?"

"Who knows?" Michael said, reaching out for her. She came close, pressing her body against his.

"What is it?"

"I just thought of something."

"What?" Natalya said worried.

"My mortgage," Michael said thinking out loud. "I forgot to pay it this month."

Philippe Bertrand, the French official who was Ross's counterpart in the study group set up to monitor Phoenix, looked at his counterparts; those who could come at short notice to meet with Michael Ross at Kandersteg.

"You flew over last night?" Bertrand asked the Secretary of the Treasury Bradley Stevens.

"Yes. I'm exhausted, but pleased to be here."

"This has not been an easy week." Bertrand said in a deadpan tone.

"Hardly the kind that I'd like to repeat," said Stevens. There had been little he could do all week, except read the depressing reports that crossed his desk. They were out of options.

"Come and have some lunch. I'm sure you must be hungry," suggested Michael, motioning his guests towards the luncheon table that had been set up inside. The weather had turned warmer and the sun was bright, but it was too cool to eat outdoors.

Stevens stared at his watch. It was noon in Europe, but his internal clock suggested it was six a.m. He yawned.

"Did you know," Natalya said, coming up with Fred Schurz on one arm, "that Fred and I were classmates?"

"When?"

"When we were at Harvard."

"And I was in love with her too, Michael," said Schurz smiling. He was short and stocky. They had not agreed on a single Fed policy since Schurz had been appointed to the Vice Chairmanship the year before, as a political payback.

"Well, Fred, she's mine now!" Michael said, impulsively taking Natalya's other arm and pulling her away from Schurz

"I was simply buttering up Fred Schulz. You never know when you may need an ally. You were jealous, weren't you?" Natalya whispered when they were out of earshot.

"I guess so."

"You shouldn't be, she said with a laugh, seeing suddenly the stern, conservative, Swiss German in Schurz for the first time. "He's far too German for my tastes." She leaned up and kissed Michael lightly on the cheek.

Earlier that morning, Lilly Masters and Beth had been moved from Kanderschloss and given rooms at the Oberschloss. Once she was certain that Beth was resting comfortably at the Oberschloss under the care of Frau Bundt, Lilly returned and asked Natalya for a job. She was bored, and needed work to make her feel worthwhile again.

"We'll find something for you to do," Natalya had assured her.

"I want to go home soon, too."

"I am afraid that that would be inconvenient, both for you, and for the US Government, if you went back as yourself. But Mr. Turner informs me that a new identity is being prepared for both you and Beth."

"When will this be ready?"

"I don't know."

"And if I don't like it? If I want to recover what was lost?"

"I suppose we couldn't stop you, but it wouldn't be easy. Even if anyone believed the story that you and Beth were sex slaves in Asia, how normal a life could she have after that? Besides, everything you once owned is lost. Latimer saw to that."

Lilly knew that Natalya was right. "Then what can I do to help?" she asked after a few moments of thought.

"We can offer you a job at the Kanderschloss, starting immediately. I suggest that you take it."

"What would be my duties?" she asked.

"Helping around the house, especially now that we are having so many guests. So, for now it will just be serving and cleaning, but in time, there may be other things that you will be better suited for." Natalya smiled because she had far greater sympathy for Lillian Masters than for Beth or Ben.

"And how much will it pay?" asked Lilly, suddenly feeling that she must be practical about money from now on.

"I think that 1,500 Swiss Francs a week will be adequate, plus your room and board," replied Natalya.

Lilly Masters adjusted the ill-fitting maid's outfit. She waited for Peter Mueller, who had managed the staff at Kanderschloss for many years, to hand her the tray of hors d'oeuvres.

"You must learn to smile more," Peter said, bringing Lilly back to the present. "Come. It isn't that bad."

"I'm sorry Herr Mueller."

"Peter, please" he said, lightly touching her hand. "After all, we are colleagues, yes?"

Mueller had a pleasant, open face, and kind eyes. Taking the tray, she walked towards the door, then out to the living room. The guests were milling around. They barely noticed her.

Michael had known Phillippe Bertrand for years, and he had also gone to school with Natalya at Harvard. With the Americans here, Natalya had suggested that Phillippe could represent the interests of the European Union. As one of the founding members of the Phoenix Group that had met in Annecy at the start of the summer, Phillippe was in a unique position to help.

"Are you going to tell us the truth then, Michael?" Philippe Bertrand asked as the last course was served at lunch.

"What would you like to know?"

"The connection, Michael, between Von Kleise and Phoenix," he asked. "There is one, I sense it."

"I'm afraid that I have little to tell on that, Philippe. As far as I know there's no connection. At heart, Heinrich was a trader. He traded hard goods that the Russians needed for gold. The trades had to be in secret. If it had become public, the ruble would have collapsed."

"And can you sell this gold?" Bradley Stevens asked.

"We expect that, by early next week, we will have the legal right to do that." Michael lied. The amount of gold far surpassed the Russian hoard. And they had the legal rights to sell. They were already selling, but selling slowly. "We'll sell most of it. The proceeds will flow to the Kleise Foundation."

"Is it enough to break the downward drift?"

"Who knows. The winds are blowing pretty hard in the wrong direction," Michael answered. If Michelle's analysis was correct, by the end of the programmed portion of the buying and selling, the Dow would have recovered more than half of its loss.

"But you could stop the increase in the gold price at least, and possibly influence the market as well."

"Brad, it will take more than the gold we have to break the downward spiral. We have to assure the markets that we are serious about solving problems, and God knows there are enough of those to scare anyone from investing. We have fundamental problems that have been put on the back burner for years, ranging from climate change to staggering youth unemployment. Leaving these problems to the 'markets to decide'," Michael said, staring at Harley Mumford, "will not work this time."

"You're sounding quite radical, Michael," Bertrand suggested, "asking us to sell our gold and buy shares. Perhaps it comes from living with a former socialist." He looked at Natalya and winked.

"And if we do nothing? Don't you think that the markets will eventually right themselves?" Fred Schurz suggested. He had remained silent throughout most of the lunch, preferring to listen.

"The markets will recover. It will just take more time, and the cost in terms of individuals and companies will be great," Michael warned. "The calculated losses on paper are in the trillions of dollars."

Michael continued. "And there are other worries. The most dangerous one, given the huge equity that is invested, is what's happening to property values. With mortgage rates rising as fast as they are now," he stared at the Fed Chairman, "this could trigger a severe contraction in aggregate spending. We need low rates and some kind of business compact so they don't cut back, and don't lay off workers. We can't let the post 2008 fall out happen again."

After the meeting had concluded, Michael sat alone with Natalya in the gathering darkness of the late afternoon.

"What did you think?"

"I think we tried, Michael."

"And you don't think they're convinced?"

"I don't know. Perhaps Stevens was swayed, but his eyes lit up at the thought that we would act on our own."

In the distance, they could hear the phone ring. It stopped and Peter Mueller came in carrying the portable phone.

"It's for Miss Avramowitz," he said, handing the phone to Natalya.

Natalya put the telephone receiver to her ear. Through the static, she heard Pyotr's voice sounding far away as if on another planet. He spoke in Russian, and as she listened, she cried. Finally, she answered his single question about Michael. The phone line went dead. She dropped the portable phone on the couch, and then began to sob loudly.

"What did he say?"

"On the streets of Moscow there's open warfare. Many people are dying, the city is in a panic, and people are fleeing. The electricity and the gas have been cut off, and winter is coming. They have established a line of defense north of Moscow with the troops they have, and are trying to bring in more. It's turning out to be a fight within the Army itself, north against south; conservatives against; more liberal elements. But don't think that they are pro-American, or even happy with the pirate form of capitalism that developed in Russia after the collapse of the Soviet Union. They are Russian nationalists, and that includes my father. In short, my love," she said, "a god-awful mess."

Michael reached for her. He pulled her close and she nuzzled into his chest, burrowing her head under his arms.

"He'll be okay," said Michael, trying to be reassuring, without feeling any assurance himself.

"I have to believe that my father knew this could happen, and that he planned for this. He loves his country, and said he was prepared to fight, but I can't let him die there." The part she did not relay from the call was that the fear she'd heard in Pyotr's voice. It meant that he didn't think they could win. It was like a repeat of 1917, when the Bolsheviks defeated the more liberal Kerensky Government that had been established after the abdication by the Czar. History was repeating itself. It would be another fight between the Whites and Reds, but this time, each side was armed with nuclear weapons.

"You can't help him, not yet. But perhaps in time, when we know more, there will be something we can do."

She walked with Michael towards the master bedroom at the Kanderschloss, and stood still while he helped her undress. The pressure of the past weeks had finally caught up with her, and she was frightened and tired. Anger at her father had given way to love. Michael pulled back the covers, and she lay down. Michael slid next to her, but they didn't make love then. Halfway through the night, she came to him. She caressed his chest with her fingers, making furrows in the dark hairs. They then made love. It was not the slow pleasure of a long night, but the hurried passions of two lovers traveling on passing trains, who happened to have met in a lonely station for the night. And, as Natalya pressed her body against Michael, and as she squeezed her hips down against his loins, she cried.

40. The Gift of the Phoenix

The President looked out across the Oeschinensee, towards the snow-covered peaks of the Bluemlisalpenhorn. The election, which had been held earlier in the week, had miraculously, left his party in charge. The new President was a woman, Kirsten Anderson. He didn't envy her the job. She would inherit a worse mess than he had inherited. Towards the end of the campaign, it seemed that neither candidate was fighting for the job very hard, almost willing the other one to win. With the economy in shambles, and the world seemingly going mad, people were, in the end, too afraid to change leaders. The market had rallied strongly on Monday and Tuesday, the week of the election, which had helped too.

"It's beautiful, Mike, just breathtaking." He looked around at the main room with its thirty-foot ceiling and floor-to-ceiling windows looking out over the lake, and up towards the Blumlisalp Rothorn, where the Oberschloss was perched, but at that moment, was hidden in clouds that were swirling around its summit. "And all of this is yours now?"

"That's still unclear. The lawyers are working out the details," Michael replied.

All in all, things had not turned out as badly as it had appeared weeks before. The President decided not to pry too deeply, and was grateful that things seemed to be working out. Germany had given indications that it would remain a part of the European Union, and for now at least, continue with the euro, but there was still the problem of the Bavarian State President Brantheim and his New Deutschland Nationalist Party, with its platform of withdrawing from the EU and the euro. The Russian problem remained serious, but it was largely political and military, not economic. At least some Russian gas was starting to flow into Western Europe again. The strike at the ports had been halted temporarily while talks were begun, but it hung over the world like a shroud, making even the smallest rays of hope dimmer. The threat of the cancellation of debt remained, but both parties were talking, which had calmed the markets. Of course, the Dow remained depressed, but it was stable and well off its lows.

There remained the mystery of how this had all happened, and whether anyone was behind it. But the President was a realist, pragmatic in his thinking that there were things best left unsaid or unknown. He decided not to pry into Michael and Natalya's involvement.

Bradley Stevens came over to where Michael and the President were talking.

"Sure glad it's starting to improve, Brad," Michael said.

"So am I," Bradley said, thinking about the *Miracle of Wall Street* that had occurred the week following their previous meeting.

"We didn't have to sell any gold either, did we?"

"No," Michael answered. "Probably wouldn't have worked anyway." He smiled, but thought to himself, you asshole, it was a missed opportunity that would have bought security for millions of retirees long into the future.

"I did seriously think about it you know," said the President with a bemused grin. "Now, there they are." He looked towards where Katherine Holtz had come into the room.

On seeing the President, Walter directed Katherine towards him. Their meeting with the world's leaders would start the next day, but tonight's affair was a private gathering.

"Walter Holtz and Katherine Holtz." Brad Stevens introduced the Holtz's to the President.

The President extended his hand. He noted that the woman's grip was stronger than the man's.

"I guess you two have caused some trouble," the President said cheerfully, as Brad Stevens looked on nervously. One could never be certain when that informal tone was being put on as a way of hiding the President's keen intelligence. "But then maybe we had it coming to us. We've been sidestepping this problem for too many years."

Walter Holtz smiled. The Pact of Geneva, worked out last Wednesday, with Michael serving as mediator, had called for a 90-day moratorium on the default, and the promise of new approaches to solving the crisis of debt without forcing further destructive austerity. This had given the global economy a shot in the arm. Monday's Kandersteg Forum on World Debt would begin the process of identifying these approaches, but it was more talk, and probably wouldn't amount to anything more than another lofty communique at the end that lacked teeth for enforcement.

Katherine Holtz looked around the room. Where was Natalya? There were fifty invited guests, mostly senior ministers of Western governments.

It was billed as a social gathering, but Katherine had been surprised when Michael had called to invite them personally.

"You're looking very healthy, Michael." Katherine came up to where Michael was waiting by the door. She kissed him lightly on one cheek. "And when will you start to call me mother?" she said with a smile.

"Not yet," he smiled back.

"If Walter and I could do it over again," Katherine said lightly, "then we would certainly not have asked you and your wife to come with us to Kandersteg to meet Papa twenty-five years ago." She then chuckled as if this were a joke, but Michael suspected that that thought had crossed both their minds many times since Von Kleise had changed his will.

Michael looked towards the staircase as Natalya entered the room. She was dressed in a white wedding gown that had been fitted in Bern that morning. She had taken Lillian Masters with her. Her taste in clothes had always been extraordinary, and her advice didn't disappoint. The decision to have the wedding that evening, before the meeting, had been Natalya's. It was important, she felt, that this be a public expression, so there would be no doubts about the control of the Von Kleise charitable trusts.

Conversation came to a halt when she appeared. Michael went to where she stood on the steps leading down into the living area.

"I have an announcement," he said, clapping his hands to get everyone's attention. "I suppose that some of you may have guessed, but this evening, aside from allowing some quiet socializing before the start of tomorrow's gathering, is also to be Natalya's and my wedding night." Michael reached for Natalya's hand and gripped it. She pressed in close to him.

A little later, Natalya saw Katherine standing alone. "Shall we drink to Carlos, Mother?" she asked, raising the glass of wine, while staring directly at her mother.

"You made a lovely bride, my dear," said Katherine, ignoring her daughter's words. Studying her, without rancor, Katherine noted that in many ways they were alike. "Michael is very, very lucky to have found you, Natalya."

Turning, Katherine walked off without looking back, leaving Michael holding Natalya's hand. She was trembling.

"Come, the President is waiting."

Francis Turner stood to one side of Natalya, standing in for her father, and Kim served as her Maid of Honor. Brad Stevens was Michael's best man and held the rings, hastily picked out that morning from a Kandersteg jeweler. The gold of the rings, the jeweler had claimed, was old, dating back to the seventeenth century.

Lilly watched through the window as the last guest passed through the guarded check points that surrounded the house. Outside, she could see the Swiss military patrols moving across the grounds. She turned and went back into the living room, picking up a final dish that had been missed. The President of the United States, the Prime Minister of Great Britain, the President of France, as well as the Japanese and Chinese Premiers were sleeping there tonight. Swiss security personnel, mixed with protection services of the five nations, rested in the living room, and stood guard outside the house. Troops patrolled the grounds, and no tourists had been allowed to come up the cableway to the lake for almost a week.

"Is that the last of them?"

"Yes," she said, relieved that all the guests other than the Presidents and Prime Ministers had left. She had never thought much about the staff at the parties that she and Ben used to throw. She was exhausted.

Despite her exhaustion, Lilly looked at the man who, in the past week, had taken hold of her life and given it direction. He wasn't Ben, but then few men were like Ben. He wasn't Brett Latimer either, for there wasn't anything that was smooth or silky about him, but he did his job well, running the estate, and when the party had to be arranged at short notice, he had managed it without showing any concern or fear. But most of all, she liked the way that he treated her. He was friendly, but not overly familiar with her.

"Are you tired?" he asked her.

"Exhausted," she smiled. She pushed back a strand of gold hair. "Did you think that any of them recognized me dressed like this?"

"No, of course not. You see, most guests don't ever look at the staff. Now come, there's coffee in the kitchen, and we deserve a slice of that torte that I had Francois work up, just in case we ran out of wedding cake."

Lilly followed him into the kitchen.

It was after two o'clock. She would have at least a half-hour ride up to the Oberschloss, and then she would have to return for breakfast in just three hours.

"It's too late for you to go," Mueller said.

"Where can I stay?"

"Come, I will give you my bed," he said putting the coffee in the sink. "I will sleep on the couch."

She followed him. Entering the small, two-room suite that he had, she looked at the pictures that lined the wall. There was Peter with many of the greats who had come to Kandersteg to discuss politics, business, and economics with Von Kleise. Did she hate the man who had destroyed her life so completely? She tried not to think about it.

"I have an extra pair of pajamas," Peter said, showing her the folded cotton shorts and top. "There's a bathroom in there. I'll dress here."

Lilly went inside and undressed. She washed quickly, and then dressed in the too big pajamas.

"I have turned back the bed," he said with a smile. "You will be comfortable." He turned and went towards the door to the second room.

"Peter," Lilly said quietly.

He stopped and turned.

"There's room for two here," she said, pulling back the sheets some more. "Come into bed with me."

He looked at her and waited. "Are you sure?"

"Yes, yes, please." She said blushing like a schoolgirl. "Come now, it's late and the morning will come before we know it."

He turned out the light before sliding into the bed next to her. He felt her press her body against his. Despite their exhaustion, they made love. And for once, in a long, long time, it felt right.

It was close to morning when Natalya awoke. The dim light coming in from the east began to send long beams of light across the chain of the far off Alps. She stared at the still strange surroundings, and then at the man sleeping next to her. Sitting up in bed she pulled her legs up, and wrapping her arms around them stared out the window towards the open sky. She had had a dream about Pyotr and it had frightened her.

Michael sat up in bed next to her. He reached out, pulling her close.

"What are you thinking about?"

"Destiny … karma … fate." Natalya looked at Michael.

He had never thought much of destiny. He could define it, but not understand the truth behind the overused word. Yet, the events of the last few weeks had thrust the fate of billions into his hands. If that wasn't destiny, then what was? His meeting with Natalya and falling in love; was that destiny?

Von Kleise had given him the tool to do good, but not the instructions as to what to do. Was he the right one to wield it? His skills as a manager were inadequate. At best, he was a hopeless academic, not a charismatic champion of the disadvantaged. At last Friday's market close, the value of the portfolio that was owned outright by the Foundation, or by the Von Kleise Groupe, came to nearly $775 billion. With the momentum in the market, the value would only increase as equity values moved back towards more normal levels.

For Michael, however, the doubts remained as to what he should do. And then, there were the others in the Order to contend with. He didn't even know all the players' names, nor was it clear what their relationship to the Foundation and the Kleise Trust was. Natalya stood up and went to the window. The light was now stronger, and the outlines of the green valley of the Kander were visible below. The blue lake seemed distant.

She heard him push the sheets away, and turned as he approached. He put his hands around her shoulders and embraced her from behind. The warmth of her skin, the slight fragrance of her perfume, lulled him to distraction from the problems that plagued each waking moment. She turned in his arms and leaned her mouth up so that he could kiss her.

"Hold me, Michael." She thought about her father. There was no word, and the situation in Russia was chaotic. The regions were fragmenting into private fiefs, controlled by military units which in time, would become warlords.

He held her tight. She was like a tiger one moment, and then could be vulnerable like a child. She broke away, and turned back towards the window.

Michael saw it first from a distance. He stared, as the small dot came closer and became more visible. It was a bird, a golden eagle searching for its first meal of the day in the morning light. It soared up in the air and came closer to the window. The growing morning light touched its wings turning dark to light; the wings looked a fiery red. Michael pointed it out to Natalya without letting go of her.

"Do you see it?" he asked.

She didn't answer, but then she saw it too. It came closer and closer.

"It looks like the phoenix rising from the ashes to herald a new age, Natalya." Michael stared at the bird, watching it soar and dive. "It will be our age to make, and build and guide." He started, for the first time, to feel the power and self-belief that he could make a difference. "It's a great opportunity. We must use it wisely."

Natalya now looked closely at Michael. The light was shining in, illuminating his face. Was it a sign of the favor of the gods, or simply an illusion that would deceive them both?

"Perhaps," Natalya said, looking at this man to whom she had pledged her love and life. "Perhaps it will, my love, but perhaps it won't. It's all in the hands of the gods."

Wattle Publishing

Wattle Publishing is an independent
publishing house based in London.
We publish fiction and non-fiction
works in a range of categories.

'Join us' on Twitter: @wattlepub

'Like us' on Facebook: Wattle Publishing

www.wattlepublishing.com